Treason in the North

Path of the Ranger Book 4

Pedro Urvi

COMMUNITY:
Mail: pedrourvi@hotmail.com
Facebook: https://www.facebook.com/PedroUrviAuthor/
My Website: http://pedrourvi.com
Twitter: https://twitter.com/PedroUrvi

Copyright ©2020 Pedro Urvi
All rights reserved

Translation by:
Christy Cox
Edited by:
Peter Gauld

DEDICATION

To my good friend Guiller.

Thank you for all your support since day one.

Map

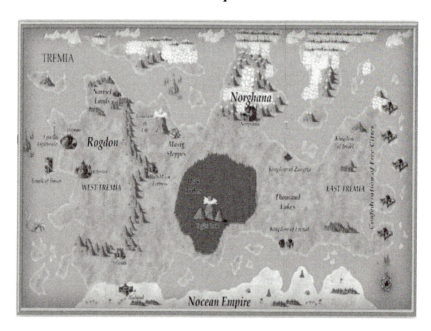

Chapter 1

Lasgol heard clashing sounds of metal, followed by distant shouting. He recognized them at once.

Armed combat!

He tugged at Trotter's reins. The good Norghanian pony stopped at the edge of the snow-covered forest, without moving out on to the plain. A cold rain mingled with thick snowflakes was falling from a black sky.

"Why are we stopping?" Viggo asked behind him. He was barely recognizable, with his hood covered with crystalline dots of snow.

Lasgol put his finger to his lips and turned his head toward his comrade.

Viggo understood the warning look. He stopped his own mount and was silent, staring around him.

It was noon, but even so, the weather did not allow them to make out much amid the dense ash forest. Lasgol concentrated and used his Gift to communicate mentally with Camu. He searched for the small pool of blue energy within his chest. When he called upon his *Animal Communication* skill, he caught the mind of the creature, who was following them a few paces behind, playing in the snow of the path that crossed the great forest.

Danger. Hide and no noise, he transmitted.

Camu looked at him with his bulging eyes and eternal smile and began to camouflage himself among a clump of snow-covered ferns. An instant later he was gone from sight.

Lasgol jumped nimbly off his horse. Crouching by a tree, without leaving the shelter of the forest, he watched the scene which was unfolding near a wide bridge of rock and wood four hundred paces to the northeast.

Two groups of armed men were fighting for control of the bridge.

Viggo crouched beside him. "How many?" he whispered. He had tethered both horses to a tree further back.

"About twenty on one side, thirty on the other," Lasgol replied in an almost inaudible whisper.

"Soldiers or militia?"

"A mixture of both."

Viggo shaded his eyes with his hand to avoid the watery flakes that were now falling more heavily.

"I can make out Uthar's colors in the group attacking from the East. And the colors of the Western League on the other side."

"Yeah, it's almost a metaphor for what's happening in the realm."

Viggo looked at him in puzzlement. "Don't go all Egil on me," he said, and grimaced.

"I mean we have an armed conflict in front of us between a bigger group on the East serving Uthar, and a smaller group on the West serving the League."

"Huh! And why didn't you say just that, instead of complicating it all?"

Lasgol shook his head. "I must be spending too much time with Egil."

"You can say that again. Way too much."

"Don't say that, you know that deep down you're fond of him."

"Yeah, sure," Viggo replied and mimicked hanging himself.

Lasgol smiled. "You're a pain."

Viggo gave a shrug. They watched the fighting for a moment.

Viggo readied his bow. "Whose side are we on?" he asked suddenly.

"Neither of them."

"What do you mean, neither of them? We're Rangers. Besides, I'm from the East. I was born there."

"Yeah, but the East is with Uthar."

"Right..." Viggo shrugged again. "Then we shoot against the East."

Lasgol shook his head firmly. "We don't shoot against anybody."

"I've got an idea. What about you shooting at the East and me at the West? That way we do our duty as Rangers, and we also do the right thing, which is going against Uthar." Viggo's casualness suggested that this was the wisest choice they could make.

Lasgol rolled his eyes. "Nobody's going to shoot at anybody here."

"Spoilsport."

The battle went on. The sound of steel against steel and the cries of fighting intensified. Several men had fallen on both sides. The

Eastern forces were fighting with metal shields and spears; those of the West with war axes and round wooden shields, in the traditional Norghanian style. The soldiers wore light scaled chainmail armor. The militia wore reinforced leather jerkins decorated with the coat of arms of whichever duchy or county they belonged to. The fighting was fierce, in the purest Norghanian style. The blood had begun to stain the snow and the wood of the bridge. The wind changed, and the cries of fury and death reached them as if they were in the middle of the fight. One man was pierced through with a spear and fell into the river. Another received an axe blow in the head which went through both helmet and skull.

"We ought to join in," Viggo insisted.

"We're passing through, we don't have to join in."

"They won't see us in the storm. We shoot, kill them all and that's that. Battle over."

Lasgol looked aside at his partner and saw that he had already tensed his bow and was aiming.

"They're more than four hundred paces away, they're moving, and you're going to release with a storm raging, when you aren't exactly our best archer... are you really sure you're going to hit the targets?"

Viggo thought for a moment. "The officers who're barking orders, yes, I'm sure of that. I've improved a lot with the bow."

"You've improved a bit. Not a lot. You'd miss at this distance. And we're not going to step in."

"Oh, you're such a wet blanket. It'd be fun to see their surprise at seeing their officers falling and not knowing what's going on. What's more, they're not carrying bows, and even if they spotted us, by the time they caught up with us we'd have killed more than half of them."

"We're not going to kill anyone," Lasgol said, and his voice was firm and definite.

Viggo gave up. "Fine..." he said, and lowered his bow.

The fight went on. The eastern forces were gaining the upper hand. The men of the west were fighting with all they had, but there were fewer of them.

"It's awful to watch Norghanians fighting Norghanians," Lasgol said with real feeling.

"Civil wars are like that."

"I can't believe we've reached that extreme."

"King Uthar isn't going to hand over the kingdom to the Western League and the Peoples of the Ice."

"I wish there was some way of stopping this madness…"

"Killing Uthar?"

"That'd be a good start, but I think it's quite a difficult thing to manage. He's taken cover in Norghania, the capital, and he's regrouping his forces. Or at least, that's what people are saying."

"No sooner said than done. He's only got the Invincibles, the Ice Mages, the Rangers, and the best of the Norghanian army with him. It's a piece of cake."

"Sure, really easy."

"I trust Darthor and the Western League. And above all, the Peoples of the Frozen Continent and their creatures and monsters of the ice."

At the mention of his mother, Lasgol wished he were with her now. But there was no way he could be. Soon, though. It was still not the time for another encounter. It was such a short time ago that they had said goodbye.

"Darthor and the League are regrouping and getting ready, the same as Uthar," Lasgol said, wishing that some solution could be found to stop it. "Soon the conflict will be on a bigger scale… it'll be horrible…"

"We could always let Uthar win."

"Never!"

Viggo smiled. "Easy, man, I was just twisting your arm a bit. I don't want you to go soft on me."

"No need. I know perfectly well what's at stake for us, for the Western League, for all Norghana. Uthar must fall. He's an impostor, a murderous shifter."

"And the King."

"And the Rangers are with him."

"I'm surprised Dolbarar's given us a few weeks' rest, with things as they are," Viggo said. He waved his hand toward the fighting, which was ending. The westerners, defeated, were withdrawing, while the easterners secured the position.

"Yeah… I believe he's done it for a reason."

"So we can clear our heads and relax?"

"No. So that those westerners who don't want to go on fighting can go home and not come back."

"Huh... I hadn't thought of that. He's smart, the old man."

"And he has a good heart."

"Yes. Anyone else wouldn't have allowed it. He's letting desertions go unchallenged, and Uthar won't like that."

"The realm's splitting in two. Men choose sides, they choose allegiances. Let's hope Dolbarar's actions don't come back to bite him."

"We'll soon know. For the moment, let's make the most of the four weeks. They'll fly past, and we'll have to come back for more training."

"This'll be the fourth year... the last one before we graduate as Rangers."

"And choose an elite specialty."

"If we're chosen."

"Yeah, because we won't be chosen. We aren't that good."

"That's what I think... maybe Ingrid."

Viggo nodded. "Miss Bossy-Boots might manage it, yes."

"Don't tease her so much. Deep down you like her, however much you pretend otherwise."

"No way!"

The fighting ended, and the easterners tended to their wounded. The Westerners they found alive had their throats cut ruthlessly.

Lasgol shook his head. The sight filled him with an impotent rage.

Viggo raised his bow. "We're still in time," he said. "They deserve to die, if only for what they just did."

"I know. But we're not judge and executioner."

"If you let me, that's what we could be today."

"No, my friend, let's move on. We've seen enough. If there's justice, they'll pay for it."

"You're too good," Viggo said, shaking his head. "Someday it'll be the death of you."

They exchanged glances. Viggo's was cold, deadly. Lasgol knew he himself did not have it in him and his partner was right; one day he would pay dearly for that lack. He only hoped that day would be as long as possible in coming.

"Let's hope not," he said, without conviction.

"Start thinking about how to solve this mess of a civil war and how we unmask Uthar."

"Me?"

"Well, obviously. You don't seriously think I'm going to come up with an idea myself?"

"And why d'you think I will?"

"Because you got us into this mess, and you're the one who's got to get us out of it."

Lasgol was thoughtful. They would have to do something to stop the madness, however small or insignificant their effort might appear. Thousands of lives were at stake.

"I'll try."

"Attaboy!"

The two friends mounted again and went on their way to the West amid the snowstorm.

Chapter 2

Lasgol tugged on Trotter's reins gently so that the strong Norghanian pony would stop before setting out across the wide snow-covered pasture-land which spread out before them. The forest was behind them, and his village of Skad was in sight ahead in the distance.

Viggo was looking at the winter landscape and the flock of sheep to one side. "Why are we stopping?"

"This is my village," Lasgol said. He pointed to the end of the green fields, currently partly covered in white.

Suddenly they heard a commotion among the sheep, which began to move restlessly. They bleated in fright for no apparent reason. There was no-one nearby.

Viggo put his hand to his forehead and threw his head back. "Here we go again!" he moaned desperately.

"I can't help it... you know what he's like..."

Lasgol could not see him because he was camouflaged and practically invisible to the human eye. When he looked carefully, he made out the tiny prints on the snow and guessed his position along by the empty space the sheep were leaving between them.

"Leave them alone," he said.

Viggo shook his head. "That animal is totally insane."

"Don't call him 'animal, you know perfectly well his name's Camu, and he doesn't like you to call him that."

"I don't like him, or her, or it either, or whatever the animal is, and even so I put up with him."

"And he does the same with you," Lasgol said with a half-smile.

Suddenly Camu became visible amid the sheep. With a happy shriek, he bounced on all four legs in delight. The little creature wanted to play with them.

"Oh, no..." Viggo said.

The sheep fled in a stampede of bleating terror.

"Camu, don't do that," Lasgol reprimanded him, even though he knew that half the time the little creature paid no attention to him.

He stared back at him with his bulging eyes and eternal smile, wagging his tail and flexing his four legs as he liked to do when he was happy.

"Camu bad," Lasgol said, and wagged his finger at him. He knew Camu understood. Whether he cared was a different matter.

Camu gave a little shriek of puzzlement, as if he had not done anything wrong. He stared back as if he did not understand why he was being reprimanded.

"Don't play the fool," Viggo told him. "You know perfectly well why he's scolding you."

Camu put his head to one side with a look of innocence, then shrieked again as if he had not done anything.

Viggo frowned thoughtfully. "He's a top-class comedian. He ought to go into the circus, or a street theater."

Lasgol nodded. "That's true," he admitted, smiling.

"Hey, suppose we sold him to a traveling circus or a theater in the capital? I bet we'd get quite a bit for him."

Camu gave a questioning shriek, and his everlasting smile vanished.

"Don't say that," Lasgol said sharply. "Don't you see he understands us?"

"I'm not really sure that creature understands us, however much you insist he does."

"He doesn't understand every word, but he does understand certain things. Egil's making a study of him, and that's one of the conclusions he's reached."

"I think it's just a coincidence that he sometimes reacts to what we say in a way that makes it look as if he understood what we're saying."

Lasgol watched Camu, who was running and leaping all over the field. The sheep had fled in terror. Luckily there was no shepherd nearby. The mischievous little creature had grown a lot. He seemed always to do this toward the end of winter, as if he had been waiting for this moment. He had just put on this spurt of growth, and by now had reached the size of a large cat. He still climbed up on to Lasgol's shoulders, but now the little creature's weight was beginning to be too much. Soon, probably by the end of this new year, if he went on growing at the same rate, Lasgol would not be able to carry him at all. Egil had spent some time recording everything they found out about Camu in his notebook, as well as his size, weight and growth. His friend was doing a real field study, and enjoying every moment.

"Why are we coming down from the forest through the fields and not following the path I can see over there?" Viggo asked.

"These are dangerous times, and it's better not to follow the roads. Besides, you and I are Rangers, and Rangers don't often follow roads or paths. That's what *The Path of the Ranger* says. Have you forgotten?"

"Yeah... yeah.... we only follow *The Path*." Viggo gave him a whimsical look.

"It's impossible to talk to you," Lasgol said with a smile.

Viggo shrugged. "I'm what I am, what can I do about it? I'm pretty happy about the way I came out, in the circumstances." He smiled from ear to ear.

Lasgol laughed.

"I'm virtuous in some areas, a bit shadowy in others..."

This made Lasgol wonder, as he stroked Trotter's rump. Camu still made the good pony quite nervous.

"Why did you want to come with me during this end-of-year break?" Lasgol asked, his head on one side.

"Wow, at last you're asking. I thought you never would."

"I know it's none of my business. If you don't want to tell me there's no need, you're a friend of mine and you're welcome."

"I don't mind telling you. After all, we're friends and partners. I didn't want to stay at the Camp and waste these weeks of leisure. I felt like a change of air. So much time surrounded by Rangers ends up affecting anybody."

Lasgol had to agree. It was quite true.

"But why come with me? Why didn't you go home?"

Viggo's face shadowed. In his eyes appeared that gleam Lasgol knew so well: the lethal gleam.

"Let's just say I can't go back home – well, to my city – for a while... for a good while."

"Oh, no! What have you done?"

"Why do you think I've done anything?"

"Because when you came back at the beginning of the course you mentioned some quarrel you'd had about settling an old score, and now it turns out that you can't go back to your city."

"You have a pretty good memory, I have to say. That's a good quality."

"Don't pretend, and tell me what happened."

"You'd better not know... all I can tell you is that at the moment I can't go back to my city."

Lasgol shook his head. "I hope you haven't killed anybody..."

"If I had, you can be sure it would've been because they deserved it." From his sleeve Viggo drew the sharp personal dagger he always carried on him.

"Maybe it's best if I don't know, after all."

"Wise decision."

"But if you change your mind and want to tell me, I'm here for you."

"Thanks, pal... better leave it for now."

Lasgol sighed. "All right, then."

"That way you won't have to judge me," said Viggo, who always had to have the last word. He smiled ironically.

Lasgol rolled his eyes, "But tell me, why with me? Why didn't you go with Gerd or Ingrid, or Nilsa or even Egil? Why me? You don't even like Camu."

"Gerd and the girls are going back to see their families. I don't feel like all that business of family relations, hugs and kisses. Not my style."

Lasgol nodded in agreement.

"And as for Egil, we'll probably go and see him anyway, right?"

"Yup. If there's nothing to get in the way I'd like to see him, but we'll have to wait and see if he gives us the all-clear. The situation's very complicated after what happened about his father, his brothers and the Western League."

"He'll probably need our help."

"Yeah, that's what I think too."

"Good. We'll wait and see whether he wants us to go. My instinct tells me that things are going to get very ugly soon, so..."

Lasgol nodded. "I'm afraid of the same thing."

"Don't worry, you're with me," Viggo said. He twirled his dagger in the air and caught it again with amazing skill.

"So I see I was your last option."

"You've always been that, hero," Viggo said with a broad, satirical grin. He spurred his pony on down the hill toward the village.

Lasgol threw his head back and laughed. Viggo was Viggo. You either loved him or hated him, and he loved him. He concentrated, using his Gift to call on his skill in order to communicate with Camu.

Invisible until I say otherwise, and behave, he ordered him.

The little creature looked at him for a moment with his bulging eyes, then blinked and vanished with a smile. He came to Lasgol, who heard his footsteps as he approached. Trotter became nervous and snorted several times.

Lasgol stroked the pony's neck. "Easy, friend. Come on, then, the village is waiting for us. We'll be able to rest, and I'll give you some hay and fresh grass."

It did not take them long to reach the village from the northern end, which was the least-used, given the steep hill that led down to it. Even so, as they came to the street they saw three soldiers guarding the entrance. Lasgol recognized Count Malason's emblem. He felt some relief, as the Count was the lord of these lands and was allied to the Western League. They ought not to have any trouble, at least as long as they were not found out to be Rangers. Although in the kingdom's current situation, any encounter with soldiers was dangerous.

"Halt! Who goes there?" called the most senior of the soldiers as he came out into the middle of the street to bar their way. The other two soldiers came up behind him. They carried spears and round wooden shields and wore blue clothes over their light scaled armor, typical of the Norghanian warriors.

"My name is Lasgol. I'm the lord of the big house in Skad, Eklund's house."

The soldiers exchanged uncertain glances.

"Lasgol, Dakon Eklund's son, is with the Rangers," said the soldier in command.

Lasgol glanced at Viggo. They knew who they were. The situation might turn ugly very quickly.

"That's correct, and I'm back on leave."

The soldiers exchanged glances again.

"We can't let a Ranger through."

"Why not?"

"You serve the East."

"And you?"

"We serve the West."

There was a tense silence. The soldiers readied their weapons.

Lasgol and Viggo tensed.

"The eastern dogs aren't welcome in Skad," said the most solidly-built of the soldiers. "Leave now or else you'll pay in blood." And he meant it.

Lasgol could not tell them that even though he was a Ranger, he was with the Western League. They would not believe him.

Viggo was ready to attack by now. He could tell by the lethal gleam in those half-closed eyes.

"We don't want any trouble," Lasgol said.

"In that case, leave at once."

Lasgol had no desire to fight, least of all against someone from the West, his own land.

"Lasgol has leave to enter," a voice thundered.

Lasgol looked past the soldiers and saw the impressive figure which was approaching. He smiled. It was the Village Chief Gondar Vollan.

"Chief... they're Rangers...."

"I vouch for him."

"In that case they may enter."

"Thanks, soldier."

"We have orders to be very wary of all strangers."

"And you're quite right to do so," the Chief said. He patted his shoulder as he passed him. "Chief," said Lasgol with a nod.

"You look well. From what I've heard, you're in quite a lot of trouble."

"I see that rumors keep arriving before I do."

The Chief quoted a Norghanian proverb. "That's right, the icy winds bring fresh news here in the north."

He offered him a massive hand, and Lasgol shook it.

"And who's this?" Gondar asked with a wave at Viggo.

"This is Viggo Kron," Viggo replied sardonically.

"He's my teammate in the Rangers."

"Is he trustworthy?"

"He is," Lasgol assured him.

"In that case he may enter too."

"What's happened?" Lasgol asked. "How are things in the village?"

Gondar glanced around. "There'll be time to talk about all that."

Lasgol understood. The Chief wanted to talk in private. It was not a good sign, but he decided that until he knew what was going on it would be best not to worry: at least, not too much.

"All right, Chief, We'll be at my house."

"I'll see you there. I'm very glad to see you."

"Me too, Chief."

The soldiers let Lasgol and Viggo pass, and they went into the village slowly. As they went forward on their mounts the people glanced at them suspiciously at first, but when they recognized Lasgol they smiled, though fleetingly. They must have been wondering which side the Hero of Skad was on.

They arrived at Lasgol's property. The entrance gate was shut. They dismounted, and Lasgol rang the bell on the wall. A moment later the door of the big house opened, and a woman appeared in it. She stared at them for a moment.

Then she recognized Lasgol.

"Lasgol! Master! Welcome!" Marta cried, and ran down to welcome him.

Lasgol smiled at the sight of his housekeeper.

"Master! How are you?" She opened the gate and hugged him as if he were the prodigal son returning home.

"Hi Marta. I'm very well, thanks."

"Let me look at you," she said. She stepped back and studied him from head to foot.

He blushed a little. "I'm the same as ever, Marta."

"You're taller, more grownup."

Viggo laughed. "More grownup," he said mockingly.

"A friend of yours?" she asked, eyeing Viggo suspiciously.

"Yes, this is my partner Viggo. He's going to stay with us until we have to leave."

"Pleased to meet you, sir," Marta said with a small curtsy.

"Don't 'sir' me and don't bow. I'm from the lower class. 'Viggo' is more than enough."

The comment amused Marta, who smiled.

"Curious friends you make in the Rangers."

"Oh, if you only knew," Viggo replied, and smiled broadly.

Lasgol nodded. "How are things in the village?"

"Come on in and I'll tell you. These are bad times, very bad times."

Chapter 3

They led their horses to the stable and took care of them before they went into the house. The *Path of the Ranger* was clear about this: a Ranger always took care of his mount before he tended to himself.

"As promised, grass and hay," Lasgol said to Trotter, who neighed and nodded with pleasure several times. Lasgol stroked his neck, and the animal relaxed and began to eat.

Inside the house a pleasant fire was burning in the hearth, and they made straight for it. The cold of the journey had got into their bones, and a good fire was the only thing that could clear it. That and strong liquor.

Martha was unable to wait any longer. "How is Mayra?" she asked eagerly.

"She's fine. She sends her regards."

"I'm so glad. I still find it hard to believe that she's... you know..."

"Darthor," Viggo said, as if it were the most natural thing in the world.

Lasgol glared at him.

Viggo's expression suggested that he could not understand why he was being criticized. "We're alone, and you told me your housekeeper and your old master, the lame one-eyed soldier, knew the secret."

"Even so, we shouldn't speak of it openly. We need to be very careful."

Viggo shrugged. "As you wish..." He stretched out his hands to the fire.

"There are terrible rumors about Darthor... Mayra... going round. They say he corrupts men and dominates them with his Dark Magic... he makes them kill for him... they say wherever he goes everybody dies, women and children included... they say he destroys villages and towns just to kill and plunder. They say that the few who survive have lost their sanity at his hands... during his interrogations... and all sorts of other awful things..."

"Those are all lies that Uthar makes people believe. You know Mayra better than anyone, don't you? D'you really think she'd do things like that?"

Martha shook her head emphatically. "Mayra wouldn't do the atrocities they're accusing her of. I can't believe it."

"Uthar is trying to poison the minds of all Norghanians with horror stories so that they'll support him against Darthor and his allies. We know the stories are false. The one who's been committing all those atrocities is Uthar himself."

Mayra nodded several times. "So you found her well?"

"As strong and determined as she always was."

"Oh, I'm so glad to hear that. I've been very afraid for her. I could barely see her for a moment when she came for you last year. I'd have loved to spend some time with her... to enjoy her company for a few days... to talk like we used to... for hours, sometimes until dawn... we were so young and so full of dreams and ideals...life drove us apart... and now... we're who we are."

"I'd have liked to be with her more too... but we're in the middle of a war, and she's the leader of one of the sides. Unfortunately there's no time for friends."

"And for sons?"

Lasgol shook his head sadly.

"When you see her again, give her a big hug from me. Give her all my love. Tell her I'll be waiting here, in her house, to go on with those conversations we used to have in the old days."

"I will," Lasgol promised.

Martha smiled at him fondly.

"Have you brought that little creature with you?" Martha asked, remembering what had happened during their last meeting.

"Yes. He's brought the beast, he always takes him everywhere he goes," Viggo said without taking his eyes off the fire.

Lasgol shook his head. "Don't call him 'beast'... and yes, I've brought Camu. I hope you don't mind."

"This is your house, Master," Martha said.

"Even so..."

"I don't mind. I'm not as much afraid of magical things as other people are."

"I'm glad to know that." He went over to the travelling knapsack he had left by the door and took Camu out. He was sleeping like a baby.

"I fed him at the stables. When he eats..."

"He sleeps like a log," Viggo finished the sentence.

Martha came over to look at him closely.

"He's certainly a funny creature,"

"Particularly when he does magic," Viggo said.

"Don't talk about him like that."

"Do you need anything special for the little one?" Martha asked.

"Vegetables. The fresher the better. He loves them."

"That's no problem. I keep the garden going."

"Thank you."

"You must be quite tired from your journey. I'll get the rooms ready."

"Thanks a lot, Martha."

"I'm delighted. The master's come back home and I'm overjoyed." She hugged Lasgol, and he was grateful for the affection.

Martha got the rooms ready for them to wash and rest. Viggo lost no time in going to his. Lasgol and Martha followed him to the door. He left his travelling knapsack to one side, his cloak on the floor and his weapons on an armchair, and stretched out on the bed.

"How nice..." he said, trying to find a comfortable posture.

Martha shook her head. "Your boots..."

"Oh, yes, sorry," Viggo said. He took them off.

"There's a washbowl with fresh water and soap so you can freshen up."

Viggo did not feel like washing, only sleeping and resting. "No need –"

"Yes there is, you stink," Martha insisted with an air of finality.

"It was a long, hard journey..."

"If you want to eat, you'll have to wash first."

That did it.

"Yes, of course, I'll wash right away," Viggo said at her look of reproach. His stomach was rumbling.

"I'll prepare a good hot meal for you," she said to Lasgol with a friendly smile.

"There's no need, Martha..."

"Of course there is, you need rest and food. You relax from your journey while I prepare the meal. I'll let you know when it's ready." She went back downstairs with her usual energy and grace.

Lasgol went to his own room and left his things on the bed. He shut the door, and following Martha's instructions he had a wash.

After this he used his Gift to communicate with Camu, who had woken up and was already bouncing on the bed.

Play silently.

Camu flexed his four legs and wagged his tail happily. He gave a big bounce on the bed. Lasgol smiled and went on grooming himself.

Come here, little one, he said to Camu when he had finished.

Camu leapt to him in two bounces, clung to his chest and licked his cheek.

Lasgol smiled cheerfully. He felt very happy; he was with Camu and at home. A feeling of delight and warmth enveloped him for a moment. He forgot all his problems and worries in this moment of happiness. If his mother had been there with him, the joy of that moment would have been complete. He imagined that it was so and relaxed with a long sigh.

He looked into Camu's bulging eyes. *I'll let you play in the attic.*

Like it, the creature transmitted. He understood more and more of what Camu was trying to communicate to him. There were still no full messages, rather specific feelings and sensations, but he had the impression that they were getting deeper and easier to understand all the time. Perhaps in the not-too-distant future he and the creature would discover how to communicate with more elaborate messages. He had this hope, and according to Egil it was perfectly feasible.

I know you do, because it's full of junk and you love playing hide-and-seek and messing it all up.

Camu put his head to one side and smiled with the look of a very good little creature who never does anything wrong.

You don't fool me, I know you perfectly well. Don't make a noise and don't break anything.

Camu gave a little shriek of complaint.

Don't pretend to be offended. I'll bring you some greens later on.

Delicious.

Yes, delicious vegetables.

Camu leapt off the bed and ran toward the trap-door that gave access to the attic at the end of the corridor. Lasgol had to run after him, cursing silently. He left the mischievous creature in the attic and went in search of Viggo in the guest room, where he found him asleep. He decided to let him rest a while longer. As he turned, the wooden floor creaked under his weight.

He heard a thump.

He turned his head at the sound and saw Viggo's throwing-dagger buried in the doorframe two fingers from his ear.

"You could have hit me!"

"You could have avoided making a noise and startling me."

"All I did was turn round!"

"You know I hate being startled, I hate it. I react badly."

"And I hate having daggers thrown at me. You might have killed me!"

"Bah, I never miss at that distance."

"You're hopeless."

Viggo smiled. "Lots of people say that."

Lasgol muttered curses under his breath.

"Is dinner ready? I could eat an elephant."

Lasgol shook his head. "Let's go downstairs. Judging by the delicious smell, I'd say yes."

They went down to the kitchen.

"I'm so glad to have you home, Lasgol," Martha said with an affectionate smile.

"I'm happy to be here with you too, Martha."

"Sit down at the table and I'll bring in the food."

Viggo was already sniffing the roast.

"No touching the food until it's served," Martha warned him, and he drew back the hand that was already reaching out towards the sauce.

"It smells delicious," he said. His stomach rumbled.

"It'll taste even better. To the table!"

They both sat down, and the first thing they enjoyed was a hot winter broth. Strong, spicy and heart-warming.

"This broth has alcohol in it," Viggo said in surprise.

"So it does," Martha said. "It's an old recipe from this region. It raises the spirits and warms the bones."

"I say it does!" said Viggo, and asked for a second helping.

Then she served them a roast with mashed potatoes and carrots and blueberry sauce. They devoured the entire roast and the side dishes as if they had not eaten in days.

Viggo licked his lips. "Everything's delicious!"

"Martha's an exceptional cook."

"Not really, it's just that you've been on the road for days without a decent hot meal."

"Ho there, the Norghanian household!" they heard suddenly from outside, like a roar.

Viggo was instantly as tense as a bowstring. He reached for his dagger. Martha looked at the front door and Viggo got to his feet, ready to go into action.

Lasgol smiled to himself and gestured to him to relax. He had recognized the voice at once.

Martha went to the door and opened it to reveal a huge Norghanian, past middle-age. He was massive, ugly as a bear. His hair and beard were reddish, and always rumpled. He was one-eyed, and never hid his empty eye-socket under a patch. His expression was unfriendly. He was leaning on a crutch, because one leg was missing below the knee, and he was armed with a sword and a long knife.

"A Norghanian soldier begs audience with the Hero Lasgol!" he roared.

It was Ulf. The one and only.

"A retired soldier, you mean," Martha said.

"A soldier of the glorious Snow Army. A soldier decorated in multiple battles."

"Yeah, the terror of the Rogdonians, the horror of the Noceans..." Martha said. She moved aside to let him into the house.

"Greetings, Martha," he said with a half-bow. "It's always a pleasure to be in your presence."

"Come in. I hope you haven't had too much of the Nocean *painkiller* at the inn."

"Two glasses, no more than that, I swear."

"Sure, and I believe you. Come on in."

Lasgol ran to hug Ulf. Viggo got up too and watched them. The enormous warrior embraced him so hard that Lasgol began to think a bear was hugging him. He was still as strong and rough as ever. Lasgol enjoyed his old master's hug.

"You're the same as ever," he said.

It was true. He was unchanged from the year before; it seemed that time did not pass as quickly for Ulf as for the other villagers of Skad. Maybe it was due to all the Nocean wine he drank; that may have been what preserved him. His red cheeks and nose indicated that he had already had a drink too many, which did not surprise Lasgol.

The enormous warrior gave him another hug, which nearly broke his back.

"I'm so glad to see you! I thought you wouldn't be back alive from the Frozen Continent!"

"We had some complicated moments, but we came out of it alive."

"I heard it was a hellish campaign."

"It certainly was. The hostile climate, the hosts of the People of the Ice, the magical creatures... quite an experience."

"By the Frozen Gods! This is how good Norghanian warriors are forged!"

"That's true."

"I can see in your eyes that you've grown a lot, lad."

"I feel the same."

"Those experiences change you, they make you stronger. They make you a true fighter."

"I've learned and lived through a lot, that much I can't deny. Although I'd rather not have experienced the horror of war."

"Bullshit. There've always been wars, and there always will be. If it's not against the Rogdonians in the West, it'll be against the Noceans in the South, or against the Masig tribes of the prairies, or against the accursed Zangrians of the Southeast." He glanced down at his lame leg. "There'll always be someone who covets our land, or we theirs. That's the way it's been for thousands of years and that's the way it'll always be. Heed what this old soldier says."

"It's not a promising view of things, particularly after what we went through in the Frozen Continent."

"I'd have given an arm to have been able to fight in the final battle."

"But not the one that holds the crut...—" Viggo started to say.

Lasgol glowered at him to stop him finishing the sentence.

Ulf glowered at him. "Friend of yours?"

"Yes, my fellow-Ranger. He has my back."

Ulf went over to Viggo and stood over him, like a mountain bear on two legs in front of a young human, glaring at him ferociously.

Viggo did not cower. He stood up to the scrutiny. A moment went by, and Lasgol thought that Ulf was going to tear his friend's head off.

"Ha! I like him. He has a warrior's spirit," Ulf said suddenly. He slapped Viggo hard on the back.

Viggo was propelled several paces forward and had to struggle to keep his balance so as not to fall to the floor.

"So do I... I like the bear..." Viggo said. He straightened his sore back.

"Let's sit down," Lasgol suggested.

Ulf nodded, and (not without difficulty) tried to sit down. Both Lasgol and Viggo made to help him, but his ferocious glance was enough to make them sit down again at once. Finally he managed to settle into the chair, or rather let himself drop into it. Luckily it was a robust one. The crutch fell to the floor.

"By the snow-covered mountains, I don't understand this situation!" he barked in his usual direct style.

"What do you mean?" Lasgol asked.

"This civil war! East against West! What else could I mean? It's what everybody's talking about all the time. At the inn all they do is spread all kind of rumors, lies and half-truths, and I don't know what the hell to think any more." He shook his head heavily.

"Perhaps you shouldn't go to the inn so much..." Martha pointed out.

"Sure, and tomorrow I'll grow a new leg."

Viggo laughed out loud.

Martha protested loudly, then went to fetch the dessert.

Viggo arched one eyebrow. "What side is a retired soldier of the Snow Army on?"

Ulf stared at him for a moment.

"I know what you're thinking, that because I've been a soldier in the king's army my loyalty's to the East."

"Isn't that so?" Viggo asked.

"I don't have to explain my loyalties to a child who isn't a full Ranger yet."

"True, but that's evading a direct question. East or West?"

"See this fist? Well it's going to make direct contact with your nose."

Viggo threw his head back and raised his hands. "It was just a question."

"Yeah... well, be careful, or else this old soldier'll tear your head off in one go."

"I can clear this up for you and tell you what's true and what isn't," Lasgol offered.

"You're one of the very few people I trust in the whole of Tremia. I'll listen to you."

Lasgol took a deep breath. Whatever he said next would either put Ulf on his side or against him. He had to be very persuasive. As far as Ulf was concerned, the Royal Norghanian Army was everything: the Eastern Army, Uthar's army...

He took a deep breath and prepared to tell him the story.

Chapter 4

"Try to understand," Lasgol told Ulf, though he knew it was like asking a lion not to eat an antelope. "Don't let your temper get the better of you."

"I'll try, but I'm not promising anything."

Lasgol nodded and took a deep breath. He wanted the big bear to understand, so he told him everything that had happened to him right from the start, from the moment he had joined the Rangers. He told him all about the attempts on his life during the first year, about the discoveries they had been making. He told him about Camu, about the Rangers, about how he had saved the King and exonerated his own father.

"So far so good, except for the little magical creature. I hate magic and anything to do with it! Did you bring it with you?"

Lasgol pointed at the ceiling.

"Are you telling me it's here right now?"

Lasgol nodded. "I told him to stay playing in the attic, but he's heard us and come down to investigate."

You can show yourself, you're with friends, he told Camu with his Gift.

Camu became visible above the table, hanging upside-down from the ceiling, like a giant lizard. He shrieked in greeting.

"By all the snowy mornings in the kingdom!" Ulf cried, and nearly fell off his chair.

Viggo snorted. "Nobody can do a thing with the creature."

"Cursed magic! He gave me one hell of a shock!"

Camu let out a small shriek, as if by way of apology.

"He won't do anything to you, Ulf, and he's a great ally. He detects magic and stops it."

"Now then, that's better, I like that."

"As long as you're with him you can't be bewitched, and no spell will have any effect on you."

"I'm beginning to like this giant lizard a bit better. Go on." He did not take his good eye off Camu.

"Fine."

Lasgol went on to tell him everything that had happened during the second year. As he did so Ulf's face darkened, and when he came to his discovery that Darthor was in fact Mayra, his mother, Ulf's face twisted, but he said nothing. Lasgol went on to describe how he had been the prisoner of the Wild People of the Snow, the atrocities he had seen the King's men commit against them, and the end of the year at the Camp when Camu had interfered with the shifter magic and they had seen that Uthar was not really the King but a shifter himself.

"That's impossible! Even if a God of the Ice came and stood in front of me and told me himself, I wouldn't believe that!"

"Take it easy... I know it's hard to take in..."

"Hard to take in? Impossible! By all the thunder and lightning of the mother of all winter storms!"

Ulf was ranting now, beside himself with fury. He banged the table with his fists, so that the dish of cooked apples which Martha had served him while he listened flew through the air.

Viggo covered his mouth to muffle a guffaw.

"Ulf! Behave yourself!" Martha scolded him.

Lasgol waited patiently for the old soldier to calm down.

"D'you believe this story about Uthar?" Ulf asked Viggo.

"Not at first. It took us a while to accept it, the same with Darthor being his mother. But now we believe it."

"You all do?"

"The whole team, yes."

"And you, Martha?"

"If Lasgol says that Uthar's a shifter, then he is."

"Thanks, Martha."

Ulf shook his head.

"This is too much, I need something to soothe my nerves. Martha, you wouldn't have something from the cellar?"

Martha threw her head back. "Why don't you eat my delicious dessert instead of asking me for wine?"

"I'm sure it's delicious, but you see, what Lasgol's telling me has taken away my appetite."

"But not your thirst."

"Look, woman, it's only wine, I could have asked for brandy."

"And I could have been a sorceress and cast a spell of Curse Magic on you."

There was a moment of silence. Viggo looked at Martha, his eyes full of suspicion.

"No..." Ulf began.

"Lucky for you I'm not."

Ulf snorted. Viggo smiled from ear to ear.

"I'll bring some wine from the cellar, but only if you promise to behave."

"I promise, better than a Rogdonian prince."

"Ha! A Rogdonian prince he says! Sure, with those perfect manners of yours! The things I have to hear..." She went to fetch the wine.

Ulf shrugged. "I'm a pure-bred Norghanian, you can't expect any different from me," he said apologetically.

Viggo laughed.

"What's the creature doing?" Ulf asked.

"He's eating the cooked apples you upset. He loves fruit and vegetables."

Ulf raised his arms. "By the sea of ice! How I hate magic!"

Lasgol went on to tell him about what had happened during the third year: everything his mother had revealed to him, how Uthar was a shifter, which they had already discovered, and how his own father had tried to kill Uthar and failed.

Martha brought the wine, but Ulf seized the bottle from her hand.

"I'm going to need a lot of wine if I'm going to be able to swallow all this."

Martha shook her head, but said nothing and left him the bottle.

Lasgol went on to tell him about the campaign in the Frozen Continent, Uthar's blackmailing of Duke Olafstone by kidnapping his sons, the final battle, and the alliance of the Western League with the People of the Ice brought about by Mayra, who was also Darthor.

Ulf said nothing. He took a long swig, shook his head and took another.

"Now I understand why Mayra disappeared," Martha said. "They faked her death. She found out about Uthar, and she's been trying to stop him ever since."

"Yes," Lasgol said. "It's not easy when your enemy is the king of Norghana himself, and he knows it."

"Lasgol, I'm sorry about Dakon. It was a heroic deed. He was like that, he had the kind of spirit that only heroes and great men have."

"Thanks. That's why we have to stop Uthar and end what my father started and couldn't finish."

"I understand how you must feel," Martha said, sounding very concerned, "but it's very dangerous..."

"We're used to it," Viggo said, as if danger were his middle name.

"I can't believe it..." Ulf mumbled. Wine was trickling down his beard.

"I'd never lie to you, Ulf, you know that."

The old soldier nodded.

"I couldn't understand what was going on, how we'd reached this situation in Norghana. I was very upset. The kingdom divided in two, east fighting west. Norghanians killing Norghanians. It's a disgrace. Barbaric. Everybody knows about the dispute over the crown between Uthar's family and the Olafstones, but I never thought it'd get as far as a civil war! I'm from this village, Skad, in the West, and my loyalty's to the West. But I've been a soldier most of my life, I've served the king... the east... and I feel divided... and it makes me bloody furious!"

"The east is led by an impostor, and that's one of the reasons why it's come to this."

"You think if the true Uthar had been sitting in the throne, this wouldn't have happened?" Martha asked.

"I'd like to believe it. That he wouldn't have gone against the People of the Frozen Continent, that he wouldn't have forced a civil war."

"I'm not so sure," Viggo said. "All monarchs are the same, all they want is power. Maybe the situation would be even worse."

"How?"

"We might be at war with the Kingdom of Rogdon or the Nocean Empire and be losing... they might be devastating our country. Monarchs are like that, that's politics."

"The lad isn't so wrong there," Ulf said.

"You think so?"

"How many decent Norghanian kings can you name in our glorious history? Most of them have been bloodthirsty conquerors and looters without any scruples whatsoever. The great war against the Zangrians, where I lost my leg, started because our great king, Uthar's father, decided to take some of their land. And he was an arrogant brute. I know that, I met him. He awarded me a medal himself."

"Yes, you're right," Martha agreed. "Our monarchs leave a lot to be desired..."

"And those of other kingdoms aren't much better," Viggo added.

"I know what I've told you is hard to believe, Ulf. But I swear to you it's the truth."

"I believe you, Lasgol, it's not that... I just find it hard to swallow."

"Perhaps another bottle would help," Martha suggested.

"You mean that?"

She shrugged. "You're old enough to know what you're doing. But if you fall flat on your face I'll tell these two lads to take you to the stable to sleep it off."

"Deal!"

Martha rolled her eyes and left.

"You've got the best housekeeper in the whole county," Ulf said to Lasgol, who laughed.

Martha came back with another bottle and put it on the table. Ulf made a grab for it. Suddenly there came a knock at the door.

"Are we expecting anybody?" Ulf asked.

Martha looked at Lasgol. "No, not that I know of."

"Me neither."

"It's Chief Gondar," came a voice from outside.

"I'll go and let him in." Martha said.

"Wait a moment," Lasgol said suddenly. He looked to see where Camu was, but could not see him. He closed his eyes and concentrated. In order to call the little creature he needed to locate his mind's aura; he searched throughout the room and the kitchen but could not find it.

"What's he doing?" Ulf asked.

"Looking for the beast," Viggo replied.

"He looks for him with his eyes shut?"

"He's using his... skills..."

"Skills? What skills?"

Viggo smiled. "Hmm, you'd better ask him yourself. That'll be another interesting conversation."

Martha opened her eyes very wide. She had understood. Ulf grunted. He did not want to understand.

Lasgol finally managed to locate Camu's magical aura, and was surprised. The little creature was back in the attic. It was quite a distance, and yet he had been able to locate him. His skill was improving, evolving and growing. This always made him feel happy.

Camu, stay there. Don't come down.

The reply did not take long.

Play. Happy.

Good. Go on playing. I'll be up soon.

They could communicate at greater distances; he wondered how far. And with other creatures? He would have to try with Trotter, who had no magical aura. Probably only if he was able to see him. He needed to experiment more and develop his skills, but it was difficult at the Camp, and outside it practically impossible, what with missions and dangerous situations.

He opened his eyes.

"That's done. You can open the door now."

"You'll have to explain this business of 'that's done,'" Ulf said with a grimace.

Martha opened the door and Chief Gondar came in, followed by his assistant Limus, they all exchanged greetings.

"The return of the hero of Skad is an honor," Limus said with a broad smile.

"Just 'Lasgol', none of this 'hero' business, please."

"It's good for the village to have such a notable hero," Limus replied, still smiling,

"Well, for the village's reputation and finances it is," Gondar said. He too was smiling.

"Very true."

"Can I offer you anything?" Martha asked.

"Nothing, thank you," Gondar said. "We're here on official business."

Martha's face took on a worried look. "Official business? That sounds serious."

"Count Malason was expecting the hero's arrival," Limus explained.

"It wouldn't be to enlist him, would it?" Ulf asked. "He's already enlisted all the men over fifteen who can bear arms."

"And some women too," Martha said.

"The enlistment of women is voluntary," Limus explained. "If they wish to fight to defend their homes, they're allowed to."

"As long as there's someone left to look after the family," Martha put in.

"Well," Limus said, "if the man and the woman both go to war, who'll look after the children and the farms?"

"He's got something there," Ulf commented.

"Mmm..." Martha said, not sounding very convinced.

Lasgol wondered whether she would want to fight. She was still young and strong. Norghanian women were renowned in Tremia for going to war beside their men."

"Martha... if you want to enlist in Count Malason's militia... that's fine by me."

"And who'll take care of the property?"

"I'm afraid it won't be me," Gondar said. "I'll be joining the Count's forces as soon as he mobilizes us, and that won't be long."

"My place is beside my master," Martha said. "I'll look after his home until he returns."

Lasgol nodded. "Fine with me."

"Count Malason wishes to inform the hero of Skad that his presence is required at Duke Olafstone's castle," Limus said.

"When did he tell you?"

"A few days ago," Gondar said. "He sent a messenger. Somehow he knew you were on your way."

"I see."

"These are difficult times," Limus pointed out. "There are spies behind every shadow. It's best to be wary. That's why we had to come in person."

"You did the right thing," Viggo said. "If the Count knew we were coming, I bet a big fat cow that Uthar knows as well."

"That doesn't sound too good..." Lasgol said thoughtfully.

"Not for our health, no..."

"Nothing will happen to you here," Chief Gondar said. "My men and I will see to that. That's why Count Malason warned us."

"A smart man," Viggo said.

"We'll leave at dawn," said Lasgol.

"So soon?" Martha exclaimed. "You've only just got here."

"The situation's very complicated, and if the Duke wants to see me, it's because there's something going on. I must go as soon as possible. Besides, if I stay I'll be putting you all in danger."

"Don't you worry about me," Gondar said. He reached for the

axe which hung at his waist.

Ulf reached for the pommel of his sword. "Or for me either."

"I know you can manage, especially here in your own village, but I don't want to take any unnecessary risks. We'll leave at dawn."

"Very well," Gondar said, "but if you need anything, you only have to let me know. After all, I owe you my life, and that's a debt I'll never be able to repay."

"Nobody owes anybody anything," Lasgol said. "We're all friends, that's what counts, and we need to look after one another."

Martha nodded. "Well said."

Gondar said goodbye to Lasgol with a hug.

"Be very careful, and if you need me I'll be there."

"You protect Skad, protect Martha."

He stroked his axe. "That's on my bill, don't you worry."

"An honor, sir," Limus said, and took Lasgol's hand in his own. "We'll look after your estate and the village of Skad in the absence of our hero." There was a gleam of admiration in his eyes.

"Thanks, Limus."

And they left the house.

"If we have to get up early, then I'm off to bed," Viggo said. "Martha, dinner was delicious. Every time Lasgol invites me I'll come to enjoy all those delicacies again."

She smiled with pleasure. "Give me notice next time and the food'll be spectacular."

"I'll send messengers by land and by air."

She laughed.

"Ulf, it's been a real pleasure," Viggo said, and offered him his hand.

Ulf stared at it. For a long moment. It did not look as if he were going to take it. Lasgol stared at him, not knowing what to say.

Then suddenly Ulf smiled from ear to ear.

"Keep an eye on Lasgol, he's going to need friends to cover his back,"

"His back is my back. I'll kill anybody who comes near it."

Ulf shook his hand firmly. "I'll hold you to that."

"I'll be true to my word," Viggo promised.

Ulf nodded and let go of his hand, and he went upstairs.

"If you'll excuse me, I'll finish cleaning up." Martha said. She winked at Lasgol and went into the kitchen. He and Ulf were left alone at the table.

Ulf grunted. Lasgol did not know how to tell him...

There was a tense silence.

"A Norghanian always says what's in his mind," Ulf said.

"I..."

"Come on, spill it..."

Lasgol sighed. "Well, you see..."

"I haven't got all night."

"I have the Gift... the Talent..."

Ulf's eyebrows arched.

"I need a drink," he said. He put the bottle to his lips and downed half the bottle in one swig.

"I wanted to tell you..."

"Since when have you had it?"

"Since I was a kid..."

"And all that time with me, you forgot to mention it?"

"No... it's just that..."

"Just nothing! By all the Gods!"

Lasgol said nothing, fearing Ulf's unbridled fury.

But it did not come. Ulf finished the bottle of wine in one final swig.

"I'm ready. Tell me."

Lasgol breathed out heavily. He summoned all his courage and described, as best he could, his Gift and the skills he had developed with it.

When he had finished, Ulf was silent for a long time, his head bowed.

"I..." Lasgol tried to explain.

"Filthy magic, that's what it is!"

Lasgol readied himself for the outburst.

But it did not come.

Ulf got to his one foot, with great difficulty.

"Don't leave like this..." Lasgol begged him unhappily.

Ulf looked up. "Who told you I was leaving?"

Lasgol looked at him blankly, and Ulf spread his arms wide.

"Come here, give me a hug."

Lasgol was left speechless.

"Don't make me say it again..."

Lasgol stood up and ran to hug the old soldier. He almost threw the crutch from under Ulf's arm.

Ulf gave him a true Norghanian bear-hug.

"I don't care whether you're a lad or a hero, whether you have the Gift or you're the King. To me you'll always be Lasgol and I'll always love you."

Lasgol, paralyzed by shock, and tears appeared in his eyes.

"There's only one thing I ask."

Lasgol stared at him, his eyes brimming with tears of emotion.

"Don't turn me into a toad."

Lasgol, with eyes moist, began to laugh. It was a moment he would never forget.

Chapter 5

The journey to the Vigons-Olafstone Duchy turned out to be pleasant, though somewhat tense. They enjoyed the journey there, the forests and rivers, the beauty of the snow-covered lands of the west of the realm. Despite this, the towns, small villages and isolated communities they passed through denied them the typical northern hospitality. They behaved with the coldness of the harsh winter that had just finished. Presumably this was a result of the tense political situation and the closeness of bloodshed.

Viggo did not mind being treated coldly. He was used to it, and to a certain extent he preferred it. He did not need to pretend and be nice. He could be himself: cold and cynical. So he enjoyed the journey a lot.

Lasgol, on the other hand, did not enjoy it so much. It saddened him to see his people, the Norghanians, behave like this, with such chilliness. The Norghanians were brave, brutal, surly, fond of fighting and alcohol, but there was one thing they were not: cold. They were direct as an arrow to the heart. The distance, the wariness, that everybody showed them wherever they went was not typical of the north. It worried Lasgol. His fellow-countrymen were behaving in a manner that hinted at coming changes, bad times for everyone. It was a foretaste of conflict... of war and death.

They went up a snow-covered hill, following a path that ran parallel to the main road but was more discreet and offered better shelter. From the top they saw the fortress-city of Estocos, the capital of the Duchy of Vigons-Olafstone.

Viggo was surprised by how substantial the big city turned out to be. "Hey, get a load of that!" he cried.

"Impressive, eh?"

"I was expecting the castle of a fairly well-off nobleman, but this is something else altogether."

Lasgol looked down at the walled city with the magnificent square castle in the middle, with its three high, square towers, the whole ensemble regal, sober and stoical. Thousands of houses surrounded it in all directions as far as the wall, which was more than sixty feet high, imposing and protective. The lands surrounding it were divided into pastures and cultivated fields, with no snow cover, and gave the Duchy the air of a small nation. And that was what it really was. Thousands of people lived there and in the surroundings.

"That wall and the castle on the hill in the center of the city look as though they'll be there for a thousand years," Viggo said.

"From what I remember from my previous visit, the walls are more than six feet thick and seemed indestructible to me. Although I don't know very much about walls and fortresses."

"This city'll stand up to years of siege, that's my opinion."

"Yeah, I think so too."

"Remind me to tease Egil for being a stinking noble, rotten with riches," Viggo said with deep sarcasm.

Lasgol smiled. "I don't think you'll need me to remind you. You're going to rub it all over his face the first chance you get."

Viggo's mouth twisted into a smile. "You're right. I'm going to enjoy it, really enjoy it."

Camu became visible in the snow and gave a little questioning shriek, as if asking whether they were making for the castle.

"Do you remember the castle?" Lasgol asked him. He was not very sure whether he would.

Camu started to flex his legs.

"I believe he does remember."

"Yeah, looks like it. And that's funny."

"Why's that?"

"He's only been here once, and that was two years ago. He was very young."

"If I were taken to a castle full of all kinds of luxury, I can assure you I'd remember too. You can bet on that."

Lasgol smiled. "I think you're right. He had a whale of a time with Egil. Besides, this was where he found the Sorcerer Muladin. It's sure to have left a mark on him."

Camu gave a huge leap and dived into the snow.

Viggo shook his head. "Isn't he ever cold?"

"Apparently not. From what we know... we think he comes from the Frozen Continent."

"That explains it."

Camu gave another enormous leap, shrieked in the air and buried himself in the snow again.

Viggo shook his head. "Crazy as a monkey."

"He is a bit daft," Lasgol admitted.

They went on. They found various lines of people who were also making for the city. They were mostly farm-workers, but there were also many armed men, mostly militia.

"Times of war," said Viggo.

"Who are they?"

"I would guess they're refugees from the towns on the border with the East. They're coming to the city for protection. Western soldiers and militia are going with them. To guarantee their safety."

"From what I've heard, Estocos is the western capital now."

"That's right, it was in the old times and it looks as if it's regained that position."

Lasgol used his Gift to communicate with Camu and get him to stay hidden and quiet.

"Let's join one of those lines of people," Viggo suggested.

"Good idea, we'll look less suspicious."

Lasgol gently spurred Trotter, and they went down to join the end of the second line. A couple of armed men came up to them and stared at them without a word, then allowed them to go on with them to the city.

They went through the great walled gate that gave access to the city inside. It was open, entrance was permitted. But there were armed soldiers at the gates watching them distrustfully. The wall too was strongly guarded. Lasgol calculated that there must have been hundreds of soldiers watching the entrance to the city alone. Viggo stared at the great wall which surrounded the city.

"Plenty of soldiers, more than a thousand of them on the wall," he whispered.

Lasgol nodded.

When they reached the main square of the city the two lines stopped. They had reached their destination. Lasgol and Viggo went on up the street, toward the imposing castle.

They stopped their mounts at the end of the road that gave access to the fortress of the Duchy. The drawbridge was raised, and on the buttresses and towers many soldiers on duty could be glimpsed. Many more than Lasgol remembered from his previous visit.

"Who goes there?" a voice called from one of the towers.

"My name's Lasgol Eklund, of the County of Malason."

"And my name's Viggo Kron, of the County of Ericsson," Viggo lied, as he was really from the East.

"You're from the West," the voice said. "But are you loyal to the League?"

This time Lasgol was able to see who was speaking. It was an officer, wearing the badge of the House of Olafstone. He was probably the one in charge of the drawbridge and access to the fortress.

Lasgol considered what to say. It was complicated. They could say they were, but if they were found out to be Rangers they would be taken for spies and hanged without a second thought. The Rangers were with King Uthar, not with the Western League. To explain their strange situation would be even more difficult. No, better not to say anything.

He avoided the question. "We've come to see Egil Olafstone."

"It's wartime. The castle is closed. Nobody's to enter or leave without authorization."

"Your lord Egil will see us," Viggo said, which put the officer in an uncomfortable situation, since Egil was one of the lords of the castle, together with his two brothers.

"Duke Austin has given the order. Nobody comes or goes without authorization."

Viggo's attempt was not working. Now the Duke was Austin, Egil's older brother, after the death of Duke Vikar in the great battle on the Frozen Continent. And so he outranked Egil.

"They're not going to allow us in," Viggo whispered unobtrusively.

Lasgol looked at the soldiers and had to agree with him. Better not to insist. One of those archers might accidentally release, and they would be in a tight spot. Better not to argue with armed men.

"Fine, we'll go," Lasgol said. He turned Trotter away, and Viggo followed his example.

They began to leave, slowly, without any sudden moves.

"Halt!"

They reined in their mounts and stayed still, listening to the sound of the wind. If they suddenly heard a whistle, it would be an arrow cutting the air.

"Come back!"

They obeyed. They were within shooting range. They had no

option.

Suddenly, and to their enormous surprise, they heard the metallic sound of the drawbridge chains, and the great gate opened.

"You may enter," the officer said, and signaled to them to move forward. They exchanged a surprised glance and spurred their horses on.

They crossed the bridge and went through the great gate to find a small figure waiting for them. Behind him were thirty or so soldiers, heavily armed.

"Welcome, my friends!" Egil greeted them with a broad smile.

Lasgol and Viggo leapt down from their mounts.

"Egil!" Lasgol cried and went to hug him. As he did, several soldiers thrust themselves in between. Lasgol stepped back.

"Easy, they're friends," Egil told the soldiers.

They hesitated for a moment, then withdrew.

"Excuse them, they have orders to protect me."

"Don't know why," Viggo said. "Who'd want to make an attempt against the life of a pompous, worthless noble?"

There was a dreadful silence. The soldiers readied themselves to kill this insolent brat.

Egil burst out laughing. Lasgol joined him, and Viggo smiled. The three of them joined in a close embrace.

"You certainly have a knack of saying the wrong thing at the wrong moment," Lasgol said.

"Yeah, but we laughed, didn't we?"

"That's true."

Egil turned to the soldiers.

"There's nothing to fear. They're my very good friends, I trust them completely."

"Do you also trust them with your family's lives?" a voice said.

They turned and saw Egil's other brother Arnold coming towards them. He was tall, strong and athletic, the complete opposite to his younger brother. He was dressed in battle armor, of very good quality. He came up to them with a sure step and a lordly presence. He was the lord of the place, there was no doubt about that.

"Yes, brother, I trust them with my life and that of my people."

Arnold came to stand in front of them and looked them up and down, his grey eyes bright with distrust. He wore his brown hair short, more in the style of the West of Tremia than that of the North.

"I recognize Lasgol," he said, and greeted him with a nod. He turned to Viggo. "You must be another teammate, am I right?"

"I am."

Arnold nodded in acknowledgement. "You're welcome here. Because of my little brother and because of what happened in the Frozen Continent... I won't forget your help... even though you are Rangers in the service of Uthar..."

"Thanks," Lasgol said.

"Captain of the Guard!" Arnold called.

Olvan came at once, and Lasgol recognized him. He was as big and almost as ugly as Ulf. The unmistakable scar on his face went from his forehead all the way down his right cheek. Unlike Ulf's, his eye had been spared.

The captain gave a respectful salute. "My lord."

"Get accommodation prepared for our guests, and have their mounts looked after."

"At once, my lord."

The captain made a sign and several men came to take charge of everything.

"I must go down to the city," Arnold said. "Business that can't wait. But I'll be back for dinner. We need to talk."

"We'll wait for you," Egil said.

"Right. See you later, then."

Arnold left, together with a guard of two dozen soldiers.

"These are difficult times for the West," Egil said. "However many precautions you take, it's never enough."

"Yes, I can see that."

"Let's go inside," he added. "Out here we're just getting in the soldiers' way, and we'll be able to talk about our affairs in private."

Inside the castle, Viggo stared at the massive labyrinth of blackish rock and the multitude of soldiers who were getting their weapons and supplies ready, or practicing in the courtyard.

"These people here aren't exactly getting ready for peace," he commented.

Egil sighed. "My brothers are preparing for the worst."

"I can see that."

"It's a wise position to take."

"Unfortunately, it is."

Lasgol said nothing, but the idea worried him. He had the distant hope that war might be avoided, that a truce might be managed, but it did not seem as though it was going to be.

"This way, follow me," Egil said. They went up a grand staircase to the second floor, then down a long corridor, through the great dining-hall, then up another staircase and along another long corridor with a library and several doors which were firmly closed and guarded by soldiers.

"This place is huge," Viggo said.

"Don't get lost," Egil said with a smile.

"I've never been lost in my life."

Lasgol muffled a laugh.

Egil went into an adjoining part of the building, and Lasgol realized that he was taking them to the great tower. They went up an endless winding stair surrounded by a wall of rock. Finally they came out on to the parapet of the great tower. From up here, the highest spot in the castle and the city, they could see the whole landscape for more than two thousand paces. This was its function in times of war. Times like those approaching.

"We'll be left in peace here for a while."

"No patrols?" Viggo asked.

"Only at night. At least, for the moment. If things get worse, it'll be all day."

"I get you. Something tells me they will get worse."

"Unfortunately I too think that the war will reach us soon."

"Let me have a proper look at you," Viggo said to Egil.

The scholar turned slowly, with his arms stretched out as though a tailor were measuring him for a new set of clothes. Viggo looked him up and down, pretending disapproval.

"You're just as skinny a shrimp as ever," he said.

"Don't say that," Lasgol snapped. "You know it's not true."

"What d'you mean, it's not true? When you see him in front of your eyes, the only thing he's done is grow older, but he's still the same scrawny rabbit."

"With friends like this, who needs enemies?" Egil said, and shrugged.

"You've said it," Lasgol agreed.

"You know perfectly well that I'm an honest man and I say what I feel."

Egil shook his head. "You're as much an honest man as I'm a

great fighter."

"And just as much as I'm a great scholar," Lasgol added.

Viggo made a sham gesture of deprecation. "Only truths come out of my mouth."

"And plenty of nonsense," Lasgol added.

Egil burst out laughing. "The honest truth is that I've missed you both a lot."

"I've missed you too," Lasgol said. He put his arm around Egil's shoulders.

"Well, I haven't in the least," Viggo said, trying to keep a straight face. But he could not keep it up for long, and he could not help chuckling.

All three of them burst into loud laughter.

Lasgol felt Camu sending him a thought. He felt it more and more strongly, more and more undeniably. He wanted to be part of this. He looked around; they were alone. He used his Gift. *Go on, Camu, appear.*

The little creature made himself visible on top of the buttress behind them.

"Look who wants to say hello," Lasgol said to Egil, who turned, saw the creature and spread his arms wide. "Camu!" he cried.

Camu jumped into his arms, and he clasped him happily. The little creature licked his cheek with his blue tongue, all the time giving little shrieks of happiness.

Egil laughed delightedly.

"I don't understand how you can let that beast lick your face with that weird tongue of his. It's disgusting. He's going to infect you with something or other, you wait and see."

"Don't be like that."

Camu licked his other cheek, and Egil laughed again. Viggo rolled his eyes.

"He's very happy to see you," Lasgol said.

"And I'm glad to see him, or her,"

"It," Viggo corrected him.

Lasgol shrugged. "One day we'll find out what he is."

While Egil played with Camu, Lasgol and Viggo looked out at the impressive views from the tower. From that height they had a clear view of the entire walled city, in all its busy beauty.

"They look like ants from up here," Viggo commented, pointing at the passers-by below.

Lasgol was looking at the distant horizon. The forests and snow-capped mountains of the kingdom always gave him a feeling of serenity. It was as if nothing affected them, as if the problems of men were insignificant. And for beings thousands of years old, like those forests and mountains, they certainly were.

"It's a fantastic view," Lasgol commented.

Viggo nodded, and they were silent for a moment, enjoying the peace and quiet the landscape communicated. They both knew it would not last.

"Watch out, someone's coming," Viggo said suddenly. He turned his head to hear better.

Camu, hide.

The creature obeyed.

"Sir..." said an elderly man as he appeared on the tower, hunched over as he walked.

"Albertsen, my faithful butler," Egil said, "you shouldn't have come all the way up here, at your age."

"Nonsense! The day I can't serve my masters will be my last day in this castle. Your brother Duke Austin sent me to look for you. It's time to get ready for dinner. The rooms are ready. I took the liberty of having baths prepared for our distinguished guests."

Viggo stared at him in amazement. "They've prepared baths for us?" he asked Egil in surprise and delight.

"I hope they will be to your liking," the servant said.

"I'm sure they will," said Viggo, for whom nobody had ever prepared a bath in his life.

"Fine," said Egil. "We'll come down right away."

Albertsen made a small bow and hobbled away slowly.

"You certainly are rotten with riches," Viggo said mockingly.

"Because I have Albertsen?"

"Him, baths, exquisite dinners and many other things."

"Those are things that come with the title."

"Now I'm starting to wish I could have a butler myself."

"Albertsen has served my family his whole life. He's not mine."

"Yeah, but it's as if he were."

"He's a faithful assistant to my family."

"You give an order and he obeys. That's what I'd like! I've always been ordered around."

"Maybe one day you'll get to be a Duke," Lasgol said.

"Yeah, sure. Once I've rescued a princess from a dragon's dungeon."

Lasgol and Egil laughed.

"I think you're perfectly capable," Egil said.

"Me too," said Lasgol.

Viggo shook his head. "Very funny."

"But you said it yourself," Lasgol said.

"So what? Let's go down. I want a bath. Will they have aromatic bath-salts?"

"We're in a Norghanian castle," Lasgol pointed out.

"Ah, you're right. There'll only be ale and weapons."

"You might be surprised," Egil said with a mischievous smile.

"Are you serious? Let's go!"

Chapter 6

Dinner would be served in the intimacy of the Duke's studio, and the three friends were told they were expected. They met in the corridor that gave access to the Duke's studio, all well-groomed and wearing clean clothes.

Lasgol caught a whiff of something sweet, strong, which delighted him. It came from Viggo.

He put his nose to his partner's dark hair. "You smell of roses," he said accusingly

"Would you believe it, they have perfumed bath salts!" Viggo said, as if this were the most amazing thing that had happened to him in a long time.

Egil gave him a friendly nudge in the ribs. "You liked them, didn't you?"

"Of course I liked them. I smell like a princess from some exotic court of the far south. For someone like me, who always smells of trouble, it's a miracle."

Egil laughed. "I've never heard it better put. You're becoming more articulate every day."

"I've no idea what 'articulate' is, but I'm sure I'm not it."

This time it was Lasgol who laughed.

"I used the salts too, but more moderately," he confessed when he finished laughing. "Camu got in the tub and started to make bubbles. It seems he loves baths too."

"Where is he?" Egil asked.

"I left him in the tub with orders to stay in the room."

"Ah, that's fine. Let him enjoy his bath."

"The problem is that he's taking less notice of me all the time."

"It must be cause he's growing."

"Yeah... too fast..."

"Don't talk about the beast as if it were your child," Viggo protested. "It gives me the creeps."

"You have to help me watch him. Very soon I won't be able to manage him."

"Don't count on me."

47

"You have my complete and absolute cooperation," Egil offered.

"Thanks, pal," Lasgol said. He knew they would both help, even Viggo, no matter how much he complained.

Viggo frowned at Egil. "I can't believe the luxury you live in. You're a filthy rich nobleman."

"They're comforts of the nobility. Don't imagine my family's very much given to luxury and eccentricity. The opposite, if anything."

"Yeah... yeah... silk sheets, embroidered cushions, tapestries on the walls, Rogdonian curtains, Nocean rugs, and all sorts of other things I haven't seen yet."

"And how do you know where the curtains and rugs are from?"

"I... well, let's say I have some 'background knowledge'… from the street..."

"From low life, you mean."

"Yes, and I'm proud of it. In the depths of the sewers and the shadows of darkness you can learn a lot, especially about the value of what you don't have."

"Or what you can steal and sell..."

Viggo looked offended. Lasgol and Egil exchanged glances. They both knew he was pretending.

"I've no idea what you're getting at, you plutocrat..."

"Nothing. Just that you have an eye for expensive tastes."

"I always have that," Viggo said, with an edge to his smile.

They arrived at the studio door, which was guarded by two soldiers. Seeing Egil they nodded and opened it. Inside, Austin, the Duke of Olafstone and his brother Arnold were waiting.

"Welcome," the Duke said.

Egil bowed his head respectfully.

"Thank you, sir," Lasgol said.

Viggo gave a slight bow.

"You must be famished after your journey."

"Just a little," Viggo replied. His eyes had gone directly to the food Albertsen was serving at his usual dormouse-like pace.

Austin waved them to the table which had been set in front of the low fire at the other end of the studio. "Let's dine first, then we'll talk."

"It's always better to talk with a full stomach," Arnold said as he sat down.

Viggo enjoyed every bite. For him, every single thing Albertsen served was a delicacy, though in fact it was the usual food at the castle, from the hands of a good cook, but not at all exotic. The dishes were traditional northern ones. Lasgol was not surprised; Austin, the Lord of the castle, did not have the look of someone who paid much attention to food and cooks. Lasgol watched him as they ate. He was tall, strong and square-jawed, and he wore his blond hair very short, like his brother Arnold. He was six years older than Egil, and his blue eyes were heavy with the enormous responsibility of the position he now held. The life of all those in the room, and of half Norghana, depended on the decisions he might make.

Once they had finished dessert – which was delicious – Albertsen asked Austin if he required anything else.

"No, that'll be all for tonight. Thank you."

The servant withdrew after cleaning up the table. The guards closed the door so that they could be alone.

"I'm glad to see you again, Lasgol," the Duke said.

"The honor is mine, sir."

"You needn't 'sir' me."

Lasgol thanked him with a respectful nod.

"And you're Viggo, aren't you?"

"Yes, sir, that's me."

"Were you at the battle of the Frozen Continent?"

"Yes, along with Lasgol and Egil. We're teammates."

Austin smiled. "I'm glad to know that. Thanks for looking after my little brother."

"You're welcome. He's inclined to be a know-all, but he's a good partner."

Arnold laughed and patted Egil's shoulder. "He knows you well," he said.

Egil nodded, smiling. "We've been together for three years, we sleep in neighboring bunk beds in the same cabin. He knows me perfectly well."

"I know I can trust Lasgol. But what about him?" Austin asked, with a wave towards Viggo.

"Yes, I'd trust him with my life," Egil replied with complete conviction.

The comment took Viggo by surprise. He nodded, deeply touched.

"Then we're among friends," Austin said.

"We are," Egil assured him.

"What we say here tonight must go no further. We're all risking our lives."

"Ours and those of the whole West," Arnold added.

"Of course," Egil said. Lasgol and Viggo gave their word.

"Right then. I'll explain the situation we're in. Uthar and his forces have withdrawn to the capital, Norghania. He's wounded and his armies are badly affected after the defeat in the Frozen Continent."

"Seems like a good moment to attack him and finish him off," Viggo said.

"That's my opinion too," Arnold said. "Now that he's weakened and wounded, we ought to finish him off for good."

Austin shook his head.

"We all want to end this situation, make Uthar pay for what he's done, but if we rush in, we'll lose."

"To get to Uthar, the capital has to be taken," Egil said, "and that's not going to be easy. The opposite, if anything."

"That's the big obstacle," Austin said.

Arnold nodded towards Egil. "We could take it. Let me be the one to lead the attack."

"No, brother, at this particular moment we can't. We're alone, and without the support of the Hosts of the Ice we can't lay siege to the city and take it."

"But we have all the forces of the West on our side. The other Counts and Dukes have sworn fealty to us. They'll support us if we give the order to attack Norghania."

"We're not ready, brother. We've just come back from the campaign in the Frozen Continent. To start a new one to take the capital would involve a lot of preparation and planning. We can't amass soldiers and march just like that. It would be a tragic mistake."

"But we have the advantage now! If we wait for spring, or if the campaign delays even more and summer comes, we'll lose all the advantage we have at the moment. Uthar will build up his strength again, and we won't be able to stand up to his armies."

"I understand you, brother. We can't afford to be hasty, but neither can we wait until Summer..."

"Brothers, if you'll allow me..." said Egil.

"Go ahead, we're listening."

"Uthar has enough forces to defend the capital. I'd remind you that the walls and defenses of the city were strengthened after the last war, which makes it very difficult to conquer. It's not impregnable, because a city as big as that is hard to defend if it's attacked from all directions. On the other hand, the West doesn't have enough forces to attack like that and put Uthar in a tight spot. To attempt a siege would be very expensive for us. Uthar can hold out behind the city walls, I calculate, for between four and six seasons."

Arnold raised his arms. "Six seasons?" he repeated despairingly.

Egil nodded.

"We can't take the capital without the help of the hosts of the Frozen Continent," said Austin, acknowledging this. "We haven't enough forces, and Uthar, even with his army reduced, can defend Norghania."

"But it'll take Darthor's forces more than one season to cross from the Frozen Continent all the way to here," said Arnold.

"One season if everything goes well," Egil said, "but most likely two."

"That brings us to Summer! Uthar will already have recovered by then and strengthened his army and defenses. We'll have lost all our current advantage."

Lasgol could not offer much to this debate between the brothers; he knew little of wars, walled cities, armies or campaigns. But he knew that whatever was decided here would affect thousands of lives, those of both Norghanians and the Peoples of the Frozen Continent. Viggo too was listening in silence. In his eyes was a dark look, as if he could foresee all the death and horror to come.

"You're the Duke," Arnold said to Austin. "It will be as you decide, since you're now the head of the family. I would only remind you of the promise we made over our father's body."

"I remember it. We'll get justice for our father."

"Justice, not revenge," Egil added.

Austin nodded. "There'll be no retaliation, only justice."

Egil acknowledged this with a nod.

"I too want to march on the capital with our forces," Austin said to Arnold. "Don't think otherwise. I want it as much as you do. But the responsibility is mine. I don't want to be over-hasty and make a wrong decision that will bring to an end all we're fighting for and usher in death and ruin to the West, to our lands."

"It's not the time for hasty decisions," Egil said, trying to support his elder brother. "Take all the time you need, my lord Duke of Olafstone. The future of the West and of Norghana falls on your shoulders at this moment in the history of the kingdom. May your decisions be remembered as wise ones."

"Thank you, brother," Austin said. "Your words are a help to me."

"We will obtain justice for our father. We will manage to unite Norghana into a strong, prosperous realm again. We will recover the crown for our house. All these things we will obtain, but I can't afford to be hasty. I'll wait for Darthor and the hosts of the Frozen Continent."

"Is that your final decision?" Arnold asked him.

"It is."

Arnold thought for a moment "I accept it, then," he then said.

"So it is decided," Austin said, ending the discussion.

"When will you speak with Darthor?" Egil asked.

"I'm expecting news from him. I need to speak to him urgently. I've sent messages by land and air. We ought to hear from him soon. Or at least so I hope."

"Good."

"Until then, we'll prepare our forces for the final attack and take the western passes so as to have them under our control."

"Leave that in my hands," Arnold said.

"What would you like me to do?" Egil asked.

Austin's face twisted in worry. "I'd like you to stay with me, but I know that's not what you want."

"I believe I can be of more help at the Rangers' Camp."

"Spying for the West?"

"That's right."

"It's very dangerous. You'll be hanged if you're found out."

"But only if I'm found out." He nodded at Lasgol and Viggo. "And my friends will help me."

Arnold sought reassurance on this. "Will they?"

"They will," Lasgol promised.

Austin and Arnold looked at Viggo, who considered this for a moment.

"They will," he said.

"Fine," Austin said, and turned back to Egil. "I won't stop you.

But promise me you won't take any unnecessary risks. I don't want your death on my conscience."

"Don't worry, Austin, everything will be fine."

Austin nodded, although his concern was obvious. Arnold stood up and raised his fist.

"For the King of the West!" he said bending one knee. "For the rightful King of Norghana!"

Lasgol, Viggo and Egil stood up and echoed the cheer.

Chapter 7

The three companions rode all day, away from wide paths or roads, always seeking the shelter of forests and the protection of hollows. This was what they had been trained to do, and they let themselves be guided by their teachings. If they had not been in a hurry, they would have travelled only under the cover of night. During their journey they saw movement of people and troops. The war was palpable in the landscape and the people, and even in the wind, which brought them smells more bitter than usual: the smell of death and destruction.

They camped not far from the river, a league from their starting-point, in the shelter of a forest. They made sure there was no danger around and made a small fire to warm themselves. Here they ate some of their supplies, in silence, sheltering from the wind that blew through trees and snow-covered branches. It was the only sound around them.

Egil shivered. He huddled deeper in his cloak and put his hands to the fire.

"I can't manage to get warm," he muttered.

"Spring'll soon be here, and then we'll be a bit more comfortable," Lasgol said.

"Perhaps the young master isn't comfortable a long way away from his castle, his servants and his wealth?" Viggo said teasingly.

Egil looked up at the sky and shook his head. "You know my body isn't especially compatible with the absence of heat."

"Cold, say cold, not 'absence of heat'. Why are you always showing off your weird vocabulary?"

"Leave him alone," Lasgol warned him.

"Don't you defend him all the time. He's grown-up enough, he can manage by himself. Besides his older brother is the heir to the crown of Norghana, so he's practically royalty."

"Contender, not heir."

"Who ought to be King by blood, Uthar or your brother?"

"My brother, by lineage and descent."

"Well, there you are. You're grown-up and royalty."

"Almost..." Egil said. "But I'm not going to fall into the vain provocations you always try to tease us with. That won't work with me. It's a waste of time."

Viggo smiled and bowed his head. "We'll see."

Lasgol took a bite of smoked meat. "I think he does it because otherwise he gets bored."

"Well, you two aren't exactly a barrelful of laughs..."

"You could be in worse company. You're fortunate enough to be travelling with a nobleman from one of the most illustrious and powerful families of Norghana, and with a national hero. Most people would be honored beyond all expectations."

Viggo considered this for a moment, then gave a disdainful wave.

"You're right. I'm beside myself with the joy of it," he said, and bit into a piece of cured cheese.

Egil and Lasgol laughed.

"I don't understand why such illustrious personages don't include wine in their provisions," Viggo said as he searched the contents of their knapsack.

"Because Rangers don't drink," Lasgol said.

"That's when they're on a mission, which we aren't, and besides, we're not full Rangers yet."

"We will be at the end of this year."

"If we get through, you mean,"

"We will get through, all of us," Lasgol said firmly.

Viggo looked at Egil. They were not so sure. It showed in their eyes.

They went on eating, alert to the sounds of the forest. When they had finished, Viggo put his hand on Egil's arm.

"Maybe you shouldn't come... you're still in time to go back to your brothers. You'll be safe with them."

Egil looked at him in surprise.

"Does it really worry you whether I live or not?"

Viggo nodded. "The last year is the most difficult. People have died... stronger ones than you..."

"I'm not giving up."

"Well said," Lasgol put in encouragingly.

"Think about it. It's a very tough year, and your situation's a very delicate one. They could hang you at any moment, as soon as Uthar gives the order. And you know he's capable of it. He's done it already."

"I swore fealty to him."

"That won't convince him. He'll use you against your brothers."

"Maybe, but I'm not going to back down. I'm going to be a Ranger and fight against Uthar." There was a determination and conviction in his voice that left no room for doubt.

Viggo shook his head. "Both of those things will end up killing you."

"Not if we protect him," Lasgol said.

"Thank you, my friend, but I don't want to put you in danger on my account. I know what I'm risking, and I'm coming of my own free will."

Viggo was still shaking his head.

"Are you sure? In your place I'd go back to the castle. I swear it."

"I am, Viggo."

"Fine," Viggo conceded, and he bent over to give Egil a brief hug.

Which was such an unexpected gesture in him that it left both Egil and Lasgol speechless.

Before settling down to sleep they tended to their horses, which were resting a few paces away under cover of a large oak. Then they checked their weapons and equipment, something every Ranger must always do before resting. Lasgol was waxing his composite bow and the arrows which he had already put together in case of anything unexpected. Viggo was honing his axe and long knife with a stone, passing it over and over so methodically that it was obvious that he had done it a thousand times. Egil was going over the contents of his Ranger's belt. He carried endless compounds and preparations in different containers in its many pockets.

"I love this belt, it's the best gift we've ever been given," he commented as he finished.

"No way," Viggo said. "The first-year gifts, the Ranger's knife and axe, are the best." He held up the weapons Dolbarar had given them as a present for graduating from the first year.

Lasgol shook his head. "I don't agree. The best gift is the Ranger's composite bow we were given at the end of the second year." He held it up. "I was really pleased when Dolbarar gave it to me."

"It seems each of us prefers a different gift."

"But how could we like the bloody belt with all its pockets and nooks?" Viggo protested.

"Because it's extremely functional. We carry all our paraphernalia in it, the things we need to confront dangers."

Viggo twirled his axe and knife. "To confront danger, you use weapons."

"You're both right," said Lasgol. "Weapons" – he showed them his bow – "need their separate parts." He showed them an arrow with a special head.

"Well then, all of us are right," Viggo said.

"Sure, as long as you're in the right yourself."

"Of course," Viggo said, and smiled from ear to ear.

Egil laughed.

They settled down to rest; by now it was already dark.

"We'll have to set a watch," Lasgol said.

Viggo pretended an innocent smile. "That's fine, I'll take the last one."

"No problem with me," Egil said. "The first or the last. I don't care."

"In that case we'll do it like this: as Viggo wants the last one and you don't mind which one you do, you take the first, I'll do the second and Viggo the last."

"Perfect."

Lasgol rested for a while as Egil took the first watch, and relaxed, although he did not sleep well. His dreams were plagued with nightmares of war, battles, blood and death. When Egil woke him up to take his turn, he was grateful; he had no desire to go on dreaming. With that partial rest his body had recovered by now, so that he was happier keeping watch than going on sleeping.

As he got up, Camu too rose as he felt him moving. Viggo, on the other hand, was sleeping like a baby under a tree.

Lasgol stretched, and as if in imitation, so did Camu. A moment later the mischievous creature was exploring their surroundings. So as not to make any noise, Lasgol concentrated, used his Gift and communicated with him.

Don't go far, and be careful.

The creature turned toward him and sent him a feeling: *Discover. Fun.*

Lasgol nodded. He knew perfectly well that his companion loved to explore, and that for him everything was fun. While the creature was enjoying running around their camp-site, he stretched his legs and investigated in his turn in case there was any danger. When he was sure that everything was calm, he settled down to take care of his short weapons.

While he honed the knife he lost himself in thought, and the face of a beautiful brunette appeared in his mind. A brunette with fierce eyes and soft, warm lips: Astrid. He was looking forward to seeing her, kissing her again, and as he thought about holding her in his arms again, doubt came over him. Suppose she no longer wanted to kiss him? Suppose she had changed her mind about him? They had spent several weeks apart and had both lived through some intense situations. Would she still want to see him? He shook his head to clear it of these doubts, this insecurity he felt. Whichever way, when he got back to the Camp and met her again, he would find out. What he knew beyond doubt was that he yearned to be with her with all his being. Every time he thought about it he felt a void in his stomach, followed by a strange feeling of warmth that rose through his body all the way up to his ears.

He sighed. The truth was that Astrid was producing some very strange effects in him: some of them very pleasant ones which he wanted to experience again as soon as possible.

Suddenly he received a feeling in his mind. It was Camu. The message hit him like a blow from a fist.

Danger!

He stood up at once and looked for the little creature, but could not see him. He used his Gift, searched for Camu's mental aura and found it twenty paces or so east. Very carefully he readied his bow and set off toward that position. He thought of waking Egil and Viggo, but it might be a false alarm, or else the creature might simply have found some animal he did not recognize. He decided to make sure there was genuine danger before he raised the alarm.

He went forward very carefully, with an arrow nocked. He tried, as he always did, to tread without making any sound and move in the shadows, hiding from the revealing light of the moon and stars. Thanks to those three years of training he could almost do it without thinking, instinctively, just as easily as he used the bow. All his senses were alert, in particular his hearing, which in the darkness of the forest was his best ally in detecting any hidden threat.

He skirted a thick oak, taking great care not to trip over its roots, and found Camu. He was very still, with his tail pointing towards another oak a few paces away.

Danger. Magic. came the warning.

He raised his bow at once and aimed it at the oak. There was something, or someone, hiding behind the tree, and there was magic about it. The hair on the back of his neck rose, so there was no doubt of it.

"Come out from behind there, very slowly," he said.

There was silence. Nothing moved, but Lasgol knew it was there.

"Come out if you want to stay alive," he said, and now his voice was threatening.

Suddenly he saw a hand appear on the other side of the tree. Then a second hand. Whoever it was wanted him to know he was unarmed, but as it was a mage that hardly mattered. A mage's power, not a sword or bow, was his weapon.

"Come on, out," Lasgol said, and tensed the string ready to shoot.

He saw a leg, followed by a body. The figure revealed itself, coming out very slowly, with its hands outspread. Lasgol recognized the black garments and the horrifying helmet that covered the mage's face at once.

It was Darthor!

"Mother..." he stammered in utter surprise.

"Hello, Lasgol. I see your restless companion is still keeping you safe from all magic."

When Camu saw her come out he relaxed. He stopped pointing his tail and gave a little shriek of joy, of recognition.

Lasgol smiled. "Yes, he's my fierce protector."

Darthor took off his helmet and Lasgol was able to see his mother's sweet face.

"I can't believe you're here," he said. He was still in shock from the unexpected nocturnal encounter.

She came over to him and hugged him tightly.

"Mother, I'm so happy."

"Seeing my son fills my heart with joy."

Mother and son embraced, sharing a moment of love and tenderness. Lasgol did not want to let go of his mother. He had the feeling that if he did, she would vanish and he would never see her ever again.

He looked around. They were on the enemy side, in the east of the kingdom. "What are you doing here? Why take the risk?"

She kissed his forehead. "I needed to see you, talk to you," she said.

He was so happy to see her, so moved that his eyes moistened. "I thought you'd be in the Frozen Continent."

"That's what we want Uthar to believe. But I'm not, I've already crossed over."

"Did you come alone?"

"No, I have a select escort with me: Wild Ones and Glacial Arcanes. They're camped inside the forest, further in. We don't want to be seen, so we only travel at night. For the moment we've managed to pass undetected. And if anyone did see us, I can manage..."

She was moving her hands as if she were about to cast a spell. Lasgol knew that his mother's power was immense. She was one of the most powerful sorcerers of all Tremia. Or so everybody said. She could cast a spell and dominate whoever she wanted, whole groups of people. He himself had witnessed this during the great battle in the Frozen Continent. And even so, he felt he needed to protect her, look after her. At least when she showed herself to him without that horrifying helmet. Once she put it on she became Darthor and did not seem to need anybody's help. Darthor seemed capable of conquering any kingdom on his own.

"How did you know you'd find me here?"

"The Rangers have taken new precautions this year, changing the frequency of the trips to the Camp and the points of embarkation. But I knew you'd have to come through here, so I've been waiting for you."

"Why, is there anything wrong, Mother?"

"Yes, my son, I need to talk to you. But first, let me look at you." She took a step back and looked him over from head to toe. "Every time I see you, you look more like your father, and you have no idea how happy it makes me and what joy it fills my heart with."

Camu came over to her, and like a kitten, got in between her feet.

"He doesn't seem to be afraid of you," Lasgol said.

"That's because he senses that I'm not going to hurt you. This is a very special creature. It took me a long time to find him. There are hardly any of its kind left."

"Is he from the Frozen Continent?"

She shook her head. "From a frozen place beyond, a land far to the north."

"Beyond? I didn't know there was anything beyond the Frozen Continent."

"Yes, there is. A land to the northeast which hasn't been discovered yet, where exceptional and magical creatures still survive. It's a remote place, and the climate is so extreme that it's practically uninhabitable. Very few have managed to come back alive. I'm one of those exceptions."

"Is the climate more extreme than that of the Frozen Continent?"

She nodded. "Even the Wild of the Ice have trouble travelling through it."

"Then it must be a terrible place."

"I wouldn't say that, it's a place where a man has very rarely been seen. Or in my case a woman."

"But you went there, and that's where you found Camu."

She nodded. "And it cost me a lot. I almost lost my life. He'll be a wonderful protector and friend to you, he'll save you from many dangers. That's why I went in search of him, so that he'd be your guardian. I don't want what happened to your father to happen to you... As far as it's possible I want to help you."

Lasgol looked at Camu, who began to flex his legs happily, and smiled. "Right now, with the amount of time he spends asleep, he'd find it pretty hard to save my life."

"Wait until he grows, and then you'll agree with me."

"In fact when it comes to detecting magic and countering it, he's already been very useful."

"Well then, keep using him. And take good care of him. I'd thought they were extinct. Luckily I was wrong."

"Why don't you keep him? You need him more than I do."

Mayra hugged her son.

"It makes me very happy that you should put my safety before your own."

"You're my mother."

"A mother who's been absent all your life."

"But my mother, after all."

"You have no idea how happy your words make me."

"I mean it from the bottom of my heart, that's how I feel."

"I know, and that's why it fills me with joy," Mayra said with tears in her eyes.

"I don't want anything to happen to you..."

"I don't want anything to happen to you either. I couldn't forgive myself, after what happened with your father. That's why Camu must stay with you, to protect you. That's my wish. Promise me you won't part from him and that you'll look after him."

"I will, Mother, I promise."

Mayra hugged him tightly again.

"Listen to me carefully, son," she said, her face now very serious. "We're uniting the forces of the People of the Ice, in the Frozen Continent. With summer the moment to invade Norghana will come. That's why we must be very careful and very wary and take every possible precaution. One false move, one mistake, and everything will fall apart. Once we cross and set foot in Norghana, the attack will begin. It'll be all or nothing. It's critical that nobody should know our plans. Uthar mustn't find out either where or when we cross."

"I've just come from Duke Olafstone's castle, and they're waiting for your news. They're worried and nervous. They feel they're alone, they say they haven't heard from you or the Peoples of the Ice. Uthar's building up his strength in the capital and rebuilding his army."

"You've been in the castle with Austin?"

"Yes, I'm travelling with Egil, I went to pick him up before setting off for the Camp. Egil had already calculated that you wouldn't be able to cross until the summer. That's what he told his brothers."

"He's very intelligent, your friend Egil."

Lasgol nodded. "So he is." He looked back at their camp where they were asleep.

"Keep him close, he'll give you good advice."

"I'll do that, Mother."

"You must be very careful at the Rangers' Camp. Uthar's going to try something against Egil."

"And against me?"

"I don't think he suspects you. He doesn't know about us. Nobody knows." She looked around to make sure no one was watching them. "If Uthar finds out you're my son... he won't stop until he captures you or kills you. If you were captured, he'd use the fact against me. If he killed you... I couldn't bear it..."

"He won't."

"The Peoples of the Ice mustn't know who you are, or who I am. If they found out I'm a Norghanian woman... that my husband and son belong to the Rangers... they wouldn't understand. The Northern League is very fragile and the People of the Ice are distrustful. We must be very careful. If we're found out, by one side or the other, everything will end in disaster..."

"Don't worry, Mother, it won't happen. They won't find out through me."

"It's crucial that they don't know. That's why I came to warn you. I'm not so worried about you. I'm worried about them." She nodded towards where Egil and Viggo were sleeping. "They know who I am, don't they? You've told them."

"Yes... but you can trust them."

"Who else knows?"

"Only the members of my team, the Snow Panthers: Ingrid, Nilsa, Gerd, Egil and Viggo. But I trust them completely. They've saved my life. I can vouch for them."

"I don't doubt it, my son. But a secret that six people know isn't a secret any longer..."

"I understand, Mother. And I'll make them swear they'll never reveal it to anyone."

Suddenly Camu turned, stiffened and pointed his tail to the West, into the forest.

"He's picking up magic, Mother..."

Mayra looked in the direction Camu was pointing in.

"It must be the Arcanes who're with me. They must be looking for me. I've been away for a while, and they'll be concerned. We'd better say goodbye."

"You're leaving?"

"I must," Mayra said, and hugged him tightly. "I love you very much, my son. I'm very proud of you. One day you'll be a great man. I know it."

"Mother, I love you."

Mayra put on her helmet and vanished through the trees to become Darthor. She left in the direction Camu was pointing in.

Lasgol thought he glimpsed a pair of violet eyes, but they vanished immediately.

He was left alone with Camu, wishing he had been able to spend more time with his mother.

Chapter 8

This year the journey up-river was going to be rather different. The Rangers had changed the details and timing of the trips to the Camp because of the war. As the *Path of the Ranger* laid down, they needed to be very wary, careful never to repeat schedules that the enemy might intercept or guess.

Viggo looked around. "This is the point we used to leave from. It's deserted."

Lasgol knelt and saw a clear trail that followed the riverbank. "I think we have to go upriver," he said.

"Dolbarar already warned us that the journey back would be more complicated," Egil said. "He told us not to wait for the assault ships, but to find our own way."

"I thought it was one of his metaphors about life and the *Path of the Ranger*," Viggo said with his hands on his hips.

Egil shook his head. "This time his meaning was literal. The Rangers are taking precautions. There won't be any ships or journeys in groups. We'll have to manage on our own."

"Are you sure we have to follow this trail?" Viggo asked Lasgol.

"Well, not absolutely sure… but there's nobody here… or rather nobody to be seen, although my instinct tells me we're being watched from the forest." He glanced to the east and shivered.

"Your instinct or your Gift?"

"Both…"

"Then it must be true," said Viggo, squinting to see if he could glimpse a hidden Ranger, something which was extremely difficult, or even impossible when they were camouflaged in woodland.

"I think the fact that we can see such a clear trail at the precise meeting-point is a more than significant sign," Egil said. "We'll follow it to the end and see what's in store for us."

Viggo shrugged. "Whatever you say."

"Well then," Lasgol said cheerfully, "on we go."

They went on for a day and a night at an easy pace, following the trail, which ran parallel to the river. They met no surprises on the way, but Lasgol could not shake off the feeling that he was being watched. Even Camu seemed to feel the same, because he barely put his head out of the travelling satchel, and it was something he usually loved to do.

They came to a sharp bend, and Lasgol called a halt.

"We'd better look into what's on the other side before we take this sharp bend. I don't like it."

"One wary man is worth two careless ones," Egil said.

"I don't know whether he'd be worth two," Viggo said with a sinister smile, "but he'd certainly live longer."

Lasgol smiled and was about to go forward, but Viggo raised his hand.

"I'll do this," he said with a wink. "I'm better at this game than either of you."

He leapt off his Norghanian pony and with absolute stealth, crouched double, he went up the hill which formed the bend. When he disappeared between the trees, they lost sight of him. Lasgol knew Viggo was right; he was much better than they were at the art of stealth, of hiding his presence, or at anything to do with the School of Expertise. He seemed to have a natural affinity with it. And despite what had happened the year before when he had been kidnapped by the bandits, it did not seem to have affected him. Lasgol found this unbelievable; anybody else would never have volunteered after what Viggo had gone through. And yet he was doing it without a thought. It said a lot about him, about his character and inner strength. It also spoke volumes about how much he had changed. Three years before, he would never have dreamed of taking a risk on their behalf; Lasgol was sure of that. He smiled at the memory of his first encounter with Viggo. Now his comrade was stepping forward without a second thought. He knew it was a situation that suited his own skills, and he preferred to endanger himself rather than put his friends at risk.

It's surprising how much a person can change and how mistaken you can be when you come to judge him.

Lasgol felt very lucky to have him as a teammate and friend, however much of a pain he could be.

It took Viggo a long time to come back, and Lasgol and Egil were beginning to worry. Luckily he finally reappeared at the point he had left from.

"Everything all right?" Lasgol asked him.

"Yes, but I had a pretty funny meeting on the way." He pointed back at the forest he had just come out of. "I met a Ranger in there."

"Curious," Egil said.

"Yes, it was. He was hiding in a treetop. It took me a good while to find him, but in the end I did."

"Is that why you took so long?"

Viggo laughed. "No, it wasn't that. What happened was that I didn't see him and he didn't see me. It was quite comical."

Lasgol smiled. "That means you're getting better at passing unnoticed in the forest."

"Or else that Ranger was taking a nap."

Egil burst out laughing. "I doubt that very much."

"He told me we have to keep going north for two more leagues. A small boat'll be there to pick us up. It looks as though this year we've dodged Captain Astol's shouting and bad temper."

"Most likely his fast assault ship is being used in the war," Egil said. "I very much doubt whether he'll be allowed to use it to transport students to the Camp. The war's a lot more important, and they need that ship."

Camu put out his head and gave a small inquisitive shriek. Lasgol scratched his head.

"It's nothing. Don't worry and sleep a little longer. I'll let you know when we get there"

The little creature licked his hand, then gave another shriek and dived back inside.

They went on north for two leagues until they came to a small clearing in the middle of the forest that gave on to the river. There they found another Ranger waiting, with several small boats. The place was surrounded by the forest and could barely be glimpsed from the river. A good place to embark; nobody would see them. The Ranger barely spoke to them. He pointed to the boat they had to take, then sent them upriver.

"And what about our horses?" Lasgol asked. He was concerned about Trotter.

"I'll take care of them," was the only reply.

He nearly asked more, but the Ranger's gesture of displeasure told him it would be better not to.

They boarded the small boat, took the oars and rowed upriver.

"Oh what unbelievable fun we're going to have," said Viggo.

"Shut up and row," said Lasgol. "We'll get there sooner that way."

"The distance to be covered is unalterable, so whether Viggo talks or not makes no difference to whether we arrive sooner or later," Egil commented.

"Very nicely put, know-all."

"You're wrong," Lasgol said.

"Oh yes? How's that?"

"If he doesn't shut up I'll hit him on the head with an oar and he'll make us waste time, then we'll take longer."

Egil smiled. "Right, but then we won't arrive any sooner, just not quite so late."

"Nobody's going to hit me with any oar," said Viggo, who was seated at the prow glowering back at them.

Lasgol had to hold back his laughter.

They rowed at a good pace. He enjoyed the journey, the calm waters, the company of his friends. He felt at peace, and as far as he was concerned the journey was shorter than he would have liked. They reached the Foot of the Camp and left the boat there, then presented themselves to the Rangers on watch-duty, who gave them their instructions. Eventually they came to the Camp.

It was dawn, and the huge natural barrier that surrounded the southern entrance received them impassively. A moment later the hidden gate was opened and they were allowed in.

Lasgol felt a strange mixture of longing and nervousness at once again entering that secluded world where he had learned so many things.

Egil was more serious than usual. He knew what he was gambling.

Before they could adjust to their surroundings, two Rangers approached them, grim-faced, bows at the ready.

"Identify yourselves,"

"Lasgol, Egil and Viggo, Fourth-Year students," Lasgol said, trying to sound as official as possible. "We're here to start the year as we were told to."

The two Rangers inspected them from head to foot.

"Which teams do you belong to?"

"All from the Snow Panthers, sir."

The two Rangers looked at one another, then at another Ranger who was watching from a little further away. In his hands was a scroll, and he was studying the three of them as he read it. After a brief, intense scrutiny, he nodded.

"Right, you can come in."

Lasgol did not know the Ranger who had granted them passage, nor had he ever seen him at the Camp before. He would have remembered him, since one remarkable feature made him unmistakable: his skin was red.

"That's a Masig of the Prairies," Egil whispered to Lasgol excitedly as they moved away.

"Now that really is weird," Viggo said. He was looking back to make sure he was not hallucinating.

Lasgol too glanced back over his shoulder and could confirm that this wiry man with an aquiline nose, small black eyes and long jet-black hair was certainly a Masig.

"Why's it so strange?" he asked.

"Because Norghanians and Masig hate each other to death," Egil pointed out.

"Or rather," Viggo added, "the Masig hate us to death because of the atrocities we've committed against them,"

Lasgol tried to remember what he knew of them. He recalled his father telling him that the Masig were the People of the Steppes, nomadic hunters scattered across hundreds of small tribes that dominated the prairies. They were ferocious fighters and great horsemen. They tamed wild pinto horses and used them for hunting and war. It was true that the Norghanians considered them a semi-wild people, illiterate and aggressive. Savages. Lasgol had seen one or two Masig before being taken to Count Malason's castle in chains as prisoners.

"The way we've treated them for hundreds of years is a disgrace," Egil said, sounding embarrassed. "They're our closest neighbors to the southeast, and we treat them like rabid wild animals."

"You mean like we treat the Peoples of the Frozen Continent," Viggo insisted.

Egil bowed his head in shame. "Yes, or even worse. Often I'm ashamed of being Norghanian."

"What have we done to them?" Lasgol asked, and regretted the question as soon as he had asked it.

"Pillage, plunder, massacres, torture, and other delights," said

Viggo.

"I can't believe it."

"Remember, Norghana's one of the most powerful kingdoms of the continent, and you don't get there without bloodshed."

"That's horrible."

"It's life," said Viggo. "The strong beat the weak. It's always been like that."

"Well, it shouldn't be!" Lasgol said furiously.

"That's why we're here," Egil said, "to prevent it as far as possible."

"I doubt very much whether we could break a tradition that's hundreds of years old. The Norghanians have always attacked the weaker tribes and lived off plunder. It's part of our culture. Why do you think we have such fast assault ships? Precisely for that, for raids on lands belonging to weaker tribes and kingdoms."

"To me that way of life's abominable."

"Well, it's the Norghanian way of life. That's why the other kingdoms fear us, and especially the semi-wild tribes like the Peoples of the Ice, the Masig, Usik and others."

"New blood, new ideals," Egil said, looking at his partners. "We'll begin the change. The Norghanians will reject that way of life and become respected for their virtues."

Viggo laughed. "You're a naïve goody-two-shoes. We Norghanians have no other virtue beyond being a race of giant brutes who for hundreds of years have done nothing but loot and plunder."

"I think we're more than that."

"You'll have to show me, because I can't see anything else."

Lasgol sighed. He knew Viggo was right, even though it was hard to admit. He remembered that in Skad stories were told of the feats of those captains who plundered the north coast, and the ones who went south down the great rivers as far as the prairies... the Masig lands. He felt downhearted. To realize that his people, the Norghanians, were not as glorious as they ought to be was not easy to swallow. But after seeing what they were doing to the Peoples of the Ice there could be no doubt. It was easy for him to believe that they were doing the same to the Masig. It was deeply depressing to find out that the Norghanians were just brutes and bullies who loved war, plunder and pillage.

"Let's not give up hope," Egil said. "There are much worse

kingdoms: the Noceans, the people of the desert, for instance. The brutalities they're capable of are well known and they have a dreadful reputation. We need to keep our chins up. We're the People of the Snow, strong warriors, tall, blond and pale like our land, who wield axes and whom nobody can defeat in the battlefield. The best infantry in the continent. We must be proud. Not all of us behave like bandits."

Egil's words lightened Lasgol's spirits a little.

"Sure," Viggo said. "Wait till you're sent on a pillaging mission on the King's orders."

"I'll refuse to go."

"Then you'll hang."

Lasgol looked round the center of the camp, trying to locate the rest of his friends. One in particular... but he could not see any of them. Rangers and pupils of all four years were going from one end to the other, carrying out their routine tasks. They all looked very busy.

Viggo was standing beside him, watching what went on with suspicious eyes. "Everything's very messy," he commented.

"It must be because of the war," Egil said. He indicated several Rangers who were carrying wicker baskets containing hundreds of arrows.

And at last Lasgol saw the one person he longed to see.

The Captain of the Owls.

Astrid.

Chapter 9

Lasgol took a step toward Astrid. His heart began to beat violently and his stomach lurched. He could not take his eyes off her, and found himself longing to kiss her. He started to walk towards her; she had not noticed him and was chatting with one of her teammates. He forgot where he was and who he was with, so that he left Egil and Viggo behind and went toward Astrid like a moth seeking the light.

"Lasgol!" cried a powerful voice.

Before he could even realize who was calling his name, someone lifted him off the ground in a powerful bear-hug.

Someone huge.

Gerd.

Lasgol found himself in the air, unable to breathe.

"It's great to see you!" Gerd said. He was spinning around without allowing Lasgol to put his feet back on the ground. The giant was smiling from ear to ear, and joy was obvious on his face.

Lasgol had to laugh. "Let me down before you break my back!"

Gerd laughed too and gave another twirl without letting go of him.

"In the end that big slob is going to get dizzy and both of them'll end up on the ground," said Viggo.

"Hey, pal! How glad I am to see you!

Viggo clapped his hands to his face. "Don't even come anywhere near me!"

Too late. The giant caught him in another huge bear-hug and lifted him off the ground. He began to spin, with Viggo protesting and launching a stream of curses. He looked like a talking puppet in the arms of a giant.

Egil watched the scene, grinning. Knowing what was in store for him once Gerd realized he was there too, he was trying to avoid being noticed.

Lasgol filled his lungs with air and recovered from his friend's affectionate embrace.

"Put me down at once, you brainless giant!" Viggo yelled. He was still trapped in the bear-hug.

Gerd took one more spin, became dizzy and had to drop him before they both fell over.

"What a half-witted oversized lump he is!" Viggo moaned while he regained his balance.

Gerd put his hands to his head while he did the same. A moment later he saw Egil, yelled his name and lunged to hug him.

Egil, who knew what was coming, closed his eyes and smiled. Gerd gave him a bear-hug and lifted him off the ground, but this time did not spin.

"I've missed you so much!" he shouted.

"We've missed you too," Egil said.

"But it's only been a few weeks," Viggo said.

"It seemed like a whole season to me," Gerd said.

Lasgol was happy to see old Gerd again. The giant always made him feel happy.

"Where are the girls?" he asked.

"Ingrid and Nilsa are at the Quartermaster's depot." Gerd's face changed and became somber. "The moment we arrived we were all put to work. It seems a great battle's on its way, or so say the rumors in the Camp, and all the Rangers and pupils are working to help with the war effort."

"I see Dolbarar's got you all very busy," Egil said. He was looking around at the constant bustle of weapons and supplies.

"How long ago did you arrive?" Lasgol asked Gerd.

"Three days ago, and the girls, two. You're late, as always." There was an enormous smile on his face.

"We should've delayed a few more days," Viggo said making a face. "They're going to make us work like slaves..."

"But you love to cooperate!" Egil said with heavy irony

"Sure, there's nothing I'd like more – apart from all the drilling we'll have to endure– than loading crates and sacks for the good of the army."

"And the Rangers," Gerd noted.

"Well, let's see if I can manage to get out of it..."

Suddenly a voice giving orders sounded behind Viggo.

"Look lively! You all look like a bunch of weaklings who've never worked a day in their lives!"

"I recognize that voice!" Viggo said without turning round.

"It's Master Instructor Oden," Egil said.

Viggo frowned. "Tell me he's not coming for us."

Oden barked out several orders at a Second-Year group, then headed for the stables.

"It seems we're free for the moment," Egil said.

Viggo snorted with relief. "We'd better get out of here before he sees us and sends us to load carts."

"I don't know why they say you never have any good ideas," Egil said with a smile.

"Shut up, book-head, and let's go."

They headed toward the Fourth-Year cabins, which were the furthest from the center of the Camp, in the middle of a dense forest north of the Command House.

Lasgol looked around for Astrid, but could not find her. She must have gone to carry out some task Oden had ordered.

There were a few fellow-pupils outside the cabins, and they exchanged greetings. The badge of the Snow Panthers was hanging on the door of one of the cabins. When they went in they saw that these cabins were bigger and more comfortable than in previous years, as if they were being given a reward for reaching the final year of instruction.

"Oh, I really like this shack," Viggo said. He hurried to lie down on one of the bunks.

Gerd was about to protest that it was the one he wanted himself, but a glower from Viggo clearly indicated that he was not prepared to give it up.

"This year I fancied sleeping in the upper bunk."

"Yeah, so it caves in with your colossal weight and I get squashed to death by your great body."

"The bunk won't give. I've already slept in it."

"Yeah, and you expect me to trust you? Besides it's very soft, I love it." Viggo made himself as comfortable as he could.

Gerd snorted in disgust.

Lasgol patted his shoulder encouragingly. He and Egil organized their bunks with no problem, as they always did.

Gerd closed the door at Lasgol's suggestion, and he let Camu out of the travelling satchel on his back. The creature leapt on the beds at once and began to play, giving a series of small, happy shrieks. When he saw Gerd he hurled himself on him.

The big guy had no time to react. He found Camu clasped to his chest. "Oh, no!"

Camu climbed up his massive torso and licked his cheek.

Gerd, wide-eyed, did not know whether to be frightened or glad, or both. So he decided on both. The creature still awoke an irrational fear in him, since it was magical; on the other hand, after spending three years running away from him he had become used to him and knew he would not harm him, that he only wanted to play. He tried, forced himself to ignore his fear and stroked Camu.

"Good Camu," he said.

The little creature licked his hand and let out a joyful shriek.

Lasgol noticed the effort Gerd had made to control his irrational fear. He could tell from his face. One instant he was pale as a ghost and his eyes seemed about to pop out in that moment of panic. Then his eyes half-closed and he frowned; he was fighting his fear, he wanted to control it. And finally the color came back to his face, his eyes and forehead returned to their normal state. He had conquered his fear. Lasgol was glad for the big guy. In those earlier years he had not succeeded in conquering it and had panicked, fleeing from Camu like an elephant from a mouse that was chasing him all over the room. What he had managed seemed a mere trifle, but in fact it was nothing of the sort, because the fear Camu awoke in him was the same fear he showed in many other situations. Gerd was overcoming some of his fears, and that was very significant and something to celebrate. Camu was having a very positive effect on him.

The big guy was patting the little creature. "He's gotten huge."

Lasgol nodded. "Yeah, it looks as though he's beginning to grow quite a bit more."

"And his weight is now decidedly substantial," Egil said as he came over to pet him too.

Camu was in seventh heaven with their attentions.

Suddenly there came a knock at the door. Gerd hastened to hide Camu, and they waited for him to vanish into a corner. The little creature knew he had to hide whenever someone knocked at the door or opened it. There was no need to tell him.

"Come in," Lasgol called.

The door opened and Ingrid appeared.

"Hey, Panthers! Fourth year!" the Captain said with a smile in her usually serious face.

"I'm delighted to see you, Captain," Lasgol said and they hugged.

"Me too, hero."

They both smiled. Ingrid was more mature, more womanly. Or at least, that was how it seemed to Lasgol.

"As much a leader as ever," Egil said, and gave her a hug.

Nilsa ran in after Ingrid, tripped and pulled Viggo down with her.

"Of all the clodhoppers in Norghana!" he grumbled from the floor.

"Sorry... it's the excitement." She stood up and fell on Lasgol and Egil, who were instantly enfolded in a warm embrace.

Gerd went to the door and closed it. "Come on, group hug," he said.

"No, no gushy stuff, I refuse," Viggo protested.

"Come on, don't be like that."

Viggo grumbled a little, but then he joined Gerd who was already spreading his arms wide.

The six partners joined in a group hug. For a moment they all felt very well, happy even, with smiling faces and jubilant souls. Inevitably it was Viggo who broke up the group.

"That's enough. All this gush makes me want to puke."

"Shut up, blockhead," Ingrid said.

"You shut up, Miss Bossy-Boots."

"You're going to swallow my fist."

"That'll be if you catch me, which you won't because I'm faster than you."

Nilsa laughed. "Looks as though everything's still just the same."

Camu made himself visible suddenly and jumped at Gerd to keep playing. Nilsa was so startled that she fell on her butt.

Gerd covered his mouth with his hands to muffle a guffaw.

Lasgol watched the scene, so familiar, so normal, and felt happy to be there with his friends, to be sharing those moments with them. He could not help smiling from ear to ear.

"You're the best," he said.

"Of course we are," Ingrid said. "We're the Snow Panthers!"

"Thanks, Lasgol," Nilsa said as he helped her up.

"See? He's got all sensitive," said Viggo.

"I think you're the best too, and I'm happy we're all back," said Gerd.

"We're all a little sensitive because of the war," Egil said.

Ingrid nodded. "Yeah, this is going to be a very interesting final year."

"And a difficult one," Nilsa said as she rubbed her backside.

"Not just difficult, but pretty intense and dangerous," said Viggo.

"Well, the last three years haven't been exactly easy," Gerd commented.

"Sure but this one loops the loop," Viggo went on. "We have to graduate as Rangers, and the fourth year is the most difficult. And on top of that, we're in the middle of a war, and we're going to find ourselves in the thick of it, that's for sure. And just to add a bit more excitement to it all, we're on the wrong side, Uthar's. Who, in case you've forgotten, is a shifter who wants to conquer half Tremia and kill anyone who gets in his way, among them Egil, who he already tried to hang last year. And if it's not Uthar it might be Darthor and his Wild of the Ice, because if we're not careful they'll be wanting to kill us too for being on Uthar's side."

There was a moment's silence.

"When you put like that..." Ingrid said, sounding troubled.

Nilsa was biting her nails and looking at Gerd, who by now was pale as a ghost.

Egil made sure the door was firmly closed. "You've forgotten that Lasgol and I support the West..."

"And so we can add high treason to the list of complications," Viggo said in a voice of despair.

Lasgol said nothing. It was going to be a very complicated year. They were risking their lives in more than one way.

Chapter 10

Lasgol was unable to sleep that first night at the Camp. He got up from his bunk and went out to breathe the fresh winter air and clear his mind. Viggo's words had affected him, and he could not stop turning them over in his mind. The situation he found himself in was so dangerous that he could see no possible way out.

He inhaled the icy air, and the cold reached his brain. He shook his head. He enjoyed that feeling. It smelt of winter, of the north, of Norghana. He felt a little better. The most important thing at the moment was to start their training and make sure the Rangers, or the King, did not find out that they were working for Darthor and the Western League. If he could manage that, they would survive. Or at least, so he hoped. Then there was the great problem of the war. Viggo was right: one way or another, they would be involved in it. He thought about his mother and shivered.

Please don't let anything happen to her, he prayed to the Gods of the Ice, looking up at the cloudy sky.

"The hero is thoughtful tonight," came a voice suddenly.

Lasgol turned and saw Astrid. His heart skipped a beat.

"Astrid!" he murmured with a smile that came directly from his soul.

She came up to him, looked into his eyes, smiled back at him and embraced him. Lasgol's heart filled with joy. He felt a wave of heat climb up his belly, chest and neck as far as his face.

"Have you missed me?" she asked, her fierce green eyes gleaming.

"A little, yes," he said, trying to play it tough. After all, he was a boy and as she said, a hero. And from what Viggo said, boys ought not to appear too interested when they were trying to gain the attention of girls.

"So just a little," she replied in an icy voice, and tossed her jet-black mane to one side in a gesture of clear rejection.

Lasgol saw the angry expression on her face and was forced to think again. What the hell did Vigo know about girls, anyway?

"Well... perhaps more than a little."

Her gaze softened. "I thought I meant something to you. Maybe I was wrong..." she countered in a voice half-sweet, half-sensual, which trapped him completely.

He realized that things were going badly and felt an emptiness in the pit of his stomach. The last thing he wanted was to lose Astrid.

"Of course you mean something to me. You mean a lot."

She looked at him for a moment and cocked her head.

"Then you've missed me?" she asked, for a second time.

"Yes, I missed you a lot."

A delightful smile appeared on Astrid's face, and her fierce expression vanished, giving way to a sweet one that she rarely allowed to be seen.

"That's much better."

"You're..." he complained, defeated. The fierce beauty of her face, and eyes, her jet-black hair, her well-honed body with certain additional curves he could not help but notice, trapped him and left him speechless. He was left stunned just looking at her. And he felt a wellbeing, a warmth, along with various intense and pleasant feelings throughout his body that he could not avoid.

"Don't play the hard-to-get hero with me, it won't work."

"Sorry..."

She smiled. "I know you, and I like you just the way you are."

Her words made his heart beat faster. He needed confirmation to calm what his soul was feeling at that moment. "Do you really like me?"

"Yes, I do, a lot," she replied, and winked.

Lasgol felt as though something was exploding inside him, filling him with uncontrollable joy. For a single instant he thought his heart would leap out of his chest with elation.

"I like you too."

"Come here, you dummy," she said. Taking his hand, she pulled him towards her.

They were now body to body. His heart was begging him to embrace her, kiss her, love her.

"Kiss me," she said.

And he did. He felt her lips on his own, and the sweetest and most pleasurable of feelings enveloped him, as if he were in some midsummer dream. A moment later an overwhelming passion surged from his soul and he kissed her as if this were the last moment they would ever share.

At dawn Oden's little bell and its infernal ringing woke everybody up, except Lasgol, who refused to wake, still immersed in a sweet, intense and passionate dream.

"Wake up, Lasgol, or else we'll be late for the assembly," Egil said.

Lasgol managed to open one eye. "Line up? Already?"

"It seems we were the last ones to arrive. The term's beginning."

"The fourth and final year," Gerd said, looking scared.

Lasgol sat up in his bunk, trying to clear his mind of sleep.

"You had a good night, didn't you?" Viggo said teasingly as he put on his pants.

"Er… yes…"

"I'd say more than yes. You're a real Romeo."

Egil and Gerd looked at him in surprise.

"I… I didn't…"

"Don't pretend, I saw you."

"What d'you mean, you saw me?"

"I see practically everything that goes on around me," Viggo said with a triumphant smile.

"What's he talking about?" Gerd asked Lasgol.

"Nothing."

"What do you mean, nothing? Romeo here was out wooing last night. No more and no less than that fierce brunette the Captain of the Owls."

Lasgol did not want the subject mentioned. "Viggo!"

"Astrid?" Gerd said, obviously wanting to know more.

"It's not gentlemanly to talk about delicate subjects like this," Egil said, "and of course the lady's name should never be mentioned."

"That's the pompous nobleman speaking. Where I come from you do talk about it, and you're proud of it."

"That's vile and contemptible," Egil said, "but on the other hand you come from the sewers of a great city…"

"Very true," Viggo replied, puffing out his chest, "And I'm proud of it!"

"Viggo," said Lasgol, "stop following me. And not one single word about Astrid or any other girl."

"You really aren't a lot of fun to be with, are you?"

"A young lady's honor isn't something you toy with," Egil said reproachfully.

"Yeah, yeah, you wet blanket. Just when we've got a succulent bit of gossip, and about one of us no less..."

"What succulent bit of gossip?" Nilsa asked as she came in.

Lasgol glared at Viggo, who shrugged and adopted a resigned expression. "Nothing, just my nonsense."

"That's all you ever say, nonsense," Ingrid said as she came in after Nilsa.

Viggo finished dressing, cursing his luck for having fallen in with a team of wet blankets, know-alls, scaredy-cats, butterfingers and bossy-boots.

They went out to line up in the new brown cloaks they had found in the trunk which each of them had assigned to them beside their bunks. The color was quite close to that of the Rangers' cloaks, which made them feel a little nearer succeeding, a little better, more confident in the path they had been following till that moment.

Oden was waiting for them with his usual lack of good humor. "Line up! Quick!" he barked, still ringing his little bell.

They all fell in, with one knee on the ground, looking straight ahead, Ranger-style.

Lasgol's gaze searched for Astrid and hers for him. Their eyes met and they smiled with happiness.

"Today you begin your Fourth-Year instruction. You'll certainly be feeling revitalized, because this is your last year and you think you're going to make it."

"I don't..." Gerd whispered to Egil.

"Courage, big guy," Egil replied, and winked at him.

"Well, don't be so smug, not everybody makes it through the final year. There are always casualties. I wonder which of you won't make it. I have my bets." He looked at the Panthers.

Gerd swallowed.

"Don't pay any attention to him," Ingrid muttered.

"This year, the last, is the hardest."

There was a murmur among the teams. "We hear that every year," said a voice.

"And isn't it true?"

They had to admit it was.

"Besides, this year we have an added complication: the war."

The murmurs broke out again.

"I don't want to see a single altercation because of the war. I won't tolerate it. There are some westerners here who've decided to support Uthar and remain with the Rangers. You will respect that decision."

The murmurs now grew into protests.

"They're traitors," the same voice said, and Lasgol recognized that of Isgord.

The whispers were in favor of this assessment.

"No. A traitor is someone who commits an act of treason. Until it's committed, everybody is innocent. So you'll respect them. I don't want any squabbles about whether people are from the east or the west. Here we're all Rangers and we support the King, the Norghanian crown."

Isgord did not agree, and neither did his team. Nor did the Boars, the Bears and other teams seem very convinced. Lasgol knew there was trouble ahead.

"Not another word!"

The protests died down slowly, and finally there was silence.

"And now we'll go and see Dolbarar so he can officially inaugurate the beginning of the Fourth Year of instruction."

The Camp Leader was waiting for them in front of the Command House on the small island in the center of the lake. The Four Master Rangers were lined up behind him. The Fourth-Year pupils crossed the bridge and assembled before them.

Dolbarar welcomed them with a slight smile. Lasgol noticed that it was not his usual one; it was more restrained, not so kind or reassuring. This surprised him and made him a little nervous. There might be bad news. He looked at Egil beside him and sighed.

"Welcome to you all," Dolbarar greeted them, his staff in one hand and the *Path of the Ranger* in the other. "Now begins your final year of training as Rangers. This will be a year you won't forget for the rest of your lives, both those who succeed in graduating and those who do not. I am not going to lie to you, it will be more difficult because it's the final one, and not all of you will pass it. So says the *Path* and so we must respect it. Only by following the difficult path will we obtain a strong group of Rangers worthy of the name."

Gerd breathed out heavily, looking worried. Egil shivered restlessly.

"This course is a little different from the three previous ones. The structure of the classes will change. In the mornings you will continue improving your physical condition in teams as you've done until now. In the evenings you'll assemble according to the School you now belong to, and this will be special as the Master Rangers themselves will be instructing you." Dolbarar turned to the Master Rangers. "Ivana the Infallible will be in charge of teaching you advanced concepts of the School of Archery. Eyra the Erudite will be teaching you the grandeur of the School of Nature. Esben the Tamer, the necessity of the School of Wildlife. Haakon, the importance of the School of Expertise for the survival of Rangers after they graduate."

"Good!" Ingrid said eagerly. "They'll be teaching us themselves all year. It'll be fantastic."

"I'm not so sure," Viggo said. "We've already had some instruction with them, and it didn't go so well."

Nilsa was biting her nails. "It increases the pressure," she said.

"You can say that again," Gerd said. "I feel a lot of respect for them."

Lasgol understood what they meant, but there was something more important.

"Whatever they teach us this final year is going to save our lives in the future. I'm positive about that."

The four Master Rangers gave Dolbarar a respectful bow, and he returned the salute. before he turned back to the pupils. "This year you become Contenders."

They looked at one another with pride and restlessness. There were murmurs of approval.

"This year we have an added difficulty. The kingdom is at war... and not only this, which we have borne the burden of since last year, but the country is divided in two. Norghanians fight Norghanians, brothers against brothers, which gives me immense pain. Fighting against a foreign enemy is hard. Fighting against your own people is traumatic and devastating, something that marks the soul. It will take the kingdom a long time to recover from this horror. Many lives will be lost that should never have been, but we're all Norghanian, whether we're from the east or the west. The differences which separate us and which have caused bloodshed are something we will suffer for generations. The same thing happened the first time, for this has happened before, on the death of Misgof Ragnarssen when he died childless, when Ivar Vigons and Olav Haugen fought for the crown. And that was a horror and a shame."

Now the murmur was one of unease and fear.

"Unfortunately we find ourselves amid another Civil War. There are two sides which are clearly divided, both by blood and by land of birth. The Rangers owe their loyalty to the Crown, and it is the Crown which we will defend. It doesn't matter who the King may be, what his virtues or defects may be. We Rangers don't judge the Crown. We defend it, from external and internal enemies. There must be no doubt about this. Those who are here today will defend the King to the last drop of blood, because that is the duty of the Rangers and so says the *Path*." He raised the book to let them all see it.

Isgord threw a poisoned glance at Lasgol and Egil and pointed at them. Many saw it.

Dolbarar went on. "Some have decided not to continue their training as Rangers this year as a result of the situation we are in. Most of them are from the west of the realm. I understand this and accept it. Because of this, I would like to offer one last chance to those who don't want to defend the Crown and believe their loyalty is with the Western League. They may leave. Nobody will stop them or prevent them from reaching their own people. Think about it carefully. There will be no other chance. The punishment for treason is to be hanged by the neck until you are dead. Remember and choose well now, because afterwards it will be too late. This is your final opportunity."

Egil and Lasgol exchanged glances. The beginnings of doubt had appeared in their eyes. Lasgol wanted to help his mother, and he knew he could do it better here than anywhere else. But if they were found out, they would be hanged. He swallowed, then realized that his hands were shaking in the fact of the scrutiny of Dolbarar and the Four Master Rangers, and he clenched his fists.

Egil half-closed his eyes. A look of determination with a touch of pain appeared in them. He was the one risking most, because of who he was. In civil wars it was not strange for members of the same family to find themselves fighting on opposite sides; it was a way of ensuring that whichever side won, the family would survive, or at least half of it, without losing their titles and properties. But the risk for him was immense.

Lasgol watched him expectantly, and he shook his head. He would go on to the end.

Lasgol understood. Egil would not back off, for his father, for his family.

"Very well," Dolbarar said. You have until midnight to leave if you so decide."

The murmuring broke out again. Apart from Lasgol and Egil there were at least six more westerners among the Fourth-Years. Lasgol wondered how many there were left in the whole Camp. And among all the Rangers? Would they all be loyal to Uthar, even though their families were from the West and with the League?

Dolbarar spread his arms wide. "It's time to begin the year, Contenders. I wish you the best of luck. I hope to see you all at the graduation ceremony at the end of the year and to be able to give you the Ranger medallion, each one for the School he or she belongs to."

Everybody applauded. Ingrid and Nilsa looked self-confident, convinced they would succeed. The four boys of the Snow Panthers, on the other hand, lowered their heads and looked down. None of them had the least confidence that they would do so themselves.

Chapter 11

And the first day of training began. They assembled in the northern part of the Camp, which indicated that they would probably be heading for the high forests. They were not mistaken. After a long walk they reached the dark forests, so called because they were so dense and there was so much foliage that the daylight barely penetrated through the trees.

Nilsa was looking around nervously at the dense vegetation around them. "I don't like these woods at all," she said.

"Well if you don't like them, just imagine what I feel..." Gerd said. He was staring at the forest with fear in his eyes.

"What d'you think they want us to do here?" Ingrid wondered.

"We'll soon find out," Egil said. He nodded at Instructor Ivan, in charge of the physical training of the Fourth-Years, who was coming to give them the appropriate instructions.

Lasgol had an ominous feeling. With Ivan were six huge wolfhounds, with a truly ferocious look about them.

"All line up at the edge of the forest," he said, and all the teams did so obediently.

Ivan was an imposing Ranger. He was almost six feet tall, broad and muscular. He gave the impression that he was constantly in training. Seeing him, and as this was their final year of training, they guessed that they had been assigned a very tough, fully fit trainer.

"I want you all to pay close attention."

In fact there was no need for him to have said this, as all eyes were fixed on him and the six hounds with him. Two of them were growling and showing their fangs in a display of aggression. Lasgol felt a shiver run down his spine. Nilsa jumped backwards when one of them barked.

"Those war-hounds really look like wolves," she said nervously once she had recovered from the fright.

"They're Great Danes crossed with wolves," Gerd explained. "They're used to defend villages, or for personal defense, and they're extremely strong. Once they attack it's hard to control them."

"How nice," Viggo said. "This looks very promising, and he's obviously brought them for us to pet."

"My reasoning leads me to the conclusion that this is to be a combined exercise between humans and wolfhounds," said Egil.

"Well, that's great," Viggo grumbled. "Now we're screwed."

Lasgol looked in the direction of the Owls and saw that Astrid and her team were looking as pale as they were themselves. Everybody was nervous, even Isgord, who usually kept cool in complicated situations and was always in the front row, puffing up his chest and trying to make the instructors notice him. Today he was further back behind the twins in his team.

"Good," Ivan said with a twisted smile that added to Lasgol's uneasiness. "I see I have your entire attention, or rather I'd say my little friends here have your entire attention."

"Are they wolves?" asked Jobas, Captain of the Boars.

"Yes and no. They're half-mastiff and half-wolf. You ought to know this already. I made sure to talk to Esben so he'd get you to spend some time with them."

The six animals were watching them restlessly. They did not look at all tame; their eyes showed that they were ready to pounce at any moment, and to Lasgol it did not seem as though they would mind whether it was pupil, Ranger or enemy.

"But this is the physical training class, not a School of Wildlife class," said Gonars, Captain of the Falcons.

"Correct, but for this final year we're going to use these little ones to make the Contenders' progress a lot quicker" – and once again he gave that smile which Lasgol did not like at all.

"I think now I understand what's going to happen," Egil said.

"Tell me, please," said Gerd, whose forehead was moist with perspiration and tension.

But before Egil could tell him what was going to happen, Ivan went on:

"It's time you all finished getting fit. I'm going to make sure you do just that. By the end of the year you'll be in better shape than any active Ranger. I want you to remember the training you've got from me forever, because it'll help you for the rest of your lives. We Rangers survive in forests, mountains and rivers in the worst of conditions, in the worst of storms, where soldiers, bandits and enemies weaken and fail. We succeed thanks to our fantastic physical training and understanding. Without them we're nothing, and let me tell you that anyone who has a body well prepared for any eventuality will survive all adverse situations. There'll be no one in the whole kingdom better prepared than you. You'll be able to confront any situation you're faced with, and my aim is to reach that goal. The king's soldiers, with all their training, will look like children beside you. You'll leave them behind in any terrain. You'll make a laughing-stock of them. I know that at the moment you don't see it and don't understand it, but one day, in some life-or-death situation, when you survive thanks to the strength of your body and mind, you'll remember the training you got from me, and you'll be grateful."

There was a long silence, during which they all considered the Instructor's words. Lasgol knew that Ivan was right, and that they might easily find themselves in more than one life-or-death moment, and that they would need all their physical strength to come out of them alive. He had already experienced some in the Frozen Continent.

"The first team who wants to volunteer, step forward."

Nobody did, not even the Eagles.

"Right then, if nobody wants to volunteer I'll choose the volunteers myself." The wolfhounds growled again, revealing fangs that could tear a man apart.

Ivan was looking from one team to the other. Egil's and Gerd's faces reflected their fear. Finally he singled out the Owls.

"You'll be the first. Who's the Captain?"

Astrid stepped forward.

"Very good. Listen carefully. Today's test will be to work on your speed, and nothing better to work on your speed than my dear little friends. The test is very simple, you have to cross the forest, uphill, and reach the other end as quickly as you can."

Lasgol felt easier. This was not so different from the training they were used to.

"But there'll be a small incentive... I'm going to count to twenty, then I'm going to release my friends, and they'll go after you."

They were all so paralyzed for a moment that they could not even react.

Lasgol thought he could not have understood correctly. "They'll go after us?"

"That's what I was afraid of," Egil said.

"What does that mean?" Astrid asked.

Ivan looked her in the eye. "It means they'll go after you and if they catch you, you'll get some... affectionate petting."

Everybody began to protest. The test bordered on the inhuman.

"Don't worry," Ivan said, looking amused. "The healer has been warned."

Lasgol could not believe he was serious. Those wolfhounds were huge and their jaws were lethal. It was madness.

"But we're unarmed," Astrid said. "We can't defend ourselves against them."

"That's exactly the point of this test. It's not a matter of fighting against wolves, that's not the goal: you must be faster than them, that's the aim. You must cross the forest before they reach you. Anyone who doesn't make it will suffer the consequences."

"That's barbaric," protested Luca, the Captain of the Wolves.

"You don't have to take part. You can leave whenever you wish. You know where the Camp exit is. Give up and leave."

The murmurs and protests became audible once again.

"You always have that option if the tests seem too hard this year. Those who wish to go on, those who want to become Rangers, can stay and do the test."

The teams thought about the consequences of abandoning it. They looked at the wolfhounds, then at the forest, and finally at their fellow-contenders. Several of them seemed to want to give up, but in the end nobody did, despite their fear of the animals.

"Right then. Owls, get ready."

The team took up their place at the entrance to the forest. Astrid nodded encouragingly at her partners.

"We'll do it," she said. "Run with everything you've got!"

"Ready? Go!" Ivan shouted.

The Owls went into the forest and began to run up the mountain. Ivan started to count: one, two, three...

When they heard this, the beasts tensed with their ears pricked, ready to pounce.

Lasgol hoped with all his heart that Astrid would make it. She was an excellent runner. She had to make it. But his fear for her made him shiver.

Ivan reached twenty and released the wolfhounds. At once they ran into the forest like lightning.

"Catch them, boys," he called after them.

Gerd muffled a cry of horror.

"I hope they make it," Nilsa said, but her voice shook.

For a while they all waited in silence, unsure what was going to happen. Suddenly there came a barking from the depths of the forest. Lasgol tensed, as did his partners.

Suddenly there came human cries.

"Oh no!" Gerd cried.

"They've been caught," Egil concluded.

More barking was heard, followed by more cries. Then they heard the wolfhounds howling: long-drawn howls more like those of wolves than dogs.

"Looks as though the boys have brought the test to an end," Ivan said. He put two fingers to his mouth and gave three long very loud whistles. A little later the beasts emerged from the forest.

Lasgol was startled, as were many others. The animals came to stand beside Ivan, like the docile puppies they were not.

"Very good, boys," he said, and rewarded them with some food he carried in his Ranger's belt.

"Those animals are trained for this exercise," Egil said, watching Ivan give them their reward in the form of food and petting them.

"Right, I need more volunteers, but as I imagine there won't be any, I'll choose them myself. The next team to do the test will be the Panthers."

Gerd's face turned so white that it seemed it would never take on color again. Nilsa was so nervous that in two leaps she was there, ready to run, at the entrance to the forest.

Egil glanced at Lasgol in resignation. "I don't stand a chance," he said.

"Don't worry, I'll go with you, beside you."

"No, please don't. This is a punishment I have to endure myself. I don't want you to suffer for me. Try to reach the other side of the forest without them catching you."

"Don't you worry, either of you," Ingrid said. "We're going to make it. Run with everything you've got and we'll make it."

"Ready?" Ivan asked, and before they could reply, he gave the signal: "Go!"

The six started to race uphill into the forest. Lasgol could hear Ivan counting. Ingrid went first, setting the course and looking for the straightest route as she leapt over roots, bushes and all kind of snow-covered vegetation that hindered their progress.

"Come on, quick!" she shouted encouragingly.

After Ingrid went Nilsa, then Viggo, with Lasgol in the middle and Egil and Gerd behind.

Lasgol began to feel the strain on his legs as they went deeper into the difficult forest. His breathing too became shallower. The thick layer of snow that covered the ground hampered their ascent, and the cutting cold of the still-icy wind punished both lungs and nose.

"Run! He's already reached twenty," Viggo warned them. He had been counting mentally.

Nilsa tripped and fell on her face.

The animals had already entered the forest.

Ingrid grabbed her by her shoulders and pulled her up. "Go!" she cried, and they went on running.

Lasgol glanced over his shoulder and saw that Egil and Gerd were beginning to lag behind. The rhythm Ingrid was setting was punishing. They were not going to be able to keep it up.

Ingrid looked back without stopping her climb through the snow and the vegetation. "Faster! They're right behind us! Keep on up!"

Then they heard barking behind them.

"Don't look back!" she cried.

But it was impossible not to. Gerd and Egil did, and they saw with horror that the hounds were almost upon them.

"Come on, run or they'll eat you alive!" shouted Viggo.

The barking sounded closer now. Lasgol's lungs were burning and his legs were beginning to get cramped, especially his thighs, from running on the snow.

Then there came a thump.

Lasgol looked back. The first wolfhound had reached Gerd, who was the last. With one leap it brought him down. He was nearly buried in the snow, and the hound bit him in the butt. He cried out in pain.

Lasgol, unable to believe what was happening, turned back and went to help his friend.

The second animal reached Egil and brought him down in turn with a leap. It began to bite him, and he covered his head with his arms.

Lasgol reached them, but the third beast hurled itself on him and he covered his face with his arms. The beast bit him, and he cried out in pain and fell to the ground. His arms hurt, and the beast was on top of him pressing down with all its weight to stop him getting up. The three other animals ran past them at enormous speed, without stopping.

Lasgol was about to fight back when he realized the hound was not attacking him anymore. It had bitten him on both forearms, but now it was merely stopping him from getting up. He looked at his teammates out of the corner of his eye and saw that the wolfhounds were not attacking them either. They simply stayed on top of them, barking.

A moment later he heard Viggo yell. They had caught up with him too.

Lasgol was silent, still as a statue, waiting to hear either Ingrid or Nilsa scream. But there was no such thing. The other two wolfhounds had not succeeded in catching them up.

The two girls had made it.

The wolfhounds began to howl, and a moment later Ivan whistled to call them back to him.

The hounds went back, leaving them there bleeding on the snow. Lasgol got to his feet and went over to his teammates.

"Are you all right?" he asked.

"My butt hurts like hell," Gerd said. "I think they've eaten all of it."

Lasgol checked. "No, don't worry, he only gave you a couple of nips, but of course with those fangs it hurts a lot."

"And what about you, Egil?"

"Fine... the same as him," he replied, clutching his buttocks. "And you?"

"He bit me in the forearms."

"I told you not to turn back for us."

"I couldn't help myself."

"You'd have managed to make it."

"I don't think I would. They caught Viggo too."

"Let's go to him."

Viggo was rubbing his behind, cursing the frozen gods.

"That Ivan's going to remember me. I swear he'll pay for this."

"It's just a test," Lasgol said.

"Just a test? Do you find it normal to set a batch of monstrous wolfhounds to chase us?"

"No, quite honestly it's not very normal."

"I think we're going to develop a very definite turn of speed," Egil commented.

"That or we'll end up without any backsides," Viggo protested.

"Let's go and see Ingrid and Nilsa," Lasgol said. "They made it."

They came to the way out of the forest on the northern side and found the two girls with the Owls. Both of them had made it, as had Astrid and another of the Owls, which delighted Lasgol even though his forearms were very sore.

Astrid was anxious to know how he was. Lasgol told her to go with her team, that he was all right. Astrid understood that they needed to keep up appearances, and after a fond smile she went back to her team.

With them was another Ranger, together with the healer Edwina.

"Come with me," she said. "I'll take care of your wounds."

Edwina used her power on the bites, which although not very deep were painful and humiliating. She gave them an ointment to put on at night so that scars would have formed by the next day.

Little by little all the teams arrived in different states, although most of them were as badly affected as the Panthers.

Finally Ivan arrived with his six canine companions.

"Tomorrow we'll repeat the exercise," he said. "Everybody here at first light."

"Everyone?" Astrid asked. "Those who didn't make it and were bitten?"

"Yes, everybody."

"But those creatures are going to tear us to pieces," Viggo protested.

Ivan shook his head. "My faithful friends are here to motivate you. For six days they'll only chase you, without attacking. But on the seventh day, they'll attack. You can't say I'm not giving you time to prepare. And the same every week. Six days of training and then a real test."

"How many times are we going to have to do the test?" Lasgol asked.

Ivan glowered at him. "As many times as necessary, until I'm satisfied."

"But once we manage to cross the forest without being caught, the test will be over... won't it?" Gerd asked.

Ivan shook his head slowly. "No way. You'll go on practicing this test every morning so that no one can relax once they've managed to pass it."

"We're screwed," Viggo said.

Lasgol felt his wounds and gave a snort of despair.

"We certainly are."

Chapter 12

Every noon the Panthers arrived at the dining hall exhausted. Sitting at the long tables had become a blessing: not for the food they were about to enjoy but because they could rest. Simply being able to sit down and relax was the greatest blessing.

"It's very tough, but we'll get used to it eventually," Ingrid said to encourage them.

Nilsa was not so sure. "You think so?"

Gerd and Egil were not even speaking. They ate to get their energy back, but their bodies and minds were so exhausted they could not manage to utter a word.

"The more effort we make, the stronger our bodies get," Ingrid went on.

"That, or we'll burst once and for all," said Viggo.

"I don't think they'll push us that far," Lasgol said.

"You sure?" Viggo asked. "Look at us. Another week of this and we won't be here to tell the story."

"The Instructor knows what he's doing," said Ingrid.

"Let's hope so..."

Night was falling by the time Lasgol was on his way back from tending to Trotter at the stables. The Rangers had to look after their animals in the Camp, even if they did not need them because of the daily lessons and because they were well-looked-after by the stable-hands. But they were each Ranger's personal responsibility.

He saw a girl by the door of the quartermaster's warehouse with a letter in her hand. She was reading it with her head cocked to one side. He was surprised by how pretty and attractive she was. Then suddenly he realized who she was.

"Valeria..." he muttered.

At the sound of his voice, she turned her head.

"Lasgol! How nice to see you back!" She ran to give him a hug.

"Hi Val," he replied in some embarrassment. "I didn't recognize you..."

"We go away for a few weeks and you've already forgotten me?" she said, pretending annoyance. "Do you care so little about me?"

"No... of course not... of course I care about you..."

She gave him a huge smile, her eyes shining. "Oh, do you? A lot?"

"I... well... of course, we're friends..."

Valeria's face shadowed. "Friends... because you don't want us to be more than that," she said bluntly.

"Val... I..."

She gazed at him intensely.

"You know that..."

Valeria raised her hand. "Easy, I shouldn't have embarrassed you. Sometimes I'm a little too determined." She smiled.

"And forward," Lasgol added.

She laughed. "That too. You know me well. You're right, we're friends. For now..." She gave him a little nudge and smiled mischievously.

Lasgol smiled. Val was like that.

"Did you get into a lot of trouble these weeks outside the Camp?"

He waved a hand. "No, not at all."

"Yeah, sure, heroes have a tendency to get into trouble wherever they go."

"Don't call me a hero, you know I don't like it."

"But I like to make you a little bit uncomfortable," she replied with another roguish smile.

"Really, Val..."

"I think you're a little more grown-up, more serious."

"Do you? Nah, I don't think so..."

"And how do you think I look? she asked. She spun round with her arms outspread so that he could get a good look at her.

She looked prettier than the year before, if that were possible. She also looked older, more attractive. As she moved, her blonde mane waved in the air around her and her Nordic beauty shone in all its splendor. She was very pretty, with her snow-white skin and her little up-turned nose. Those blue eyes and red lips would be the perdition of many. There was no doubt that she was the most attractive girl in the whole Camp.

"You're just the same," he lied.

She wagged her finger at him. "The same? You're hateful." She had not liked the comment at all.

Lasgol smiled and nodded at the letter to change the subject.

"News from home?"

Val frowned and stared at the letter in her hand. "Yes..."

"Everything all right?"

She shook her head. "No, not really."

"It's none of my business... but if I can help in any way..."

"Thanks, I know you mean it."

"I do."

She looked at him with sadness in her eyes. "What d'you know about my family?"

Lasgol shrugged. "Not much. They say you're the daughter of some nobleman, that you come from a rich and powerful family..."

"That's the gossip, huh?"

Lasgol nodded. "Probably unfounded rumors. People are jealous..."

"They're true," she interrupted.

"Oh, you never said anything to me..."

"It's complicated, more so now."

The comment surprised Lasgol. "Because of the war?"

"Yes. My father is Hans Olmossen. But I use my mother's last name, Blohm, to blend in."

"Count Olmossen?" he asked in surprise. He knew the name. And he knew he was with the Western League. He had seen him at the secret meeting of the Peoples of the Frozen Continent.

"That's him."

"But in that case... you're from the West."

"So I am."

"I don't understand. When Uthar nearly hanged Egil... he didn't go after you."

"Because my father's very smart. He'd sworn fealty to Uthar."

The comment puzzled Lasgol. Count Olmossen seemed to be playing on both sides. He would have to tell his mother. He was a risk.

"I see."

"That's one of the reasons why I'm here."

"Your father sent you to assure Uthar that he's on his side. You're a hostage of the King."

"Yes, and because I asked him myself."

"You asked him? That's taking a big risk."

"My father and I don't get along very well," she said with dull eyes. "Not well at all, in fact."

"You needn't tell me anything if you don't want to."

Valeria's usually velvety voice turned grave.

"I want to tell you. You see, I'm the elder of two siblings. My younger brother Lars is the apple of my father's eye. On the other hand I'm his 'bane' as he puts it. We've been arguing for years, about almost anything, that's how strained our relationship is, but especially about something I don't accept and which I'm never going to let my arm be twisted over."

Lasgol was looking at her with great interest, unable to think what it might be.

"My inheritance."

"Now I'm lost."

"I'm the elder, so the title, the lands, the castle, ought to pass on to me once my father dies. That's what I've been brought up to keep in mind. But he named my brother Lars as his heir. According to my father a woman can't inherit, even if she's the firstborn, even if she's better with a sword or a bow than her brother."

"I can see that. It's a deeply-rooted belief in Norghana."

"It's unfair! I'm worth as much as my brother, or more, and I have all the right in the world to inherit!"

Lasgol raised his hands in a pacifying gesture, but she went on: "We live in a kingdom, a society, which is run for and by men. I'm not going to accept it. Ever. Women deserve the same rights. Men can't always have privileges over us. I'll always fight against this injustice, starting in my own home. You'd better not be one of those dullards who think men are better than women."

"Not in the least. If there's one thing I've learnt here it's that women are formidable. I've got a couple in my team who prove it to me every day. I don't think you're father's being fair. He shouldn't reject you as his heir just because you're a woman."

"I'm glad you think that way. I was ready to throw you a right hook. Although I didn't believe you'd be so backward, or at least I hoped not."

He smiled. "I'm glad I didn't end up with a black eye," he said, trying to make her relax a little. It seemed to work.

"I'm here because my father wanted to send me to Uthar's court, me being a woman. I told him that I wouldn't even dream of it. I offered to come here. After a lot of arguments he finally agreed. The

King had given him an ultimatum, and he'd run out of time. He had to agree that I should come here and in that way comply with the King's demands for loyalty."

"Like what happened to Egil."

"With the war, the situation got more complicated," she said, looking down at her letter. "My father is ordering me to stay here so that Uthar doesn't suspect him."

"Is your father with the Western League?" he asked, hoping to find out how much she knew.

"I don't know. We barely speak. He'd never trust me with anything like that."

"I see."

"That's what my life's like. My father despises me and doesn't trust me."

"I trust you and appreciate you very much. Your father's wrong."

Valeria looked into his eyes and kissed his cheek.

"You're charming, my hero."

Lasgol blushed. "I'm not a hero…"

"Let's leave before I lose my head and one of my kisses finds your lips."

Lasgol did not know what to say. He bowed his head. His cheeks and his ears were burning.

They went on towards the cabins.

Chapter 13

Night had already begun to fall by the time Lasgol, Egil and Viggo made their way to the Fourth-Year cabins through the center of the Camp. Several Rangers on watch duty stared at them questioningly. Lasgol glanced at the lookouts and saw several Rangers posted on them. The atmosphere was tense. Dolbarar had strengthened the watch both inside the Camp and in the forests that surrounded it. They did not expect an attack from Darthor's forces, as the Camp was practically impenetrable and the passes closely watched, but what they did expect was possible trouble or even squabbles between the Rangers themselves, the soldiers and the pupils.

"Where are you going?" came an unpleasantly arrogant voice which they immediately recognized.

"None of your business," Lasgol replied without stopping.

"You ought to be more respectful to your betters."

Lasgol stopped. He turned and found himself facing Isgord. With the Captain of the Eagles was the Captain of the Boars, Jobas, a very big young man, almost as big as Gerd, and a nasty piece of work. Almost everyone in his team was afraid of him. The Captain of the Bears and several of their team members were also there.

"The only thing better than you would be a sewer rat, and only just," Lasgol said.

"To be fair, I don't think you could compare a rat with the Captain of the Eagles," Viggo said, sounding completely relaxed. "More like a crawling snake."

Isgord went red with rage. He reached for the weapons at his waist.

"I wouldn't if I were you," Lasgol warned him. "Those guards on the lookouts would finish you off before you could attack us."

Isgord looked up and realized that Lasgol was right. He took his hands off his axe and Ranger's knife, looking more relaxed, and put them behind his back. He smiled.

"You're lucky all those eyes are watching. Otherwise I'd make you pay."

"Don't be so cocky just because you're with all those other Captains."

"I'm not being cocky. It wouldn't cost me anything to finish you off. You're just treacherous scum from the West."

The two other Captains smiled at this, and several others murmured. Lasgol realized that all of them were from the East of the kingdom, like most of the Rangers and pupils who were left in the Camp.

He stiffened. Egil put a hand on his shoulder.

"It's not worth it. Don't give way to provocation."

Lasgol took a deep breath and tried to relax. He did not entirely manage to.

"We westerners are as good as easterners, if not better," he said calmly.

"No way," Isgord shot back.

"You wish it was true," Jobas said, looking superior.

"In your dreams," said Ahart, the Captain of the Bears.

The other easterners started to hurl insults. Egil and Lasgol made a point of taking no notice.

"Dolbarar ought to have thrown you all out," Isgord said disdainfully. "Nobody trusts you." He gestured at Egil. "You're traitors, especially the wise guy."

"Don't attack him," said Lasgol. "It's me you're trying to provoke."

"The two of you are spies for the Western League," Isgord said. "You don't fool us. Dolbarar's too soft, you shouldn't be here. You should be hanging from a tree, you and all the westerners still in the Camp."

"We don't belong to the League," Egil said evenly.

"Yeah, sure. We ought to hang you as traitors. Once the dog's dead, there's no more rabies."

Lasgol watched the reaction of the others and was not happy about it. Several were nodding in agreement, others making aggressive gestures. Things were turning ugly. What impressed him most was the rage he saw in their eyes, the real desire to see them hanged. And that really worried him. He knew there was great tension between the two sides, but they were all fellow pupils. No-one would raise a hand against one of their companions... or would they? At that moment he realized that they would. If the Rangers had not been watching, they would have come to arms.

"You can insult us all you want," Lasgol said. "It doesn't alter the fact that we're here to stay, finish the year and graduate."

"You maybe, though I doubt it," Isgord said. "Not the wise guy, though."

"There's more knowledge in the wise guy's little fingernail than in that empty head of yours," Viggo said.

"You shut up," Isgord said. "You're from the east. You ought to support us, not them."

"I could be from Rogdon, but I support my teammates."

"Then you'll fall with them."

"We'll see about that, bully-boy."

"You're asking for it," Isgord said. He clenched his fist and lunged at Viggo. Ahart, Captain of the Bears, stopped him.

"Not here," he said. He was looking at the Rangers, who were watching the scene unfold.

Isgord jabbed his finger at Viggo. "You've been asking for it."

"Oh yeah? And what are you going to do about it?"

"Nothing here," Isgord said with a poisonous smile, "but why don't we go to the lake and talk about it"

"Talk? Sure," Lasgol said.

"Aren't you westerners so good after all?"

"Yes, we are."

"Show us, then. A Rangers' duel. You and me," he said to Lasgol. "Hand to hand. One easterner against one westerner. Let's see who's better."

"It's a trap," Egil whispered. "Don't yield to provocation."

"If you don't turn up we'll be proved right, you westerners are all cowards and traitors only fit to hang from a tree."

"Exactly," Jobas agreed.

Lasgol considered it. Egil was right. A fight was not a good idea; he had already learnt that lesson when the village bullies had beaten him on the bridge. No, confronting Isgord by the lake was a very bad idea. He started to shake his head.

"He'll be there and he'll tear you to pieces," Viggo said.

Isgord smiled from ear to ear, and all the easterners cheered.

"Duel! Duel! Duel!" they chanted.

Lasgol glared at Viggo, who shrugged and looked innocent.

"Then we'll meet at the lake. Tonight. At midnight."

"We'll see you there," Viggo said.

The two groups went their separate ways, with Isgord giving a final look of triumph at Lasgol, who knew he was in deep trouble.

Back at the cabin, they dropped on their bunks. Camu had poor Gerd cornered, but he ran to greet them.

"But why on earth did you do that?" Lasgol shouted angrily at Viggo.

"It got a little out of hand..."

"A little?"

"I'd say quite a lot," Egil said.

"That's a pretty tight spot you've put me in."

"All of us," Egil added.

Viggo looked apologetic. "That's my specialty."

Lasgol rolled his eyes and muttered curses at the sky. Egil was shaking his head.

"What happened? Is it serious?" Gerd asked.

"We need to calculate the repercussions that could follow from our actions," Egil said to Viggo.

"Are you telling me or asking me? Don't worry, I'll be there with you."

"But you're an easterner," Lasgol said. "You're in no danger."

He smiled. "Well, I am a little, I'm with you guys, my dear teammates."

"Don't try and sweet-talk us after the mess you've created."

Egil explained to Gerd what had happened, while Lasgol played with Camu to relax and forget what he had just been through.

When Egil had finished telling him the story, Gerd wagged his enormous finger in front of Lasgol's face. "Don't go," he said.

"If I don't go I'll look a total coward... me and all westerners..."

"Well," Viggo pointed out, "it wouldn't be either the first or the last time we've been laughed at."

"You in particular," Ingrid said as she came in, followed by Nilsa.

"We already know about it," the redhead said.

"I see news has wings here," Lasgol said resignedly.

"Isgord and those boneheads of the Boars and Bears have been telling everybody," Ingrid said.

"In that case I have no choice but to go..."

"No. Listen to me: I'm your Captain, and I forbid you to go."

"They'll say I'm a coward, a spy, a traitor... that we westerners are no better than worms..."

"Let them say whatever they want. If you go, anything might happen, with things the way they are... it'd be better not to risk it."

"Don't go," Nilsa begged him, her eyes full of concern.

"You don't understand... you're all easterners, and only Egil and I are from the West. If I don't go, I'm giving them a reason to do as they please with the few westerners left at the Camp."

"That's not your problem," Ingrid said.

"No?"

"No, it isn't. Your problem is to graduate as a Ranger. The rest shouldn't matter."

"And what about this civil war?"

"Not even that. If East and West tear each other to pieces, we – you – still have the same goal: to graduate as Rangers."

"To serve the East."

"To serve the kingdom."

"Not the King," Egil said.

Ingrid looked at him. "That's more complicated."

"I know. I only wanted to point out that your views, although perfectly valid, also have ramifications and consequences."

"I'm already lost," Gerd said.

"When he gets into wise-mode..." Viggo said.

They argued for hours, trying to dissuade Lasgol from going to the encounter with Isgord. Lasgol felt divided. On the one hand he knew his teammates were right; it was a very bad idea to go, both risky and dangerous. Things could turn ugly, more so considering that he was facing Isgord. On the other hand he would love to teach the pretentious, unbearable captain of the Eagles a lesson. But he could not let himself be driven by his pride. Pride was a very bad counselor, his father Dakon had taught him. *Always seek to be a good person first. Pride is necessary, but it can lead you down the wrong path. Listen to your heart.* He did not know what to do. The simple thing to do was not to go. He would have to listen to the insults of Isgord's and others like him for the rest of the year. He could cope with it, it was true. He had been the Traitor's Son, he had been through that before and he could do it again. An inner voice told him not to go, that it was better to stay with his friends in the cabin.

They left him in peace at last so that he could decide for himself. He went out behind the cabin with Camu, then a little way into the forest, and spent a good while playing with him.

"What about you, little one, what would you do?" he asked him.

Camu looked back at him, moving his head from side to side in amusement.

Play hide-and-seek, was the answer that came to Lasgol.

"You always want to play. That's all you care about. Lucky you! Enjoy it while you can. Life changes and the joy of playing starts to fade."

Camu looked at him with sad eyes.

"But you still have plenty of time left to play. All right then, let's play."

The two friends played for quite a while, and Lasgol enjoyed both the game and Camu's company. During this time he forgot all the problems that lay in wait for him.

Almost on the stroke of midnight he came back to the cabin with Camu. He found all his friends waiting for him.

"What have you decided?" Ingrid asked him directly.

Lasgol breathed deeply.

"I've decided to go."

His friends burst out into protests.

Ingrid raised her hands high. "Shut up, all of you!"

There was silence.

"I've thought about it a lot, and I think it's the best thing."

"If that's what you think, we'll support you," Ingrid said.

"We're coming with you," said Nilsa.

"We'll defend you," Gerd put in.

Lasgol was touched. "Thanks, you're the best."

"Let's get our weapons ready," Ingrid said.

When they left the cabin, there was a surprise waiting for Lasgol. The westerners still at the camp, both boys and girls, were waiting for him. There were not many of them, but all the Years were represented.

"We're coming with you," Valeria told him, her eyes shining with admiration.

Lasgol remembered that she too was from the West.

"There's no need... you're putting yourselves in danger..."

"We already are. We've talked about it and we're coming with you. You're defending us, so we'll cover your back."

Lasgol felt so touched that his eyes moistened. He fortified himself inwardly. He was not coming to the encounter for himself, but for all of them. He could not back down. He had already known this in his guts, but now, watching all those faces, he had no doubt. It was what he had to do, no matter what might happen.

The Panthers came out after him and were astonished at the sight.

"It seems you're not only fighting for yourself," Egil whispered in his ear, and winked.

They set off for the lake with Lasgol in the lead, the Panthers behind him and the rest of the westerners following.

When they reached the lake they found themselves confronted with another scene they had not expected at all. Isgord was waiting for them.

Surrounded by a crowd of easterners.

Chapter 14

Lasgol swallowed. Things looked very bad. There were a lot of people there, their bodies hidden by the hooded cloaks in the characteristic colors of each of the four different Years. Nerves made his stomach churn. He swallowed again, took a deep breath and managed to regain a little calm.

Ingrid was looking round the crowd. "I can't see any Rangers or Instructors."

"The Rangers and Instructors wouldn't get involved in this," Viggo said.

"How do you know?"

"It's a matter between us. They'll let us settle it ourselves."

"Even if there's bloodshed?"

Viggo nodded. "I'm afraid so."

"I think he's right," Egil said. "They're all pupils, from all the Years. There's nobody of authority or rank here."

"And they're all armed under their cloaks," Viggo added.

Lasgol wondered how he could know that, but being Viggo he knew and was not mistaken. Of that Lasgol was sure.

Nilsa walked round him in a circle. "This doesn't look good to me," she said.

"You've still got time to turn back," Gerd said. It sounded more like a plea than a piece of advice.

Lasgol glanced behind him and saw all the westerners who had come with him. He shook his head.

"I can't. I have to do this."

He breathed out in a snort, trying to rid his body of all its nerves. Then he walked on to the lake, toward Isgord, who was waiting for him with a malicious smile of pure satisfaction.

"That moron thinks he's got the bear skin before he's caught it," Viggo commented.

Ingrid nodded in Lasgol's direction. "This bear's going to teach him a lesson."

Lasgol did not feel at all sure of this, but he appreciated the comment and above all the support of his friends.

They stopped five paces from Isgord and the thirty or so eastern boys and girls who seemed to be his personal guard. The rest were further back, forming a long line in front of the lake.

Someone separated from the Eastern group and came running to Lasgol. Immediately everybody stiffened and reached for their weapons.

"Don't move," Lasgol said. He knew who it was.

"Why didn't you tell me?" Astrid asked him reproachfully when she reached his side.

"I didn't want to worry you."

"How could I not be worried?" she said, and stroked his cheek. Her eyes showed her fear for him.

"Don't be afraid, I'll be all right," he said, but his voice did not sound as confident as he would have liked. Perhaps because he did not feel that way.

"Don't do it."

"I must."

"It's too dangerous. For you, for everyone."

He looked at the westerners who were with him. "I know, but I can't back down."

Astrid saw Valeria among them. Her expression darkened and she glared at her defiantly. Valeria did not flinch, but remained grave, impassive.

"You don't owe them anything."

"I know, but they're like me. Someone has to defend them."

"Leave it to somebody else."

"I can't."

"Heroes end up in a nameless grave. You've already been a hero once, don't take any more risks. Don't push your luck."

"I don't want to be a hero, but I can't let Isgord get away with this. If I back down, they'll go after all of us, one way or another. You know that. I can't let it happen."

"I know, but I don't want you to defend them. I'm afraid for you."

"Thanks. Your concern for me... means a lot..."

"Then back down."

"I can't..."

"Isgord will seize the moment to kill you if he can," she said. Her voice was anguished.

"Even so, I've got to do it."

Astrid shook her head, and the flame, the fiery look that was so typical of her appeared in her eyes.

"Then finish him off, don't show any mercy."

Lasgol nodded. "I won't show any."

"Have you finished with all the farewell hugs and kisses?" Isgord asked him disdainfully.

Lasgol drew himself up to his full height and walked toward him.

"Here I am, as I said I would be."

"I see you've come with all the spies and traitors of the West."

"They're neither spies nor traitors. Did you need to bring half the Camp with you?"

"They came because they wanted to. Rumor must have spread..."

"Or rather, you spread it."

"They have a right to witness the champion of the traitors of the West falling before the champion of the East."

"I knew you'd turn it into a conflict between both sides."

"Aren't we at war? Aren't we on opposite sides?"

"We're at war, but not on opposite sides. Here we're all Rangers."

"Yeah, but some are loyal to the King and some aren't."

"You can't make that distinction. Everybody here has sworn fealty to Uthar."

"Sure, with a sword at their necks. D'you really think that convinces us easterners? Well you're wrong. Very wrong."

Lasgol shook his head. He had known that Isgord would make the duel into something more, and what was worse, he had the clear feeling that tonight blood would be shed. It was something he wanted to avoid at all costs.

"You've gone very quiet suddenly. Is it fear that's not letting you speak?"

"I'm not afraid of you."

Isgord grinned. "Well you should be."

"That day'll never come," Lasgol said, although deep down he was afraid. But he would never let it show.

"Who are your seconds for the Duel?" Isgord asked. "Mine are Jobas the Captain of the Boars on my left, and Ahart the Captain of the Bears on my right." They both gave a curt nod.

"Mine are Ingrid, Captain of the Panthers –" Ingrid came to stand on his right "– and..." He had no other. Tradition demanded two seconds, with some seniority. He could not use his teammates.

"And Astrid, Captain of the Owls," she said, stepping forward to stand on Lasgol's left.

Isgord's face twisted. "You're from the East. Don't get mixed up with this bunch of traitors."

She gave him a fiery look. "Don't tell me what I ought to do."

"As you like. You're disgracing your team, and you'll pay for this." He gestured towards the Owls, whose faces were grave. None of them said anything. They were all from the east.

"What are the rules of the duel?" Lasgol asked.

Jobas spoke. "It'll be a traditional Ranger's Duel. You'll carry your basic Ranger weapons and gear. Distance will be four hundred paces. Classic rules. Each one will carry a standard composite bow and a quiver with three arrows. You'll have three shots at three different distances: four hundred paces, three hundred and two hundred. It's forbidden to release before you reach the position. It's forbidden to move once you reach the releasing position, and you don't shoot until your opponent reaches his mark too. The first one to disable the other wins. Are the rules clear?"

Lasgol nodded.

"Very clear," Isgord said haughtily.

"The witnesses will inspect the equipment now," Jobas said. Propped against a boulder were two sets of weapons and gear.

Ingrid and Astrid inspected them to make sure they were in perfect condition and that there was no hidden trap, as did Ahart. It took them a while, because they both did so thoroughly.

Finally Ingrid and Astrid went back to Lasgol.

"The arrows have real heads," Astrid whispered. She sounded very worried.

"Rangers' Duels are fought with real arrows," Ingrid whispered. "It's the tradition."

"We're wearing a reinforced corselet to cover our chests," Lasgol said.

"It only covers your torso," Astrid said. "It's light armor. I doubt whether it'll stop an arrow from going through." Her voice was sounding more and more concerned.

"We'll have to trust it will."

"Everything all right?" Jobas asked, arching an eyebrow.

Ingrid glanced doubtfully at Lasgol. His eyes were scanning the crowd, which was watching them with close attention. He recognized the Bears: Osvak, Harkom, Mulok, Groose and Polse, all of them as big and burly as their captain. Beside them he saw Gonars, the Captain of the Falcons, with Arvid, small and brown, and big blond Rasmus from his team. He also saw the Snakes, red-blond Erik and Gustav, with Sugesen, their Captain, in front of them. The Foxes, with their Captain Azer to one side, were further to the right. Seeing them, all from the East and decidedly unfriendly, made him nervous. But he could not back down; the situation might explode.

He nodded to Ingrid. He was determined. He would do it. If anything disastrous happened, it would be in a good cause.

"All correct," Ingrid said, and Astrid nodded.

A moment later the Captain of the Bears went over to Isgord and nodded as well.

"Everything's in order."

"Right," Jobas said. "In that case we'll toss a coin to decide on the gear, then to choose sides."

Lasgol nodded, and Jobas brought out a silver coin,

"Heads, Isgord chooses his gear. Tails, Lasgol does."

Both nodded their agreement.

The Captain of the Boars tossed the coin, grasped it in the air and checked.

"Heads. Isgord chooses first."

The Captain of the Eagles smiled triumphantly. Standing very erect, he went toward the gear, then after checking it he chose one set and put it on. Lasgol did the same with the other one.

"Bows crossed behind you," Jobas ordered. "Now I'll toss again to choose sides."

Lasgol swallowed. The wind was northeast, so that whoever was allotted the west would be at a disadvantage.

Luck did not smile on him.

"Heads again. Isgord chooses."

Isgord's satisfied smile and look of disdain were so strong that Lasgol felt as if he had slapped him.

"I choose East, which is appropriate enough," he said, and raised his chin.

Lasgol felt the poetic irony of the situation.

The murmuring of satisfaction among the easterners grew louder. The westerners were silent, aware that Lasgol was going to have difficulties with the wind.

"I'm going to put an end to you!" Isgord said with a murderous glare.

"We'll see about that."

"And then we'll teach all those traitors of the West a lesson. They'll remember tonight for a long time."

"You won't dare."

"I certainly will."

"You'll pay for what you do."

Isgord gave him a deathly smile. "We're at war, and all's fair in love and war, or didn't you know that?"

"Dolbarar will hand out justice if you harm them."

"Maybe, but the King needs Rangers... I don't think the punishment will be too severe."

"You have neither scruples nor conscience."

"I seem to remember you called me a snake."

"Yes, that's exactly what you are."

"Well, you're going to try my poison, you and all of them." He waved his arm toward the westerners behind Lasgol.

"One day you'll pay."

"Perhaps, but not today."

"We'll see."

Jobas sent two Captains to stand a thousand paces away: five hundred to the east and fifty to the west. When they were in position, they raised one hand.

"Marks set," Jobas said.

Lasgol swallowed and looked at Astrid, who clenched her fist to give him confidence.

"Are the Duelists ready?"

"More than ready," Isgord said.

Lasgol was not at all ready, but the moment of truth had arrived and he had no choice but to say yes.

"Right. Back to back."

The two of them stood back to back in front of Jobas, one facing east, the other west.

"Start," said Jobas. "Now. I'm going to count the steps"

All the attendants closed in to get a better view.

Isgord took the first step, and Lasgol followed suit. They started walking the two hundred paces, each in an opposite direction, to the first and furthest shooting position.

"One, two, three..."

While they advanced practically simultaneously, the people began to cheer Isgord's name. Lasgol began to feel nervous once again, but at that moment he heard Ingrid's voice cheering his name and the voices of all the westerners joining in. He gave thanks to the Gods of Ice for the fantastic friends he had. He walked on, trying to keep the beat and not get nervous.

"Twenty, twenty-one, twenty-two..."

With each step, he was growing more nervous. Possibly that was the reason for the count. He felt the reinforced corselet and had the feeling that it would not stop a swift arrow.

"A hundred and one, a hundred and two..."

Lasgol felt his stomach being squeezed like a wet cloth.

"A hundred and fifty-five..."

He walked on, his heart beating like a war-drum.

Each step brought him closer to his mark. He saw the judge for his side: Luca, Captain of the Wolves, who was holding a torch aloft.

"A hundred and ninety...ninety-one..."

Once they came alongside Luca he would have to release. He needed to be ready, to be mentally prepared to make the move.

"...ninety-seven."

He visualized what he had to do and crushed all the nervousness he was feeling.

"...ninety-eight."

Isgord was a better shot than he was. But he had the Gift. He hesitated whether to use it or not.

"...ninety-nine."

And he did not use it.

Isgord arrived at his mark an instant before Jobas pronounced the number two hundred and began the release movement.

"Two hundred."

Lasgol arrived. He saw the line marked out on the snow, crossed it and half-turned, very fast. He reached for the bow he was carrying across his back, nocked an arrow, pulled the string as far as his cheek and aimed.

Isgord had already finished the same movement. He released.

Lasgol feared for his life. But he could not move. He could only hope that Isgord would miss. At a distance of four hundred paces –

at night, with only torchlight and with a composite bow – hitting the target was going to be difficult.

He released.

Isgord's arrow buried itself in the ground ten paces away from his foot. He let out his breath. It had not reached him.

His eyes followed the flight of his own arrow. It buried itself fifteen paces away from Isgord, a little to his left.

The wind...

The cries and cheers echoed once again on both sides.

"Second position," Jobas called.

The two opponents began to run. The second mark was fifty paces further on. They ran as if Ivan's wolfhounds were after them. The first one to arrive could shoot first and so have an advantage.

The judge at the second mark was Ahart, the captain of the Bears. He was holding the torch aloft, and Lasgol saw the line on the snow. He clenched his teeth and ran as fast as he could.

But Isgord was not only a better shot than he was himself, he was faster and stronger. He arrived a long moment before him.

Lasgol kept running.

Isgord was aiming. He had enough time to avoid missing. He had him.

Lasgol reached the line, turned and stood sideways on, to offer less of a target, even though it would make his own shot more difficult.

Isgord grinned and released.

Lasgol saw the arrow leave the bow, but had to keep calm and avoid losing his concentration. There were three hundred paces between them, and it was not an easy shot. He released an instant before the arrow hit him.

It buried itself in his left arm, the one he used for support, and he felt a cold sharp pain. He looked at his arm and saw the arrow, buried almost at the level of his shoulder.

It's not lethal, he told himself, and let out his breath. The pain was intense, so that he could barely hold the bow.

The audience was now cheering encouragingly. He heard Astrid call out his name. But he could not afford to lose his focus; he was gambling with his life.

He looked to see whether he had hit Isgord. No; he was intact and smiling. He had missed.

"Final position," called Jobas.

Isgord was already running.

Lasgol thought about giving up. He was wounded, and if he said he had been disabled it would be accepted. He thought about it for a single instant. No, he could not let himself be defeated. Never.

He launched himself into a run. He could not let Isgord get away with this.

He saw the last judge at the third mark. It was Ingrid, and this encouraged him.

He put body and soul into running. But Isgord was faster. Once again he got there before him. Long before.

Lasgol went on running.

Isgord prepared to release. He was smiling. The light of the torch shone in his malicious eyes.

When Lasgol reached the line he started to turn, knowing that Isgord had the advantage and that at two hundred paces there was no way he would miss.

Isgord was beside himself by now. "Gotcha!" he shouted.

And he was too hasty, so that he released too soon.

Lasgol, sideways by now, saw the arrow heading for his torso. It was going to hit him.

He held his breath, and as he did so he noticed something. The arrow was flying slightly off-course.

He stayed where he was, without moving.

The arrow brushed his ear, and he felt it cut his earlobe.

Isgord was staring at him with an insane glare in his eyes. He took a step backwards.

"No!" he cried when he realized he had missed.

"You can't move!" Ingrid yelled at him. "Hold your position like a Norghanian!"

Lasgol aimed.

Isgord was on the brink of running away, and his face showed the terror he was feeling. His leg gave way, and he almost fell on his knees.

"Stand still Isgord!" Jobas ordered.

Everybody was watching in silence now.

"Release, Lasgol," Jobas called. "Those are the rules of the duel."

Lasgol thought about it. At two hundred paces he could hit his target with no trouble. *I don't want to kill him... not even wound him badly.*

He was a despicable creature, but Lasgol had no desire to kill him. As a punishment it was excessive. He could not do it.

He released.

The arrow cut through the winter air and flew the two hundred paces in the blink of an eye. Isgord screamed.

The arrow had buried itself in his thigh, deeply.

Lasgol smiled. He had not maimed him, but Ivan's dogs were going to have a wonderful time with Isgord. The wound would stop him running for a long time.

At that moment there came a thunderous voice.

"By all the Gods of the Ice! What is all this?"

It was Master Instructor Oden. Val had gone to fetch him.

"What's going on here? By all the frozen heavens!"

Oden went up to Lasgol and saw the arrow in his arm. Then he saw the one in Isgord's leg.

"This is outrageous! You're going to pay very dearly for this! Disperse, all of you, now!"

The crowd ran off in the face of his fury.

"Run before my rage falls upon you all! You fools!"

Astrid looked at Lasgol. He signaled to her to leave, which she did as fast as she could.

Oden wagged an accusing finger at Lasgol and Isgord. "You two are in colossal trouble," he told them.

Chapter 15

Dolbarar was furious. Very furious indeed. Lasgol had never seen him so angry. He was waving his arms in the air with his staff in one hand and *The Path of the Ranger* in the other. In one of these violent waves he nearly lost the tome, which would have been a disaster; it meant an enormous amount to the Leader of the Camp and to all the Rangers. His usual smile and peaceful expression had vanished, to be replaced by a hostile glare and a somber face. His eyes were sparkling with fire.

The four Master Rangers looked no happier. They were staring at Lasgol and Isgord with grim faces and expressions that went from rage to deep disappointment.

The healer Edwina was sitting by the fire, saying nothing. Lasgol was very grateful to her. Oden had taken them to her so that she could tend to their wounds, and she had used her healing power on them, closing the wounds and preventing any possible infection. They still needed to recover, but the wounds were not serious and would heal in due course. As the good Healer used to say, all she could do was help Nature, but that Nature must follow her course. His wound did not hurt him, and he was sure that in a couple of weeks – three at the most – he would be as good as new. Isgord's wound was deeper and more bothersome, and it would take him longer to recover.

Nobody was speaking inside the Command House, which made things even worse.

Dolbarar had not spoken to them. Lasgol was waiting, with growing anticipation and fear, for the moment when he would stop gesticulating and decide to address them. They waited, hands behind their backs and heads bowed, for the tremendous scolding and subsequent punishment which was certain to descend on them.

And the moment arrived.

"A Ranger's Duel? Are you out of your minds?" Dolbarar yelled at them with such intensity that Lasgol was genuinely scared. Isgord went very white.

Lasgol did not say a word; he swallowed, not even daring to raise his eyes to the leader of the camp.

"Sir..." Isgord began.

"Shut up if you don't want to spend the whole year digging latrines for the Invincibles of the Ice! I can assure you it's not the most agreeable of experiences!"

Isgord fell silent at once.

Dolbarar took up his scolding. "You could have maimed each other! Worse than that, you might have killed each other!" As he spoke he was walking around the two of them, glaring at them.

"It was a mistake," Lasgol acknowledged.

"It was much more than that," Dolbarar corrected him. "It was a gigantic piece of stupidity."

They were in a tight spot. The leader of the Camp was more than furious, he was beside himself, and they had never seen him that way before.

"Yes sir," was all Lasgol could say.

"Your stupidity deserves an exemplary punishment."

Isgord tried to object. "But... sir..."

"Not one word. Your actions speak for themselves." He pointed his staff at them. "You know perfectly well, and don't dare say you don't, that a Ranger's Duel is forbidden in the Camp."

They nodded.

"And you're not even Rangers yet, which makes it even more serious, because you don't know what you're doing and you're not sufficiently prepared for it."

"They ought to be expelled at once," Haakon said. He folded his arms.

Lasgol felt as though his stomach was churning. Isgord shifted restlessly beside him.

"Yes, that ought to be their punishment," Dolbarar said.

Now Lasgol was terrified. Dolbarar was going to expel them, and with that his dream of becoming a Ranger would die. And what was worse, he would not be able to help his mother in her fight against Uthar.

"Expelling them wouldn't teach them a lesson," Esben said. "A more painful and immediate punishment would be better. That's how it works with animals, and these two are nothing more than a couple of large animals without much brain."

"Of course they're animals," Dolbarar said, and his face

shadowed again. "They were on the point not only of killing each other but of making half of the pupils kill the other half. A terrible catastrophe might have occurred. If it hadn't been for Master Instructor Oden's prompt intervention, it might have all ended in a bloodbath."

Ivana shook her head. "I'm with Haakon in this. The best thing would be to expel them. It's not as if they'd infringed some minor rule, this is very serious and far-reaching. They must be expelled," the icy Master Ranger of the School of Archery concluded.

Dolbarar was thoughtful.

If two of the Master Rangers insisted on expelling them, they were lost.

Eyra, the old Master Ranger of the School of Nature, intervened at this point. "What was the purpose of this duel?"

"It was a duel of honor," Isgord said.

"For what reason?" Eyra insisted, as if she were not convinced by the answer she had been given.

"For the honor of the East," Isgord said.

"Oh, I see. The honor of the East against that of the West. Two young men, one from each side, fighting a Ranger's Duel to safeguard the honor of his land."

"Yes, exactly," Isgord said.

"Here there is no East or West," Dolbarar told them. "Here there are only Rangers. We are one, and we all serve the kingdom."

"That's what I said, we serve the East," Isgord said.

"No, we don't serve the East," Dolbarar corrected him. "We serve Norghana, we serve the Crown, there is no East or West. The Rangers don't divide into sides, we've never done it and we never will. We're faithful to the Crown, and it's the Crown that we defend. So says *The Path of the Ranger*." He showed him the book in his hand.

"But the East defends the crown and the King. The Westerners are traitors."

"Incorrect," Dolbarar snapped back. "The kingdom is divided in two, that's true, but not all westerners are against the King. The Rangers of the West are loyal to the Crown and the principles we defend. There cannot be, nor will there be, divisions or confrontations among us."

"But among those of the West there are trait—"

"There's nothing," said Eyra, cutting him off. "What you imagine, young Contender, isn't necessarily the truth. In your youth you're unable to discern what's in the hearts of men. Those of the West who decided to stay as Rangers have done so knowing the consequences, and they've put the Rangers and the kingdom above their own land, which is what ought to be done. When we become part of the Rangers we leave behind our past, because it weighs us down, and when we leave this place we must learn to live as Rangers, and only as Rangers. That's something you learn with time, time which you haven't yet enjoyed."

Isgord bowed his head.

"The punishment for such an act ought to be expulsion," Dolbarar said. "And all the more so now, with the times as they are and the state the realm is in. Particularly for all the bloodshed you might have caused."

Lasgol felt he was already out. A shiver ran down his back, and he felt nauseous,

"On the other hand we do need new blood," Esben said. "And these animals, though they have little brain, are certainly good Ranger material."

Dolbarar nodded, considering the advice his counselors had given him.

"I vote for expulsion," Haakon said.

"As do I," said Ivana. "What's happened is too serious for us not to make an example for the others. It might happen again, and this time blood would run."

Dolbarar turned to Eyra, seeking the old lady's wise counsel.

"I agree that it's necessary to punish them in order to make an example of them. It must serve as warning for those who have stayed on here that this cannot be repeated."

"The King won't tolerate the least sign of insurrection among his people," Haakon said.

"It won't be permitted," Dolbarar assured him sternly. "This is a Rangers' matter but let me remind you that King Uthar needs each and every one of these young men and women to help his armies defeat Darthor and his allies; as you are all aware of it they are right now preparing to attack Norghana," he was thoughtful for a moment…

Then he announced: "I have made my decision,"

There was a tense silence, with everyone hanging on the Leader's words.

Lasgol swallowed. There was such a knot in his stomach that he felt it would rip apart. Isgord was white and tense as a newly-strung bow.

"They will not be expelled."

Lasgol breathed out so hard that his relief almost reached the ceiling.

Isgord let out a long-drawn breath.

"But they're going to receive an exemplary punishment."

Lasgol knew he was going to suffer. A lot.

Chapter 16

With dawn came the punishment.

Dolbarar gathered everybody together in the center of the Camp, both Rangers and pupils, as it was a matter of public humiliation and he wanted everyone to witness it. They must know what had happened and the punishment it entailed. His speech was curt, and he showed the extent of his anger to all those who were there.

"For their unacceptable behavior they will receive a traditional punishment among our people: the Scorn of the Ranger. Proceed."

"What are they going to do to them?" Gerd asked. He was deeply worried.

"Don't know," said Viggo, "but it sounds bad."

"I've never seen Dolbarar speak so angrily," Ingrid said.

Nilsa was shaking herself to relieve her tension. "I'm so nervous..."

Egil knew the punishment; he had read about it in the library. He bowed his head and said nothing. His eyes turned to the Eagles who were wondering as much as they were themselves. Among the Owls, Astrid was watching with her eyes fixed on Lasgol and her fists clenched tightly. Fear about the fate of the two who were about to be disciplined was unmistakable.

Oden went up to Lasgol and Isgord, escorted by two veteran Rangers.

"Strip to the waist."

Lasgol and Isgord exchanged blank looks, wondering what was about to be done to them. They did not know what the punishment was to be.

"I said strip to the waist! I won't say it again!"

They did as they had been ordered, and were left naked from the waist up in front of everyone else.

"On your knees, with your hands behind your backs."

Lasgol did so at once. Isgord opened his mouth to protest, but a glare from Oden made it clear that he would tolerate neither protest nor plea. Isgord shut his mouth and did as he was told.

The two veteran Rangers roped them hand and foot, then joined the ties with another rope.

"Why are they being tied like that?" Nilsa asked. She was biting her nails.

"Something bad," Viggo said.

"Maybe the punishment won't be so bad," Gerd said, almost as a plea.

"If they're tying them up like prisoners, it'll be to stop them escaping or defending themselves," Ingrid said.

Oden made a sign, and four Rangers took both boys away by the arms. They left them under one of the lookout-points in the center of the Camp. Suddenly the ends of two long ropes came down. The Rangers tied them to the rope that joined the bonds which linked hands and feet.

Everyone who was there watched in silence. Most were as confused as the Panthers and the Eagles.

Oden gave an order and they were raised half a man's height from the ground and then left hanging there, arched under the weight of their own bodies. Their faces showed how painful the position was.

Gerd put his hands to his head. "They're going to break!"

"This is terrible!" Nilsa cried.

"No, they won't break," Ingrid reassured them. "Their bodies will bear it, though it'll be painful."

"How d'you know?" Nilsa asked her.

"Because otherwise Dolbarar wouldn't allow it."

"Ingrid is right," Egil said.

"Are they going to leave them hanging there?" asked Gerd incredulously.

"I'm afraid that's not all," Viggo said. He nodded towards a group of three Rangers, who were approaching with something in their hands.

The Rangers went up to Lasgol, then stopped and looked at Dolbarar.

"Let the punishment begin!" the leader announced. "Let the Scorn of the Ranger begin!"

The Ranger beside Lasgol slapped something spiky against his back. He could not see what it was, though he glimpsed what might have been a branch. Then he felt the sting, a sting that began to grow more and more intense. He recognized it: it was a bunch of thorns. The Ranger moved on and did the same to Isgord.

"What are you doing to me?" he asked. But there was no answer.

A moment later he let out a grunt.

The next Ranger rubbed Lasgol with a small plant. Pain surged in his back. Before it subsided, the third of the Rangers in turn rubbed poison ivy all over his back. The combination of the three pains exploded in his mind. He groaned; the pain was intense and did not go away, even though the Rangers were no longer beside him.

"They're torturing them!" Gerd said in disbelief.

"It's a public punishment, what did you expect?" Viggo said.

Egil was shaking his head. He could sense his friend's suffering.

"Defying the law of the Rangers has its consequences," Ingrid said.

"You're not defending this punishment?" Gerd asked her angrily.

"It's fair. They disobeyed a rule, and they must pay for it."

"But it's a disproportionate punishment," Gerd insisted.

"They could have literally hanged them!" she fired back. "It doesn't seem disproportionate to me."

"I agree with Ingrid there," Nilsa said.

"You always agree with her," Viggo muttered.

Gerd agreed with a grunt. He was furious at the sight of his friend suffering.

Someone else was suffering as much as Gerd, or even more: a brunette with fiery eyes. Astrid stepped forward to go and help Lasgol, but her teammate Leana pulled her back.

"Nobody can interfere with a public punishment," she whispered in her ear.

"But he's in pain..."

"I know, but you can't do anything to help him."

Astrid tried to take another step forward, but Leana stopped her and shook her head.

"They'll hang all day and all night," Dolbarar said. "The Rangers will inflict the punishment every hour until dawn."

"Oh no!" cried Astrid.

"Nobody will interfere," Dolbarar said sternly. "Whoever does will be expelled. The Rangers' punishments are irrefutable."

The Panthers murmured among themselves, but they knew that Dolbarar was both firm and fair. There was nothing they could do.

"And now go on with your duties."

The Rangers left. The students whispered, and for a moment

nobody moved.

"You heard!" Oden ordered. "Everyone to their tasks!"

In response to the Master Instructor's shouts, they all left gradually, except for a few. The Panthers stayed. So did Astrid. A third person did not move either; it was Valeria.

Oden waited until everyone else had left the area, Dolbarar and the Master Rangers included, then he went up to the Panthers.

"Didn't you hear what I said?"

"Yes, sir," Gerd said, "but we're worried about him."

Oden seemed surprised that Gerd should have stood up to him. It was something very unlike him.

"I won't say it again. I gave you an order, so follow it."

"But..." Gerd began.

Oden gave him a furious look, but he did not flinch.

"We're going," Ingrid said,

"That's better," Oden replied, arms akimbo.

Ingrid tugged at Gerd's arm, and he finally yielded. They went past Astrid as they left.

"Come on," Ingrid whispered. "We can't do anything for him. We'll come back at dawn."

Astrid hesitated, but in the end she left with them.

Oden scanned the area and found the last person still watching: Valeria. The Master Instructor was about to yell at her when she turned and set off toward the cabins. He turned to Lasgol and Isgord.

"I hope you learn your lesson. For your own good."

He left, leaving two Rangers on watch duty.

Lasgol snorted with pain, and because of the mess they had got themselves into.

"This is all your fault," Isgord spat out.

"It's not, and you know it."

"You bloody traitor!"

Lasgol shook his head. "One day that hatred of yours is going to kill you."

"Maybe, but before that happens I'll kill you."

Lasgol did not bother to reply. It was useless to reason with an enraged Isgord. He prepared himself for the next torture, which came punctually. Three other Rangers came and hit them repeatedly with bare, hard, flexible, branches, like whips. He groaned with the pain. Isgord cursed them all.

When they left, Lasgol's spirits sank even further. It was going to be a hellish night. The pain of each new torture would be added to the one they were already feeling.

And then he saw something that helped to raise his spirits. Hiding behind a tree, Astrid was watching him.

He was not alone.

He would bear the punishment.

It was the longest night in his life. The tortures arrived punctually, bringing new pain to his body, but not to his heart, which was happy because Astrid was there with him, helping him to get through the punishment.

They were let down at the first light of dawn.

"Take them to the healer to be examined," Oden ordered.

Edwina worked all morning on their wounds, using her Gift, together with potions and healing cures. At last she bandaged their wounds.

"I don't want to see you back here until the year is over."

"Yes, ma'am," Lasgol replied.

"We're not here out of choice," Isgord said.

"Just don't come, make sure you take care."

The two of them left. Outside, the Panthers and the Eagles were waiting and they were welcomed with hugs of joy.

And Astrid too was there.

Lasgol gave her a huge smile of gratitude. She hugged him and kissed him on the cheek.

"Don't get into any more trouble. Promise me."

"I'll try."

She smiled at him and hugged him again.

Chapter 17

The wounds from his punishment did not take long to heal, and before he had time to think about what had happened Lasgol was back training with his teammates.

The morning tests with Ivan were turning out to be real purgatory for all of them, especially Isgord. The day they had the 'real' test nobody was safe from the jaws of Ivan's six wolfhounds. Not even Ingrid or Nilsa, who were very fast, because at the slightest mistake – a trip, a slip – the animals would pounce on them. And they were merciless; they bit everyone alike.

Egil had deduced that Ivan had trained them specifically for this test, to make the pupils suffer.

"I don't want to go," Gerd said on the day of that week's 'real' test. He had been through four weeks of suffering in which he had been bitten three times already, and he had no doubt that during this test it would happen again.

The animals were clever, and did not bite twice in a row in the same area of the body. Egil reasoned that this was to give the bite time to heal. Sometimes it was on the buttocks, sometimes the right or left leg, at different heights, sometimes the arms, and not knowing which it would be made it even more horrible. Gerd was terrified.

"Come on, you've got to go," Lasgol said.

He shook his head. "No, I'll get bitten again. I can't stand it."

"I know it's very hard, but you'll get there."

"No, I'm not like you. You and Viggo have already done it, you don't often get bitten now, but I always do."

"Me too," said Egil.

"Yeah, but you're closer to making it. I'm not."

"Don't say that," Egil said. "You've improved a lot, you'll soon get there."

"You say that to encourage me, but I know I'm not going to make it. I can't be like this all year... it's too much..."

Viggo wagged a threatening finger at him. "Don't you dare even think about giving up!"

"Can't you see I'm never going to graduate? Why go through this torture for a whole year?"

"You're going to graduate with me," Viggo said firmly. "I haven't put up with three years of you, your snoring, and your poisonous farts in bed for nothing."

Gerd bowed his head and looked at the ground.

"We knew this last year was going to be very tough," Egil said. "But they won't break us, we'll make it."

"I'm terrified of those wolfhounds..."

"So am I, but I'm not going to let myself be defeated." Egil said.

"You're strong in spirit."

"And weak in body."

"You have more chance than Egil," Viggo told him. "You just have to go on making the effort, and that big body of yours'll do the rest."

Egil looked at Viggo, who shrugged. "It's the truth, you're a puny specimen. He has a resource he can count on, and you don't."

"Well, thanks very much."

"I'm being honest."

"That's true," Egil agreed.

"I'm really afraid... not only the pain of the bite... long before that... running, suffering, and then the fear of not knowing when they're going to catch you and bite you... I just can't stand it."

"It's in your head," Lasgol told him. "The fear, I mean,"

"I know, but I can't get rid of it... I know they're coming for me, to hurt me... I don't know when it'll happen, but I know it will. It scares me stiff."

"Sometimes fear is worse than the pain itself," said Viggo.

The other three looked at him in surprise.

"I know some things too."

"I don't want to go, Gerd complained.

"Well then, we'll have to drag you there," Viggo said cheerfully.

"You wouldn't dare."

"Of course we would."

Gerd looked at Lasgol in search of support. Lasgol merely folded his arms.

"Nobody's giving up here."

Gerd snorted in despair.

When they arrived where Ivan was waiting with his six wolfhounds, the faces they saw could be divided into two large groups: on the one hand the ones who knew they could beat the dogs in the race, and on the other those who were resigned to the fact that they could not, and hence would suffer the bites of the hounds.

"Welcome," Ivan said. "We've been training for some time, and it's nearly summer, so we'll go from just working on our speed to working on our endurance too."

They all exchanged looks and murmurs, and whispers of surprise began to be heard.

"Don't fret," Ivan said with his crooked smile. "It's not going to be as painful as the training you've been through so far – at least I think so, though I can't be sure." He smiled again, this time with a certain malice.

"What kind of test has he got in store for us?" Gerd wondered.

"I'm not good at endurance," said Nilsa, "I'm fast, but I don't have much stamina."

"Stop worrying," Ingrid said. "Whatever's on Ivan's mind, we'll conquer it."

Viggo looked at her doubtfully. "These two haven't passed the previous test, so why do you say that?"

"Because they need courage, you blockhead."

"Oh yeah, they're sure to be super-encouraged now."

Lasgol looked at his two friends' faces and saw that they were not in the least encouraged. He did not feel too confident himself. He knew that this endurance test of Ivan's would be designed to improve their stamina, but whatever it was, it would be both difficult and painful.

"I see you're all quite worried, muttering among yourselves and wondering about this new test... but let me repeat what I told you when we started these training sessions: Rangers need to be very well-prepared, to be fast and also to have powers of endurance. We need to be able to run through the forests and mountains of our realm for long periods at a time. And that's what we're going to work on now."

"Oh, we're fast enough already," said Viggo.

"Well then, now we'll have stamina too," Ingrid said.

"The training system will be as follows: two teams and one dog. The distances will increase during the next few weeks. You'll be wondering why one dog goes with every pair of teams, right? It's very simple: to improve your endurance you need to push your bodies.

What we're going to do is train so that you run till you can't manage any more, and the dog will go after you to make sure none of you stops to rest. Any educated guesses as to what'll happen if you stop...?"

"Oh no," Gerd muttered.

The complaints and protests grew louder.

"I see this new exercise is to your liking, and I expected no less. Today, as it's the first day, we'll go easy. You're going to run up to the top of Bald Mountain and then back. Anyone who stops, even to get their breath back, will get a bit of loving attention from my friends here." He indicated the wolfhounds.

"This is going to be awful," Egil said. He sounded utterly downhearted.

"The peak is a long way away!" Gerd protested.

"Remember: go to the top and come back, no rests, no stops under any circumstances, and follow the pace set by the dog. If any of you goes slower, you'll feel the loving attention; if any of you stops or takes a detour, you'll feel the loving attention. Is all that clear?"

"As stream water, sir," Ingrid said.

"Right then, everybody ready. I'll choose the teams. We'll start with the Owls and the Panthers."

Lasgol felt his hair stand on end, thinking of what might be in store, not only for his partners but also for Astrid.

"My dear Howler will go with you in all the training sessions from now until the end of the year," Ivan went on. He pointed at the largest and ugliest of the six wolfhounds. At his wave the brute growled, showing enormous fangs.

Lasgol felt a stab of fear. This animal would be a match for wolves and bears. A young Ranger Contender would be no problem for him.

"Now then," Ivan said. "Ready, steady, go!" He gave the signal to start. As soon as they broke into a run he bent over Howler, patted him, said something and pointed at the group. The beast howled and ran off after them.

The Owls ran ahead, with Astrid in the lead. Howler overtook all of them and took his place beside Astrid, who glanced at him anxiously. Howler began setting the pace and set off to the northeast, showing her where she was required to go. The other Owls followed their leader. Howler slowed down a little to fall back in with Ingrid, who was followed by the remaining Panthers. As with Astrid, he pushed her a little to the northeast, setting both route and pace. Ingrid gave the hound an unfriendly glare, and Howler snapped at the air to intimidate her. She did not like this at all, but she knew that if she protested she would be bitten, so she was forced to hold her temper to avoid provoking the wolfhound.

They went on through forests and broken terrain, and Howler fell back until he was bringing up the rear, very close to Gerd and Egil. He might have been watching them in case they lagged too far behind.

"Why's he chasing us?" Gerd asked Egil.

Egil was keeping up the pace as best he could. "It's just that he's placed himself behind us to make sure nobody stops or lags too far."

"I think he's giving me the evil eye," Gerd said. He was looking back as he made an effort to move on amid the snow.

"Don't be afraid of him, he's a bully," Viggo said. He was running beside Lasgol, a little ahead of them.

Ingrid was running at the head of the Panthers, with Nilsa beside her. "Don't lag behind, and don't stop."

Lasgol looked ahead and saw Astrid glancing back to see how they were doing.

"We've got to keep up this pace," Lasgol said. "Or else I'm afraid Howler's going to make us pay."

They went on running through the snowy woods, trying not to go any faster than the speed Howler expected of them. For some time they kept up the pace, but gradually the weakest started to flag.

Viggo shook his head. "I can't believe we're going wherever this dog leads us, whatever pace he sets, just as if we were so many sheep rounded up by a sheepdog."

"A sheepdog in a very bad mood with an urge to bite," panted Nilsa. She was having a tough time.

Egil glanced back and saw that the hound was not taking his eyes off them. "In fact this animal has been very well trained. Ivan knows what he's doing. I'm sure that if we stray from our path, he'll attack us and guide us back to the fold."

"Well, that's just great," Viggo said despairingly.

They ran through forests and plains all morning. Around noon the strength began to drain from their bodies.

"I'm going to bring the rhythm down a notch," Astrid warned

Ingrid. "Let's see what happens. We won't be able to keep this pace up all day."

"Good idea."

Astrid slowed down a little, then a little more. The two groups merged into one.

The hound howled and moved to her side. He overtook her and set the pace again, but slightly slower than the one they had been keeping up so far.

Ingrid noticed this. "Let's repeat the move a bit further ahead," she said to Astrid, who nodded in acknowledgement.

They repeated the same stratagem twice more, but the third time Howler realized and snapped at Astrid, almost getting her in the arm. Luckily her reflexes were fast enough and he did not manage to bite her.

"I think he's realized what we're doing," Ingrid said, and Astrid nodded.

By mid-afternoon Egil and Gerd were exhausted. Nilsa was not doing so well either, and nor were several of the Owls. They began to lag behind, and Howler barked threateningly.

"He's going to bite us," Gerd panted.

"Keep going, don't stop," Lasgol told him.

"I can't keep it up any longer," muttered Egil.

"Don't give up," said Ingrid. "We have to go on, we'll make it."

And the moment they feared came at last. In fact it was not Gerd who first suffered but Egil. Howler bit him in the buttock, and he cried out in pain.

Gerd, unable to go on, stopped in turn, received the same punishment and groaned.

Astrid and Ingrid stopped, followed by the others. This enraged Howler, who went for them, barking and looking very aggressive.

"Keep running!" Lasgol shouted. "Or else he'll attack!"

Astrid, seeing that Howler was going to attack her, started running again. Gerd started to walk, after her, then Egil did the same. Howler turned toward them but did not attack again. He barked at them, warning them not to stop.

"Come on, keep going," Lasgol called. "Even if all you can manage is to walk fast."

And at last they arrived at the burnt hill.

"What now?" Astrid asked Ingrid, while the remainder of the

teams straggled in.

"Now we have to go back any way we can."

"That's what I was afraid of."

They waited until everyone had arrived, and immediately set off in the opposite direction so as not to give Howler any reason to attack them. On the faces of Egil and Gerd, together with those of both teams who could not keep up the pace, was an expression of absolute terror.

"We'll do it," said Ingrid. "We've got to go on. Don't stop, don't give this bloody animal an excuse to bite you."

The way up might have been a torture, but the way back was far worse. Several of them were forced to stop because they could not even walk, and Howler bit them mercilessly.

"Come on, we're nearly there!" Astrid said, even though it was not true.

Their fear of Howler meant that finally the departure point loomed into sight. Here they collapsed in front of Ivan. Howler, seeing them all lying on the ground breathless and exhausted, went over to Ivan nonchalantly to receive a pat or two and some food, then howled at the night.

"Very good boy," Ivan said to him. "You did wonderfully."

The last teams arrived one by one after night had fallen. Ivan was waiting for them with his arms crossed, looking distinctly displeased. Nearly everyone dropped to the ground as soon as they arrived, utterly exhausted, unable to take a single step further. Some of those who had not been able to keep up the pace and who had been punished relentlessly by the hounds would need a visit to the healer.

A few, among them the Captains of the teams, as well as a few with a strong physique and enormous endurance, had managed to finish the test without being bitten. But they were the minority.

"I'm very disappointed," Ivan said. "I'd hoped my dear friends wouldn't have to work so hard, but of course you're in a very sad shape and you won't be able to graduate as Rangers like that, so you'll have to train and train a lot." He was patting his dogs as he spoke.

Lasgol snorted in disgust and looked at his friends on the ground, exhausted and bitten.

"And you need to understand that the endurance test isn't going to replace the speed test. You'll have to keep working on both. We'll alternate them."

Protests and fears returned to all those who could barely cope with the tests.

"A bit less protesting, and you're all going to have to train harder, or else you're going to end up full of scars." He went back to patting his wolfhounds.

Lasgol shook his head. These tests of speed and endurance looked like being hell for them.

Chapter 18

They had just woken up and were getting ready to face the day when Egil went to Lasgol's side, looking worried.

"What's up, pal?"

"Well, you see... this evening I've got to go to School of Nature with Eyra and I'm rather worried... that I'm not good enough..."

"You? Not good enough? You know more about any number of different subjects than anybody in the Camp. Not even the veteran Rangers know half as much as you do!"

"I'm not arguing that point... but remember what happened at the Schools selection test last year. None of the Master Rangers wanted to accept me in their School because I failed the tests. I wasn't up to the level expected of a Ranger."

"But in the end Eyra accepted you in her School."

"Yeah, but it was just as a favor to Dolbarar, so that in the end I'd become a Librarian here at the Camp."

"And that worries you, becoming a librarian?"

"No, not at all, it would be an honor and I'd love to be one. I could spend a lot of my time among books, learning and studying, which is what I like most. Apart from keeping an eye on everything that goes on in the Camp, that is, and telling the West anything that might be of interest."

"Then you've got nothing to worry about. Or is it because you're who you are, and sooner or later you'll have to go back with the Western League to take up your position alongside your brothers?"

"No, I'm relaxed about that. Austin's the Duke now, and may the Gods protect him from anything bad, because I don't want his position at all. To become the Duke and lead the West is something I have no interest in. In fact, the complete reverse, I'd never want to do that. Luckily my two brothers are there to run the duchy and carry on my father's legacy."

"You'd be a great Duke, the best the West has had in generations."

"No, that should never happen, because for me to become Duke would mean both my brothers were dead, and the thought terrifies me."

"I'm sorry, that was a stupid thing to say. I hadn't even stopped to think that something bad would have to happen to your brothers first."

"Even if nothing happened to them, even if they deferred to me and left me the title, which frankly I think is impossible as both Austin and Arnold were born and groomed to bear the title, I don't want it, it's not what I want to do with my life. I'd a thousand times rather be a librarian here in this Camp. Besides, at this moment, in the situation we're in, my brother Austin could be crowned King of Norghana."

"That's right. He's the heir to the Crown."

"I wouldn't want to be king."

"You'd make a very wise one."

Egil grimaced. "When has Norghana ever had a wise king?"

Lasgol smiled. "Never?"

"Correct. They've all been warriors and strong leaders, but as for *wise*... not a single one."

"Well then, you've got nothing to worry about. You're already on the right way to becoming a librarian-spy." Lasgol gave him an encouraging pat on the shoulder.

"We'll see what Eyra thinks."

"I'm sure she'll be delighted to have you in her School."

Egil gave a sardonic snort. He did not look very sure about this.

At dinner-time Lasgol was waiting for Egil at the door to the dining-hall instead of rushing in to eat as soon as possible, as Gerd liked to do. The giant was already inside, devouring everything that was put in front of him.

Astrid, who was with Leana, Asgar, Borj and Kotar of the Owls, came to say "hi" before they went in.

"How's everything going?" she asked Lasgol with a smile.

"It's all going wonderfully."

"You're a terrible liar."

They both laughed.

The Owls went into the dining-hall, while Astrid stayed chatting with Lasgol. They both welcomed one another's company.

"How did you do in School of Expertise?" Lasgol was asking Astrid, when Egil arrived.

"It went very well. Every day we learn something new and

surprising from Haakon."

"I can believe that," Egil said.

"I still find it hard to believe that you were chosen for School of Expertise."

She tilted her head a little to one side. "What did you expect me to choose?"

"Well... I figured it would be Archery, or if not, then Nature..."

Astrid smiled, and her lips curved dangerously.

"Ah, now I realize how you see me. I like it, except that you don't see everything that's inside me. I'm not an archer, I'm not bad with a bow and other weapons, but that's not my strength. And I don't think I've got a real feeling for nature, though I'm not bad at that either."

"So are you happy in Expertise?"

"More than happy. That's where I belong."

"Really?"

"Yes. There are parts of me you don't know, that belong to the arts we're learning in School of Expertise and are absolutely in harmony with it."

Lasgol was left rather at a loss by this. "Does this mean you have a dark side I don't know about?"

Astrid smiled roguishly. "I certainly do."

Lasgol was left unsure what to think.

"There's still a lot of me that you don't know, my dear hero," she said with a warmer smile.

"I'd like to get to know it..."

"All in good time. There has to be some mystery."

Egil chuckled.

"But Viggo is in Expertise," Lasgol said.

"I know. He was my partner in today's exercises. He's very good."

Lasgol and Egil exchanged a look of surprise.

"You praised Viggo. There must be something wrong with my hearing."

"I praised him. Your friend is very good at the dark arts, and he certainly gives a good account of himself in the shadows."

"I can't believe a Captain is praising Viggo," Lasgol said.

"Yeah, the fact is that he hasn't told us much about his past."

"And there must be something to tell," Egil said. "Something deep and, if I'm not mistaken, sinister."

"I agree with you on that," Astrid said. "Sometimes he has a lethal look in his eyes, cold, like someone who'd be capable of killing without hesitation."

"Do you think he's dangerous?" Lasgol asked, a little put off. He thought he knew Viggo quite well and he doubted he would ever go against his allies, but against others...

"All those of us in School of Expertise are dangerous."

Egil nodded. "That's true, otherwise you wouldn't be in that School."

"We all have a past," she said, "and in some cases it's a complicated one. I have the feeling that your friend Viggo has had a very tough, complicated past."

"Yeah, we think so too," said Egil.

"I'd like to know what that past could have been," said Lasgol, "but I'm afraid Viggo'll never open up enough to tell us."

"It's sometimes best to leave the past behind and buried," Astrid said. "Stirring up some things is never a good idea."

Lasgol was a little taken aback.

"Well, I'll leave you now and go and dine with my people."

As she passed Lasgol she brushed her hand against his. He felt happy about that little gesture. They could not publicly demonstrate their feelings for each other in the middle of the Camp. On the other hand they could keep these little gestures toward each other, sweet and secret.

He watched her go into the dining-hall, thinking that perhaps he did not know Astrid so well. He realized that he really knew very little about her past.

"What's worrying you, my friend?" Egil asked him.

"The fact that I don't know much about Astrid's past, or even her present, because I was totally wrong about the School she was going to belong to."

"Don't worry too much, you'll get to know her. Follow your feelings and your instincts. Everything'll be fine."

"Yeah... but I feel a bit strange. You know all about my past and I know all about yours, and yet we know very little about Astrid and even less about Viggo."

"That's because to know someone's past you need to earn their trust, and that person needs to want to trust you with it."

"Astrid and Viggo trust me. I've no doubt about that."

"Nor have I."

"So why don't they tell me about their past?"

"Because the moment hasn't come."

"And will it?"

"That's a question to which I have no answer to give."

Lasgol understood him.

"Let's go eat. I've been puzzling over these things so much, I've almost lost my appetite."

Egil patted him on the shoulder, and they went into the dining-hall.

Ingrid and Nilsa hailed them from one of the tables. "Tell us, what did you do today in School of Nature?" Nilsa asked Egil.

"In fact it was a very interesting class. When I got to the workshops I was rather uneasy, because of what happened in the Schools selection..."

"And how did Eyra receive you?" Ingrid asked.

"Actually, very well. I wasn't expecting it. She was very kind to me. She greeted me and told me she was very happy to have me among her own people. I told her about my misgivings, as my merits weren't good enough for me to be there with the rest of her group. She smiled as she doesn't often do, sweetly, and I can assure you that when she did, the expression on her face changed completely. She no longer looked like a witch, as she usually does, but instead like a very kind, wise old lady, which is what I believe she really is. She told me not to think too much about what had happened at the ceremony and that I belong in her School."

"I told you, you had nothing to worry about," Lasgol said.

Nilsa giggled. "Kind old lady… I wouldn't be so sure about that…"

"I was surprised by her kindness to me. And I thanked her for it. Besides, today we started learning about something new which is essential for all Rangers and which you only learn about in this particular School."

"Advanced healing potions?" Lasgol asked.

"Probably new, very powerful poisons," said Ingrid.

"Invisible arrows?" That was Nilsa.

"No, something much more useful. The Ranger's belt."

"The what?" Ingrid said, sounding disappointed.

Egil took off the belt he was wearing and showed it to them.

"That great ugly thing?" Nilsa said with a wave of distaste.

"Eyra told us that this belt is absolutely basic for every Ranger, and we're going to learn how to make them. We've started to study them, and I can assure you that the designs of the patterns are really complex and intricate. Eyra explained that the Belt is based on a more advanced one used by the Alchemists in the cities of the far East."

Lasgol's interest was aroused. "Alchemists?"

"Yes, I've become very interested in them. It turns out that there in the far East, where Tremia ends and the endless sea begins, there are city-states which in some ways are more advanced than us."

Ingrid was intrigued. "More advanced? In what way?"

"From what Eyra told us, they have Alchemy, which in some ways is like our process of elaborating potions and poisons or elemental arrows, but with a lot more reactive agents and effects. They can make small balls of fire like those of the Mages, but using more advanced chemical compounds. They also have weapons like a short bow, but which shoot iron wands with great power at short range. They call them crossbows. At a distance of a few paces they're devastating, and anybody can use them with very little in the way of instruction."

"That's what I find particularly interesting," said Ingrid.

"But to get back to the belt: the patterns are very complex and the belt lets us carry an array of different components without getting them mixed up or breaking their containers. Eyra told us that the *Path of the Ranger* teaches us always to be prepared, and to carry the things we need for the different situations we might come across. It's no good learning to make a poison or an elemental arrow if when we really need them we don't have the components. That's why this belt is so important. According to the story, the first belt was made by Uldritch the Brisk. He was on a mission for the King in the far East and he met a renowned alchemist. He was astonished by the things they could do. They became friends, and he showed Uldritch the belts they wore to carry their preparations. Uldritch asked him if he could have one, and the Alchemist gave it to him. When he came back to Norghana he took it to the Leader of the Rangers, who saw how useful it could be and decided to adopt it. It was modified so it would be better suited to our needs, and thus the Ranger Belt was born."

"How curious," Lasgol said.

"I want to see a crossbow," said Nilsa and Ingrid together.

Egil rolled his eyes, and Lasgol laughed.

"I see that the belt and its history don't interest you. If it's any consolation, we're going to learn to prepare new, powerful poisons, advanced healing potions and arrows that are almost invisible."

"That's much better," said Ingrid, and Nilsa nodded.

Lasgol, unlike them, was now convinced of the value of the belts. They sounded as though they were likely to get them out of a whole range of complicated situations. And if they were experts in anything, it was getting into that kind of situation.

Chapter 19

The way the training was carried out was different in the Fourth Year. Having to separate themselves into different Schools gave Lasgol mixed feelings. On the one hand he was happy to go to the School he had entered for and learn things that genuinely interested him; on the other hand he had to be away from his friends, which always gave him a feeling of sadness and even of unease.

The best part of the day was when they all came together in the dining-hall and exchanged their daily experiences. That evening, while they enjoyed a dessert of fruits and berries, Ingrid and Nilsa explained what had happened in the School of Archery.

"It was fantastic," Ingrid said.

"More than fantastic," Nilsa elaborated. "It was spectacular."

"Do tell us about it," Egil said with great interest.

Ingrid nodded. "We got to the shooting range and none other than Master Ranger Ivana the Infallible was waiting for us."

"Let me guess," Viggo put in "as cold and dry as usual."

"Yeah, she does have an icy nature," Nilsa said, "and eyes that go right through you."

"Those are the qualities of a born leader," said Ingrid. "There's nothing to criticize about that."

Seeing that Ingrid was in total support of Ivana, Nilsa and Viggo held back their criticisms, although they exchanged a look of secret agreement.

"Do go on," said Egil.

"The Master Ranger gathered us around her and showed us a very powerful weapon. We're going to train with it until we've mastered it."

Lasgol was interested. "A weapon?"

"Yes, the great yew bow."

"Oh," Lasgol exclaimed. "My father had one at home. They're beauties."

"My jaw dropped when Ivana showed us hers," said Nilsa. "It's very powerful, and far bigger than a composite one."

"I suppose that's so it has a longer range," said Egil.

"Ivana explained that it reaches two hundred and fifty paces, or even three hundred, easily." Ingrid said.

"Wow, that's quite an improvement," said Gerd.

"She gave us a demonstration. She took an arrow that was longer and heavier than a normal one, nocked it, tensed, aimed in an arc and then let fly. The arrow covered almost three hundred paces before it buried itself in the grass."

"That's fantastic," said Egil.

"Especially for killing Mages and Sorcerers," Nilsa added.

"True, generally the Mage can't cast spells beyond a hundred and fifty or two hundred paces, according to what I've read in the tomes of magic I've studied. Nor can sorcerers and shamans. The range of their spells is rarely more than two hundred paces, and only the more powerful can manage that, and there are very few of them.

"She also told us that although the bow's very powerful and can launch an arrow farther than any other known bow, it also has one great disadvantage."

"Accuracy," Egil said.

"Exactly."

"It sounds reasonable: more strength, less accuracy. It happens with the composite bows and the short ones too."

"Not only that," said Ingrid, "but using it takes someone strong, with a well-trained arm. That's why we're going to have to develop our strength a lot. Not everybody's going to be able to use it."

"I will, that's for sure," Nilsa said.

"There's no doubt about that," Viggo said with smug sarcasm. "I bet you'll be the best at managing a bow that's almost as big as you are yourself. Considering how nimble you are, I can see it clearly as I'm sitting at this table,"

Nilsa poked her tongue out at him. "You're an idiot," she said, "and you can mock all you like, but I'm going to manage to master that bow. It's going to let me attain my dream and become a Mage Hunter."

Viggo shook his head openly. "Hey... that's an elite specialty, isn't it? D'you really believe you'll be able to get into an elite specialty of the School of Archery?"

"Don't be a blockhead," said Ingrid. "Of course she'll do it. She's with me. I'll help her, and we'll both do it. Not only will we pass the School of Archery tests, we'll both be chosen for an elite specialty.

You just wait and see."

"Of course!" Nilsa said triumphantly, her arms raised.

Gerd was looking concerned. "I'm not sure that becoming a Mage Hunter with the sole aim of killing Mage in revenge for what happened to your father is a good goal to follow..."

The redhead's answering glare was a mixture of furious and guilty. "And what does it matter to you anyway? Mind your own business."

The comment hurt Gerd, who threw his head back as if she had slapped him and reddened.

"Sorry... I only meant to help... I didn't mean..."

"I don't need your help, I can take care of myself."

Lasgol stepped in before the tension increased.

"I'm sure Gerd didn't mean anything insulting, and up to a point I agree with him. Revenge isn't a good adviser. I'm telling you from experience, after what happened to me."

"Yeah, but you kept on till you cleared your father's good name. Nothing stopped you. So I'm asking the same of all of you, don't stop me. Let me do what I have to do. I'm going to be a Mage Hunter. It's my dream, and it's why I'm here."

Lasgol realized that Nilsa was partly in the right, although not completely, so he did not insist any further.

"Fine," Viggo retorted, "but I still say that whatever your goal may be it doesn't matter, because you're so clumsy you'll never make it in a thousand years!"

"Sure, and I still say that you're such a brainless idiot that all you'll manage in life is to annoy everyone around you."

Viggo's eyes widened at her reply, and he smiled. "That's one of my aims in life."

Ingrid and Nilsa rolled their eyes and treated him to a number of extremely negative comments.

"Please go on telling us about what you've learnt," Egil insisted. "It's extremely interesting."

Ingrid managed to calm down a little. Taking a deep breath and snorting angrily in Viggo's face, she went on:

"They made us stand in a line and gave us the great bows. When Ivana explained how we had to hold them, I realized that these long-range bows are much more difficult to handle than the composite ones we're used to. It's incredible, but the first problem is something as simple as trying to aim at a target in front of you. When I took the bow and nocked an arrow to see how I could manage it, I couldn't aim straight ahead. I was knocked sideways. For a moment I thought the bow was badly made, that the measurements weren't right. But then I saw I wasn't the only one. I think everyone else there felt the same. The bow's so big that it won't let you aim the way we're used to, because to clear the ground the nocked arrow sits pointing a little upwards, not parallel to the ground."

"This is fascinating." Egil said.

"Don't you believe it. This bow is bigger than you are. I'd like to see you try it."

"Oh no, of course I wouldn't try to handle a bow as big as that. I know my limitations perfectly well. I wouldn't be able to hold it."

"I can assure you that you wouldn't," said Nilsa. "I could barely do it myself."

"Actually, it's much more complicated to use than a composite bow. All day they had us nocking and aiming, and as the arrows are bigger too, what looked like a small thing turned into a whole new experience. We spent half the evening simply trying to handle the bow, and there were plenty who couldn't. In the end we had to aim at a cart full of hay at a hundred and fifty paces. It was a big target, easy to reach, or at least so I thought. But how wrong I was! I nocked my arrow the way I usually do with my composite bow, and it was a lot harder because the tension of the string is much greater and you need more strength to be able to pull it right back to your cheek. I released and missed by a lot. And I not only fell short, but my shot went way to the right."

"And mine went way to the left and fell very short too," Nilsa added.

"Ivana told us that with the long bows we always have to tense them and keep up the tension for a moment before we release. And also that we have to aim a little higher than the target, because these arrows fly in an arc at that distance and not straight, or almost straight. She took a shot to show us how to hold the bow and aim in an arc to hit targets so far away that it was amazing. The arrow flew perfectly and hit the cart dead center. After that she asked us to do it ourselves, but no matter how often we tried we couldn't hit it, not even Isgord, until the very last time, when we were already being told to go back for dinner."

"You didn't manage either?" Lasgol asked her.

"Oh yes, she did," said Nilsa.

"Well, I wouldn't say I did it. I hit the hay in the cart, and basically I think it was because I was compensating for the other shots. So it wasn't really as a successful shot, more like a whole series of corrections which finally succeeded."

"But what matters is that you hit it," said Gerd.

Ingrid was not so sure. "It's going to take us months to be able to hit something properly with that bow and at that distance."

"Did you manage it, Nilsa?" Egil asked her.

She shook her head. There was a look of sadness in her eyes, but she clenched her fists on the table and said: "I don't know how long it's going to take me, but I'm going to do it. I'm going to be able to hit not just a cart full of hay at a hundred and fifty paces but a person, a mage. And the arrow'll go right through him."

Ingrid put her arm round her shoulder. "That's the way to talk."

"It really does sound pretty complicated and exciting," Lasgol said. "I'm a little envious about not being able to practice with you. I'd like to master the big bow too."

"From what Ivana told us," Ingrid said, "only those who are accepted in the School of Archery learn to use it. I can understand how you feel, because it really is a beautiful, powerful weapon." They could see that her eyes were shining.

"To end the day," Nilsa went on, "Ivana gave us an amazing demonstration. Instead of the cart, they put three man-sized dummies stuffed with hay three paces from one another and two hundred paces deep. Ivana ordered us to keep absolutely quiet. In a single swift movement she drew a long arrow from her quiver and nocked it, then aimed for only a moment and released. While the arrow was still in the air she repeated the movement, tilting the bow slightly to the left this time. The first arrow hit the dummy in the chest. Before the second arrow hit the dummy on the left she released again very swiftly, barely aiming, without thinking, although I'm sure she must have been. The second arrow hit the dummy in the chest too and then we all looked to the one on the right and saw the arrow hit it in the middle of the forehead. Ivana lowered the bow, looked at us and said: 'Before the year ends you'll have to be able to do what I just did if you want to graduate as Rangers.' She left us all open-mouthed."

"Three hits at more than two hundred paces in three consecutive shots," Viggo murmured, "practically before the arrows reached each target... not even in your wildest dreams, young ladies."

"Shut up, blockhead," Ingrid snapped back. "Of course we'll manage it."

"Sure, and I'll be able to fly from tree to tree."

"You will be from the kick I'm going to give you!"

Nilsa shook her head. "Honestly, I was quite miffed. Particularly seeing I can't even hit a hay cart..."

"You will," Ingrid assured her. "If Ivana chose you for the School of Archery it's because you've got talent, not like this one here" – she gestured at Viggo – "who wasn't chosen, so don't worry, you just practice a lot and you'll get there. Tomorrow we'll stay back for a while after the class to practice with the long bow. And as sure as my name's Ingrid, we're going to master this weapon!"

Lasgol knew they would have to work hard, since that was the rule at the Camp: practice and suffer to gain a place as a Ranger. He was sure these two would strive to the limit. He hoped the Gods of the Ice would smile on them and that they would succeed.

Chapter 20

That evening Lasgol was watching the School of Expertise. On certain days they were allowed to observe the other Schools in order to have some notion of what their colleagues were learning. Lasgol liked the School of Expertise the least of the four, particularly because of the constant presence of Haakon, whom he still did not entirely trust. But on the other hand the techniques they were learning were so amazing and so useful that he found them fascinating, and he had to admit this.

Haakon had summoned all those in his group in front of the School cabins. Viggo had explained to Lasgol that they had spent weeks practicing the technique of 'walking among the forest shadows', and today they had to show how much progress they had made. Hence they were being allowed to watch, which Lasgol appreciated.

"Warm up and get ready," Haakon said.

Astrid was in this School, and she was the main reason Lasgol was so interested in watching the practice, although he had not admitted the fact to Viggo.

She gave her partners an encouraging gesture. "We've practiced a lot," she said. "We've got it under control."

"We'll do it!" Asgar agreed. He was a slim, very nimble boy with copper hair, from the Owls.

Viggo said nothing, but grimaced. Marta of the Eagles, Einar of the Wolves and Erik of the Snakes did not seem altogether convinced.

Astrid stepped forward confidently when Haakon called her name and gave her a Ranger's cloak to wear instead of her Fourth-Year one. The Rangers' cloaks were greenish-brown on one side and completely white on the other so that they could be used in both bare and snowy forests, helping to melt into either kind of surroundings, as long as the wearer knew what he was doing.

Haakon entered the forest, following a cleared path. At the center he turned round.

"Walk among the shadows till you reach me. Remember: the

forest is your ally. Use it well."

Astrid nodded. She looked at the cloak, then at the forest. The area she would have to cross was not very snowy and fairly densely-grown; she chose the greenish-brown side. No sooner had she covered her head with it than she seemed to blend into the landscape. She went into the forest very slowly, one step at a time, with very slow movements, seeking vegetation and shadows that would allow her to hide.

Lasgol, who was watching with great interest, felt she was doing it very well. Suddenly she was no longer visible. He scanned the forest, fruitlessly trying to spot her.

"She's doing great," Asgar told his teammates.

"I can't see her," Marta said.

"Nor me," said Einar.

Viggo pointed to the final area near Haakon, where there was very little vegetation. "We'll see when she reaches the high part."

"We'll have to trust the training," said Erik.

Astrid went on getting closer to Haakon, slowly, crouching, placing each foot in the shadow, under the cover of the vegetation and tree-trunks. Once she had located the area of shadow, she moved her body very slowly until she melted into it. She waited motionlessly, invisibly, thinking out her next move before she attempted it, making sure that the light filtering through the tree-tops would not reach her.

She reached the highest area. By now she was very near Haakon. A little more and she would be there. But there was less shadow there, and when she tried to step into an area further away, part of her body was revealed.

"Oh no!" said Asgar.

"She's been seen!" Marta cried.

Astrid hid again and finished the exercise. She appeared beside Haakon, who was waiting with folded arms. He shook his head.

"You did quite well. But you were too hasty at the end. You failed."

Astrid cursed under her breath, but did not protest. She went back to her teammates with her head bowed.

"Next, Marta of the Eagles. On you go."

Astrid handed the cloak to Marta, who began the exercise. The result was very similar. She almost made it, but not quite. Asgar and Einar did worse. Erik made a very good attempt and nearly succeeded. He was very pleased; he had done better than Astrid, which was a genuine feat. The rest took their turns, then came Viggo. He made his usual grimace, put on his cloak and set off.

He vanished the moment he went into the forest, and they did not see him again until he appeared beside Haakon.

"Very well. You succeeded," the Master told him.

Everybody was impressed. Marta clapped her hands enthusiastically. "He did it!"

"Awesome," Astrid said, looking incredulous.

Asgar nodded. "Viggo has a real gift for this School."

Lasgol felt very proud of his friend. Very surprised, but also very proud. All the Panthers knew that Viggo had certain skills, but the fact that he was so good at Expertise was something else altogether. Lasgol remembered that his friend had grown up in the slums of a dangerous city, and had been forced to manage on his own from an early age. This had made him develop skills which were now serving him very well. He did not normally talk about it, but from comments he had made it seemed that night and shadows had been his natural allies in making a living for himself, which hinted at illegal activities. The fact that he had no desire to go back there was another clue to the fact that he might be in trouble...

Lasgol was delighted that at least in Expertise, things were going so well for Viggo.

During the weeks that followed Haakon set his students to work on improving their skills for confronting enemies. Lasgol went back to watch their practice.

"Soldiers, mercenaries and ruffians in general," Haakon explained, "might have plenty of experience in the use of weapons and tricks, but they all have one defect that we Rangers learn to exploit. Any suggestions as to what these might be?"

"They're clumsy?" Marta suggested.

"You're not completely off the mark there. It's true that many of them are rather clumsy and put their trust in brute force, of which they usually have plenty. Don't make that mistake. But no, that's not their biggest flaw."

"They use short weapons like swords, axes, and knives, which are less effective than a good bow?" Einar said.

"That's a correct assumption. But in enclosed spaces, or in a forest at midnight, a bow isn't a lot of use."

"They don't use their brains," suggested Astrid.

"Wrong. They might not be very intelligent, but they're clever, treacherous and ruthless. They'll bury a dagger in your back the moment you're distracted."

Now it was Erik's turn to suggest an answer. "They're not as fit as we are?"

"Soldiers practice once a day. They're not in such good shape as we are, but they're not a lost cause either."

"And so?" asked Viggo, looking as though he was tired of waiting for one of his teammates to give the right answer.

Haakon turned to him. "And so, their flaw is that they basically use only one sense, that of sight."

There were murmurs of understanding among the group.

"We Rangers use all our senses when the moment comes to act, and particularly when it's the moment to fight. Anyone who only uses sight isn't using his full potential. That's why we train our hearing and sense of smell so that we have an advantage over our enemies in combat."

"And touch and taste?" Viggo asked.

Haakon smiled. "Those two senses are developed in the elite specialty. If you want to work on them, you have to reach the level of specialization."

Viggo looked defeated. He had no chance of being elected for any of the elite specializations of this School. Well, of this one or any other.

"Right then. Let's begin. The exercise will be as follows. Get into groups of six. First make a circle of five. The sixth member of the group will go into the circle and his eyes will be covered. You each take one of these." He showed them a stick with a long needle at the end. "You'll move around your blindfolded partner, two paces from him. When I raise my arm, one of you will step forward and jab him."

"But that's going to hurt," Marta protested. Others joined her.

"Of course it'll hurt. That's the whole point. That's the only way the mind will learn. It'll try to avoid the pain and so sharpen the senses of hearing and smell in order to guess where the next jab will come from and avoid it. Pain and suffering are great teachers."

"Can't we do it without hurting him?" Astrid asked.

"No, it has to be through pain, otherwise it would take too long.

We don't have that much time to practice. This is your last year, and time goes by very fast. We need to take advantage of what time we have and make the most of it."

The protests went on growing, but Haakon shushed them.

"If you can't stand up to a little punishment, you don't deserve to be Rangers. Choose. Anyone who doesn't want to do the test is free to go now and leave the Camp."

There was silence. Nobody said another word. Nor did anybody leave.

"Right. Begin."

They were not very happy, but they knew there was nothing they could do. If they refused they would be out, and they were not going to give up now, not after all they had gone through in order to be here. They would put up with the pain.

They drew lots, and Viggo was selected.

"Courage," said Astrid, who was in his group.

"We'll try not to hurt you too much," Marta said with an unconvincing smile.

Viggo wrinkled his nose at her, snorted in disgust and went to stand in the center, blindfolded.

"At my signal start moving around, and when I lower my arm, jab. A different person every time."

At his signal, the group began moving around the blindfolded person in the center. Haakon raised his arm and the moment came. Astrid was the first to jab Viggo, though she did it carefully.

Viggo felt the jab in his back and jumped, more from surprise than from pain. He tried to relax and concentrate. He had caught the sound of a step forward just before the jab.

"Harder! I don't want to have to say it again."

Marta gave the second jab. This time Viggo had clearly heard a step to his right, but had not been able to react in time. After Marta came Erik, whom Viggo scented rather than heard. Einar took two steps instead of one, and Viggo heard him clearly behind him. He tried to move away, but was jabbed in the arm. He had almost managed to dodge the attack. Finally it was Asgar's turn. As he was so nimble Viggo could not hear him, so he focused on scenting him. Asgar had a characteristic smell, of the mentholated herbs he washed with, so Viggo concentrated on his scent and caught it to his left. He sidestepped and completely avoided the jab.

They continued with this exercise for a couple of further rounds. Lasgol, who was watching spellbound, was amazed at what they were managing to do because of fear and the fact that they could not use their eyes to guide them. They got better with every try, even though they ended up covered in painful stings.

"Change over!" Haakon ordered.

Asgar took off the blindfold and handed it to Marta. "If you concentrate hard you can hear the moment just before the attack, even smell the person." he told her in an attempt to encourage her.

"We'll see," she said with very little confidence.

Marta did not do very well. Her senses did not seem to be very well-developed. Einar did no better, and Erik was the worst by far. Astrid, on the other hand, did very well. Lasgol was surprised at how well Viggo had done. Having grown up in the sewers of the city, he had evidently learnt how to survive in that cruel dark world, had developed his senses. Lasgol stared at him, wondering what he could have done to manage that.

Viggo noticed. He shook his head, "You don't want to know," he told him with that glare of his that froze the blood, a lethal glare.

Lasgol nodded to his friend and let the subject drop. In fact he would rather not have known. He was sure it was nothing good.

Chapter 21

During the afternoon a week later, after finishing the class, two members of the Snow Panthers entered the wood north of the Camp, while the remainder of the team went back to the cabins to rest before dinner.

"You needn't come with me," Lasgol said to Egil.

"Of course I need to. This is something of great significance, and I want to be a part of it. I couldn't allow myself to miss it."

"I probably won't achieve anything... just like all these other days you've come with me."

"That's not the important thing. What matters is the way you experiment to develop new skills. That's something worth studying, something I'd like to experience."

"Why do you want to analyze what I do?"

"Because from study and analysis comes progress."

Lasgol stopped and looked at him in amusement. "You know, you really ought to write that down."

"What I say is of no interest to anybody. What someone chosen, with the Gift, does to discover new skills, on the other hand, is of great interest."

"I don't think so... at least not what this 'chosen one' does, because he's got no idea what he's doing."

"The fact that you let your instinct guide you doesn't mean you're not doing the right thing."

"But I haven't the slightest idea of what the hell I'm doing... and you scribbling everything down..."

"I have to write everything down so that later it can be analyzed by minds more brilliant than ours, who may reach conclusions which allow them to make unthinkable advancements in this complex field."

Lasgol shook his head and went on deeper into the forest. The snow was thicker in this area, but not enough to be an obstacle. They came to a clearing in the middle of the forest, and Lasgol stopped.

"It looks like a lake of snow in the middle of a fir-wood," he commented.

"It's an optical effect that results from two uncommon circumstances: nobody has set foot on this clearing since the snow fell, and it's in the form of a circle. A pretty effect."

"Well, let's destroy it," Lasgol said. He pretended to smile maliciously and walked into the clearing until he reached the center.

"Now you've broken the magic of the place," Egil said in mock-reproach as he joined him.

"We'll be safe from prying eyes here. I don't want anyone to see me using the Gift. I've had enough trouble as it is already. I've no desire for any more. If anybody found out, I'd go back to being a weirdo that everyone looks down on."

Egil sighed and shook his head. "It's terrible, the harm that ignorant, narrow-minded people can do."

"Aye to that... let's hope I'm not found out."

Egil looked round. "We're safe here. I can't see a soul."

"Good. I'm going to get ready," Lasgol said. He began to check his bow and quiver.

"What are you going to try today?" asked Egil. He had already taken out his notebook and was preparing to write down Lasgol's experiences.

"The same thing I've been trying for the last three weeks without any luck."

"Don't get frustrated. It's only natural if you don't get it at the first attempt."

"I've tried a thousand times..."

"The path to discovery is hard and ungrateful, my friend, but success deserves all the effort along the way."

Lasgol stared at his friend. "Write that down. That's valuable. A lot more than anything we might do here today, which is going to add up to precisely nothing."

"Don't lose hope. I'm positive today is going to be your day."

"You said the same thing three days ago."

Egil smiled. "But today I'm more sure of it."

Lasgol laughed. "You're always sure!"

"It'll be fantastic!"

"I'm not sure you realize that you use the word 'fantastic' all the time."

"It's a word I love."

"Yeah... I've noticed."

Both friends laughed.

"D'you mind setting up the target?"

"Right away." Egil walked to a tree at the edge of the forest two hundred paces or so away. He set up a practice target they had borrowed and nailed it to the tree with his axe.

Lasgol finished inspecting his bow and arrows. He was not as optimistic as Egil that afternoon, but he was still going to try. He knew he did not stand very much chance, but after all, unless he tried he had no hope of success.

"Ready," Egil said as he went back to his side.

Lasgol closed his eyes and concentrated. Deep inside himself he sought the small pool that represented his inner energy. He focused on what he was seeking to accomplish, the skill he was seeking to develop, and released. The arrow flew straight to the tree a hundred paces away and hit the bull's eye. Immediately he reached for the quiver on his back, nocked a new arrow and released, all as fast as he could. The arrow hit the target, but on its right-hand edge. He repeated the movement still more quickly, and the third arrow flew off course to the right of the tree.

"Ufff…"

"Don't get discouraged. Keep trying."

"I can't manage to call on my Gift."

"Well, you know, without the Gift there's no new skill…"

"Know-it-all…"

"Half-Chosen…"

Lasgol laughed, and Egil joined him.

In a somewhat better mood he tried again. But the result was the same. His Gift was not responding. He tried again, but once more: nothing. He went to retrieve his arrows and went on trying until night began to fall. He was getting nowhere. He did not want to give up, but his fingers and arms were sore and every time it was harder to make the movement fluidly.

"We haven't got much time left," said Egil.

Lasgol looked up at the sky and grimaced. He was feeling very frustrated. He always found it hard to develop a new skill, but he had thought this one would not be so difficult. After all, it only implied great speed and, of course, accuracy.

"I think I have a name for this skill," Egil said. He was holding his notebook.

"The one I still haven't managed to develop?"

"Yes, it's a matter of time, but I'm sure you'll make it."

"I'm not so sure myself..."

"Want to know the name?"

"If I must..."

"I'm going to call it *Fast Shots*."

Lasgol heaved a deep sigh.

"Don't you like it?"

"Sure, the name's fine."

"Think about it while you try to reach your Gift."

"About the name you've given it?"

"Yes, and what it means."

Lasgol shrugged. "All right."

He took up his position once again and looked up at the sky. They only had time for one more attempt, then he would no longer be able to see the target in the dark. There was nothing to be lost by following Egil's advice, though he doubted it would be any use. He closed his eyes, concentrated and sought the pool of blue energy inside his chest. *fast shots... very swift shots... three consecutive rapid shots... come on, three in a row... like lightning... I can do it...* He went on repeating in his mind what he was trying to do: to make three shots in the time others would take to manage a single one. It would give him an enormous advantage over any enemy.

He took a deep breath, focused on what he wanted to happen, then released. And it happened. He felt the characteristic tingling as the Gift was summoned. A green flash which only he could see ran up his arms and head. *Yes! I've got it!* He looked in the direction of the target, but could no longer see it. He had waited too long, and night had fallen. *But the target's there, I know!* He had lost his chance. Without being able to see his target he could not release three times in a row. There was nothing to shoot at.

He snorted in frustration and released blindly.

"Don't worry," Egil said teasingly "We'll do it next time. It's gotten late, and night waits for no one, not even for two intrepid scholars like us."

Lasgol smiled. "True. Tomorrow's a new day, we'll have better luck." But he did not really believe it. He had been trying for this skill unsuccessfully for too long. By now he did not think he would be able to manage it. Normally when a skill proved itself resistant, he could not manage to acquire it. The question was knowing how long to go on trying before he gave up. He thought he was near that point by now, but he was unwilling to tell his friend, who was full of unshakable optimism.

"Let's get our things and go back," he said.

"I'm so hungry, tonight I'm going to eat as if I were Gerd."

Lasgol shook his head, smiling at the comment. Egil was half the size of Gerd, who got taller and stronger every year. Egil went into the darkness to retrieve the target while Lasgol waited with his bow and arrows.

"Lasgol..."

"Yeah?"

"This last shot you took, could you see the target?"

"Nah. I must have missed by a lot. Don't look for the arrow, you won't find it."

"Come here a moment."

Lasgol went over, puzzled.

"What is it?"

Egil pointed to the target. "Look," he said.

Lasgol went close enough to see the target, and his jaw dropped. The arrow was buried in the center. A perfect bull's eye.

"It... it can't be. Must be a coincidence. Sheer luck."

"Maybe. Or maybe it was your unconscious mind."

"What d'you mean?"

"Did you notice whether your Gift responded?"

"Well, yes... but I didn't manage the *Lightning Shots*."

"True, very true, but all the same, you managed to achieve something else."

"Another skill? Can't be, I wasn't trying for anything else."

"Many of the greatest discoveries of our time are due to chance or serendipity. They were discovered accidentally when something very different was being attempted."

"I didn't know... but I don't think..."

"We've got to try it."

Lasgol looked at him blankly.

"Another blind shot like the one you just made."

"But I can't even see the target."

"All the same, you know where it is."

"You don't seriously think..."

"Come on, what do you lose by trying?"

"Looking like a fool?"

Egil smiled. "It'll be our secret."

Lasgol waved his hand in resignation. "All right then, one shot and then we go back for dinner."

Egil nodded. They went back to the position, and Lasgol readied his bow. He concentrated, and called on his Gift. *I have to hit the target, even though I can't see it. I know where it is, I've seen it before.* He took a deep breath and prepared to release. It seemed ridiculous to release blindly. But for Egil…

A green flash ran through his arms and eyes.

He released.

Both friends ran to see the result.

"It's not possible…"

"It's fantastic! Right in the center again!"

Lasgol shook his head. Egil meanwhile was hopping around excitedly.

"I'm going to call it *Blind Shot*."

"I call it incredible."

Egil laughed.

That evening they did not arrive in time for dinner. They repeated the shot in different positions and places until they were sure they had found a new skill. Lasgol could release at targets he could not see as long as he knew where they were. And once again, Egil was right.

Chapter 22

Esben, the Master Ranger of the School of Wildlife, had assembled them for training at nightfall instead of in the afternoon, which was usual. Considering that they were doing more and more nocturnal exercises, Lasgol and Gerd were not altogether surprised.

"I hope they won't have us going round in circles in the forest all night till we drop," Gerd said.

Lasgol laughed. "Let's hope not."

The other pupils arrived one by one, and they all waited at the door of the School of Wildlife cabin. The temperature was cool, even though they were huddled in their cloaks, and it would get colder during the night. Gerd had gone to greet the animals, especially Strong Boy, the white bear he knew would be there, as he was not let loose at night, for his own good. The panthers and wolves were let out at night so that they could go back to their natural habitat. They were so well trained that they came back when they were called.

"Gather around, all of you!" Esben shouted from outside the cabin. "Today we have a very special session."

The teams looked at one another, wondering, but no one had the slightest idea what was going to happen.

"The next School of Wildlife lessons will all be held at night," he announced.

There were cries of surprise and some murmured protests.

"For how long?" asked Luca, the Captain of the Wolves.

"Until you've mastered the subject."

The comments and murmurs returned, but died out when they realized Esben was not prepared to relent.

"Today we're going to begin learning an art which we Rangers of the School of Wildlife have been practicing secretly for over a hundred years."

The comment caught Gerd's attention "*Secretly*," he said. "This is going to get ugly…"

"Let's hope it's not dangerous," Lasgol said.

Leana of the Owls patted Gerd's shoulder affectionately and winked. "Easy, big guy. You've got me to protect you."

Gerd went as red as a ripe tomato.

Esben looked up at the sky and the moon, which was shining timidly through the clouds. Night had fallen by now, and visibility was limited. He put a reinforced leather glove on his right hand. It covered his whole forearm, up to the elbow. Then he put his left hand to his mouth and imitated the hoot of a bird.

They all watched, intrigued.

From the dark sky an owl came down, very quickly and stealthily, and landed on his strong arm.

"This albino beauty is Mote," he said. The owl was a large one, with feathers white as snow and intensely yellow eyes. "It's a Snowy Owl, an adult male, so his plumage is practically all white. Can anybody tell me how it's different from other owls?"

"Is it stronger?" Luca ventured.

"No, that's not a quality of this particular family."

"Can they fly greater distances?" asked Osvak of the Bears.

Esben shook his head. "Not especially."

"They nest on the ground and fight other predators like foxes and even wolves, fearlessly," said Leana.

"That's correct, but it's not limited to this family."

Gerd dared to make a suggestion. "They hunt by day as well as by night."

"Very good, that's correct. Now that's a unique characteristic of this family. In fact during the day you'll find them always looking toward the sun. They do this to orient themselves. It's a well-known feature of these beautiful birds. And it's because of this that they're the Rangers' favorites. That and the fact that they're originally from the north, and acclimatize well to the cold." He went to Leana's side. "Try to stroke him. Slowly."

Leana reached out, very slowly. Mote turned his head and looked at her with his huge yellow eyes.

She spread out her hand to stroke him, and the owl gave a loud snap with his beak.

"He didn't like you," Esben said. "He's protesting."

Leana moved her hand away, and Mote snapped again.

"He has a rather unusual personality, but in the end he'll accept you, don't worry. It takes time. He doesn't accept strangers at first sight." He moved his arm, and the owl flew away. It was spellbinding to watch him fly in total silence.

"The Rangers use owls as messengers. That you already knew. In fact we're the only ones to do so. Mages and some nobles do it too. But what we Rangers specialize in, and we're the only ones who do, is the 'Night Hunt'."

Gerd was shaking his head. "We're not going to like this..."

Esben waved his arm. "Now form teams of five."

Leana, who knew them, joined Lasgol and Gerd, and so did Luca, which did not particularly please Lasgol, as he recalled their rivalry over Astrid. Finally Igor of the Tigers joined them too. Lasgol remembered that he had a way with animals. One by one the other groups formed.

Esben gave each group a glove, explained how to use it and asked for a volunteer from each group. Leana was the one from theirs. She put on the glove and stepped forward. Esben led them to the back of the cabins. It was some time before they came back, and the others were growing restless. When the volunteers finally came back, each had a snowy owl on their arm. They were different sizes, some completely white, others salt-and-pepper.

"Right. Now split into groups. I'll go round and explain how to interact with the owls. They're trained, so don't worry. The important thing is to gain their trust. They're a bit wayward, so it'll take time."

And he was right: it took them a long time. Every night for the following four weeks, when they had School of Wildlife, they assembled in front of the Wildlife Cabin and brought out the owls. Esben had explained how to handle them, and they did practice exercises to gain their trust. The owl assigned to Lasgol's group was Milton, a young male and one of the most self-willed. He was beautiful, completely white but for the tips of his tail-feathers.

"This bird does whatever he wants," Igor complained. He could not make it pay attention to him, however hard he tried.

"He's a very clever owl," said Leana, smiling. "That's why he ignores you."

"I don't find it amusing."

"Not much sense of humor," Leana replied. She nudged Gerd, who was trying hard not to giggle.

"The thing is, this bird's a male, and I think he only pays attention to the females."

"He pays attention to Gerd too," Leana corrected him.

"Well, it must be because Gerd always looks scared, and the bird knows it."

Leana came to Gerd's defense. "Maybe he's better than you with animals."

Milton snapped his beak, annoyed at all the commotion. Gerd stroked his feathers. "Gently, they're just playing."

Esben re-assembled them in a forest north of the cabins.

"Today we'll start practicing the Night Hunt. Each group will take turns with the owl. One student will handle it while another hides in the forest. The owl's been trained to 'hunt' you. You have to hide: remember you're the prey. Don't let him find you, if you can. It won't be easy to trick him, so I'm expecting you to do your best. Don't make me angry, because I have a rather bad temper, according to some."

Lasgol swallowed. Gerd was pale.

"This stupid owl won't find me in a forest at night," Igor said. "Not even by accident."

"Oh, really?" said Leana. "We'll see soon enough. I'll handle him, you're the prey. Put this Ranger scarf on your arm. Now run and hide."

"Okay then," Igor said. He tied the scarf to his arm and set off toward the forest at a run.

"This is going to be fun," Luca said.

They waited until Igor was well hidden. It was a dark night, so he had a chance. Lasgol was watching Milton and wondering whether he would be able to find him. It was not going to be easy.

"Milton, hunt!" Leana said to the bird. She gave the hunting-call Esben had taught them.

Milton turned his large eyes toward Leana, apparently considering whether to heed her or not. He finally decided that he would, and flew off. They followed him with their eyes until he had vanished into the darkness of the night-forest. A long time went by, until they were beginning to think he would not manage to find Igor. Suddenly a white shadow appeared behind them, and without the slightest sound he landed on Leana's gloved arm.

"Look who's back," Gerd said.

"And look what he's brought," Luca added.

In Milton's claws was the red scarf.

"He did it!" Leana cried happily.

Luca arched an eyebrow. "We'd better make sure this is Igor's scarf. There are other teams doing the test in the forest."

They did not have long to wait. Igor came back without the scarf, protesting and wagging his finger at Milton.

"He clawed my arm to get the scarf off. He almost took off half my arm." he protested, wagging his finger at Milton.

"That's because he doesn't like you," Gerd said.

Milton snapped his beak several times.

"See?"

"I don't like this test one little bit," Igor said, and dropped to the ground. He stayed sitting there, checking his arm, which was bleeding, and bandaged the wound with the Ranger scarf.

"Next volunteer?" Leana suggested.

The sight of Igor's wound had dampened their spirits. Milton's claws were very sharp.

"Come on, we all have to do the exercise."

"I'll go," Lasgol said.

Gerd smiled broadly. "Great, I'll handle Milton."

Milton did not show any aggressiveness toward the giant.

The forest was very dark, and it took Lasgol a while to get his eyes used to that, and to the reigning silence. He concentrated on remembering what he had learned in School of Expertise. *And the sense of smell,* he reminded himself. He took a deep breath, and the fresh scent of the night filled his lungs. It comforted him, it always did. He loved the freshness and the silence of the forest.

He went further in, all his senses on the alert. The year before, Haakon had had them doing a similar exercise for weeks. In this they had gone into the wood at night and had to reach designated spots, while avoiding being detected by an instructor. He had to admit that the tests of the School of Expertise were by far the worst, but also the ones which would help them the most in the future. Navigating a forest in complete darkness as if it were day was impossible for almost everybody, and if they knew how to do it, it was thanks to their tough training in Expertise these past three years.

Suddenly he heard a twig snap from a footstep, five paces or so to his right. He could see nothing, but he knew there must be someone there. So as not to interfere with anybody else's test he turned left and went on up through the trees, careful not to take any unwise step. Suddenly he saw a white owl swoop down over his head. There was a cry of pain where he had heard the twig snap, and the owl flew off with the scarf in his claws.

"Bloody owl," complained Jared, one of the two giant twins of the Eagles team,.

It was curious how he could distinguish the twins' voices without seeing them. Yes definitely, Expertise had taught them some very useful and surprising things. *I'd better focus. Milton must be lurking around.* He crouched and went on cautiously. He knew that he himself was now the prey and that a snow-white hunter with fantastic night vision was seeking to grab the Ranger scarf from his arm.

He went a little further on, carefully, as far as the center of the forest, the thickest part. It was the best place to hide as the vegetation grew tall here. He lay down and dragged himself to the foot of a great fir surrounded by underbrush. It would be very difficult for anyone to catch him there; it was a perfect spot. Except for one thing: he was not alone. He could hear rhythmic breathing on the other side of the fir. Very slowly, he looked to see who it was.

A feminine face appeared on the other side of the trunk.

"Hello, Lasgol," she whispered.

He was stunned. He recognized the golden mane and sea-blue eyes.

"Val?"

"Surprised to see me?"

"Hiding in the depths of the forest at night in the middle of a Fourth-Year School of Wildlife test? Well, yes, I'd say so."

Val smiled as innocently as though she had never broken so much as a plate in her life.

"And suppose I told you I was out for a stroll to clear my mind?"

"I wouldn't believe you."

She smiled beguilingly. "You've always been very smart, besides being handsome."

He was still puzzled. "But what on earth are you doing here? We're practicing!"

"I saw you taking the owls and I followed you."

"Why?"

"I like to watch you practice."

"The Fourth-Years?"

Valeria cocked her head slightly to one side, smiled and winked at him.

"One Fourth-Year in particular."

Lasgol realized who she meant, and blushed. He was about to protest when she embraced and kissed him passionately. Taken by surprise, he was unable to react.

She let him go after a moment.

"Val, don't..." he started to protest.

She put her finger on his lips. "We'll see each other again," she said, and left under cover of the bushes.

Before he could think clearly about what had just happened, Milton brought him back to reality by digging his claws into his arm and flying off with the Ranger scarf in them. He had not seen him coming.

"Ouch! Where on earth did you come from?"

He straightened up and set off back down toward the entrance to the forest.

"Girls..." he complained bitterly.

Chapter 23

A week had gone by, and Lasgol and Viggo were waiting for Egil at the library door. Their friend had gone in to change some books he was consulting.

"I don't know why he reads so much," Viggo said. "He already knows everything."

"He says he never knows enough."

"Well, I don't know where he finds to put everything he learns."

"According to him, knowledge doesn't take up space."

"He talks too much nonsense."

Lasgol laughed.

Suddenly they saw Ingrid coming, with Molak beside her. Viggo stiffened and clenched his jaw. Lasgol replied pleasantly enough to their greeting.

"What are you still doing in the Camp, Molak?" Viggo asked, sounding unfriendly.

Ingrid glared at him, and Lasgol stepped in, trying to ease the tension.

"That's right, you've already graduated. Haven't you been told where you're going yet?"

Molak gave him a friendly smile. "Actually I was posted to the Camp."

"Why the Camp?" Viggo asked.

"Because he's a hero, and the best of his year," Ingrid replied.

"Well..." Molak began.

"The best," Ingrid said, passing judgment.

"I've been assigned to the School of Archery. I'll be helping with training the First-Years."

"Because he's an exceptional archer."

"If he's so exceptional, why wasn't he chosen for the elite specialization?"

"Well, actually he was chosen, but he refused."

"Yeah, sure."

"I postponed it... for a year. I want to do something for the Camp... after what happened to my team... I think it's the best thing for me to do. I want to help so it won't happen to others. I feel it's my duty."

Lasgol was pleasantly surprised. "That does you credit."

"Doesn't it?" said Ingrid, and smiled at Molak.

That smile was as though a dagger had been buried in Viggo's stomach. Ingrid never smiled much, and for her to do so, openly, at Molak... it was killing him.

"I wouldn't give up an elite specialization for the sake of a bunch of ungrateful newbies," he said, more because he felt snubbed than because he really felt it.

"What a strange thing to think," Ingrid said.

"Well, I'm glad to see you, take care," Molak said, and they went on their way.

When they were a few paces away Viggo exploded.

"What an arrogant poser!"

"You really don't think..."

"Of course I do, don't you see he's acting like Mister Perfect the outstanding Captain?"

"It's what he is..."

"Well, he lost half his team, that's how perfect he is."

"That's not what you really think, it's just jealousy talking."

"Jealous? Me? Of what?"

"Jealous about Ingrid," Egil said as he appeared at the door with two heavy books under his arms.

"And what do you know about it! You weren't even here!"

"Didn't need to. Anybody can see you're jealous from a league away."

"Bullshit! I can't stand her! I loathe her!"

Egil stared at him, wide-eyed. "In that case, why are you yelling at us?"

Viggo was about to curse, but instead he turned round and left like a whirlwind.

"Touchy..." Lasgol said.

"We haven't seen the half of it."

Lasgol sighed.

That evening, with dusk falling, Viggo and Lasgol were practicing their knife-throwing against a nearby tree. They saw Ingrid and Nilsa coming toward them with their long bows.

"Here come our archers," Lasgol said.

Nilsa smiled at them. "Hi there, guys, how was your day?"

"Pretty hard," said Lasgol, who had suffered during the day's classes.

"Actually, it wasn't so bad," said Viggo.

They turned to him, not expecting the comment, since he had been complaining bitterly that School of Expertise was becoming a real torture and the suffering was unbearable.

He shrugged. "Today things went well."

Ingrid rolled her eyes.

Lasgol indicated Ingrid's long bow. "May I have a look at it?"

"Yeah sure, I trust you."

Lasgol took the bow and became aware of its size and weight at once.

"Could I have an arrow?"

"Yeah, sure, but be careful. The string tension is a lot stronger than it is with the composite bow. You have to pull back hard and use all your strength to keep your arm straight."

Lasgol nocked the arrow carefully. He began to pull the string back to his cheek and felt the truth of what Ingrid had said. Trying to keep the bow straight, he made sure there was nobody in the area and aimed at a nearby tree.

"It's no more than thirty paces away. I ought to be able to hit it."

Ingrid and Nilsa exchanged a conspiratorial look.

"By all means," Ingrid said. "Go ahead."

Lasgol felt a thrill at being able to try the weapon thanks to his friends' generosity. He would never miss a shot like this with a composite bow, so he concentrated on his aim, relaxed. And released.

He missed completely. The shot went too high and to the right. Ingrid and Nilsa burst out laughing.

"I don't understand. How could I have missed?"

"We've been asking the same question again and again," Nilsa said with a mischievous smile.

"It's because of your position," Ingrid explained. "Just today we were practicing short shots with the long bow under Ivana's iron hand. Now I know why they call her Infallible."

"She never misses," Nilsa said, "whether the target's less than a hundred paces away or more than two hundred. And that's with this great bow. With a composite one or a short one she could probably hit the bulls-eye with her eyes closed."

"She can't be that good," Viggo said.

"She is, and much more than that. It's as if she puts her arrow where she puts her eye."

Lasgol's interest was aroused. "Tell me what you did today."

"Today Ivana taught us to shoot short distances with the long bow, less than fifty paces. At first we thought it'd be a piece of cake, because at that distance we almost never miss with the composite bow, but we were in for a really big disappointment."

"Disappointment?" Viggo repeated. "This is getting better. Tell us."

"She asked us to shoot at a target about forty paces away, with long arrows, as if we were making a long-distance shot but had been surprised by an attacker at close range and had no time to switch weapons. In an ideal situation we'd have had our composite at hand and we'd have switched, but she wouldn't let us, she said we'd have to use the long bow. At first, like you, Lasgol, I thought it would be easy. I missed by a hand-span. I could barely believe it."

"I missed by two hand-spans." Nilsa said, shaking her head.

"After all of us had done badly, she showed us how to release in this situation. What puzzled us was that she didn't hold the bow vertically when she released but horizontally, at chest level. The reason she gave us was that at close range, and more so if the attacker's running toward us, releasing with an upright bow makes the arrow fly upwards in most cases, and then you completely miss. But holding the bow horizontally you can release directly and powerfully and the arrow flies straight with only the slightest curve up, which you need to compensate for. She had us practicing all day releasing at different distances, forcing the pace."

"It was terrible at first," Nilsa said, "but then it got really good."

"Once we started hitting the target, she means! Because at first we missed more than if we'd been moles."

"So," Lasgol said, trying to understand, "if you have to make a long-range shot it's better if you do it with the bow vertical, but at close range it needs to be horizontal."

"That's right, especially if the attacker's closing in on you."

"That's really interesting."

"In fact Ivana even released from the hip, which left us all open-mouthed. They set up a dummy with heavy Rogdonian steel-plated armor, a lot tougher than the scaled Norghanian kind, at twenty paces. She released at full speed, pulling the arrow out of her quiver, nocking it horizontally at hip level and releasing fast as if the soldier were coming at her."

"What happened? Did she hit it?"

"Not only did she hit it in the heart, but the arrow pierced the heavy armor and buried itself deep in the dummy. If it had been a soldier, she'd have killed him instantly."

"She managed to pierce heavy armor. That's awesome."

"Ivana's shown us that with a long bow and the right arrow, always at less than a hundred paces, you can pierce armor."

"That's really cool," Egil said, feeling slightly envious of the girls.

"The problem is being able to use the bow fast enough and skillfully enough to make that kind of shot before the soldier jumps on you and runs a spear or a sword through you," Ingrid said.

"And that isn't easy at all," Nilsa said. "What with the size of the bow, its weight, and the difficulty of handling it, releasing so fast at hip level is really difficult. We've had to suffer the whole afternoon because she had us practicing without a break. As she said, we must be able to use the long bow as if it were the composite one at close range, or else it'll mean losing our lives in some chance encounter we might not be prepared for. It's taken me ages to hit the targets, and I won't even start on how long it took me to pierce the armored dummy..."

Viggo laughed. "Seeing how coordinated you are, I'm not surprised."

"Mock all you want, but in the end I did it!"

"Did you? That seems pretty surprising to me."

"Well I did. I hit it in the head and the arrow pierced the helmet visor."

Viggo looked at her in disbelief, his head on one side. "Wow, that's quite a shot. So you aimed at the head instead of the chest where you'd have more chances of hitting the target. You're a real archer."

"Well, I didn't really aim at the head... it's just that I was aiming at the chest but the arrow went a little high, which is the usual thing when you use the bow that way."

Viggo burst out laughing. "I thought so!"

"I don't care how it happened, the fact is that I managed to pierce the armor with an arrow and in the head at that. I'm proud of myself."

"So you should be," Ingrid said encouragingly.

"The next time aim at the feet, then you might hit him in the chest!"

"You're utterly impossible," Nilsa said.

He smiled from ear to ear. "Yeah, that's why you love me so."

"Have you done any other practice with the bow?" said Lasgol, who was now trying a horizontal shot at the same tree as before.

"No, not yet, but the next thing we're going to have to do is short releases against moving targets with the long bow, which should be interesting. I'm dying to try it."

Nilsa stretched. "It's also going to be really frustrating, because if we have trouble hitting a fixed target, imagine what it'll be like with moving ones."

"I wish I could see it," Viggo said roguishly. "I'd enjoy that."

"Lucky for us you have Expertise instruction, and you won't be able to," Ingrid replied.

Lasgol released again, this time keeping the bow horizontal, and missed again. The arrow bore to the left.

"It's really difficult to handle this bow," he said. What with the size and the weight and the tension of the string, it's really hard to aim."

"Yes, that's the main problem," Ingrid agreed. "It's got power, but aiming with it is a major feat."

"I'd like to learn to use it," Lasgol said.

"You can come and practice with us whenever you want. We'll let you try and teach you how."

"Of course!" Nilsa said excitedly.

"And I'm not invited?" Viggo put in.

"So that you can laugh at us all the time?" said Nilsa. "Of course not."

Ingrid was shaking her head very visibly. Her expression said, 'no way'. "Not for all the gold in the world."

"You really are lousy friends," Viggo said.

"They're good to me," Lasgol said. "It must be for some reason..."

"That's because you're too good."

"And you're a pain in the neck," Nilsa retorted.

At that moment they saw a figure approaching their cabin: a tall Ranger, with an athletic build and a light step. Lasgol did not recognize him until he was already by their side.

"Hello, Panthers,"

"Hello, Molak," Ingrid replied with an immediate smile.

"To what do we owe the honor?" Viggo asked, in a voice which showed that he was not at all happy with the visit.

"The other day Ingrid asked me to help them with the long bow. I thought now I had a moment and my duties leave me free, I could make an appointment with them for tomorrow at the shooting field."

"That would be fantastic," Ingrid said, still smiling.

"Actually, we need it badly," said Nilsa. "Me in particular."

"Don't worry, Nilsa, the long bow's difficult to handle, and it takes time to get used to it. Tomorrow I'll show you a couple of tricks I learnt that'll help you."

"Tricks?" Viggo repeated. "That's cheating."

"Not necessarily. They're improvements in handling, if you don't like the word 'trick'."

"Don't pay any attention to him," Ingrid said. "Any advice you give us and any trick you can teach us will be great."

"We need to master it if we're going to end the year well," Nilsa said, "or we won't graduate. And quite honestly, this weapon is a bit too much for me."

"Don't worry, either of you. I'll help you, and with a bit of practice you'll manage it."

"Would you mind if Lasgol came along?" Ingrid asked.

"Of course not. It'll be my pleasure."

Lasgol nodded gratefully. "Thank you."

"Then we'll meet tomorrow at the shooting field."

"Thanks so much for helping us," Ingrid said. "I really appreciate it." Her gaze lingered on him. Viggo clenched his fists, but said nothing.

Ingrid followed Molak with her gaze until he disappeared further down.

"He's so nice," Nilsa said.

"Yeah, he's a real gentleman."

"Sure, and he's not doing all this so as to win your affections,"

Viggo said, folding his arms.

"What do you mean?" Ingrid asked.

"Just what I said. He's using his archery lessons to win you over, and don't tell me you hadn't noticed, because I know perfectly well you have."

"He does it because he's a good person, unlike you."

"Sure and pigs have wings. That one's come to see if he can score with you, and the archery's only an excuse to spend time with you."

"And why should that be any concern of yours?"

"Me? I don't care. I'm only saying that he's not doing it out of the goodness of his heart."

"Well then, if it's no concern of yours, you might as well shut up."

"Or is it just that you're jealous?" Nilsa asked with her head on one side.

"Of course I'm not jealous! Why should I be?"

"Maybe because he's trying to woo Ingrid."

Viggo suddenly went red, then wrinkled his nose. He glowered.

"I'm going inside. All this nonsense is giving me a headache." He turned and went into the cabin.

Lasgol looked at Nilsa, who smiled mischievously.

"He can be impossible," Ingrid said.

"Yes, especially when Molak is around you..."

"Don't you start as well."

"Fine, whatever you say, I'm just saying..."

"Bah! It's all nonsense. I'm going inside too."

Lasgol and Nilsa burst out laughing.

"Even a blind man would see what's going on between these three," she said, still laughing.

Lasgol was laughing too. "Even I see it, and I never notice these things."

Nilsa chuckled. "Quite honestly, I'm a bit sorry for Viggo. The poor man hasn't a single chance beside Molak. He really has it tough. But knowing Ingrid, it's quite possible that neither of them will get her."

"That's true too. It'll be interesting to see how it all ends."

"Well, I hope."

"Yeah, let's hope so."

Chapter 24

The days slipped rapidly by at the Camp, and the news that arrived was not at all good. The rumors the river brought told that the war was not going well for King Uthar, which was bad for the Rangers, although not of course for Lasgol and Egil.

It was rumored that the Western League had assembled an army at Estocos, the capital of the Viggons-Olafstone Duchy, and was getting ready to march at any moment. It was also rumored that the hosts of the Peoples of the Frozen Continent had already crossed into Norghana and were heading South with the intention of reaching Norghania, the capital city of the realm where Uthar had his army.

How much of this was true and how much speculation nobody knew, but if there were rumors at all, there must be some truth in them.

Lasgol wished that a ceasefire would somehow be reached and that no more blood would be shed on either side. He longed for peace, longed for Norghana to be able to go back to being a peaceful, prosperous kingdom where people lived good, flourishing lives. On the other hand, given the situation, it seemed highly unlikely. He knew that under Uthar's yoke his wish would never come true. After this war would come another, a new conquest of some other, weaker, kingdom or people. That was why they must fight him, not because he was not the legitimate king, not because he was an impostor. He wished there was some way of putting an end to the war, of bringing Uthar down and seeing a good, just king on the throne in his place. Unfortunately kings tended to be anything but good and just, and even more so in the North. Viggo had told him more than once that his wishes were as naïve as those of a five-year-old, that he ought to wake up to crude, hard reality, but he did not want to wake up. He wanted to go on hoping that in the end there would be peace and joy for everyone. Just thinking this he knew that Viggo was right, but he still did not want to give in to despair.

My mother will help crown Austin Olafstone King of Norghana, and all this nightmare will come to an end, he told himself.

On the other hand, the quarrels among the few Westerners who had stayed in the Camp and the Eastern majority were still there under the surface, even though there had been no other incident after the duel and the public punishment which had followed. Lasgol's back still bothered him, but he had to admit that the punishment had worked.

That morning Oden made them assemble, and his face showed a concern that was not usual in him.

"Dolbarar has asked me to take you Fourth-Years to see him, so not a word and no questions. You know I won't tell you anything, so we go straight on to the Command House."

Lasgol and Egil exchanged a glance of doubt and worry.

"This looks great," Viggo commented.

"Don't get ahead of yourself," said Ingrid.

Astrid came over to Lasgol as they went to the Command House. "D'you have any idea of what's up? Any news? There are several people in the other teams who are saying it's to do with the war."

"Oh, are they?" Egil asked.

"Yeah, it seems that several Royal Rangers have come to the Camp."

"We didn't know any of that," Lasgol said.

"I did," Viggo said.

"So why on earth didn't you tell us?" Ingrid asked angrily.

"Because when I tell you things you give me a nasty look and ask me how I found out, and say it's because of some low-life trick or other, so this time I kept it to myself."

"You're hopeless," Ingrid said, sounding frustrated.

"Yeah, I'm hopeless when I tell you because it's me telling you, then when I don't tell you, I'm hopeless because I haven't told you. It's always me that's at fault."

Astrid smiled at Viggo's outburst. "Actually, he does have a point," she said to Lasgol.

"Don't side with him, because we'll be screwed."

"Of course I have a point, and the hot brunette here knows it."

"Hot brunette?" Astrid narrowed her eyes and turned to Viggo.

"I mean the Captain of the Owls, whose hair is a beautiful jet black,"

Astrid laughed out loud. "This Viggo of yours sure is something!"

"You really wish I was in your team."

Astrid stared at him for a moment. "Well, you'd come in handy. You're very good at Expertise. I like that."

"Thank you. At least someone recognizes my abilities."

Lasgol smiled at Astrid, assuming the comment had not been serious. She whispered in his ear: "I mean it. He's very good."

Lasgol was surprised, but nodded.

At the Command House, as on all important occasions, they found Dolbarar together with the Four Master Rangers. But beside them this time were four Royal Rangers. This changed things; their presence meant that whatever Dolbarar had to tell them would be to do with the war, not with daily life at the Camp.

"Line up in silence," Oden ordered.

"Welcome, everybody," Dolbarar began.

Lasgol always tried to guess the severity of what was going on by the leader's expression. As he watched him he had an ominous feeling. The usual reassuring smile was on his face, but it was not as strongly marked. This meant that something was going on, and he was worried.

"The first thing I'd like to do is to congratulate you all, because you're in your final year and you're doing very well. If you pass this year's tests you'll become Rangers, and I know that's what your hearts are truly set on. Let me give you due notice that the fourth year has two tests, one in Summer and the other in Winter. These tests are actually missions. They're quite special, and we call them war missions because they are carried out together with the army and must be real. I've gathered you here because it's time for you to face your first war mission."

They all looked at one another uncertainly.

"We have news from the King. He asks us to help him in the war efforts. You Fourth-Years are the only ones sufficiently ready for the mission he has entrusted us with. If it were a normal year, if we weren't at war, the war test would take place in the summer. This is a test in which the Fourth-Years carry out maneuvers with the Rangers and the royal army, but unfortunately this year these maneuvers will be a genuine war mission."

There were murmurs and comments among the Contenders.

"It will be real and dangerous, and for that reason I need you all to take the greatest possible care."

"I knew it would be bad news," Viggo said.

"Don't be so worried," Ingrid said. "We took part in the war in the Frozen Continent, and we survived."

"I worry every time someone wants to kill me, and just in case you hadn't noticed, that's what happens in wars."

"Everything'll be all right," Nilsa said. "Nothing happened to us in the Frozen Continent, and nothing'll happen to us now."

"Yeah? Well say it again with a little more conviction, because your voice shook there at the end, redhead."

"The King," Dolbarar went on, "is entrusting us with a mission of vital importance: to search the eastern area and keep watch on it to find out where Darthor's hosts are planning to land."

"This mission is going to be dangerous," Gerd said, "and besides, we're going to be in a difficult situation… bearing in mind the side we support."

Egil glared at him. "Not a word, they might hear you."

Gerd put his hand to his mouth. "Sorry…"

Lasgol knew what Gerd was trying to say: if they found where Darthor's troops were planning to land and had to inform the King's army, it would be going against themselves, against Egil. The Peoples of the Frozen Continent were allies of the forces of the west, the forces of Egil's family.

"Tomorrow you set out on your mission. The Royal Rangers will go with you. Always follow their instructions. Don't stray from them under any circumstances. This war mission will act as your Fourth-Year Summer Test. Those of you who come back alive will have passed the first half of your final year. You'll each be awarded an Oak Leaf. Remember, it'll help you in moments of difficulty. And most of all, be very cautious and take no unnecessary risks."

"It's us that danger goes looking for," Viggo commented.

"Very true," Gerd agreed.

"I want you all back to face the last part of the year. I want no incidents. Make use of everything you've learnt during these four years of instruction and training. And don't deviate from the orders of the Royal Rangers, that's absolutely essential."

Murmurs and worried expressions were now tangible everywhere.

"You heard!" Oden said. "Go back to your cabins and get ready to leave at dawn."

Lasgol and Egil looked at one another. Things were beginning to get complicated, and they both knew that they would turn distinctly nasty before very long.

Chapter 25

It took them a little over three weeks to reach the east coast. At first the nine teams went in a group, since there is always safety in numbers. But the coast of the kingdom was vast, and they had to cover the whole of it. The Royal Rangers divided it into nine sectors and entrusted one sector to each team. The Snow Panthers were sent to cover Killer Whale Bay, together with the cliffs at either end.

It took them several days to reach the cliffs that overlooked the enormous bay, and here they camped for the night. Royal Ranger Mostassen had been appointed leader of their group. He was the living image of a Norghanian warrior: tall, strong-armed and broad-shouldered, with long unbound blond hair. His eyes were light green, and his jaw appeared to be capable of absorbing a right-hand punch with no trouble. What disconcerted Lasgol was that unlike the typical brutal, barking Norghanian soldier, Mostassen barely spoke. In fact whenever he could convey his orders with a gesture, that was all he did. During those weeks of travel after they had left the Camp he had not addressed any of them other than to give them orders. Lasgol, remembering Ulf, knew that most of the Norghanians were as tall and strong as they were loud-mouthed. The Rangers were rather less so, but they were still Norghanians, and every once in a while they barked and shouted. Yet it was as if a panther had bitten off this Royal Ranger's tongue.

Mostassen went out on patrol. Not wanting to take anyone with him, he simply waved at them to stay put until he returned, which was what they did. They prepared a small fire behind a large rock on the cliff which overlooked the bay. It smelt of salt and the sea, and the evening views were beautiful from that height, with the ocean stretching out to infinity. The only sound was that of the waves breaking in the distance.

"My mother said it was essential that Uthar should never find out anything about where or when the Peoples of the Frozen Continent crossed into Norghana," Lasgol whispered to his partners.

"Interesting situation," said Nilsa, "because that's exactly the mission they've given us, to find the spot on the east coast where

Darthor's army is going to land."

"Well, I think the situation's rather more than 'interesting'," Viggo said, "if we bear in mind that we're right in the middle of two sides at war."

Lasgol frowned. "What do you mean, in the middle of two sides?"

"Just that things aren't entirely clear. They might be to you, because of whose son you are, and also to Egil for the same reason. You two have a reason by blood for supporting Darthor, the Peoples of the Ice and the Western League. But yours truly here, the giant and the redhead have no loyalty by blood to that side. Our loyalty's to the other side, the Eastern Norghanians."

"You can't be serious," Egil said. "You know perfectly well that Uthar's a threat to the whole North, the whole of Tremia. He's not even Uthar, he's an impostor, a shifter who's going to lead the kingdom to misery and destruction."

"Yeah, I know that and I understand, but what'll happen when I have to fight one of my own, an eastern Norghanian? Do I put an arrow through him?"

There was a moment's silence.

"Besides, I'm wondering about it, and I know Nilsa and the giant are doing the same even though they may not say anything about it. I personally don't mind killing Norghanians, eastern or western, or Wild from the Frozen Continent. I'm like that, but I'd like to be clear beforehand about who I have to shoot. It would help a lot."

"You're right," Egil said. "We need to talk about this, because up to now we haven't, or at least not openly."

"What d'you think, Gerd?" Lasgol asked.

"Pretty much the same as Viggo… although as usual, he's twisted everything. I'm an eastern Norghanian by roots, and so my loyalty's to the east. But on the other hand I can understand the problem we have with Uthar, the false king. I realize that we're going to have to commit ourselves. I don't think we can go on avoiding the situation much longer. Sooner or later we're going to meet either a Wild One of the Ice or a Norghanian from the Western League, and then what? Because we're Rangers, and I'm from the East myself."

Lasgol realized that he was expecting a lot from his friends, perhaps too much. They now found themselves at a crossroads. They had tried so far to be supportive and were aware that they would have to do something about the problem of Uthar, but now they were all trapped in the war and were going to have to take part in it, one way or another. This was going to create problems for all of them, and they were going to have to go against their own principles. Lasgol knew this very well; at the moment he was serving the Rangers, serving Uthar, and this was very much against his will. And if the Peoples of the Ice should attack the Rangers, which side would he take? The invaders and his mother? Or the Rangers and Uthar? They needed to be very careful, because if they hesitated and failed to act with conviction and determination when the moment came, it might cost the life of one or other of them.

"I'm a bit divided too," Nilsa admitted. "I understand that we want to get rid of the King, the shifter, but we're trapped in the middle of a civil war and we belong to the Rangers. Even though I want to expose Uthar and stop this war, which is completely insane, I don't really know what to do. I wouldn't know who to shoot at." She raised her hands to the sky and then shook them to try and help herself relax.

The last to speak was Ingrid, who had been quiet and thoughtful until that moment, which was not her usual way. Normally she took the initiative, with determination and leadership.

"We're eastern Norghanians and we're Rangers, the four of us," she said, looking at Viggo, Gerd and Nilsa. "There's no doubt about that. It's something we can't change, it's in our blood, and so our loyalty must be to them."

Egil and Lasgol began to be nervous at the sound of this.

"Ingrid…" Lasgol began.

She raised her hand to stop him. "And because of this, because we're loyal to the Rangers, because we're loyal to the kingdom, we must stop Uthar. And if in order to do that we have to join the cause of the Western League and the Peoples of the Ice, that's what we'll do. Not because we're traitors, but the opposite: because that's the best thing for the kingdom at this moment, because that's the way Uthar will be unmasked and defeated."

"Are you sure of that, Blondie?" Viggo asked her. "They'll hang you for those words."

"Yes. I've thought about it a lot, and I can't see any other way out. If we four fight for the East, which could be another option, and we let these two help the West – and that's something we could do –I don't think that in the end it would be what's best for the realm. I don't think we'd solve the problem that way. I believe we need to stay united and work together. That's the only way we'll manage to get rid of Uthar and end this war which is setting Norghanian brothers against Norghanian brothers."

They were all silent, pondering her words.

Egil now spoke: "First, let me thank the four of you for your trust and your help. I know it's not easy for you to go against the East and against the Rangers for the sake of us two. I understand that perfectly well. In part I too find it hard, and for this I thank you. I believe Ingrid is right, the best thing for Norghana at this moment is to be with the West, not because my family is its leader, nor because it's fair for the Peoples of the Ice, but because if we don't fight with the West, the East might win. And if it wins, then Uthar does."

The breeze from the coast caressed their faces. The crackling of the fire seemed to indicate that their decision would be critical.

"But I can't force you to make that decision. It has to be a personal one, and whatever you decide I will respect, because I respect you with all my heart."

"I think we'll see the decision each of us makes when the time comes," Gerd said. "At this particular moment it's a hard one to make."

Nilsa nodded. "We'll have to wait till the moment comes, and then we'll see how we all react. I love you both, and you know it," she added to Lasgol and Egil, who smiled and nodded gratefully.

"Let's be prudent," Lasgol said. "We'll try to avoid the conflict as far as we can, then when the time comes, let's act for Norghana."

"Then that's what we'll do," Ingrid said. "If the situation gets complicated, come and get me, and I'll make the decision as your Captain."

"Fine," Viggo said. "Just tell me who to shoot at and I'll do it."

"I'll let you know."

"All united?" Egil asked.

"All united," they said, one after the other.

The strengthening breeze caused the fire to crackle even more intensely. An oath had been sworn between the six, one which when the time came might either save the kingdom or condemn it.

Sometime later Mostassen arrived from further inland.

"The area's clear. I haven't seen any trace of an advance party or explorers on this side. They haven't arrived yet. Or else they're very good at hiding their tracks."

Lasgol decided to try and extract some information from the Royal Ranger. "We don't know whether they're going to land here," he said.

"No, but that's our mission, and therefore we're going to assume they will."

"We assume this because it's our mission, not because there's any information to indicate it?" Egil asked.

"We assume it because in both cases it's necessary to assume it," the Royal Ranger said with a frown.

Both Egil and Lasgol realized that they could get no further information, so they asked no more questions to avoid arousing suspicion.

They were silent for a long time, taking the opportunity to rest and eat something from their supplies. Lasgol was worried because Camu was in Trotter's saddlebag, and if there was any strange movement, or if the pony started, he was sure Mostassen would notice. From what they knew, the Royal Rangers were the best among all the Rangers, which made him very nervous.

"How does someone become a Royal Ranger, sir?" Nilsa asked suddenly.

Mostassen looked at her for a moment, unsure whether to answer or stay silent. He decided to answer.

"The Royals are chosen by the Leader of the Rangers to serve directly under the King's orders."

"According to what we've been told," Gerd said, "the Royals are the best of all the Rangers."

"That's correct,"

"And how are they chosen?" Ingrid asked.

"There's more than one way. The most usual one is for him to be chosen because of his record on missions or his excellence in some School. It's the Leader of the Rangers who selects him or her when there's a vacancy. On some occasions, when there was a large number of vacancies, there've also been tests."

"That's to say when there'd been a lot of casualties," Viggo put in.

"That's correct. The position of Royal Ranger brings with it a great deal of responsibility, and also great danger. It is a position of constant risk. Many don't survive."

"What other way is there to become a Royal Ranger, sir?" Nilsa asked.

"The last way is direct choice by the King. On some occasions the monarch himself chooses the person he wants."

It was Gerd's turn now. "Apart from protecting the King, what other things does a Royal Ranger do, sir?"

"We undertake whatever mission the King wants carried out. Without questioning the reason or the consequence."

"In other words," Viggo put in, "nobody questions whether what they're doing is morally good or bad."

Mostassen glared at him murderously. "The Royal Rangers serve the King. His aims are beyond question."

Nilsa had not finished. "Are there any Specialist Rangers among the Royal Corps?"

"Yes, there are. Most of us are Specialists. It's necessary to safeguard the King and carry out his missions."

"That's very interesting, sir," Egil said. "And it makes sense, because after all, the Specialists are the best of the Rangers and the Royal Rangers are the best of the best, so it makes sense for the Corps to be made up of Specialists."

"That's right."

"Sir, are you a Specialist Ranger?" Ingrid asked.

Mostassen said nothing. All six of them waited for an answer, deeply intrigued, and at last the Royal Ranger spoke.

"Yes, I'm a Specialist Ranger."

"Which School?" Nilsa asked. She was more and more interested.

"The School of Wildlife."

This fascinated Lasgol. What elite specialty had he chosen? Before he could ask, Gerd anticipated him.

"What specialty, sir?"

Again Mostassen seemed reluctant to tell them. They all stared at him, and at last he decided to talk.

"I'm a Tireless Tracker."

"Fantastic!" said Egil. "As I understand, the Tireless Trackers can follow any trail for weeks without any wolfhounds, hawks or owls to help them."

"That's right."

Lasgol was delighted. In front of him was a specialist tracker from one of the Schools he himself had considered following.

"And now, if the interrogation's over, we'd better start on the mission we've been entrusted with."

Ingrid looked at Lasgol and Egil out of the corner of her eye. "Of course, sir."

"I want two lookouts to the East, two to the West, and two here on the top of the cliff."

They looked at him unsurely.

"Ingrid and Viggo, east. Nilsa and Gerd, west. Lasgol and Egil, up here. And no confrontation with the enemy. If you see any vessel or stranger in the area, don't engage. Release a warning fire arrow and the others will come to your aid. Is that clear?"

They all nodded.

"I'm a man of few words," Mostassen said, "but if I have to shout your head off over some mistake, I will."

"Don't worry, sir," Ingrid said, and they set off to their positions.

With him watching them they left for their positions.

Chapter 26

The following days went by without anything noteworthy happening. Time passed slowly, because most of it was spent watching sea and coast for any sign of enemy activity, of which there was none.

Mostassen disappeared in the mornings and did not come back until nightfall. As far as Lasgol knew, he spent the day keeping a ceaseless watch on the coastline. The man was like a bloodhound, and if he finally found a trail he would follow it to the end of the world. So far he had found none.

The fact that he disappeared for so long at a stretch was to Lasgol's advantage because it meant that he could let Camu loose, and the little creature had a wonderful time playing on the hill. He spent a long time looking down at the sea, which he loved. The only problem was that he wanted to go down to the water, and Lasgol had to forbid it.

Each time Mostassen came back, Lasgol ordered Camu to hide. Luckily the little animal's trail was not obvious enough to make Mostassen worry. But Lasgol made him stay hidden all night if the Royal Ranger was in the camp. He had discovered that if the little animal stayed hidden for long periods of time, he would sleep the rest of the day as if regenerating the energy he had used up in hiding for so long. This made sense, because it was more or less what he found himself doing when he used his Gift. If he used up all his inner energy he was obliged to rest until he had regained it, or else collapse in exhaustion on the spot.

They had already spent a week without seeing anything, and he was beginning to feel more at ease. This was not where his mother's forces were going to land. But he wondered where exactly they would. He remembered his mother's words: that it was deeply important that the King should not know which spot on the coast they were planning to choose. This worried him, because if the King found out, he could set a trap for them and the casualties would be enormous.

Egil too was restless. Both knew that the final confrontation was looming. The two armies had been regrouping and assembling new forces for a final campaign, and that moment was almost at hand. Summer was the best time to begin the invasion, as it would allow the hordes of the Frozen Continent to enter Norghana. Something else that worried Lasgol was that they themselves were a long way east, deep inside enemy territory. If anybody was planning anything against Egil now, they had a clear opportunity outside the Camp and far from the West, where he would have been safe.

"Don't worry," Lasgol had said, meaning to ease his mind. "Nobody knows we're here. Nothing's going to happen to you."

"We mustn't be too confident. The King might try something against me at any moment, and he's got spies everywhere. Particularly among the Rangers."

"Even so, nobody knows we're at this particular spot. It was decided at the last moment."

"True, but we'd better keep all our senses alert," Egil said, and began checking his Ranger's belt. "I'm going to go over all my equipment. I want to be sure I have everything I need."

Lasgol understood why he was nervous, and knew he ought to be just as nervous himself. Uthar would go for Egil and then, sooner or later, for him as well. It was just a matter of time. He had had this feeling ever since he had left his mother, and he could not shake it off.

At nightfall Egil and Lasgol made out a silhouette amid the shadows of the night, coming toward the camp. They both readied their bows at once.

Camu, hide, Lasgol ordered. The little creature, who was twenty paces or so away, leapt behind a boulder and vanished, using his special camouflage skills.

The silhouette stopped and hooted like an owl.

"It's a friend," Egil said, and Lasgol nodded.

It must be Mostassen, Lasgol thought, although it was a bit early, since usually it was after midnight when the Royal Ranger came back to the camp.

"Don't shoot, it's me," came a voice they both recognized at once.

"Astrid!" Lasgol said in amazement. "What on earth are you doing here?"

She came closer to the fire. "Could you please lower your bows?

Aren't you happy to see me? You're looking at me as if I were a ghost."

"Of course I am, I'm thrilled," Lasgol said, and hugged her. They both stared into one another's eyes. He felt the urge to kiss her, to tell her how much he had missed her during these days they had spent away from the other teams, and she read it in his eyes. Their lips came close, but when they were on the point of making contact, they stopped. She smiled.

Egil looked amused. "As far as I'm concerned you can kiss, there's no problem."

Lasgol was suddenly very serious. "It wouldn't be appropriate for Rangers on a mission."

Egil burst out laughing. "We're alone, for goodness' sake," he said, looking all around with his arms spread wide.

Lasgol was about to say something when Astrid took him by the back of the neck and kissed him passionately.

Egil smiled from ear to ear.

"But… Astrid…"

"We're at war," she said with a mischievous smile. "We have to seize every moment. We don't know what tomorrow will bring."

Lasgol who had turned as red as a tomato, nodded. "You're absolutely right," he said, and returned the kiss with even more enthusiasm.

"Hey, hey, if you want me to leave, just say so."

It took Lasgol more than a moment to take his lips and soul away from her. "Not at all, you're fine right where you are, with us."

"Sure, someone has to keep watch while you two kiss."

Astrid and Lasgol began to laugh, a little embarrassed.

"To what do we owe your visit?" Egil asked her.

"Royal Ranger Ulsen sent me to find out about the situation at the bay."

"Everything's quiet around here," Lasgol said.

She put on an official voice. "I need the report of the Royal Ranger in charge of this patrol."

"Oh, I see. So whatever I tell you myself is no good."

"It's always good, but I can't tell it to Ulsen."

"How about your sector?" Egil asked.

"Everything's quiet. It's a very rocky part of the coast. I don't think any boat would dare approach the coast that way. On the other hand, this is a very likely area for the landing."

"We know, Mostassen told us."

"Where is the Royal Ranger?"

"He spends the day exploring, searching for trails, in case someone lands without us seeing them. He'll be back at midnight."

"Wonderful! That way we'll have time to chat at leisure."

"Would you like something to eat or drink?" Lasgol asked her.

She showed them the backpack she was carrying. "No thanks, I haven't come a long way, we're not far from here. Besides, I'm carrying supplies with me."

"What's your Royal Ranger like?" Egil asked.

"Not bad, a bit too serious for my taste. He seems to know what he's doing. I'd say he must be very good."

"Ours doesn't talk much either," Lasgol said, "except when he has to order us about."

"I don't understand why they're so worried," Astrid said, "or to be more exact, why the King's so worried. There's no sign that Darthor's troops are going to invade from the East."

"It's not likely, but it is a viable route," said Egil.

"And why at this particular moment?"

Egil and Lasgol exchanged a glance, but neither said anything.

"Do you know something?"

Egil and Lasgol exchanged another worried glance.

"You're not saying anything, so you must know something."

"It's not that we actually know anything," Lasgol said.

"Don't lie to me. You know I can tell when you're lying from two leagues away."

Egil arched his eyebrows. "I'd better leave you two to talk in private and go and take a look around to make sure the camp's safe."

He left, but Astrid's eyes were still fixed on Lasgol's.

"Spill it, I'm waiting."

"It's not that we know anything, but we're guessing the invasion'll start straight away."

"And how do you guess that? Or do you have information we don't?"

Lasgol felt he was trapped between the sword and the wall. On the one hand he wanted to tell Astrid who he was and who his mother was, everything that had happened to them, everything about King Uthar, and involve her in their situation. On the other hand, if he did so he would be risking her life, and he did not want to do that under any circumstances. He decided not to tell her. The danger was too great, and he would have to wait until it was all resolved one way or the other and there was no danger for her.

"I'd like to be able to tell you, but I can't," he said sadly.

"What can't you tell me?"

He took both her hands in his own. "There are certain things I can't tell you, for your own good. If I did, I'd be putting your life at risk, and I don't want that. I don't want anything to happen to you."

"Whatever it is, you can tell me. You know you can trust me, I'm on your side. I'm with you, we're together."

"I know... it's not that I doubt you in any way. I know I can trust you and that you'd never betray me, but I've promised not to reveal my secret to anyone, because of the risk to me and the risk it would mean for the person who knew my secret."

"So by that you mean there are others who know, like Egil."

Lasgol nodded, and knew that the conversation was taking the wrong turn.

"So what you mean is that you trust Egil, but you don't trust me."

"It's not a question of trust. I don't want to put you in danger, a danger that could mean your life."

"And Egil's life is expendable?"

"He had no choice. He was involved in the situation just like I was."

She squeezed his hand and stared into his eyes. "I'm with you and so I'm involved too. I deserve to know what I'm getting into."

This left Lasgol utterly at a loss. She was with him, and it was true that if she continued with him she would suffer the consequences of the situations he would find himself in. It was not fair on her. It was not fair that she should be with him.

"Perhaps you shouldn't be with me... not now, not until all this is over."

"But that's nonsense! Of course I should be with you, and you should be with me."

"I don't want anything bad to happen to you, there's too much risk."

"In case you hadn't noticed, I can take perfect care of myself. Better than you, in fact."

"I know. It's not that. Things are going to get very difficult, and there might be no way out. People might die. People I love."

"In that case I want to be part of those people and I want to know what's up. It's my decision, not yours."

Lasgol breathed out heavily. He felt a sharp pain in the middle of his chest, as if someone were squeezing his heart.

"I'd love to be able to tell you all my secrets, share all my problems with you. Believe me, it would take a load off my mind. Unfortunately I can't. That's the easy way out, and it's the one I mustn't choose. What I must do is difficult, and until all this is over it's better if you're not with me. You must stay away from me. That way you won't be in danger."

She pulled him toward her by his wrists. "No way! You're going to tell me everything that's going on, right now! And you're not getting away from me!"

At that moment Egil came up to them. "Someone's coming," he said. "I saw a silhouette moving."

Astrid and Lasgol leapt to their feet and seized their bows, and the three of them aimed toward where the shadows were moving.

A figure approached and hooted like an owl.

"Friend," said Egil.

Mostassen appeared from the shadows. "And who are you?" he asked Astrid immediately.

"I'm Astrid of the Owls, sir. Ulsen sent me."

"Does he want a report?"

"Yes, sir. Shall I say there's nothing to report?"

Mostassen shook his head. "Far from it. I've found the trail."

"The trail, sir?"

"Of an enemy advance party."

"Have they already landed?" Lasgol asked in surprise.

"Yes, and they've hidden their trail very well. Almost too well, which is strange. But I managed to find it. Although it's taken me a long time... it's strange..."

Astrid pointed down to the bay. "Sir..."

Several rowing-boats were crossing the bay under cover of the night, making their way toward the beach.

"Get your weapons ready," Mostassen said. "Enemies."

Chapter 27

Mostassen, Lasgol, Egil, Astrid and the other Panthers were watching the bay from the cliff. The Royal Ranger had sent Egil and Lasgol to fetch the rest of the team; he wanted them all with him.

More than a thousand dark dots filled the bay. They were rowing-boats approaching in silence, slowly, seeking the coast under cover of the night.

"We need to get closer to get a better idea of how many of the enemy there are and what they're planning to do," Mostassen said.

"Shall I warn Ulsen?" Astrid asked.

"Not yet. It's too soon to decide. We need to make sure they're really going to land and that this really is an invasion."

"Well, it certainly looks that way to me," Viggo commented.

"I'm not saying it isn't, it's just that we have to be sure. They might turn back at any moment. It might be a distracting maneuver. We don't know, and we must be sure. And they mustn't see us."

"Sir," Egil put in, "if they're moving on to the beach it must be because they think it's clear. There must be a patrol on land."

"That's a correct assumption. That's the trail I found. I couldn't locate the patrol. They have someone very skilled with them who's hiding their tracks very well, practically making them vanish, which worries me."

"A renegade Ranger?" Nilsa suggested.

"No. I believe the tracks have been wiped out using arcane arts."

"Oh, no! Magic!" Gerd cried in terror.

"That's what I'm afraid of."

"What are we going to do, sir?" Egil asked.

"We're going to approach very carefully, so as not to be detected, then wait and watch what they do until we're sure the invasion has begun. Get ready to move."

They started down the cliff toward the southwestern end of the bay, with the Royal Ranger in the lead.

The first barges had landed in the darkness. Not a single light or fire was visible, which was significant: they were trying to land without being seen, with all the risk that involved.

They found shelter behind a group of rocks which gave them a view of the beach at their feet and the bay on their right. Mostassen ordered them to take up their positions, then they waited.

Lasgol noticed that there were a dozen or so people waiting for the landing. From where they were hiding they could not see their faces, but their clothes identified them as Norghanians rather than people from the Frozen Continent. But the ones who were coming to the beach were not Norghanians at all. They were huge figures with bluish skin and hair of ice: Wild of the Ice.

"I can't see them very well in this dim light," Viggo said, "but judging by their size and what they're wearing they're Wild Ones of the Ice."

"And the ones waiting are Norghanians," Ingrid pointed out.

"If they're Norghanians," said Viggo, "they must be from the Western League."

"Isn't it strange that they're here deep in the east?" Nilsa wondered aloud.

Viggo smiled. "I'm no strategist, but if the hosts of the Frozen Continent are landing here in the deep east and the Western League are attacking from their position, it seems to me that the King is going to be caught in a tight spot between two fronts."

"That's the reason we're here," Mostassen said, "to warn the King in case that's so."

"And where's the King's Navy?" Ingrid asked.

"It was badly damaged after the defeat on the Frozen Continent. Besides, most of the ships belong to the Western League. The King hasn't much of a navy. He has men but not ships. Those are in the West, which doesn't have so many men."

"Well, it's always best to have more men than ships," Viggo said, still smiling.

"Not necessarily," Egil said. "If you have to transport those men, it's better to have ships. Otherwise you wouldn't get to where you need to in time, and you might lose the war."

"Very true," said Ingrid. "Even the Invincibles of the Ice often need ships to reach their point of attack, even though they're heavy infantry."

"Well, it looks like the infantry of the Frozen Continent do have ships," said Viggo, "and they're arriving,"

"Lasgol, Egil, with me," Mostassen ordered. "Let's go and see what's going on from closer at hand. You others, stay here on the alert. If we have trouble, go back and inform Ranger Ulsen at once."

The Royal Ranger went on down the cliff toward the bay among the rocks, seeking the shelter of darkness at every moment. Lasgol and Egil followed him in silence, making sure they kept their footing. To their left the cliff dropped steeply to the bay. The view was spectacular, but if they put a foot wrong they would fall to their deaths on to the rocks below.

At the foot of the cliff, they hid behind boulders. They were practically on the beach by now. Mostassen was looking through a gap between the rocks, watching the Wild Ones of the Ice, who were now landing in large numbers.

Lasgol decided it was time to use his Gift. He called on his *Hawk Eye* skill and watched the Norghanians who were welcoming the Wild Ones.

He recognized a face at once. It was Arnold, Egil's brother!

"I can't make out who they're meeting," Mostassen muttered. "I'm sure it's some Duke or Count of the Western League, but I can't recognize him from here. The devils haven't lit a single fire, and it's too dark to recognize anybody."

Lasgol said nothing. He was not going to help Uthar, not then or at any other time, even if it meant going against the Rangers' orders, and he was sure Egil would do the same.

"Spying is a bad habit," came a sudden voice behind them.

The three spun round like lightning and raised their bows. Before them was Asrael, the Arcane Shaman. With him were two other Glaciers Arcanes and four huge Wild of the Ice.

Lasgol was petrified.

Mostassen threatened them with his bow. "Don't move or you'll die."

Asrael smiled calmly, as if the situation held no danger whatsoever for either him or his people.

"Do you really believe that?"

"We're three Royal Rangers. You won't get out of here alive if you try anything stupid."

Asrael smiled again and spread his arms slowly.

"You might be a Royal Ranger, but I can assure you these two with you are not."

Mostassen was taken aback by this.

"Let us change the assumption behind the conversation. You three lower your weapons, and you'll get out of here alive. Otherwise you will die."

Mostassen hesitated. They were outnumbered by the enemy, and there were several Arcanes who could easily use magic against them. In addition, with him were two Ranger Contenders. But before he could make up his mind, Lasgol and Egil lowered their bows.

"Let's do what he says," Lasgol said.

The Royal Ranger was struck dumb, unable to understand why the boys had not waited for his order. He was left aiming his bow, alone, in a state of shock.

"What do you think you're doing? Raise your bows!"

Lasgol and Egil shook their heads.

"By all the skies of the north! Raise your weapons and aim, I tell you! Or else you'll die!"

Lasgol and Egil exchanged a glance, then turned back to Mostassen.

"Sorry, sir, we can't," Egil said.

"Last chance," Asrael said. "Lower your weapon and you'll leave here alive."

Mostassen hesitated, numb with shock. But now it was him alone against the enemy group, and he knew that even if he managed to kill a few of them, in the end he would die, together with the two young Rangers who were acting so strangely.

Finally he lowered his bow, and the Wild of the Ice took away their weapons.

"The two young ones are not to be harmed," Asrael told his group. "They're friends."

Mostassen's expression went from surprise to utter confusion. Several of the Wild stared at Asrael to make sure they had understood his order.

"You heard me. They're friends of mine and are not to be harmed."

The Wild Ones nodded and tied Mostassen's hands. Asrael smiled broadly.

"I'm so glad to see you," he said.

"And so are we," Lasgol said. He came forward to give the Arcane a hug, which was returned with pleasure. The other Arcanes and Wild of the Ice looked on in surprise.

"To be honest, we might have met again in better circumstances," Egil said to Asrael as he too hugged the Arcane.

"These things happen in life, and one never knows who he is going to meet the next day. It happened to us on our first encounter in my cavern, and it's happened again today."

Lasgol looked at Mostassen, then at the bay where the barges were still arriving. "Yeah, and today it looks as though we're in a right fix."

Asrael smiled. "The next time we'll have to meet around a fire, sharing a good dinner."

"That would be much better," Egil said.

"How is Camu?" the Arcane asked Lasgol.

"He's very well. As mischievous as usual and growing very fast. He's up there on the cliff, with our horses."

"Lasgol!" Mostassen cried. "What on earth are you doing? Have you lost your wits? Don't tell him where our horses are!"

A Wild One kicked him in the ribs, and he doubled up in pain.

"Please don't hurt him," Lasgol begged.

"You heard him," Asrael said. "He is not to be hurt. I must be true to my promise. He will not die, I am a man of my word. Gag him so that he will not interrupt us."

His men did as they were told.

"And how's Misha?" Egil asked.

"Better. He suffered with the wounds he got in battle in the Frozen Continent, but he's recovering."

"Is he here with you?" Lasgol asked.

Asrael looked around.

"Certain matters are best dealt with in private. I wouldn't like the Rangers to know where Misha is, or what our plans are."

"Yes, I see that..."

"Are you alone, or is there another group with you?"

Egil pointed upwards. "The others are on that ledge."

Mostassen began to writhe furiously, trying to find some way to stop the two of them from endangering their friends and the mission the King had entrusted them with. The Wild Ones held him tightly, and although the Royal Ranger was strongly-built, compared to those People of the Ice he was no more than a man.

"There are two ways we can do this," Asrael said. "I can send my people to capture them, or we can ask them kindly to join you down here. Personally I think the second option is best, because with the first there might be some accident which I am sure you would not want, and to be honest, neither would I."

"I'll go and get them," Lasgol said.

He set off, and two of the Arcanes began to argue with Asrael.

"Lasgol is a friend of mine and has my trust. He'll come back with the Norghanian Rangers."

There was more arguing, but in the end the Arcanes yielded before Asrael's leadership.

Lasgol considered the situation as he went up the hill. He had to tell his friends to hand themselves over, or else both Egil and Mostassen would be in danger. He trusted Asrael, but not his wild companions and their leaders. Nor was he sure about his friends' reaction... and then there was an additional problem: Astrid was with them. If he did not tell her the truth he would be in trouble, but if he told her and she decided to flee to warn her own group, both her life and theirs would be in danger.

He did not have much time, and nor did he know whether his decision would be the right one or not. But he had to think of something before things turned more complicated and someone died.

"Who goes there?" came a voice which he recognized as Viggo's.

"It's me, Lasgol."

"Why didn't you hoot like an owl? I almost shot you."

"Sorry, I completely forgot, I didn't realize I was so close."

"Well, be more careful, or something nasty could happen."

"What's going on down there?" Ingrid asked him.

Lasgol stopped in the middle of his friends and looked them in the eye for a moment. He had no more time left, he had to decide. There was a lump in his throat. He hoped he was not wrong.

"Mostassen wants us all to go down to the rocks on the beach. He's waiting for us."

"Understood," Ingrid said.

"Me too?" asked Astrid. "Or should I go tell my group?"

Lasgol swallowed. On the one hand he wanted her to be safe, to run away from there and disappear. But he knew Asrael, and his intelligence. If he knew they were here, he would also know where Astrid's group was. He would never let her reach them. So there must be more patrols. It was only a guess, and he could not be sure because he had not seen any, but he decided to choose what seemed the least dangerous option at that moment. Although he was well aware that it was not necessarily the least risky in the long run.

"He asked you to come too."

Astrid looked him in the eye as if she had noticed the lie in his voice. For a moment she half-closed her eyes and stared at him intently. He looked back without flinching. He was almost certain that she was reading his soul.

"Fine, I'll come," she said at last. But her expression showed that she did not quite believe what he had said.

"On we go, then," Ingrid said. "Nilsa be careful, there's a steep drop. Don't lose your footing or overbalance."

"Don't worry, Ingrid, I'll be careful how I step."

"Gerd, you get behind her in case she loses her balance. With your size and strength you'll be able to hold her without her dragging you down with her."

"No problem," Gerd said. Strangely enough, he was not afraid of cliffs or heights.

They went down carefully and had no trouble until they reached the boulders where Lasgol had left Egil, Asrael and his people. But now the place was deserted, and what was even stranger, there was no trace or trail to reveal that they had all been there before. It was amazing, and Lasgol was left puzzled.

"Where are they?" Ingrid asked. "There's nobody here, and I can't see any tracks."

"Are you sure it was here?" Nilsa asked.

Lasgol did not answer. He was looking in all directions, unsure what to think. He was sure he would not be betrayed – or perhaps he would be.

At that moment Asrael appeared between some trees and came towards them slowly.

"Everyone stay still," Lasgol said. "Don't shoot, he's a friend."

Ingrid, Nilsa, Gerd and Viggo watched as Asrael came closer. The Arcane was smiling and coming toward them with open arms.

"By all the icebergs!" Viggo cried. "It's Asrael!"

"Yes, and please don't shoot," Lasgol repeated. Fearing Astrid would take no notice of him, he moved in front of her to block her aim.

She stared at him in bewilderment. "What's going on here?"

"Lower your bow and I'll tell you."

She did not seem at all convinced.

"Greetings to all," Asrael said as he reached them. "I'm delighted to see you all still in one piece."

Ingrid waved a hand at them, and they lowered their weapons.

"And we're pleased to see you," Gerd said. "What are you doing here?"

"What d'you think he's doing, big guy?" Viggo said. "He's come with the navy of the Peoples of the Ice."

"How's the leg, Viggo?" Asrael asked him. "Better?"

"Sure, as good as new, the only thing is that when a storm's on its way I feel a terrible cold climbing up my leg as far as my head."

"Ah yes, that's one of the secondary effects of that type of spell."

"Well, looking on the bright side, now I always know when a storm's coming."

Asrael laughed. By now Ingrid was beginning to understand the situation.

"If you're here and your people are landing, then it means you've captured the Royal Ranger and these two, right?"

Asrael nodded.

"I was afraid of that," Ingrid said. She looked hard at Lasgol, who knew he would have to explain.

"You haven't hurt them, have you?" Nilsa asked.

"Of course not. You are my friends." Asrael made a sign and Egil appeared, together with several Wild Ones and a few Arcanes. Astrid stiffened.

"Take it easy," Lasgol warned her.

The others looked at Lasgol, beginning to understand what had happened.

"You might have warned us," Viggo whispered.

Lasgol glanced aside at Astrid.

"Oh... I see."

"Will you introduce your new friend?" Asrael said.

Lasgol did the honors. "This is Astrid. Astrid, this is Asrael, he's our friend. He saved us from death on the Frozen Continent."

Astrid gave Lasgol a murderous glare, then bowed lightly to Asrael.

"Can she be trusted?" The Arcane asked Lasgol.

"She can."

"You I trust, but her I do not know."

"You can trust her," Viggo said. "She's Lasgol's girlfriend."

Asrael smiled. "Aha... interesting."

"So now what?" Ingrid asked.

"Now you must decide which side you are on."

"And if we choose wrong?" Nilsa asked.

"Then you will not be my friends anymore."

"And we'll be dead," Gerd said.

Asrael shrugged.

Chapter 28

While Asrael led the group to the beach, Lasgol was thinking about the answer he would have to give the Glacial Arcanes. He could see by their worried faces and tense expressions that his teammates were thinking the same.

Astrid meanwhile was glaring furiously at him.

He could not talk to her at that moment and explain everything that was going on, not in front of the Wild and the Glaciers Arcanes. And even if he could, how was he going to make her understand the situation they were in, make her understand what he was doing? Astrid was an Eastern Norghanian, a Ranger, honest, proud and loyal to the crown, which meant loyal to Uthar. The more he thought about it as they walked across the damp sand of the beach, the less confident he was that she would understand.

Out of the corner of his eye he watched the myriad vessels approaching the coast and knew that even if he managed to explain, Astrid would not turn against her own people. She was too honest and true. And as she also had a fierce nature, he was worried that she might do something unwise and risk her life. He could not let that happen. Ever.

When they reached the other Norghanians waiting on the sand in the middle of the bay, Lasgol recognized two more men. The presence of one of them had already surprised him: a tall, strong young man with short chestnut hair and brown eyes.

"Egil, brother!" said Arnold, the second Olafstone, in surprise.

Egil hastened to embrace him. "Brother, how are you?"

"More surprises," Viggo commented.

"I wasn't expecting this one in the least," Gerd said.

"Were you expecting to meet Asrael again, then?" Nilsa asked him.

"No, not that either. Especially not here, in Norghana."

"Too many surprises," Ingrid said, "and they all suggest that things are going to start happening soon."

"I don't understand why you haven't told me any of this," Astrid said. "Especially you, Ingrid. We're both Captains, you ought to have trusted me."

"There are things that can't be told without endangering the lives of the people you tell. We decided to keep our agreement with Asrael between ourselves."

"I don't understand. Why?"

"It's very complicated. Perhaps the right person to explain is" – she glanced at Lasgol – "you-know-who."

"Yeah, but he hasn't deigned to explain."

"He has his reasons, and they're strong ones," Ingrid said.

"I don't know whether there's a reason strong enough to make me forgive him."

"I certainly hope there is."

Astrid watched the landing for a moment, then turned back to Ingrid.

"I can't believe what's happening. And I can't believe you're all so calm. The enemy is invading us. We have to escape and tell our people."

Ingrid exchanged a worried look with Nilsa. "All in due course," she said.

"We have to give warning of the invasion before it's too late."

"We'll think of something," Nilsa said. "For the moment, don't try anything crazy or they'll kill you. And then probably they'd kill us too."

Astrid looked thoughtful. She did not say she would not try anything.

"What are you doing here?" Arnold asked Egil. "Didn't we tell you not to get into trouble?"

"I could say the same thing to you."

"And what does it look like I'm doing, little brother?"

"Leading an invasion?"

His brother smiled from ear to ear. "This might not be what it looks."

"Oh yeah, sure."

"And where's Austin?"

"Carrying out his duties in the West."

"Oh, now I see..."

"I can't tell you our plans. I hope you understand, it's for your own safety. But Austin and I are both very busy, as you can see."

"Has the moment come?"

Arnold nodded. "Yes, it's come."

"Understood. For Father," Egil said with deep feeling as he turned to look westwards.

His brother too turned to the west. "For Father."

"We must send men to the cliff and take up positions," Asrael said. "There'll be more Rangers watching."

"My men will do it," Arnold said. "The Wild Ones of the Ice are too conspicuous, even in the dead of night."

Lasgol took a good look at the Wild Ones. They were just as impressive as he remembered them: over six feet tall, strong and muscular. Their blue skin and intensely blue-white hair and beards meant that sending them to watch, or hoping that they would pass unnoticed, was unthinkable. Although what most surprised him was when they looked back at him with those eyes whose irises were so pale a grey that they looked blind. There was a quality about them that chilled the blood.

Among the troops who were still coming ashore he could see Wild Ones of the Ice and the Glacial Arcanes, unmistakable with their part-blue, part-crystal-white skin. Their heads were shaven, tattooed in white with strange runes. But for the moment he could not see the remaining forces of the Peoples of the Frozen Continent.

Arnold made some comment to the two Counts of the West who were with him, and Count Ericsson turned to address some men who were waiting further back.

"We'll secure the positions," he said, and Asrael nodded.

While the troops were landing, the Wild erected command tents at the inland side of the bay, on dry land. Lasgol and the others were taken to one of these tents and left there. Three Wild were standing guard at the entrance, and several Arcanes were keeping watch on both sides.

Viggo, as usual, was the first to comment on their problem. "What a fix we've gotten ourselves into. Although as it's us, I don't know why I should be surprised."

"Let's keep calm, and everything will be all right," Ingrid said reassuringly.

"I'm not so sure that everything will be," Gerd said. There was unease in his eyes. "We're in the middle of the landing of an invasion force..."

Nilsa was walking round in circles inside the tent. "Asrael won't let them harm us," she said.

"They might not give him a chance to step in," Viggo said. "Or else he might not get here in time."

"What do you mean?" Ingrid asked.

"We're amid a complicated war, with three very different groups. On one side we have our dear blue-skinned friends from the Frozen Continent. On the second we have the Norghanians of the East, and lastly those of the West. I think there are plenty of possibilities for alliances, betrayals, all kinds of foul play. So we can't trust anybody. Not our own people, not the Westerners, not the Wild of the Ice."

"That's a very shrewd and intelligent reading of the situation," Egil commented.

"Your brother Arnold's here," Lasgol said. "He won't let anything happen to you."

"As Viggo has already put it so shrewdly, my brother will try to prevent anything bad from happening to me, but he can't guarantee it. At the moment he's surrounded by the hosts of the Frozen Continent. If they decided to kill us, all he could do would be to lose his own life trying to stop them."

Gerd shook his head. "I told you, I don't like this situation at all."

"Let's stay calm," Ingrid said. "So far we've been treated well, and we've got Egil's brother and Asrael on our side. Nothing ought to happen to us. Don't do anything stupid, keep calm and we'll get out of this alive, the same way we have before."

"Let's hope so," Viggo said, but he did not sound very confident.

Nilsa was so nervous that she could not stop walking around in circles inside the tent. Astrid was watching and listening without a word, but her eyes shone with a gleam of enmity. Lasgol saw this, but did not dare go to her for fear of her reaction, and for fear that that same reaction might bring her harm.

They waited in silence for a long time, amid growing tension.

"I don't trust those Wild of the Ice one little bit," Viggo said.

"It's true, they look like the kind who hit out with their axes first and then think afterwards," Nilsa said. "But I like those Arcanes and their filthy magic even less. They can control your mind and make you see things that aren't there... and I don't even want to think what things."

"Don't provoke them, and everything'll be fine," Ingrid said.

"The problem is that even if we don't provoke them, they might get rid of us anyway."

"Well then, keep your distance, and most of all keep your mouth shut."

"I don't think those brutes understand a single word of what we say."

"Don't be so sure," Egil said. "Some of them know the common language of the North. They're not the brutes they seem to be."

"Well, isn't that just wonderful," Viggo muttered.

"Egil and I have been in meetings with their leaders," Lasgol said, to reassure them. "There weren't any problems then, so there shouldn't be any now."

Astrid glared furiously at both of them.

They were left undisturbed for several hours. Silence fell on the tent once again. They sat down on the floor, made themselves as comfortable as they could, and waited.

Astrid shook her head suddenly. "I can't believe you're friends with the Western League and the Peoples of the Ice. To stay here and deal with them is high treason. We have to escape and tell Dolbarar."

"That's not a good idea," Ingrid told her. "Not right now, in the situation we're in."

"But at least we have to try to escape. Someone must pass on the news that Norghana's being invaded. It's our duty. That's the whole point of the mission we were assigned."

Lasgol wanted to speak, but the words would not come out of his mouth. Egil spoke for him.

"The situation is very complex, Astrid. The King you're fighting for isn't a good king. He's not even the true king."

"You say that because you're with your brothers. I'd like to remind you that you and all of us here swore fealty to King Uthar."

Egil nodded.

"And don't tell me Uthar isn't the legitimate king and your brother Austin is. Even if Austin may have a right to the crown, even if he ought to be King, you've sworn your loyalty to Uthar, not Austin. I was there, I heard you swear. I know you're a man of your word, just like your teammates. That's what I don't understand."

"Yes, I swore fealty to King Uthar."

"So? I don't get it. Are you reneging on your oath?" She looked at Lasgol with the eyes of an interrogator. "Are you all reneging?"

Egil shook his head. "The oath we took was one we took

consciously, me above all, because of what it implied... even more so knowing that it would result in deeply compromising situations, like this one we're in, for instance. We swore loyalty to King Uthar, but that creature calling himself Uthar isn't either Uthar or the King."

"What? Have you lost your mind? Are you under some spell the Arcanes have set on you?"

"No, Astrid," Lasgol said, and she turned to stare at him. "What Egil's trying to tell you is that the King isn't Uthar. We've found out that he's a shifter passing himself off as Uthar."

There was total shock on Astrid's face. Her eyes opened wide and her jaw dropped.

"I know it's hard to believe," Egil said, "but it's the truth."

Astrid looked at Ingrid in search of a denial. But Ingrid nodded. Astrid turned to Viggo, who nodded in turn.

"I can't believe it. You've all gone crazy. No, worse still, you're all under some spell of magic that's been cast by the Glaciers Arcanes."

"I swear it's not so," Ingrid told her. "It took us all a long time to accept it, but it's the truth. The King isn't the King, he's an impostor, and for that reason doesn't have our loyalty."

"Not only does he not have it," Viggo added, "but we're going to try and expose him or kill him, whichever is the easier."

"Are we going to do that?" Gerd asked in surprise.

Nilsa nodded. "If we have the chance, of course we are. This bow of mine is going to deliver his death."

"I don't suppose we'll ever get the chance to come close enough to kill him," Egil said, "but at least we'll try to stop him winning this war, because otherwise it'll plunge the whole north into suffering and destruction, more even than it's doing already."

Astrid got to her feet. She was shaking her head in total disbelief. "This is utterly insane. You're all bewitched," she said with her hands to her head.

"If only we were," Viggo said. "If we were bewitched, this would all be easier to solve."

"Kill the sorcerer," Nilsa said. "Problem solved."

"This mess is far more complicated, and it's on an epic scale," Gerd said resignedly. "I know it sounds crazy – it did to us for a long time – but in the end, unfortunately, it's the truth. We're united in this mess. Whatever happens."

Hearing Gerd, Astrid was left speechless. She knew the giant had a noble heart, so if he said this it was because he believed it.

"Darthor himself has put a spell on you."

At that moment the entrance flap of the tent opened and a figure completely dressed in black came in.

"I see you're talking about me in my absence," came a somber voice.

They spun round.

Darthor had just entered the tent.

Chapter 29

They all stood up in a hurry. Lasgol's eyes were staring, and his jaw dropped. Behind Darthor came another Arcane. It was not Asrael but someone younger, undoubtedly a Glaciers Arcane.

"Don't worry," Darthor said, "you have nothing to fear."

Lasgol and Egil were relieved, but the others were still very tense, especially Astrid, who seemed unable to believe she was in the presence of the enemy leader, the great corrupt Mage of the Ice.

Darthor turned to his companion, whose eyes were strange, almost violet, intense and unforgettable. Lasgol shivered at the sight of that grim, determined face.

"You may leave me alone."

"My duty is to protect you, my lord. That is what our leader Azur has ordered. He's the Shaman of the Ice, Chief of the Glaciers Arcanes, and hence I must obey."

"There's no risk for me in this tent. The Norghanians are unarmed, as you can see, and they're friends."

"As you wish, my lord. I will be waiting outside in case you need me. One word and I will be in here in the blink of an eye."

He stared intensely at them all with his violet eyes, and there was a clear warning in that hostile gaze. Lasgol knew, watching him leave, that the Arcane would not hesitate to kill them all on the slightest pretext.

"Forgive my bodyguard's attitude. Sometimes he's overzealous, but I can assure you that Asoris won't cause you any harm."

Viggo's expression suggested that he was not entirely convinced.

Astrid was watching with half-closed eyes. She looked as though she was ready to pounce on Darthor at any moment.

"Lasgol, Egil, I'm glad to see you again and in one piece."

At the sight of Darthor greeting them so naturally, Astrid was so amazed that the shock was clearly visible on her face.

"My lord," Lasgol said with a slight bow.

"It's an honor and a pleasure to see you again, my lord," Egil said.

"It was a real surprise when Asrael told me. I could hardly believe it. I delayed my plans so that I could come and see with my own eyes.

I imagined you'd be at the Camp."

"The King is short of forces," Lasgol explained. "We've been ordered to join the watch patrols on the coast."

Darthor nodded. "I expected Uthar to send Rangers to keep watch on all the coast, but I never expected anybody in this particular spot. I chose it very carefully."

"We weren't expecting to find the Navy of the Ice landing here on our watch mission either," Egil said.

"Or rather, we didn't think it would happen in the sector of coast we were watching," Lasgol added. He was dying to embrace his mother, but he knew it was neither the time nor the place.

"Who are these people with you? Are these your teammates from the Camp, the Snow Panthers?"

"That's right," Lasgol replied. "This is our Captain and Leader Ingrid. She's the one who always keeps us going with her spirit and determination." The blonde captain took a step forward and gave a slight bow, which Darthor returned.

"This is Gerd, big and strong and with a great heart."

Gerd blushed and also bowed respectfully.

"That's a great quality," said Darthor, returning the bow.

"Nilsa is our skilled long-range archer."

Nilsa stepped forward and bowed nervously.

"Easy, girl, there's no need to be nervous. Nothing bad is going to happen to you under my protection."

"Oh, no, it's not that, sir," she said, "it's just that I'm naturally nervous... and meeting you... well, thanks for the protection, sir."

"This is Viggo, lethal with any hand weapon," Lasgol said.

"And with his tongue too," Egil added, and Lasgol could not help but smile.

"You have to know how to use all the weapons you have," Viggo said, bowing graciously.

Darthor returned the bow. "Well said."

"With Egil and myself, these are The Snow Panthers."

"I understand that you know what's really happening here, not just what it looks like from outside, but the problem Uthar poses for all of us."

"We know," Ingrid said. "Lasgol's told us."

"I must ask you whether you're all with him and Egil in this complicated and crucial situation."

"We are," Ingrid said determinedly, and the others nodded.

"Therefore I can trust you. You know what's best for the North and for Tremia."

"You can trust us, sir," Ingrid said.

At that moment Darthor looked at Astrid, who was still at the far end of the tent and had not said a word, but was alert to everything that happened with a look in her eyes that was half-fierce, half-worried.

Darthor turned to Lasgol. "And what about her?"

Lasgol turned to look at Astrid. He needed to be very careful about what he said next, because he was not prepared to take any risks, would not allow Astrid to endanger everything. And neither could he allow anything bad to happen to her.

He thought for a moment before he spoke.

"She's Astrid, the Captain of the Owls. She doesn't know everything, so she doesn't understand the situation, but she's a noble and honest person, and we can trust her."

Darthor looked at Astrid through his strange helmet. Nobody said anything or moved a muscle. They all knew Astrid's life was in danger.

"If she's not with us, if I can't trust her, then she's a risk."

"I know, sir. But if you give me a chance I can convince her."

"And why should I believe you can convince her? I can see in her eyes that she doesn't believe a word of this. If it was up to her, she'd lunge for my neck and cut my throat." Darthor turned to Astrid. "Am I wrong?"

There was hatred in Astrid's eyes. "No, you're not wrong. If I had a weapon you'd be dead by now."

Darthor raised a hand toward her.

"No, please," Lasgol implored, "don't hurt her."

"You heard her yourself. I can't have anyone who wants to kill me close enough to me to do so."

"Don't kill her," Lasgol said desperately. "I can make her change her mind."

"From the look in her eyes, I very much doubt it. Why do you think you can change her mind?"

"She's his sweetheart," Viggo put in.

Darthor snorted under his visor. He turned to Lasgol, but kept his hand raised toward Astrid.

"Is that true? Do you love her?"

Lasgol looked at the raised hand. He knew that a few words of power would end Astrid's life there and then. The mere thought of losing her, of not having her in his arms or kissing her ever again was making him unbearably anxious.

"Yes, I love her."

Astrid was staring at him with huge eyes, her eyebrows raised. She had not expected to hear him make this confession in front of all the others.

"Do you say it because you really mean it, or to save her life?"

"I really mean it. She's the person I love and the one I want to be with. I can't imagine a future without her. My heart belongs to her."

Darthor lowered his hand.

"On behalf of Lasgol, I'll let you live tonight. If at dawn you still think the same, I'll be forced to kill you. It's nothing personal, but I can't leave loose ends when the situation is so critical."

"Thank you, my lord," Lasgol said gratefully.

"Let me tell the others that I'm grateful for your help and that I understand how complicated your own situation is. If any of you has the slightest doubt that you're doing the right thing, let me assure you that you are. Uthar is a terrible danger, not just for Norghana but for the entire North, and when he conquers it he'll pose a danger to all Tremia, because nothing will stop his overbearing greed. I want you to consider not only Uthar but all those who serve him, as well as those who once he's gone – and believe me, after this campaign he won't be in the picture any longer – might take the reins of the kingdom."

The faces of the Panthers suggested that they did not understand this warning.

"Egil," Darthor asked him, "if Uthar falls, who of his own people would take the crown?"

"If Uthar dies, the next in line by blood on the Eastern side is his cousin Thoran."

"And if Thoran fell?"

"His brother Oden."

"Why don't you enlighten your teammates with what you know about Thoran and Oden?"

Egil nodded. "Thoran is clever and has a deeply irascible nature. He's known among his nobles for his ruthlessness and his tendency to cruelty. He enjoys causing pain and boasts of his power. He's the second most powerful man in the realm, and he knows it. He's Uthar's chief ally, and the King lets him do whatever he wants. At the Court everybody avoids angering him, because he's perfectly capable of killing someone in a rage. It's happened more than once. His duchy, which is one of the largest in the realm, suffers from his outbursts and fits of madness. He once burnt a whole village in a fit of rage because they were late in paying their taxes. He's said to kill defenseless villagers and traders simply because they weren't able to satisfy his requests."

"And his brother Oden?"

"His brother is a brute and a savage. He's said to have all the worst Norghanian qualities. He enjoys causing pain to others, and he's known to send men to the Steppes to kidnap young women so they can be brought to his castle for his personal pleasure."

"As you see," Darthor went on, "it's not just a question of Uthar. Even if we were to kill the King, the situation wouldn't be resolved. Or at least not entirely, because either Thoran or Oden would seize the crown, and as you heard from Egil, they're a pair of unscrupulous worms we ought to crush for the good of all Norghanians. In this war the Western League and their allies the People of the Ice must prevail. Not only must we win the war and get rid of Uthar, we also have to crown a new, just king, one whom we could trust to rule with justice and make Norghana into a prosperous and admired kingdom. At the moment the rest of the continent considers us a gang of barbarians of the Snows, savages and brutes who kill, pillage and torture for amusement. So it has been for a long time, and it will go on if we don't do something about it now we have the chance."

"And who's going to 'do something about it'?" Astrid asked. "You? Are we going to crown you as King?"

Darthor shook his head slowly.

"No, Astrid, I have no desire to be King. I don't want to rule Norghana or the North. When the war is over, I'll disappear, I'll leave the way I came, because my wish isn't the crown but to put a just king on the throne to lead this land on the path to becoming a great kingdom. I would like the Norghanians and the Peoples of the Ice to live in peace, like brothers, and for both to prosper. When that's achieved, I'll disappear."

"And you really want us to believe that?" Astrid shot back. "Once you've defeated Uthar, nobody will be able to stop you."

Darthor indicated Lasgol and Egil. "I don't expect you to believe me, but they do. When we've defeated Uthar, Egil's family will reign over Norghana. We'll crown Austin, who is the legitimate king. We'll forge a lasting peace between the Norghanians and the Peoples of the Ice, which Austin will protect. That day I will go back to the shadows."

Darthor's reply took Astrid aback, and she did not know what to say. She had not been expecting this.

Egil took a deep breath. "On behalf of my family I would like to thank you for all your help, my lord."

"You don't need to thank me for anything, Egil. It's the best thing for the kingdom, which is why it's the right thing to do and why I support it. Does anybody else here have any doubt as to whether you're on the right side, and doing the right thing?" He looked at them one by one.

Ingrid stepped forward. "No doubt whatsoever, my lord."

Gerd and Nilsa did the same and gave a brief nod. "No doubt, sir."

Finally Viggo too stepped forward. "I fight beside my friends, and if my friends are on this side, so am I. The rest is politics. Kings, dukes, counts, I don't care whatsoever." He bowed in turn.

"Good," Darthor said. "Very complicated times are at hand. I have the feeling that you'll find yourselves facing difficult situations in which you'll have to make very hard choices, but I believe you're ready and that you'll know what to do."

Lasgol felt that his mother was addressing him in particular, as well as the others, and was grateful for the thought.

"Whatever may happen from now until the end of the war, always bear in mind your principles and your values, and never give them up. Go on, ever forward. Use your head, which is your most powerful weapon, and always fight for what you believe in. Only by being true to yourselves will you prevail and have a full life. This is how I've lived my own life; and when things turn difficult remember who you are."

"So we will, my lord," Lasgol said

"I know that the Panthers are aware of my secret identity," Darthor went on. He came forward and stood beside Lasgol. "I hope you will preserve it with your lives and never reveal it to anybody. If this secret were to be known it would mean my end. The end of all this effort."

"Your secret is safe with us," Ingrid said.

"The Panthers won't go against one of their own," Viggo assured him. "They'll keep the secret."

Darthor nodded. "Then no more needs to be said on the subject." He put his hand on Lasgol's shoulder as if he wanted to say something to him, but then he looked toward the entrance and decided against it. He removed his hand and moved away from Lasgol.

"Urgent matters await me. Think about all we've said, and good luck to you all. You're going to need it."

With these words Darthor turned and left the tent.

Lasgol was left with a bitter-sweet feeling in his throat. On the one hand he was very glad to have been able to spend a moment with his mother, and on the other he felt sad about not being able to enjoy their relationship as mother and son. He wondered whether they would be able to do so one day, whether they would ever be Mayra and Lasgol, not Darthor and a Ranger.

Most likely not.

Chapter 30

"That was very interesting," Viggo said. "And even more intense,"

"You said it," Gerd muttered. "I was really scared. His voice, his armor and his presence... they're terrifying."

"Above all, the power he emits," Nilsa said. "Even I noticed."

"He's who he is, and we've given him our word," Ingrid said, and they all nodded.

Suddenly an enormous Wild of the Ice walked into the tent, and they all stiffened. He threw them a water-skin and a sack, then grunted and went out again.

"He doesn't like us," Viggo said.

"Him or any of his continent," Nilsa said.

"There's smoked herring in the sack," Gerd said, smiling. They would not die of hunger.

"If it weren't for Darthor and the alliance they'd kill us all," Viggo said. "And I'm sure they'd even eat us."

"Don't talk nonsense, you blockhead, how are they going to eat us? They're not cannibals!"

"Well, you never know."

"They're not cannibals and they wouldn't eat us," said Egil. "But Viggo's not altogether wrong. There's been a deep-rooted hatred between Norghanians and Peoples of the Ice for generations. The Wild, in particular: if they could, they'd destroy us."

"See? I was right," said Viggo.

Astrid was still in the far corner with her arms folded and a very unfriendly look on her face. "And you've allied yourselves with them," she said.

"Let me explain," Lasgol began.

"There's nothing to explain. You're all traitors, and you even more than the others for not telling me anything."

While the others sat down to eat, Lasgol tried to calm her down and tell her everything that had happened. With great patience, and despite her repeated denials, speaking almost in a whisper so that nobody outside the tent would hear, he told her about his relationship with Darthor, about what had happened on the Frozen Continent and the alliance he had witnessed. Astrid shook her head and interrupted him, protesting that she did not want to know anything more, that it was all a lie, that they were bewitched, that it was all impossible. Lasgol went on, summoning up all his patience and courage, and went over everything again. But there was no way of changing her opinion. It was too much for her to take in, something utterly unthinkable.

"You don't believe I love you either? You think I said that because I'm under a spell?"

Astrid hesitated.

"It's true, I love you, and that's something an Arcane couldn't have put in my heart."

"I don't know whether an Arcane could make you believe that. It might be just a trick to lower my defenses so that I trust you."

"I swear it isn't."

"And I'd like to believe that. It would fill my soul with joy if those words were sincere, that they came from your own heart and you really felt them, but at this moment, in this situation, I can't believe them, no matter how much I'd like them to be the truth."

Lasgol had to give up in the face of her steady refusal to accept the truth.

"Think about everything I've told you. I know it's crazy, but I swear it's the truth. I'd never lie to you, not openly. You know me, you know us all, we wouldn't lie to you."

"That's why I believe you're all bewitched. I'm not saying you don't believe what you're telling me, just that it's not true, it's just what you've been made to believe. It has to be that."

At that moment Arnold walked into the tent. He stopped at the entrance and signaled his brother to go over to him.

"I have to leave," he said. "I have urgent obligations to take care of."

"I understand."

"I don't want to tell you about our plans now. It would be very dangerous, especially since I understand you're going back to the Rangers."

"I think I'll be more use to you if I'm there. I'll try to warn you if we find out anything that could be relevant."

"Very well then, little brother. I'm really glad about this meeting. I see you're well, stronger, more mature."

Egil laughed. "You're saying that to cheer me up, I know that and I appreciate it. I'll always be half what you both are."

"But you're twice as intelligent as we are."

Egil went red. "No way. Both you and Austin are very intelligent."

"Be very careful. Things are going to turn nasty very quickly."

"Don't worry, I have my teammates. They'll help me."

"Keep an eye open at all times. And remember the promise we made to our father at the moment of his death."

"I'll always remember it. We'll get justice, and we'll kill Uthar."

Arnold grasped Egil by the shoulders, looked him in the eye and said: "I'm very proud of you, little brother. We need to survive this war and to use your brains to put Austin on the throne."

"We will, brother. Austin will be King by right and by blood."

"For the Olafstones! For King Austin!"

"For the true King! For Austin!"

Both brothers embraced one another firmly.

"Take great care, Egil."

"And you, brother."

Arnold turned to the others. "Take care of my brother, I beg you."

"Don't worry, sir, he'll be safe with us," Ingrid said.

"If anybody tries to lay a hand on him I'll cut his throat," Viggo added.

"Thank you, all of you," Arnold said. With a nod, he left.

Dawn came, though Lasgol had barely been able to doze off because of the tension of the situation and what was in store for them the next day. They waited for some time for Darthor to appear and pass judgment on Astrid. Lasgol, feeling very nervous, made another attempt to convince her, but without success. The fierce brunette refused to listen to him, or to his friends when they tried in their turn.

The morning went by and nobody came into the tent, which surprised them. Evening came, and only a huge Wild of the Ice came to bring them water and more smoked herring.

Lasgol asked for Darthor, but the Wild One simply grunted in reply and left.

"Something must have happened," Lasgol said to Egil.

"The situation may be very complicated now."

"I hope nothing's happened to him."

"Don't worry, your mother's the most powerful sorcerer of northern Tremia, and she has an army of Wild of the Ice with her. Nothing's going to happen to her."

Lasgol nodded, although he was not so sure. They did not know what was going on outside the tent; they could see the silhouette of the guards when the sun projected their shadows on to the canvas, but beyond that they had no idea. Night fell and nobody else came, so they slept and rested. Lasgol woke up at dawn and had a terrible shock.

Astrid was gone!

He woke his friends, but nobody had heard anything. He looked at them in disbelief.

"Did they take her while we were asleep?" Gerd asked.

"I doubt it," said Ingrid. "We'd have woken up."

"She's escaped," Egil said. He pointed to a small slit in the canvas at the back of the tent.

"How on earth did she get out through that?" said Gerd. "It's too small."

"She's one of the best in our course," Viggo said, "and very good at Expertise. That's how she got through. And if you want my opinion, I think the guards didn't even notice."

"So she must have escaped," Lasgol said.

"Viggo's right," said Ingrid. "She's very good and we didn't hear a thing, no alarm or struggle, nothing. She must have gotten away."

"But all this part of the coast is being watched by the Western League," Gerd objected. "They'll hunt her down."

Viggo smiled again. "I doubt it. She'll pass through them like a shadow and they won't even notice."

"I agree, I think that's what happened," said Ingrid. "Considering she escaped at night, and seeing how stealthy and skillful she is, I doubt whether they'll find her. Or even realize she's gone."

Lasgol snorted in frustration. There was a knot in his stomach and he did not know what to do. He could not warn his mother, because then he would put Astrid's life in danger. On the other hand, if he did not warn his mother, Astrid might reach her group, who would warn Uthar of the invasion and put its success in danger.

"We have to decide what we're going to do," Viggo said.

Egil nodded. "We'll have to tell on her. If we don't, we'll be in tremendous trouble with Darthor and his people."

"Yes, Gerd objected, "but if we do that and something happens to her, it'll be on our conscience."

"I haven't got much of that, so I'm not worried," said Viggo.

"Well, you might not have much, but I do," said Nilsa.

"Astrid has made her own choice," Ingrid said. "We can't be involved in her escape. We have to give the warning."

Lasgol was walking around the tent, trying to find a solution in his head, one that would mean neither Astrid's death nor his mother's, and could find none.

"The more time goes by, the worse it'll be," Ingrid went on. "They'll accuse us of helping her, and rightly."

Finally Egil spoke. "I'm really sorry, Lasgol, and I'm sorry for Astrid, but Ingrid's right, we must warn them. She's been gone for quite a while, and as Viggo says, if the sentinels on the cliff haven't seen her go by, she'll soon rejoin her group and they'll raise the alarm. The whole invasion will be at risk, and we can't allow that to happen. We need to warn Darthor and let him decide how to proceed, whether the plans need to be changed for the invasion, or whatever else has to be done."

Lasgol was shaking his head, unconvinced. He knew that his friends were right, but he did not want anything to happen to Astrid. He would rather die.

Egil made the decision for him and started toward the entrance.

"Wait!" Lasgol cried, and reached out to seize his arm. But Egil dodged him nimbly and went out of the tent.

"No!" Lasgol shouted.

They heard one of the guards growl at Egil. Moments later a familiar voice reached them; it was Asrael.

"You may come out of the tent."

The five friends did so, and found Egil. Beside him were Asrael, several Arcanes and half a dozen Wild of the Ice. In the bay were hundreds of empty barges, but there was no trace of the hosts of the Ice.

"Darthor had to leave. He apologizes for not saying goodbye."

"And the hosts?" Viggo asked suddenly. "Where are they?"

Asrael smiled. "They've left."

"This is very odd. And where are the ships? Now I come to think about it, we only saw barges. Where are the big naval ships?"

"Your mind is very sharp, young Viggo."

"This smells fishy. The bay ought to be full of big ships."

"As I said, they've left."

"So quickly?" Egil asked in surprise.

"It's foolish to stay at the landing spot any longer than is strictly necessary. Sooner or later the enemy will find out that we landed here and come to kill us."

Egil glanced at Lasgol sadly. "That's just what we wanted to tell you."

Lasgol knew that his friend was not being guided by malice but honesty, so he nodded in agreement.

"The seventh member of our group got away during the night," Egil went on. "She'll tell the Rangers about the landing, and they'll tell the King. You should change your plans."

"So she got away. A clever girl, by the look of it. None of our sentinels have caught her..."

"The King will send his forces to intercept your advance," Lasgol warned him.

Asrael nodded. "Very probably. You did well to tell me. We'll take measures to adjust to the situation. And now, my friends, it's time for you to go back to your people."

"You're letting us go?" Lasgol asked him, his eyebrows raised in surprise.

"That's right. On Darthor's orders. Go back to the Rangers, and when they ask, simply say that you were captured, which after all is the truth."

"What about the Royal Ranger?"

"Don't worry about him. I gave my word that nothing would happen to him, and nothing has. You'll find him at your campsite above the cliff. He might act strangely, but don't worry, he'll be all right."

Egil and Lasgol exchanged a look of surprise.

"If he comes back to the Camp with us," Lasgol said, "he'll give us away and we'll be hanged for treachery."

"He won't do that," Asrael promised him. "And now you must leave."

Lasgol was not convinced, but he did not argue. "Until next time," he said. He embraced Asrael, and one by one they took their leave of the ancient Arcane.

"We'll meet again," he promised them.

At the top of the cliff, as Asrael had told them, they found the Royal Ranger with his hands tied together, but unharmed. Ingrid cut his bonds.

He looked at them with a vague gaze. "What happened?" he muttered. "I can't remember anything."

"What's the last thing you remember?" Egil asked him.

"We were camped here..." His expression changed as memory returned. "I remember thousands of barges... an invasion! Darthor's forces! We've got to give warning!"

He tried to stand up, lost his balance and fell over.

"Take it easy," said Gerd, who had hurried to help him sit up.

"We've got to report, quickly."

"Give him some water while we check the horses," said Egil.

He and Lasgol went to see the horses and found them unharmed, together with a friend who ran out to meet them from the undergrowth. With a massive leap Camu, sprang on to Lasgol's chest and began to lick his cheek with little shrieks of joy.

Asrael come play, he transmitted mentally.

"You've seen old Asrael, haven't you? Did you have a good time with him?

Yes, happy.

"And haven't you missed me, and Egil?"

Camu jumped from Lasgol's chest to Egil's and licked his cheek.

"I think he really has missed us." Egil said pleased.

"What d'you think Asrael's done to Mostassen?" Lasgol asked.

"He's erased his memory somehow. Or rather, he's put a spell on him so he won't remember certain events."

"How long d'you think the spell will last?"

"Considering how powerful Asrael is, I'd say it could last a very long time."

"Let's hope that's true. It wouldn't do if he remembered in the middle of the camp."

"We've got another much more important problem to worry about at the Camp."

"Astrid..." Lasgol whispered.

"Yes. We're going to have a real problem with her."

Lasgol sighed. He would have given anything for things to have turned out differently, but that was the way things were.

"If we don't go back," he said, "they'll suspect and send someone to find us."

Egil nodded. "All we can do is risk it."

"If Astrid speaks to Dolbarar, we're dead."

"Let's hope she doesn't."

Lasgol shared the hope, but something inside him told him that since she was the kind of person she was, she would go and speak to the leader the moment she arrived. The worst thing was that they would not find out until they themselves arrived, and then it might already be too late for them.

Chapter 31

They rode non-stop in order to reach the Camp as soon as possible and give Dolbarar the news of the invasion. Mostassen set a cracking pace and nearly killed the animals, but luckily he had calculated the endurance of the horses well and they made it in time. Half a day more at that pace and Trotter would have been dead.

As soon as they had left the ponies in the Camp stables they met Master Instructor Oden, and they all stiffened.

"I have very important news for Dolbarar," Mostassen said to him.

Oden nodded. "Follow me. Dolbarar and the Master Rangers are waiting for you."

When he heard this, Lasgol felt his skin prickle. He and Egil exchanged a cautious look. They had gone into the wolf's den and now they might be eaten, depending on what Dolbarar and the Master Rangers knew. The faces of Ingrid and Viggo showed the same concern. Nilsa and Gerd looked like people on trial who are about to be judged and know they are guilty.

I hope they won't hang us, Lasgol told himself, but he was not at all confident about his fate or that of his friends. If things went wrong, he would try to save them by pleading guilty himself. After all, Darthor was his mother. If anybody had to die, it ought to be him. It was not his teammates' fault. He saw Egil beside him and knew his friend would not be spared either. *Egil and I are doomed, by blood, by our ancestry. We're who we are, our parents are who they are, and if we have to die for it, so be it. In times of war there'll be no mercy shown to us.*

At the Command House, where there were four duty Rangers at the door, Oden knocked and waited.

"Come in," they heard from inside, and the guards let them through.

Dolbarar was waiting for them, looking serious. He was seated at his table with the four Master Rangers around him, and their faces looked even more serious than usual.

Nerves began to wreak havoc on Lasgol. He could barely stop his hands from shaking, and rubbed one against the other in an attempt to keep them still.

At one point it looked as if Gerd would fall over when his knees buckled, but he managed to recover. Nilsa was biting her nails to her knuckles. Viggo's eyes had that cold lethal look that showed he knew they were in big trouble. And for the first time Lasgol saw Ingrid looking defeated, as if she knew the axe was about to fall on their necks.

"We bring critical and important tidings," Royal Ranger Mostassen began.

Dolbarar stood up. "Go ahead, make your report."

"Darthor's hosts are landing at Killer Whale Bay. We've just come from there, and we've seen thousands of barges full of Wild Ones of the Ice and the Glaciers Arcanes."

Dolbarar nodded slowly and put his hands behind his back.

"Thank you, Royal Ranger, this is indeed serious news. Yesterday Royal Ranger Ulsen arrived with Captain Astrid and her Owls and reported the same news. We've sent messengers and hawks to the capital. King Uthar has already been informed. His armies left yesterday to intercept the enemy advance before they could join the forces of the Western League and become unstoppable."

Lasgol tensed like a bowstring and looked out of the corner of his eye, first at Egil, then at Ingrid. If the king moved his armies, if he knew the landing-point and the most likely route for an advance on the capital, he could set a trap for Darthor's hosts. In addition, they would not have the support of the forces of the Western league. Austin's men would be starting to move about now. They would not arrive in time to help Darthor and the hosts of the Ice. He was worried sick at the thought, his stomach began to churn and he began to feel a terrible headache. And what worried him even more than this was what Astrid might have told Dolbarar about them. They might all be hanging from a tree by dawn.

"Astrid has told us –" Dolbarar began, and they all stood still as statues, with horror in their faces, in anticipation, "– that you were captured. Luckily she managed to escape during the night and warn us. I wonder how you were able to escape…"

"Well, you see, sir," Mostassen began, "I can't remember what happened…"

"Blow to the head or spell?" Eyra asked sharply.

"I think it was a spell… cast by the Glaciers Arcanes…"

"Interesting," Haakon said. "Why wouldn't they want you to remember?"

"Presumably in case he escaped and passed on the news of what he'd discovered," Ivana said.

"Why only you, and not them?" Esben asked.

"I don't know, gentlemen. I imagine that as I was in charge of the group and they were very young Rangers, they assumed it was better to put me out of action so that we wouldn't raise the alarm."

While Mostassen tried to reply, without much success, to the questions he was being asked, Lasgol was growing more and more restless. He felt bile rising up his gorge, so that he nearly threw up.

"It would make more sense if they'd put a spell on all of them," Ivana said. "In fact it would make more sense if they'd all been killed at once, unless they interrogated them to get information out of them."

"I couldn't tell, ma'am," Mostassen said.

The rest of the group said nothing. Nobody moved a muscle. They were all as taut as a branch on the point of snapping.

Haakon was the next to speak. "Perhaps they not only erased his memory but extracted the information they wanted, then covered their tracks by stopping him remembering anything at all."

"That makes sense," Dolbarar said.

"If that's so, I'm sorry I wasn't able to resist," Mostassen said apologetically.

"There's nothing you could have done," Eyra said. "The Glaciers Arcanes are very good at Illusion Magic, and some even at Domination Magic. No matter how you might have tried to resist, you wouldn't have succeeded in the face of that kind of magic. If they wanted you to see a sailing-boat, that's what you'd see and that's what you would have told us, with absolute conviction. Because of this I don't think your testimony is the most coherent or appropriate, since we don't know whether the illusion is still there in you. You'd better go to the Healer so that she can use her healing magic to get rid of any spell there may still have been left in you."

Ivana raised an eyebrow. "Will she be able to do that?"

"Probably not," Eyra explained. "Healing magic works on the body and physical wounds rather than on the mind. It's not a kind of magic that can eliminate spells that have been put on the subject's mind, but at least Edwina will examine him and see whether she can do anything more for him."

Dolbarar nodded. "It seems a good idea to me."

"In that case," Mostassen said, sounding very relieved, "if you'll excuse me, I'll go and see her right away."

"By all means," Dolbarar said, and waved him to the door.

The six members of the Snow Panthers were left standing there, and the tension was even greater now that they were alone, facing the Camp leaders, and would have to answer for what they had done.

"Going back to the main question: how did you manage to escape?"

Lasgol was about to answer, but Egil got in before him. "It wasn't so much that we managed to escape as that they'd already struck camp and were getting ready to leave."

"You mean they left you behind?"

"That's right," Egil said, very seriously and without a trace of hesitation. "They left us while the army moved on, with just a skeleton guard to keep an eye on us. We took advantage of a moment's carelessness to run off and reach our horses, which were hidden in a wood near the cliff. From there we came back as fast as we could to report."

There was a long, tense silence, as if Dolbarar and the four Master Rangers were considering the reply, seeking some gap or lie in it. But Egil's reply had been a half-truth rather than an outright lie.

Lasgol was surprised at how easily Egil had given his statement. It had sounded very convincing, and his voice had been utterly firm. He was beginning to see a change in his friend as a result of the war, of who he was and of what was at stake for him. He was turning little by little into a true Olafstone, a son worthy of his father, a noble of the Western league: an heir to the crown after his brothers.

"It's not very remarkable that you were left behind," Esben said. "The strange thing is that they didn't set a better watch."

"Exactly what I was thinking," Haakon agreed. "Why leave them alive when they could pose a risk? It doesn't make much sense. They ought to have been killed so they couldn't report."

Lasgol stared at Haakon's black eyes. They always had that dark look, always seeking some trap, some trick.

"What you're suggesting is interesting," Dolbarar said. "In fact leaving them alive makes no sense at all. The Wild Ones of the Ice aren't exactly known for the goodness of their hearts. They should have killed them. And yet you were left alive and you're here now. Perhaps there's something behind all this that we're not yet capable of seeing."

"You mean a possible deception?" Eyra said.

"Yes, I'm thinking of a lie... a well-thought-out plan that I still can't manage to see. This could certainly be some sort of trick."

Lasgol could see that Gerd was so pale that it seemed as if the blood was not reaching his head, and his hands were beginning to shake. Nilsa, who was by his side, came even closer and touched him on the arm to calm him. Although knowing Nilsa, a moment later she would be fidgeting herself.

Ingrid had remained silent until now. "We don't know what our captors' plans or intentions might have been," she said. "But it's not farfetched to think there's something else behind all this, because as has already rightly been said, we ought to be dead, and we're not."

"Exactly" Haakon said, "and I wonder why you're not."

Ingrid bore the scrutiny as if her blood were ice, her head held high, without any sign of being nervous, which Lasgol knew perfectly well that she was. Even she, harder than a rock, must have been suffering in that situation.

"The important thing is," Dolbarar said, "you're alive and you were able to return to the Camp. You've done very well. You'll be rewarded with an Oak Leaf each for a mission well carried out in the Summer Test."

Lasgol, Egil and Ingrid looked at one another in surprise. Not only had they not been found out, they were being rewarded and had passed the Summer Test. Some color came back to Gerd's face, and his hands stopped shaking. Nilsa was smiling and bouncing up and down. Viggo was frowning in disbelief.

"Rest tonight," Dolbarar said to them. "Tomorrow morning you set out."

"Sir?" Ingrid asked, taken aback.

"The rest of your fellow Contenders have already left. We need to locate the enemy forces and trace the route they'll take to the capital. That's what the King has ordered us to do."

"The King believes the hosts are on their way to besiege the capital?" Ingrid asked.

Dolbarar nodded. "That seems most likely, and that's where the forces of the Western League will join them. We'll have the Peoples of the Ice attacking our beloved capital from the East and the Western League from the West. The King has ordered us to find the route Darthor's hosts are going to take now that we know where they landed, then try to get them into a trap somewhere on the way so that they never get to join the Western League troops. If they were to reach the capital and both forces were to join together… it could be the end."

"Understood, sir," Ingrid said.

"Are we the only ones out of all the Fourth Year still left at the Camp?" Lasgol asked.

"That's right. The others have set off for different points with the order to send word the moment they detect the enemy advance."

"Our friend Astrid… is she all right?" Lasgol asked. No sooner had he done so that he regretted it.

"Yes, we were going to give her a break, but she insisted on leaving at once to locate the enemy forces. She's a courageous and honorable Captain."

Lasgol gave a silent snort of relief. Astrid was fine, and more than that, she was not there, which meant that he would not have to confront her. And what was most important, she had not told Dolbarar about them. He wondered why. In Egil's eyes he saw the same question: *Astrid hasn't given us away: why?* Why should she have pardoned their lives after the clear treason they had committed before her eyes? *I don't know. But we can live another day, and I'm grateful to her from the bottom of my heart.* He had been almost certain that she would have told Dolbarar everything.

He was left feeling very confused.

"Go and rest now, and get ready to set off at first light."

Chapter 32

They left at first light, as Dolbarar had told them to. Royal Ranger Nikessen had been chosen to lead them, along with one of the Instructor Assistants of the Camp: Molak.

When they had appeared in front of the Fourth-Year cabins, Ingrid had smiled in surprise. Unlike Viggo, who had cursed under his breath. His usual sarcastic humor had now turned much darker.

"That's all we needed, getting 'Captain Marvel' as our instructor!"

"Apparently there aren't any more Ranger Instructors available in the whole Camp," Egil said. "We're the last ones to leave. The Camp is practically deserted, except for the First- and Second-Years, and they couldn't involve them in the war."

"Well, it's going to be a very entertaining mission," Viggo grumbled bitterly. "Not only have we got a Royal Ranger with us again, we've got 'Captain Marvel' too! I feel like stabbing myself and getting all the pain of this mission over with."

"I don't know what you're moaning about," Nilsa said. "Molak's a fantastic Instructor Assistant and his help's going to be worth its weight in gold. And anyway, there aren't many in the Camp as good as he is with the bow. Not even Ingrid or myself can come anywhere near him."

"I don't care how handsome, wonderful, fantastic and good at archery he is, what I don't get is why he has to come with us."

"I think he asked for it himself. He stayed to wait for us even though he wasn't absolutely certain we'd come back, according to what Ingrid told me."

"Of course!" said Viggo, fuming. "How could it be any other way!"

They started their journey towards the south, following the river, then turned east. As they were the last to leave, all the key positions had been entrusted to other Rangers and teams. Their mission was to survey the advance of the King's army, which had now left Norghania, and give warning of any danger that might threaten them, such as attacks from the flanks.

It took them ten days to locate the head of Uthar's army. They contemplated the King's military power from the distance, wide-eyed and open-mouthed. An enormous snake of red, white and silver scales was moving slowly across the plain toward the Mountains of Oblivion. Thousands of men were on their way to crush the invading enemy.

They would reach the army the following day. They camped on a rocky hill for the night and lit an inconspicuous campfire. Here they settled to get their strength back. Royal Ranger Nikessen turned out to be pleasanter company and more talkative than Mostassen, which was a nice change, even more so in the circumstances.

"We'll let our horses rest tonight, then tomorrow at dawn I'll go up to the front line of our troops and report to Gatik."

"Isn't it a bit risky for the King to be sending his troops to intercept Darthor's advance?" Ingrid asked as they ate.

The Royal Ranger drank from his water-skin, then handed it to Molak.

"Yes. It's a risky tactic. The King could wait behind the walls of Norghania, but this opportunity is a difficult one to turn down. If he manages to crush Darthor's army before he can join the forces of the Western League, victory will be his. That's why he's sending most of his men. It's an unrivalled opportunity."

Lasgol and Egil exchanged a look of concern.

"What's strange is that the Peoples of the Ice should have decided to land so far to the east," Molak said.

"I was thinking the same thing," said Ingrid.

"They don't have many other good choices for the landing-site. If they do it further north, they'll have to come down to Norghania through the northern mountains, and Uthar can seal the passes and stop them. That was the most likely strategy, the least risky. Dolbarar's sent plenty of Rangers to the north precisely because he feared that's what Darthor might have opted for."

"Which he obviously didn't," Viggo said.

"Both strategies are risky," Egil said suddenly. "The hosts of the ice should have crossed further north. It's the shortest route, and the least dangerous one. But as Royal Ranger Nikessen rightly pointed out, the King could have located them. That's what he was expecting, and in addition the northern passes are heavily watched by the Rangers. Crossing that way would have been extremely difficult. Darthor has opted for something even riskier, which is to come by sea to the southeast and landing in the east of the kingdom. Which is a maneuver Uthar wasn't expecting."

"Luckily you discovered them," Molak said, "and the King saw his chance to act."

"I don't understand much about armies or wars or plans of attack," said Gerd, "but wouldn't it had been better if the Peoples of the Ice had landed in the West and joined the troops of the Western League there? Wouldn't that be the safest option?"

"It is," said Egil, "and that's exactly what Uthar was expecting them to do. At the same time it's also the most conservative option, and the most time-consuming. To transport the whole army through the frozen ice into western Norghana, quite apart from the risk, would take a lot of time, and then they might be caught by autumn, because they haven't been able to move until now and we're already at the height of summer. That means the offensive would take place in winter, and what with bad weather and Uthar in the capital, the Western League and the Peoples of the Ice would be likely to lose. Keeping the biggest northern city under siege during the winter would be a very bad idea. The King could withstand the siege comfortably behind those walls with the supplies he already has, while his enemies would have to endure the harsh winter with a shortage of food."

"It looks as though Darthor's opted for the most daring strategy," Molak said.

"Yes," said Nikessen. "Probably he was trying to surprise the King's army, but it didn't work because the Rangers saw him land and informed Uthar. You did very well."

Ingrid nodded and said nothing. The others followed her example.

"Don't worry, soon the King's army will repel this invasion and the war will be over. The Western League won't dare to go against the King outnumbered and without their allies of the ice. Soon Uthar will reign again over all Norghana, and law and order will rule once again."

"If that's so," Nilsa asked, "what will happen to the leaders of the Western League?"

"I very much fear that the King will have no mercy with them. They've committed high treason, and the punishment is beheading."

Egil swallowed.

Lasgol felt a knot in his stomach and thought of his mother. If the King came out victorious – and it looked as though he would – both Egil's brothers and his own mother would die. They could not let that happen, but what could they do to stop it? The Eastern army was advancing and would attack as soon as they glimpsed the enemy. He had to clench his fists to avoid shaking with fear and rage.

"Molak, you take the first watch," Nikessen said. "Ingrid, you go with him. The others watch in pairs. Next, Viggo and Nilsa, then Gerd and Lasgol, then Egil with me for the final one. Understood?"

They all nodded, except Viggo, who was not at all pleased to see Ingrid being paired with Molak.

"Remember that the enemy will probably have advanced scouts too. If you see anything, don't shoot. Wake me up first before you attack– it might be one of our own people on the trail. Understood? Right, start the first watch. You others, go and rest."

Ingrid and Molak took their places a hundred paces from each other, one to the east, the other to the west. Every hour they changed over, and when they did so they stopped for a moment and exchanged impressions in whispers.

"Seen anything?" Molak asked at the first exchange.

"Nothing. Everything's quiet, some wild animal or other, a night bird of prey, but nothing suspicious."

"Same here. Remember what the Royal Ranger said," he added with a touch of worry in his voice. "If you see anything, don't release, withdraw and report back."

"What's the matter? Are you afraid for me? I'm quite capable of looking after myself."

Molak nodded. "I know. I'm sure you're capable of killing a snow troll all by yourself. But I do worry about you, even so."

"You worry about me?"

"You know I do. I always worry about you."

"You worry the same way you would about anybody else on watch duty with you."

Molak's eyes glinted. "You know my concern for you goes further than that."

"Further?" she asked, looking puzzled.

Molak sighed. "You're going to make me say it, aren't you?"

"You can say anything you like."

"I worry more about you than I do about the others," he

admitted.

"And why's that?" she asked, still puzzled.

Molak snorted in frustration. "You're really making this difficult for me."

"People say I have a difficult temperament, it's true. Don't you like it?"

"I like everything about you," Molak finally admitted.

Ingrid was taken aback, and she took a moment to react.

"Everything?"

"That fierce gaze of yours in those deep, sea-blue eyes. The courage and determination in that blonde head of yours. Your skill with weapons and as a Ranger in that well-trained warrior's body. Your indomitable personality and fighting character. I like everything about you. I like it a lot."

Ingrid listened attentively and said nothing until he had finished his paean of praise.

"If you think you're going to woo me with pretty words and flattery, you're very much mistaken. You'll need a lot more than that to win me."

Molak bent over her, put his right hand behind her neck and kissed her passionately. She resisted for a moment, but then, suddenly feeling overwhelmed, gave in. They stayed locked in one another's arms for a long, intense kiss under the summer moon.

Someone was watching them from the camp with eyes full of disappointment.

It was Viggo.

The remaining watches were uneventful. The last one was shared by the Royal Ranger and Egil. It began with a certain tension, which Egil noticed.

"You've put me on watch with you for a reason, haven't you?" he asked.

The Ranger nodded. "I see you're as quick-witted as they say you are."

"We're alone," Egil said. "You can speak freely."

"Right. I'll be honest. I know who you are and what family you belong to, and I'm worried that you're with us."

"Worried... why?"

"Because when the moment comes, I don't want you to be a problem."

"My loyalty's to the King. That's what I swore, and that's what I'll deliver."

"Maybe that's what you believe now, but at the moment of truth feelings run deep and you might not make the right decision."

"Don't you worry, sir. I'll make the right choice."

The Royal Ranger looked him in the eye.

"I'm glad to hear it. I hope you won't disappoint me."

Chapter 33

Nikessen left the camp with the first light of dawn and set off for the vanguard of the royal army to receive his instructions.

Lasgol, who was watching the army, called upon his Gift and his *Hawk Eye* skill.

"What do you see?" Egil asked him.

"Uthar's sending most of his forces. I can make out the Blizzard Army at the head, rear and both flanks of the main column. In the vanguard I can see the Thunder Army with their winged helmets and their strong red jerkins with their diagonal white stripes."

As always they led the way. The Snow Army followed, unmistakable with their pure white breastplates over chainmail.

"Uthar is sending all he has, except for the Invincibles of the Ice..."

"I can see Commander Sven leading the troops and two Ice Mages, but not Mage Olthar."

"Can you see Gatik and the Royal Rangers?"

Lasgol shook his head

"That's odd. They ought to be there, with Sven."

"I can't see the King either..."

Egil's eyes opened wide. "That too is significant."

"D'you think he's stayed in Norghania?"

"It looks like it. It makes sense for him to stay behind in the safety of the great walled city."

"In that case Gatik will presumably be with him."

"I agree. That, or else he's been sent on a special mission with the Royal Rangers."

"Nikessen didn't say anything about that."

"I don't suppose he knows, and even if he did, I don't think he'd say anything, or at least not to us."

"True. We're only eyes and ears, we don't need to know what's really going on."

"That's right."

Viggo interrupted them. "Well, I want to know."

"Why this interest?" Egil asked.

"Anybody who isn't well informed tends to die early. I want to die as late as possible, preferably of old age and in my own palace."

"Palace?" Nilsa mocked him. "What palace are you likely to have?"

Viggo looked at her with an air of mock superiority. "One day I won't be a mere Ranger Contender, I'll be a nobleman with a grand palace, servants, riches, women, and everything you could dream of."

"Yeah, sure."

"Just wait and see."

Gerd came over to listen to the conversation. "I can see him as a nobleman. Cruel and ruthless with his subjects, that's it exactly."

"But noble, after all," said Viggo smugly.

Nilsa rolled her eyes. "You'll never become a nobleman. You come from the scum of the earth and your past is full of dark secrets."

"That's why I'm here. Once I'm a Ranger my past will disappear."

"Once you're a Ranger you'll be a Ranger, not a nobleman."

"Life is very long and it's full of twists and turns, especially in these messy times of civil wars, invasions and so on... we'll see where I end up. What I will say to you is that I won't be dead because of not knowing what's going on. I'm off to investigate for a while till Nikessen returns."

"That's not a good idea," Molak said.

"I don't care whether you think it's a good idea or not, it's what I'm going to do."

"Nikessen told us to wait for him to come back, here in this camp. That's what we ought to do."

"That's what you ought to do. I'm going to see what's happening."

"Don't be a pain and do what you're told," Ingrid said as she joined the group.

"You're not in command and neither is your beau. I'll do what I want."

Ingrid and Molak looked at one another in embarrassment.

"I'm the highest-ranking member of this group," Molak said, "and in Nikessen's absence it's my orders you have to follow."

"What rank? You're an Instructor's assistant, nothing more than that."

"I'm a Ranger, and you're not."

Viggo's eyes sparkled with hatred. Molak did not flinch.

"I saw what happened to your team in the Frozen Continent. I'd rather follow my instincts than your orders. I'll stay alive longer."

Molak tensed and clenched his fists. The comment had hurt him. He was about to come to blows with Viggo.

Ingrid moved to stand between them to prevent it. "Don't bother, it's not worth it. Believe me, I know."

Molak's jaw was clenched and his eyes shot fire. He said nothing. Ingrid turned to Viggo.

"Sometimes you're really low and hateful."

"You know what I said was the truth, whether you like it or not."

"Do whatever you have to do and come back before Nikessen does."

"Fine," he said, and went to fetch his horse.

"If anything happens to you, it'll be your responsibility. We won't be coming to help you."

Viggo stopped and turned. "Your concern for me touches my heart," he said mockingly.

Ingrid growled under her breath. Viggo mounted and disappeared into the woods.

"Let's hope he doesn't get into trouble," said Nilsa.

Gerd shook his head. "That would be a miracle."

Lasgol felt that he ought to help his friend. Viggo was what he was, but deep down he was a good person, even if it was very deep down and most of the time he was insufferable. Lasgol remembered the time he had spent shunned by everyone himself when he had been the 'Traitor's Son', and he felt sorry for his friend. He must be feeling like that at the moment, if not even worse, because of Ingrid...

"Where are you going?" she asked him when she saw him going for Trotter.

"I'm going after him."

"He's not worth it."

"Yes he is, deep down..."

Ingrid shrugged. "As you wish."

By the time Lasgol wanted to catch up with Viggo, he had already vanished during a great forest. Following his trail was not too difficult. He was not making any effort to avoid being followed. He must have assumed that nobody would go after him.

At noon, Lasgol saw Viggo's pony in the distance, tethered to a tree by the river, drinking. He approached slowly, dismounted and let Trotter drink with the other pony. He crouched and examined Viggo's trail, which went up a hill. The forest was thinning, and he caught sight of a valley in the distance, behind the hill. He was about to step out of the forest to get a view of the valley from above.

A hand covered his mouth, and a knife was pressed against his throat.

Lasgol froze as still as a statue. He had been surprised from behind and had heard nothing.

"Not a word..." a voice whispered in his ear. It was Viggo's.

His friend removed the knife from his throat and pointed below, to his right. Lasgol followed the pointing hand and saw a group of riders resting.

"Let's hide," Viggo whispered.

Lasgol nodded. They threw themselves down and watched from the undergrowth. In the group were three Norghanians and three Tundra Dwellers.

"Interesting group," Viggo commented.

"Yes, very, particularly in this area."

"I'd say it's a scouting group."

"Are they following Uthar's army?"

"Looks like it."

"There must be scouts reconnoitering, but what surprises me is that they're working together."

"They're not together," Viggo said. "They've come from different directions. They're exchanging information."

"That makes more sense. The Western Norghanians and the Peoples of the Frozen Continent don't really get along very well... not even with the alliance."

"I'm not surprised at that."

The two watched for a while in silence. Suddenly Lasgol asked: "Why can't you go back to your city?"

Viggo looked him in the eye and smiled. "It's been eating at you, huh?"

"Yeah... a little..."

"Fine. I'll tell you, though you won't like it."

"Tell me and we'll see."

"I can't go back to my city because I'd be hanged."

"What did you do?"

"Are you sure you want to know?"

"Yes, tell me."

"I killed a man."

Lasgol's blood went cold. He had expected bad news, but not as bad as this.

"You killed a man? It must have been in self-defense..."

"No."

"Was it an accident? Unintentionally?"

"No."

Lasgol was horrified. There had to be an explanation. He prayed to the Five Gods of the Ice that it had not been for any trivial reason.

"What happened?"

"I killed my mother's lover."

Lasgol was taken aback. "Why? How did it happen?"

"He was a bully, and he treated her as if she were his property to do whatever he wanted with. I couldn't defend her, I wasn't living with them. My mother went to live at that filthy scum's house. One evening I went to see her, because I was worried. I snuck into the house and found her unconscious on the kitchen floor. He'd beaten her terribly. I tried to help her, tend her wounds... and then he came back. When he saw me he grabbed a knife from the table. He should never have done it. I took out my dagger. We fought. He was forty-five and I was fifteen, but even so, I won. I killed him. My mother begged me to leave, she knew I'd be condemned. I'd killed a man in his own house and he had friends among the city guards. So I left."

"But they can't hang you for that?"

"They can and they will. If they catch me, of course."

"But you acted in self-defense and he was a bully. He deserved what happened to him."

"But I killed a man in his own house. There's an order to catch me and hang me."

"When did this happen?"

"Right before I joined the Rangers."

"Is that why you did?"

Viggo nodded.

"If you don't sort this out, then sooner or later they'll find you, even among the Rangers."

"I'm sorting it out. That's why I'm here."

"I don't follow..."

"I see that the know-it-all hasn't told you everything about the Rangers."

Lasgol shrugged. "What hasn't he told me?"

"Becoming a Ranger is hard work and not everyone succeeds, but there's a reward."

"Serving Norghana?" said Lasgol, who, knowing Viggo, was certain he did not mean that.

Viggo smiled. "Apart from that. When you enter the Rangers' Corps you leave your past behind. You begin a new life. From scratch."

"Would the crime be forgiven?"

"That's right. When I become a Ranger. Crimes, debts and anything else are forgiven when you become a Ranger because you start a new life in the service of the Crown, from scratch."

"I didn't know that."

"It's in the *Path of the Ranger*. For most people it's something inconsequential. For a few, like me, it's very important."

"You have to graduate, somehow," said Lasgol.

Viggo gave him his sarcastic grin. "I know. It's been there in my mind, since the first day."

"Why didn't you tell us?"

"We're all here for different reasons. You came to clear your father's name and I came to avoid being hanged in the main square."

"You're risking your life."

"You did the same. You're still doing it."

"That's different."

"True, but in the end it comes to the same thing. We've got to finish the year and graduate, despite the instruction, the tests and the war. The only difference between all of you and me is that I risk my life if I don't make it and get expelled."

"We'll finish the year. We'll make it. And we'll graduate."

Viggo smiled. "I'd better..."

"Thanks for telling me."

"If you don't mind, let's keep it between the two of us. I'm already getting enough bad looks as it is."

"They'd understand... but all right, I'll respect your wishes."

"Thanks. And now let's get back. Both groups are leaving." Viggo pointed down to the valley.

Royal Ranger Nikessen came back at a gallop later and leapt off his pony. "We have new orders," he told the group.

They gathered around him. Lasgol and Viggo had already returned, but had said nothing of what had happened to anyone.

"Commander Sven wants us to keep watch on the rearguard of the army. We'll be patrolling in semicircles, covering the whole southern part of the rearguard. There are other teams to cover east and west. We have to make sure we're not attacked from behind by the forces of the Western League."

"That's highly unlikely," Egil pointed out. "To do that, the forces of the league would have to cross the Wild River and then cross the whole southeast of the kingdom to get here. I don't see it as viable, not without them being spotted."

The Royal Ranger nodded several times. "That's what I think too, but orders are orders and we need to be very wary in times of war. The Commander of the kingdom's armies wants his back well covered, and that's what we'll do, cover it."

"On the other hand," Molak said, "it wouldn't be the first time a war's been lost because of a totally unexpected surprise."

"Also very true, Ranger Molak."

"We won't let the forces of the Western League make some strange or unexpected maneuver to surprise the rearguard as they're moving forward to meet the hosts of the Ice."

"Better to anticipate than to be sorry," Ingrid said.

"Is the King with the army?" Lasgol asked in a neutral voice.

"No. Uthar and the court are staying in the capital. They have to be there to prevent the troops of the West from trying to take it."

"The Western League won't try to take the city on its own," Egil said. "It hasn't got enough men to keep up a prolonged siege on a walled city as well-protected as that."

"They can't now, but they'd be able to if the enemy managed to cross the Great Central Pass of the Oriental Mountains and reach the city."

"And that's precisely what we're going to prevent," said Molak.

"Exactly. We can't allow the Hosts of the Ice to cross the Oriental Pass. The army is on its way there as we speak."

"How do we know they haven't crossed already?" Lasgol asked.

"The Rangers are watching the way out of the Pass. They haven't reported any enemy coming out of it."

They hastened to carry out these new orders. When they arrived at the rearguard of that great snake of silver, white and red scales, they took up their positions. As they had foreseen, everything was quiet and there was no trace of the forces of the Western League or any Wild of the Ice.

While they patrolled, they saw Wolves and Eagles doing the same in the southern part of the rearguard. They stopped to swap information with them, and two veteran rangers leading the groups came over, followed by Isgord and Luca.

Isgord, as arrogant as ever, glared disdainfully at Lasgol and Egil, who ignored him. Luca greeted them with a friendly wave.

"Any news?" Nikessen asked.

The first Ranger was looking south. "None," he said. The second shook his head. "No trace of the enemy."

"Have the other groups reported anything?"

"No sir. There are three other groups further east, and they haven't seen anything."

"And any news from the West?"

"As far as we know, the forces of the Western League are still getting ready to cross the river, but they haven't done it yet. Gatik and the more seasoned Rangers are watching all the fords in case the Western troops start moving."

"That leaves me feeling easier," Nikessen said. "There's less chance of being surprised from behind."

"The problem is in front, not back here," the first Ranger said.

"They haven't crossed, have they?"

"They haven't had time," the second one said. "But they'll be here soon. Sven wants to prevent their crossing at all costs. He'll stop them before they arrive, he won't let them set a foot in the gorge."

Nikessen was looking at the head of the army, which was reaching the entrance to the Pass by now. "He's moving at top speed."

"The first one to cross the Pass will have the advantage," one of the Rangers said.

"That'll be Sven."

"Let's get a move on and follow him."

"Good luck and be careful," Nikessen said. The Rangers saluted, and Isgord and Luca did the same. They went their separate ways.

"We'll follow the army," Nikessen ordered.

Lasgol had a distinctly ominous feeling.

Chapter 34

Nikessen led the group to the entrance to the pass of the Oriental Mountains the Norghanian army was already moving through. They took their position at the rear and stopped at a sign from the Royal Ranger, who was pointing back at the plain they had left behind.

"Keep your eyes open. Don't let anybody approach from behind."

Lasgol looked out at the magnificence of the mountains which rose ahead of them, their rocky peaks covered with snow and ice. The pass between them was nearly five hundred paces wide, and looked as though a god of the north had sliced the majestic mountains in two with an axe. It had certainly not been created by the hand of man.

Lasgol did not know the region well. "How deep is the gorge?" he asked.

"The pass is more than five thousand paces long," Egil said.

Viggo gave a long whistle.

"Those mountains are colossal," Ingrid said

"As impressive as the ones in the North," said Molak.

"In fact there's not a lot to envy about them," said Egil, "except that here in the east there's not so much snow and ice, because the climate's more benign."

"Is it possible to climb all the way up?" Gerd asked.

"It's pretty difficult," Nikessen said, "but it can be managed. In fact several Ranger colleagues of ours are up there right now, keeping watch."

"It's impressively high, and the walls are vertical," said Ingrid. "How did they manage to climb up there?"

"Because they're experienced Rangers," was Nikessen's response.

"And because they have a map of these mountains and their points of access," Egil added.

"That's correct. The Rangers' maps are deeply valued, and it's one of the things you learn in one of the elite specialties. My own, in fact."

They all looked at him in surprise, not having known he was an

Elite Ranger. But when they thought about it, since he was a Royal Ranger it made perfect sense.

"Which specialty is that, sir?" Lasgol asked with great interest.

"It's an elite specialization of School of Nature, and it's called *Green Cartographer*."

"Their function is to make maps?" Nilsa asked.

"That's right. We travel the whole kingdom making very detailed maps. Not only of roads, forests, mountains and rivers, but also of all the accesses to peaks and gorges, and especially the most difficult ones. Bear in mind that the royal cartographers can't reach where a Ranger does. Their maps are better, certainly, but ours go further. They're of great military value."

"Especially in situations like this war." Viggo said.

"Correct."

"I could never be a cartographer," Gerd said. "I'm terrible at drawing."

"You're also terrible at climbing," Viggo pointed out.

"You need a very well-trained physique and a good hand for doing the drawing," Nikessen said. "And to be able to climb peaks as inaccessible as the ones you can see."

"And come down from them as well," Molak added.

"Exactly. Often the descent's more dangerous than the ascent."

"Have you traveled all over the kingdom?" Ingrid asked.

Nikessen nodded. "Quite a bit. Particularly the southeast."

"Then you know these mountains and this pass well."

"That's right."

"You mean you've been up there?" Gerd said, staring up at the heights.

Nikessen nodded again. "I've been up there. In fact I collaborated in making a map of this pass and these mountains for the Rangers."

"I'd love to be able to study it," Egil murmured.

"I'd love to have gone up there with you," Ingrid said.

Viggo shook his head. "I'm perfectly happy down here. This is too high and dangerous already."

"Each of us has a different vocation. This is mine, and I certainly like it."

Lasgol stared up at the snow-covered peaks of the gorge, imagining what a strenuous business it would be to climb them. Meanwhile the great army was still moving on into the depths of the pass.

Ingrid's eyes were on the soldiers. "What do we do?" she asked Nikessen.

"We follow a hundred paces behind, and watch our backs."

As they went on, they took a last look at the distant plain they were leaving behind. Lasgol used his *Hawk Eye* skill to scan the horizon. He was able to make out four mounted groups, which he recognized as Rangers and some of their fellow Camp members.

And Astrid.

When he saw the fierce brunette his heart skipped a beat and his stomach twisted into a knot. Soon the moment would come when he had to face her, and he knew the situation was going to be a very complicated one: not only because of his feelings for her but because of what she might tell about what had happened. He still could not believe she had not given them up to Dolbarar. But how long would she keep the secret? According to Viggo, not much longer. Nilsa was convinced that she would not betray them, but the others were not so sure. This included himself as well.

"We're losing visibility as we go deeper into the gorge," Nikessen said.

"What do we do, sir?" Ingrid asked.

"We spread out, in stages. Ingrid, Molak, go to the end of the pass and go on watching the plain from there. If you see anything strange, sound the alarm. Nilsa and Gerd, follow them and take up a position a thousand paces from them, inside the gorge. If they sound the alarm, run and let me know."

"Right away, sir."

"Viggo, you a thousand paces more, same orders." He turned to Lasgol and Egil. "Egil, another thousand paces, Lasgol another thousand."

Egil nodded. "We're creating a warning chain."

"Exactly. Just in case. You can never be too careful."

Lasgol took a good look at the pass. "There's no trace of the enemy and we're already half-way in, if I counted the paces correctly. There doesn't seem to be any danger."

"That's exactly why we need to be more careful. Now's the most critical moment."

"If the enemy were coming into the pass, the scouts would sound the alarm."

"True. But that's if the scouts come back alive. Never assume things are going to turn out the way they should."

"Understood." Egil said.

They went on with one eye on the rear of the advance and another on the peaks around them. The weather seemed to be worsening. Dark clouds came down from the top of the gorge, casting a gloomy shadow over the advancing troops.

"I don't like the look of those clouds," Nikessen said.

Lasgol stared closely at them. There was something in them he did not quite like.

"Looks as though they've stopped over the pass."

"It's a natural effect," Egil commented. "When low clouds are about to shed their burden and reach a mountain range they can't pass over, they stay above it. There's nothing strange about that."

Lasgol was not entirely convinced by his friend's explanation, but it made sense, and besides, Egil was hardly ever wrong.

Nikessen glanced back to check for any sign of trouble. "Let's go on. We can't afford to get too far behind the troops."

As they went on, a bluish fog drifted towards them from ahead. The three of them stared at this phenomenon uneasily.

"Blue fog," Nikessen said. "Now this really is strange."

"It could be a perfectly natural climatic effect," Egil said. He reached out to touch the fog, which faded when he contacted it.

Lasgol felt the hair on the back of his neck stand on end.

"This fog is a very odd color," Nikessen said as he too tried to touch it. "It ought to be whitish, or even turn dark if there's a storm threatening, but this blue color... I don't like it at all. Forget the previous orders. We'll keep together. I don't like this."

"The soldiers are going on through it," Egil said.

"I can't see the front of the column," said Nikessen, "but they must already be nearing the end of the pass."

At Egil's unobtrusive prompting, Lasgol called upon his *Hawk Eye* skill. He managed to see the head of the troops leaving the pass at the far end, but nothing more.

Suddenly there came a prolonged, urgent horn-call. It was the alarm!

"Look out!" Nikessen cried. "Something's up! Stay here, I'll go and see what's going on."

He spurred his pony and rode fast to reach the rear of the line.

The others, unable to see much in the fog, waited for him to come back.

"I don't like this at all," Egil said.

"Yeah, me neither, neither this fog nor the fact that the enemy's there ahead of us."

Nikessen did not take long to return at a gallop. Horns were calling in the pass by now.

"The enemy's at the end of the pass! We're marching! We have to get out of the pass at a gallop and take up positions for the battle!"

"There's a battle?" Egil asked.

"Yes, we managed to arrive before the enemy and get out of the pass. We have the advantage, and we're going to finish off the enemy here and now. The King's plan was a risky one, but it's going to pay off. Luck smiles on those who take risks. On we go, to help in the battle!"

They rode as fast as the ponies were able. The whole army was maneuvering outside the end of the pass, blocking it to stop anybody else from entering it. The three armies took up a square formation: the Thunder Army in the center, the Blizzard on the left and the Snow Army on the right. Compact formation. The enemy army would not be able to reach the pass now, with a wall of men blocking the access.

And as they reached the end of the gorge, Lasgol saw the hosts of the Peoples of the Frozen Continent assembling in front of the Norghanian Army in the midst of the bluish fog. He could see the Wild of the Ice accompanied by the Glaciers Arcanes, Snow Trolls, and an enormous beast he could not identify but which looked like a giant crocodile with scales of ice.

"The enemy!" Nikessen exclaimed. "We came just in time! Now they'll find out what Norghanians are made of!"

Egil looked at Lasgol. If the Norghanian army, more numerous and better prepared, were to destroy the hosts of the Frozen Continent in this battle, everything would be lost for the Western League and his brothers. Uthar would go after them and execute them. Darthor's planned surprise landing in the east was going to fail, and fail spectacularly. The invasion would be over before it had even begun. First the Peoples of the Ice would fall here, and then the Western League. Uthar was going to come out victorious, with nobody to stop him. Lasgol could feel his stomach splitting in two.

The war horns rang out now, calling to battle.

Full of concern, he used his *Hawk Eye* skill to search for his mother among the lines of the hosts of the ice. But he could not see her.

Nor could he see the Glaciers Arcanes.

It was impossible. He shook his head and looked again. In front of the Norghanian army there was simply no-one. He pulled on Trotter's reins to bring him to a halt, shook his head again and rubbed his eyes. Something was not right. He stopped using his skill and now was able to see everything again. The hosts of the Frozen Continent were already forming in front of the Norghanian army.

But what on earth's the matter with me?

He used his skill again, and once again there was not a single dweller of the Frozen Continent to be seen there. Only the Norghanian soldiers with their weapons at the ready, waiting for the order to attack.

Egil realized that Lasgol had stopped and did the same.

Lasgol, baffled, stopped his skill once again, shut his eyes firmly a couple of times and looked again. The hosts of the Frozen Continent had come back.

But this is impossible!

He tried to part the blue fog around him to see more clearly and understand what was happening.

Nikessen too had brought his horse to a halt. "What on earth are you doing?"

"There's something strange going on here, sir," Lasgol said.

The horns called loudly again, and the troops began to move forward. He brushed aside the fog in front of his face.

And at that moment he realized.

"The fog isn't fog, it's a huge spell cast by the Glaciers Arcanes."

"What on earth are you saying?"

"There are no hosts of the Frozen Continent ahead of us."

"Don't be stupid, I can see them perfectly well."

"It's a hallucination, sir. It's a spell of the Arcanes, there's really no one out there. They're making us see it."

"That doesn't make any sense," Nikessen said.

"Yes, it does," Egil said suddenly. "It's a trap."

"How can it be a trap if we've gone through the pass and come out, and we hold the advantage?"

"I don't know, but it's a trap all the same."

"That's enough nonsense from the two of you. Come with me. We've got to get out of the pass and join in the combat."

Lasgol used his Gift one last time to confirm that he was right. The Norghanian soldiers began to march against the enemy, except that the enemy was nowhere on the plain. There was nothing but snow and trees.

Suddenly they felt a huge tremor that frightened the ponies, as if an earthquake were taking place.

Nikessen was looking all around. "What's this? What's happening?"

"I don't know," Egil said, "but I fear it's a trap."

The tremor grew stronger, and they were forced to dismount. The ponies were bucking in terror.

"Watch out!" Nikessen cried as he flung himself to one side to escape an enormous boulder which nearly crushed him.

Lasgol pointed upwards. "There are boulders coming down from above! We'd better get out before it's too late."

"No, stop!" Egil cried. "We need to do the opposite, we need to go back the way we came!"

"Are you sure?" Lasgol asked. He was finding it hard to keep his balance, what with the quakes, the crashing of the rocks as they fell and a strange jarring sound that was coming from above.

"Yes! We've got to retreat, I'm sure of it!"

Rocks and boulders kept falling, but only at the far end of the pass. Lasgol fell to the ground, and Egil with him. Nikessen managed to get back on his feet, miraculously dodging a huge rock which fell beside him. He had no choice but to retreat. He took the reins of his horse, which was panicking. Tugging at the reins, he ran to Egil and Lasgol.

"What the hell is going on? Is it an earthquake?"

"No, sir," Lasgol said. He pointed up to the summit of the range.

The whole pass seemed to be shaking. Suddenly there came a huge avalanche of rocks from their right. A strange creature appeared and gave a jarring shriek, while more boulders fell to the floor of the pass.

"What's that thing?" Nikessen asked, his eyes wide in disbelief.

"I've no idea, Egil" said, "but it's from the Frozen Continent. It has white crystal scales."

Suddenly, from the left, there came another great avalanche, and they saw a second creature. Both were colossal, and somehow they were managing to split the boulders at the top of the pass and overbalance them.

"They're sealing the far end of the pass," Nikessen muttered. "I don't understand…"

The tremors and the din went on, while the two creatures, amid jarring shrieks, shattered snow-covered rocks and tipped them into the pass.

Egil nodded. "I think I understand," he said as he struggled to maintain his balance.

"Explain yourself."

"They're sealing the pass so that the King's army can't go back through it."

"Why? It doesn't make sense. The enemy's right ahead, and we're going to destroy them. It doesn't matter if they seal the pass, all they'll manage to do is delay the celebration in Norghania."

"How long will it take the army to skirt the mountains to get back to Norghania if the pass is cut off?" Egil asked.

"I don't know, a march of six weeks or so. They'd have to go around the entire mountain range. But what does that matter? We'll have destroyed the enemy."

"Not if the enemy isn't there ahead of us," said Lasgol, who now understood what was going on.

"What do you mean, if it's not there ahead of us? I saw it with my own eyes."

"Yes, but I didn't."

"I don't understand."

"It's this blue fog. It's making us see the enemy ahead, but that's not really where they are. There's nobody there. It's a trap. A trap planned so that the royal army's caught and trapped on the far side of the pass."

Nikessen was shaking his head. "I don't believe it. There's no sense to it. I still don't understand it. I've seen the hosts of the Ice."

"Lasgol's right," said Egil. "It's a very elaborate, well-thought-out trap. They've made us believe the enemy army's right there in front of us, and now we've crossed and they've sealed the pass. The army can't come back this way."

"And why would they want to come back?" Nikessen asked.

Before Lasgol could answer, his eyes opened wide and his jaw dropped.

"They're going to attack the capital!"

"And the Royal Army won't be able to get there in time to prevent it," Egil said, passing judgment.

Chapter 35

The enormous mouth of one of the creatures of the ice tore off a ledge of rock, which added to the huge pile of boulders sealing the pass when it fell. The tremors were so strong that they could barely stay on their feet. The second creature on the opposite range shook half the mountain, and masses of broken rock fell into the pass.

Lasgol, open-mouthed, wondered how they could shatter rock like that to make it fall. They must have had some kind of unknown power.

"Those two creatures have magic from the Frozen Continent," Egil said. "These tremors aren't natural, and they're the ones who are causing the avalanches."

Lasgol nodded. "It's going to take months to re-open the pass."

As if they had heard, the two creatures vanished among the heights and the earthquake came to an end.

"We've got to warn the King!" Nikessen cried.

Lasgol and Egil exchanged worried looks. As far as they were concerned, warning the King was a very bad idea.

"On horseback! We've got to raise the alarm!"

Lasgol was thoughtful for a moment. So far they had been thinking that the King's armies would end the invasion by the forces of the Ice, and thus Darthor and the Western League would be destroyed. But his mother had thought out a magnificent plan. She had lured all the King's troops from the city and set a trap for them, one into which they had fallen headlong. Now Uthar's armies were trapped behind the Oriental Mountains and would be unable to defend the capital against a siege. And this was clearly what his mother had intended, the reason why she had behaved so strangely when they had met her on the coast. The entire landing, the array of barges, had all been a ruse. Her presence and that of Asrael, the Arcanes and the Wild: that too had all been part of the ruse.

Even the Rangers had been part of it; who would doubt the word of a group of Rangers who had witnessed the landing? Uthar had swallowed the bait, hook, line and sinker and confidently sent his troops. But everything had been an elaborate plan of Darthor's, and he had got his way.

"What are you waiting for, Lasgol?" Nikessen yelled at him. "Get on your horse!"

Lasgol came out of his reverie and mounted Trotter at a leap. He could not disobey a direct order.

"On we go! At a gallop! We've got to raise the alarm!"

Lasgol's stomach knotted again. He knew that if they warned Uthar they would be going against the plans of his mother and the Western League, who were presumably on their way to the capital at that moment to besiege it. But he decided not to act until he knew exactly what was going to happen.

They retraced their steps along the Pass, picking up the rest of the team as they went.

"Get mounted! Follow us!" Nikessen shouted, first to Viggo, then to Nilsa and Gerd and finally, at the entrance of the gorge, to Ingrid and Molak.

They all looked at him blankly, but a moment later they were following at a gallop. Without stopping, Nikessen looked back to check that they were following him, then spurred his horse.

Ingrid caught up with Lasgol and Egil, looking worried. "What's going on?" she asked.

"It was a trap. The troops crossed the pass, then Darthor sealed it and made half the mountain collapse at the far end of the gorge. It looks as though Darthor's hosts are going to attack the capital, and Uthar's army won't get there in time to defend it. They'll have to go the long way around the mountains."

Ingrid, her blonde mane blowing about her face, her hands on the reins of her Norghanian pony, stared ahead for a moment, puzzling over what this meant. She squinted against the wind, which was blowing full in their faces with the speed they were riding at.

"We're on our way to warn Uthar…"

"That's right," Lasgol replied, looking back at her with concern and doubt in his eyes.

Ingrid understood his look and nodded. "I see. I'll tell the others." And she held back so that she could do this.

Nikessen forced the horses to their limit for several days. They rode while there was daylight and rested during the night, more to avoid killing their horses than for their own sake. He would not allow them to make any fires, because the enemy was on Norghanian soil and might detect them. They rested in silence, in the darkness, and always deep within the woods where they could find a stream for drinking-water. Nikessen knew the east of Norghana like the back of his hand. And if he had any doubt, he would take out one of the precious *Green Cartographer* maps he carried with him.

"Tomorrow we'll reach Bergen, the capital of the Bergensen Duchy. We'll let Duke Ulrich know, and he'll send a pigeon to the King. That'll be the quickest way. What I'd give to have one of our hawks with us! Then the King would already know what's happened."

"He might know already," suggested Lasgol.

Nikessen shook his head. "I doubt it. The ambush has only just taken place, and we were the only witnesses. We've got to reach Bergen and warn the Duke."

"We could go to the Camp, and send hawks from there."

"Too far. We'll reach Bergen in three days if we don't meet any trouble. It's our best plan."

"Very well, sir..."

"Now let's stop and rest. I'll take the last watch with Molak. The others do your stint in pairs. Wake me up at the slightest suspicion. We're risking the kingdom. We can't afford to fail. We need to warn the King."

With the third watch there came a critical moment. It was Lasgol and Egil's turn. Ingrid and Nilsa had taken the first one, and Viggo and Gerd the second.

"We'd better talk," Lasgol said to Viggo and Gerd when they came to wake them up.

Viggo nodded and gave them his lethal stare. He knew what they were going to talk about.

They walked a little way from the camp. Viggo woke Ingrid and Nilsa carefully, and the six of them met together in the shade of a large oak. Lasgol looked back to make sure Nikessen and Molak were both asleep.

"We have to decide what we're going to do," he said.

"We can't let Nikessen warn the King," Egil said.

"It would jeopardize Darthor and the Western League's plan." Lasgol added.

There was a silence. Ingrid looked at Nilsa and Gerd, whose faces showed concern and hesitation.

"The moment has come to decide which side we're on," Ingrid said at last.

"We don't know whether we're going to have to stop the Royal Ranger," Gerd said. "Perhaps his warning won't lead to much. Darthor will have already taken that into account."

Egil nodded. "It's possible, but the later Uthar finds out, the better for the West and the Peoples of the Frozen Continent. Now that they have a chance to defeat Uthar, we need to make sure it's not wasted. In circumstances like this a single day might mean the difference between the failure and the success of an entire campaign."

"What do you suggest?" Ingrid asked.

"Stop Nikessen," Egil said.

"That'd be treachery," Nilsa said. "We'd be hanged."

"Not if the West wins," Egil said.

"If you want me to deal with the map guy, just let me know," Viggo said. He passed his thumb across his throat from left to right.

Lasgol shook his head. "We're not going to go that far."

"We're not going to do anything to Molak," Ingrid said. She gave Viggo a warning glare.

He made an apologetic gesture. "We'll have to do something if you don't want him to make his report."

"You're not going to lay a finger on him, or I'll split you in two,"

"Hang on," Lasgol interrupted, "there's no reason to go that far."

"We just have to stop them giving the warning, that's all."

"So what do you suggest?" Ingrid asked.

Lasgol and Egil told them their plan in muffled whispers.

"That's not going to work, and we'll end up hanged," Nilsa said.

Gerd was rubbing his hands together nervously. "I don't like it either."

"All right then, we'll do as you say," Ingrid said. "But very carefully."

"My plan's much better," Viggo said. "We can take care of them right now while they're asleep. They wouldn't even know."

"No way!" Ingrid spat at him with fire in her eyes.

"We don't act that way," Lasgol told him.

Viggo gave him a sarcastic smile. "We're traitors who don't get their hands dirty?"

"Not if we can help it."

"You won't be able to avoid it much longer. Sooner or later you'll have blood on your hands. We all will. This is a war, in case you've forgotten."

"I haven't forgotten, and I know the danger we're all running."

"I'm just reminding you."

"I hate to say he's right," Nilsa said, "but in this case he is. We've already committed treason by saying nothing of our meeting with Darthor, and now we're doing it again. The noose is waiting for us..."

"Not if we do things right and stick to the plan," Egil said.

"Is that a promise?" Gerd asked apprehensively.

"I promise, big guy. We'll come out of this mess alive."

Gerd nodded to his friend.

"Do we agree, then?"

They all nodded slowly.

"Right then, on with the plan," Lasgol said.

The birds of the forest began singing with the first light of dawn. Nikessen was the first to rise. He went over to where Lasgol and Egil were on watch duty.

"Everything all right?" he asked.

"Everything in order," Egil replied.

"Let's have something to eat to fortify ourselves, then we'll set off. Ingrid, Nilsa, get the horses ready. Give them the grain in the saddlebags. They'll have to run as if they were being chased by hungry wolves. Viggo, Molak, go to the stream and fill the water-skins. Then we'll hand out the rations."

Lasgol and Egil sat down under the oak and watched in silence.

Viggo and Molak came back with the water and food, and these were duly handed out.

"We still have enough for a week."

"For a week?" Nikessen said, taken aback. "There ought to be enough for two."

"The food went bad in one of the saddlebags. It's rotten."

"It doesn't matter. We'll be in Bergen in three days and we'll pick up fresh supplies there."

"What do we do once we're there?"

"Report, then wait for orders from either the King or Dolbarar."

"Understood, sir." Molak said.

With their strength restored, humans and horses set off. Nikessen set a tremendous pace, so that the ponies could barely keep up with him. They rode all day and well into the night, then rested and set off again. At noon on the second day Nikessen called a halt, and as soon as they stopped the Royal Ranger vomited from his horse. A moment later Molak did the same.

"By the icy north winds," Nikessen muttered, "what's the matter with me?"

"I don't... I feel..." Ingrid began, then vomited as well.

Viggo touched his forehead. "I think I've got a fever."

"By the snow hyenas!" Nikessen cried. "Is anybody else sick?"

Nilsa and Gerd raised their hands.

"Frozen hell! It doesn't matter, we go on! In a day and half we'll be in Bergen!"

They went on, but by nightfall Nikessen and Molak were running a high fever and were left lying incapacitated by a fire they had been obliged to make in order to boil the water.

"It has to be the water," Nikessen had told them. "Don't drink it."

Ingrid was looking after Molak. She was worried; he had a high fever. Nilsa and Gerd lay downside by side and held each other's hands, trying not to shiver.

"I'll prepare a potion to deal with the fever," Egil said.

"Good... idea... we've got to reach... warn the King..." Nikessen said, and a moment later lost consciousness.

Ingrid went over to Egil and Lasgol. "Haven't you overdone the dosage?" she whispered. "Molak's unconscious, and Nikessen looks about to die at any moment. They're turning purple."

Egil shook his head. "It's the right dose for the effects we need. I pay very close attention to Eyra's teachings. Don't worry."

"Tell me nothing's going to happen to Molak,"

"I promise."

"How long will it last?"

"They won't be able to get up for three days. In five they'll be able to ride."

"Are you absolutely sure their lives aren't in danger?"

He indicated the Ranger's Belt he wore, with all the compounds in its compartments. "I know this poison very well. I've studied it thoroughly. Don't worry."

Ingrid looked at the belt, and then into his eyes. "I just hope you haven't made any mistakes with the measures."

"I don't make that kind of mistake. They're not going to die."

Ingrid looked at Lasgol. He too was seriously worried. The plan was a risky one.

"The book-head doesn't make mistakes with this sort of thing, and you know it," Viggo said to her. He looked terrible, and there were purple circles under his eyes.

Ingrid nodded.

"Remind me to make you pay for all this when the war's over," Viggo said to Egil threateningly.

"I will, and one day we'll laugh about it all."

"It won't be tonight," Viggo said, and threw up.

"No, that it certainly won't."

When dawn came, Nikessen realized the gravity of the situation. He tried to reach his horse, but could not make it. He fell to the ground and lay there shivering.

"Who... can... ride...?"

"We can, sir," said Egil and Lasgol.

"You're not sick?"

"Not as badly as the others. Only diarrhea and throwing up now and then, but the fever doesn't seem to have hit us."

"Or it's... about to..."

"It could be, yes, sir," Egil said.

"You must get to Bergen... warn the King..."

"Yes, sir."

"Set off... now..."

They mounted and gave their friends a final glance of farewell. They were all lying beside the fire looking terrible. Gerd's eyes were tearful with fever. Nilsa waved at them. Ingrid, who was looking after Molak, nodded to them. Viggo waved them off with his fist raised.

The two of them set off at a gallop.

Chapter 36

Lasgol and Egil rode like lightning in a winter storm until they reached a crossroads where a wooden sign pointed in the direction of Bergen. In the distance was a long caravan of people heading for the city. These were refugees, seeking shelter in the great city in case of what might happen.

"The rumors of war are already circulating here," Egil said.

"Looks like it. If they knew that their army's fallen into a trap…"

"Even so, they'd seek refuge in the great city. Farms and villages aren't the places to stay when an invading army's come into the realm."

"You're right. I hope nothing happens to them."

"Unfortunately," Egil said sadly, "in wars it's innocent people who suffer, not so much the powerful and corrupt."

"Uthar will get his punishment."

"Let's hope so."

Suddenly Camu put his head out of the saddlebag and gave a little shriek. When Lasgol looked at him, the little creature sent him a message: *Play. Jump.*

"All right, you can come out, but only for a moment."

Camu shrieked with joy and jumped happily into the grass. He began to scamper among the flowers and tall grass.

Lasgol shook his head.

"It's logical that he should want to stretch his legs," Egil said with a smile. "Look at him, so happy chasing butterflies."

"He's the happiest of all, that's for sure."

"It's the advantage of being a magical creature."

Lasgol turned round on Trotter and looked back. "Do you think Nikessen suspects foul play?"

"I doubt it very much. It was a good plan, and it worked out well."

"Thanks to our teammates."

"I wasn't sure they'd be willing to go along with it."

"Because of the treachery?"

Egil shrugged. "That, and having to take poison."

"They didn't like that at all."

"And yet they did it. It says a lot about them."

"About how committed they are."

"And about what good friends they are. They put their lives in our hands. They might all have died."

"You know, you're very good with potions."

"Even so…"

"Yes, you're right. I have to admit I was afraid for them."

"Don't you ever tell them, but so was I."

Lasgol rolled his eyes. "I'll never tell them that. What do you think Nikessen will think has happened to us when he realizes we never reached Bergen?"

"The worst. That we've died, or that the enemy's captured us."

"Are you sure?"

"Yes," Egil said. He dismounted, took out his Ranger knife and trod the ground firmly in front of the road sign. He made a cut in his hand, took his Ranger's glove and staunched the blood with it, then dropped it beside the sign.

Lasgol gave him a bow. "You're intelligence personified." He got off Trotter, patted him and took several firm steps to leave good tracks. Then he took his gloves off, and as Egil had done, cut the palm of his hand. He rubbed the gloves on his bloody hand and threw them to one side of the ditch.

"He'll think we didn't get there because we were prevented by force. He won't suspect. He's got no reason to, and we'll have gained critical time."

"You have a privileged mind."

"Not so much, but at least it's more useful than my little body." He gave a resigned smile.

"That little body of yours is wiry and tough. Ranger training's been very good for you."

"Yeah, it's turned me into a man, that I have to admit."

"I'd better call Camu so we can go on."

Lasgol had some trouble trying to persuade Camu to jump back into the saddlebag, but he finally convinced him. They went on along the Royal Way, which led to Norghania. By using the great road – which the King kept in perfect condition, since it was the way he and his men travelled the kingdom – they went much faster than they would have through forests and mountains. The Royal Way took the shortest route through both.

They met soldiers and refugees on their way, but nobody stopped them because they were dressed as Rangers. Fortunately they did not come across the hosts of the Frozen Continent.

They rode without pausing to rest, careful that their ponies did not suffer too much. Finally, on the outskirts of the capital, they emerged from a huge beech-wood, and what they saw left them open-mouthed.

Norghania was under siege!

They stopped on a small hill, and from here they could see the whole plain which spread in front of the capital of the kingdom of Norghana.

The forces of the Western League had taken up their positions south of the city. Thousands of men and blue and black tents formed a huge, compact square. Lasgol used his *Hawk Eye* skill and made out groups of men being commanded by different leaders. In the center he saw the Olafstones, with the largest group of men and tents, practicing group combat. On their left were the forces of Duke Erikson, very busy with supplies. On the right, those of Duke Svensen were readying their weapons. Count Malason and his people were looking after the horses which had just arrived at the camp. Further to the right were the forces of Counts Bjorn and Axel, who were assembling ladders and hooked ropes. The forces of Count Harald and several lesser lords had taken up position to the left of the camp and were getting bows and arrows ready for the siege.

To the north, behind the city, he could make out Darthor's forces. There were almost as many of them as the forces of the Western League. They were too far away to see clearly, even with his Gift, but he could make out the Arcanes in the center. Darthor would be with them, as would Asrael and Azur. To their right were the Wild of the Ice unmistakable for their size, and more so their leaders, the semi-giants. To the left were the Tundra Dwellers, and behind them Snow Trolls and other creatures of the Frozen Continent. Lasgol would have liked to have been closer to see them better, but even from here, from a distance, the hosts of the Frozen Continent were terrifying.

He pointed. "Look! Through the Eastern Gate!"

Egil half-closed his eyes and saw a long column of soldiers in red and white, the King's colors, entering the city.

The war horns were sounding from the city battlements.

"Those are Uthar's last reinforcements. I think we've arrived at the very beginning of hostilities."

"Yeah, it looks that way. The hosts of the Frozen Continent are still taking up their places."

"And the Western league too. I can see movement in their ranks."

"What shall we do?" Lasgol asked.

"For the moment, watch and study the situation."

"We can't get closer dressed in Rangers' clothes," Lasgol said. "Both sides would attack us the moment they saw us."

"You're absolutely right. And they'll have patrols watching the area around."

"I can see several farms to the west. Let's see if we can find some clothes to help us pass unnoticed."

"Good idea."

The farms proved to be deserted. Their occupants had fled to the city, like everyone else in the area, when they saw the enemy arriving. In the first two they found nothing they could use, but in the next three they found clothes. They changed their pants and cloaks, but kept their Ranger weapons and belts, which they would need.

"How do I look?" Lasgol asked.

"Not bad. You look like an armed peasant. What about me?"

"You look like a skulking poacher."

Egil smiled. "That's fantastic."

They went back to the road and climbed another hill to get a better view of the city and the besieging forces.

"Look," Lasgol said, "they've already completely surrounded the city."

"The hosts of the Frozen Continent have got control of the north and east, while the Western League have the south and west. Nobody will be able to go in or out of the city."

"And more important, Uthar's been caught unawares."

"Yeah, I agree."

"Let's hope our friends are all right."

"They will be."

The conviction in Egil's voice reassured Lasgol. Suddenly several armed riders appeared on their right. Lasgol and Egil exchanged a quick look and reached for their bows. The patrol consisted of a dozen men in light armor, on horseback. They were dressed in black and blue, the colors of the West.

"Who goes there?" asked the one who seemed to be in command.

"A couple of hunters," Egil said.

The soldiers surrounded them. They were armed with axes and round shields, and a couple of them were carrying spears. The leading rider looked them up and down.

"Hunters?" He waved an arm at their bows. "Smells to me as though you know how to fight..."

Lasgol became aware that the soldier was no fool, and that their clothing would not work as a disguise.

"It looks as if the war has reached the capital," Egil said.

"And what's that to you?"

"Nothing. I guess you're men of the West. You're not wearing the King's colors. I can't see much red and white among you."

"And which side are you on, then? East or West?"

Lasgol noticed the men stiffen when their leader asked the question. One mistake and they could be in trouble; these men were very restless.

"West, of course."

"Oh yes? What are your names? Where are you from? What are you doing here?"

Egil hesitated for a moment, but then seemed to recognize something about the horses' saddles.

"I'm Egil of the Olafstone Duchy. My friend's name is Lasgol, and he's from Malason County."

"Oh yes? From the deep West... so what are you doing here in the heart of the east?"

"We've come to help. We want to join the troops of the West."

Lasgol swallowed. If he was wrong and these were men of the East, they were going to die. They were surrounded. These could be King's men posing as Western Soldiers. In war, all is fair.

The leader of the patrol studied them again carefully.

"My name's Eilarson. I'm not sure whether to believe you're who you say you are."

"If we were from the east, we'd already be behind the walls of the city."

"The King has left patrols in the outskirts. Spies, too."

"We're not spies."

"Perhaps. But for the moment I can't say you're not. Lower your weapons and come with us."

"Where to?"

The leader of the patrol turned toward the city. "To join the forces of the West, as you wanted," he said with a suspicious smile. "If you're from the East, or spies, you'll be hanging from a tree by nightfall."

Egil looked at Lasgol and gave a slight nod.

"Very well. We'll go with you."

At that moment another patrol appeared on their left with about twenty men. Lasgol swallowed. Now they really would be helpless if things went wrong.

"Everything all right, Eilarson?" asked the leader of the second patrol.

"All clear. We've only found these two in the area. We're taking them to the camp."

"Fine. I'll check the Royal Way as far as the next village."

"See you later."

When they set off, Eilarson made them ride in the rear, as if daring them to escape. Four men did not take their eyes off them. Lasgol and Egil followed the patrol without complaint.

At the Western League siege camp, more than fifteen hundred blue and black tents had been set up, a thousand paces or so from the city walls: close enough for Uthar and his people to see them perfectly, but out of reach of his archers.

The camp was immense, occupying a huge plain in front of the city with the forest protecting their backs. Thousands of men and women in blue and black, in clear contrast to the red and white of the Crown and Uthar's armies, were working non-stop at a multitude of war-related tasks. No-one was idle or resting. They looked like bees flying from one side to the other, making a beehive for their queen. Each bore a coat of arms on his chest, marking the duchy or county they belonged to. Lasgol recognized Count Malason's coat of arms on a group of men who carried spears: his own shield, his own county.

Near the trees the officers were training the militia, peasants, fishermen and shepherds who had been forcefully recruited. They were being taught how to use the axe and spear, these being the easiest weapons. The Norghanians, big and brutish, were perfectly able to wield an axe and many were accustomed to using it to cut timber and fences. Now they were being taught to use it to kill a man. A strong downward swing at the level of the neck or shoulder was enough. On the other hand, the spear was a safer weapon. If anybody came close, a strong, direct thrust was enough to impale an enemy. They were being trained to cleave them in a tree with a two-handed blow. Soon, instead of trees, they would have to cleave them in men.

"Those are Duke Eriksson's men," Egil said.

"That's right," Eilarson said in surprise. "How did you know?"

"Because I know the Duke."

"Now I can see you're not from the east. I think you're a spy. You'll hang today."

"And what would your lord, Count Harald, say?"

The leader's face was suddenly serious. "How do you know who my lord is? Answer, you spy!"

"From the coat of arms engraved on your horses' saddles. I know it."

"Now there's no doubt you're a spy." He unsheathed his sword.

"No, I'm not. But I am Egil Olafstone, the youngest son of Vikar Olafstone and younger brother of Austin and Arnold Olafstone."

"I'll run you through for that lie! You're not an Olafstone!"

Eilarson was about to run him through when a deep voice shouted: "Stop, you fool!"

The sword did not move. Eilarson looked to see who had shouted at him.

"My lord, Duke Eriksson."

"Lower your weapon. This is Egil Olafstone. If you touch a single hair on his head, you'll hang by the balls."

Eilarson stared at Egil with eyes wide as saucers. "I'm sorry, sir... I didn't know..."

The Duke went over to Egil and helped him dismount. "What a pleasure it is to see you, Egil. Your brothers will be delighted."

"I'm looking forward to seeing them too."

"Have you come alone?"

Lasgol dismounted. "I'm with him."

Duke Eriksson recognized him at once.

"Lasgol. Of course. I'm glad to see you too." He offered him his hand, and Lasgol shook it.

"We seem to have arrived at the right moment," Egil said.

"I'd say you have. We have that rat Uthar walled up in his city.

The attack is imminent."

"In that case, I'd like to see my brothers."

"Of course. I'll go with you to the command tent."

"Wouldn't it have been easier to tell Eilarson who you are?" Lasgol whispered in Egil's ear.

Egil smiled. "He'd never have believed me, and we were running the risk of being executed as spies. In times of war, suspicion runs high."

Lasgol nodded. He understood. He looked at the city in the background with its high walls and turrets and knew that it was not going to be easy to take. A lot of blood was likely to be shed.

Chapter 37

Duke Erikson led them through the troops of the Western League. He was middle-aged, with golden hair and deep blue eyes. He was slim and handsome, soft-featured, almost feminine: something very unusual among Norghanian men, who tended to be strong, with distinctly manly features. But his poise and powerful voice left no doubt as to his status; the soldiers made way for him at once when they recognized him.

The movement of men, supplies, weapons, horses and all manner of needs for the siege was incessant. Lasgol, watching it all as they made their way through, felt dizzy.

Stay still and don't show yourself for anything in the world, we're in the middle of thousands of soldiers, he told Camu. The little creature was on his back, clinging on to him with hands and feet. Lasgol was unable to explain how the little one managed to adhere to anything, from stone walls to people, but once he did, nothing would loosen him. As Egil was in the habit of saying, it was fascinating.

Several groups of soldiers carrying arrows and spears passed them. They were going to need a lot of both for the coming battle. A little further on a large group of soldiers were preparing ladders of wood and rope for climbing those huge walls. It was not going to be an easy feat: far from it.

Lasgol could feel Camu's weight on his back. It did not bother him much, but his little friend was growing large enough to mean that soon he would not be able to carry him like that... He put the thought out of his mind; he would face it when the moment came. But it would be a very sad moment. Camu was like a little brother for him.

"Make way!" the Duke ordered, and the soldiers moved aside to let them through.

There were both young soldiers and veterans among the Western forces. The veterans belonged to the armies of the Dukes and Counts, while the young ones had been enlisted in cities, villages and farms of the West, and they could not refuse under penalty of death. Such were wars, and nobody could escape them. Lasgol could see the fear in the eyes of those young people, who were mostly peasants, fishermen and farmers; they did not know how to fight or wield a weapon, but they would have to do so and pray to the Gods of the Ice that they came out of the conflict alive. In moments like these he felt that the Gods had squandered the Gift on him. It was a divine blessing, certainly, but why had it been granted to him and not someone with a more important destiny? Austin, for instance, Egil's older brother: he was destined to rule if they won, he could use the Gift which Lasgol himself did not really need. But as Ulf had often said: *May my beard freeze if I understand the designs of the Five Gods!*

He would have given anything to prevent the bloodshed and numberless deaths that were about to ensue. But however much he might want to, the matter was not in his hands, or even in those of the Gods. These did not normally interfere overmuch in the affairs of men, nor did they seem to care much about their suffering. They must have other priorities, and Lasgol wondered what these might be.

He sighed. He could not prevent the battle. Even if he were to kill Uthar, or expose him, it was inevitable. If he did, Uthar's cousins Duke Thoran and his brother Orten would assume power in the East, and according to hearsay, they were as brutal and degenerate as the worst of the Norghanians; the future of Norghana would fall into bad hands if the crown stayed in the East. Fortunately there was still hope. If the West won, they would unmask Uthar and Austin would become King. From what Lasgol had seen of Egil's older brother, and from what Egil himself had told him, the kingdom would be in good hands. Lasgol wished with all his heart that the West would come out victorious and with the least possible amount of bloodshed.

They came to a huge tent with shields embroidered along the sides. These were those of the Duchies and Counties of the West who supported the Western League. The command tent was surrounded by more than a hundred men, armed to the teeth.

"Announce Duke Erikson, with two guests!" the Duke told the Captain of the Guard, who nodded in recognition and respect and went into the tent.

Egil was eagerly watching everything that was going on in the war camp, trying to learn as much as he could, as he always did in any new and interesting situation.

The Captain came out after a moment and the dozen men posted in front of the entrance held the flap open to let the Duke in. Inside the tent, around an oak table, several nobles were arguing, bent over maps and plans held down by candelabras, silver goblets and daggers. Lasgol recognized Austin and Arnold, Egil's brothers, who were at the head of the table. Beside them were Duke Svensen, the true image of a Norghanian: tall, blond, strong and broad-shouldered, with the face of a woodcutter, and Count Malason, whom Lasgol of course already knew. With them were Counts Bjorn, Axel, Harald and several minor lords: all the nobles of the West who had sworn fealty to the Western League.

"Look what the northern winds have brought!" Erikson announced.

"Egil!" cried Austin in surprise. "What are you doing here?"

They embraced. "Little brother!" Arnold said.

"I've never been at the siege of a capital," Egil said, "so I decided to come and study how it's done."

Austin laughed and hugged his little brother again.

"I'm so glad to see you safe and sound. I feared the worst for you. It made me very uneasy, knowing you were among Uthar's Rangers."

"This kid knows how to handle himself," Arnold said as he wrapped him in a loving bear-hug.

"So far I've managed to cope."

"Well, now you're safe with us," Austin told him.

Egil nodded.

"Hello there, Lasgol," Austin said. "I see you're still inseparable."

Lasgol smiled broadly. "To survive, you sometimes have to join forces with brilliant minds."

Arnold laughed. "Indeed. Well said!"

Count Malason greeted Lasgol with a nod.

"My Lord Count," he replied respectfully.

"We bring news from the East," Egil said when the other noblemen had greeted them. And he told them what had happened at the Pass and whatever information he thought would be relevant for his brother.

When he finished there was a silence. The Western Nobles were thoughtful.

"That's very encouraging news," Austin said.

"Yes, we didn't know whether Darthor's plan would succeed."

"Well, it did," Egil said. "Uthar's army is trapped on the other side of the Oriental Mountains."

"That gives us at least two weeks, maybe even more," Arnold said excitedly.

"We should seize the advantage," Erikson said.

"We must speed up the preparations," said Svensen.

The other nobles began to talk and make plans all at once. Austin raised his hands for quiet.

"We mustn't be hasty. It's true that my little brother brings us good news. Darthor's plan was a risky one, and the idea that Uthar would fall into it even riskier. But it looks as though he's succeeded. This gives us a substantial advantage for a couple of weeks, until Uthar's army returns. Even so, we mustn't launch ourselves into the attack like madmen. This city is practically impregnable, and Uthar has the Invincibles of the Ice with him."

"They won't be able to do anything against all of us," said Svensen.

"Not with the help of the hosts of the Frozen Continent," said Erikson.

The nobles all began to suggest strategies at the same time. They could barely hear one another, and Austin once again asked for calm.

"Brother, the information you bring is well worth a war. I'm deeply grateful to you." He patted Egil on the back. Lasgol could see in his friend's eyes what the gesture meant to him, and was overjoyed to see him basking in his elder brother's recognition in front of all the other Western nobles.

"Let's plan our strategy," said Arnold.

They all gathered around the table and went on arguing until nightfall. Both boys sat on one side and listened. Luckily they were brought something to eat and drink, and they cat-napped a little. Then, when the strategy had finally been worked out, everyone retired to rest. One by one the nobles left the command tent until only the Olafstones and Lasgol were left.

"We'll put you up in our tent," Austin said to Egil.

"It'll be like when we were little," Arnold added, "except that we're in the middle of a war and the whole of the East wants us dead."

"You're an Olafstone by blood and merit," Austin said.

"You have to tell us everything you've done this year with the Rangers, and everything you've learned," Arnold added.

"With pleasure," Egil said, and Lasgol could tell how pleased he was.

"Lasgol, you'll sleep with my Captain of the Guard. From what I hear he doesn't snore much, and he's in the next tent to ours. Anything you need, just ask."

Lasgol thought of asking for permission to go and see Darthor, his mother, but he rejected the idea at once. It would be distinctly odd, and rather suspicious, for him, a Western Norghanian and a Ranger, to go and see Darthor, crossing the whole war camp of the hosts of the Frozen Continent to reach his destination. In fact he would not even be allowed to set foot there, knowing the nature of the Wild Ones of the Ice. He would have to wait to see his mother, even though he longed to speak to her more than anything in the world. Surely Mayra would have a plan to ensure victory. He wanted to enjoy life without wars, and most of all to enjoy his mother's company and her love. It was something he missed deeply and had always missed.

Lasgol smiled in gratitude. "I'll be fine."

"We'll give you more appropriate clothes," Austin said, seeing what they were wearing.

"And weapons," Arnold added.

"No," said Egil. "The weapons are the ones we've learnt to use. We need them."

"But you're a noble," Austin protested, "from the most important family in the West, heir to the Crown. You must carry a sword at your waist."

"It wouldn't be any use. I don't know how to use it."

Arnold nodded. "He's right. It would be better if he were to use the Ranger weapons in case of need."

"Very well then, so be it. But I don't want you coming near the fighting under any circumstances, Egil."

"I won't, brother."

Lasgol noticed a particular quality in his friend's voice. It had not been a firm promise.

"Good," Austin said. "We'll send out the orders for the night and then have supper in my tent."

Lasgol thought it was better to let Egil and his brothers discuss their affairs, and gently refused their invitation to dine with them. They had a lot to talk about, and he felt he would be a nuisance. He went to the Guard Captain's tent, had dinner by himself and went to bed early. As it turned out the Captain did not snore heavily, but even so, he was unable to get much sleep. There were all manner of noises in the camp, since the preparations for battle did not cease at night. But worse than this was the singing of the Norghanian soldiers around the campfires. They sang of victory and glory, at the top of their voices, with throats moistened by beer as tradition demanded, but their singing was loud and out of tune. This did not surprise him, as Norghanians were bad at singing as well as brutish, but even so they loved to sing, in particular when they were drinking or when the situation, as now, was very tense.

He thought about Ulf, and how much the old man would have enjoyed taking part in this war. Days of glory, as he called them. Unfortunately Lasgol knew they were also days of death, destruction and horror. Perhaps one day his people would leave behind their bad habits, but to do that they needed a just and wise leader. Without someone wise and principled ruling over Norghana, its people would never change their nature. They would go on being brutes and bullies until the snow-covered mountains were bare.

To cheer himself up, he thought about his mother. He would see her soon. And with that pleasant thought in the midst of all the chanting about glory, plunder and death, he fell asleep at last.

He woke up to the summons of the horns. The sun was not yet up. The troops got down to their chores at once, while the officers shouted orders at them. The numbers of men and women left him breathless. There were several thousand, organized in different sectors. Archers and lancers were the minority, infantry with axes and shields the overwhelming majority. This did not surprise him; Norghanians were said to be born with an axe in their hands. He could not see any mounted units; they must be watching the rearguard and the flanks.

A large number of men were on their way to a forest alongside the camp, all carrying axes, and as he watched them begin to fell trees, he wondered what this was for.

"They're for constructing siege weapons," Egil said. He had appeared by Lasgol's side, dressed like a Western Noble.

"They're going to construct siege weapons?"

"That's part of the plan. They'll be ready in a week, and we'll attack the walls day and night until we breach them."

"Do you think that's possible? They seem invincible from here."

"They're a hundred and twenty feet tall and thirty wide. It'll be quite a job, but it can be done. That's not the problem."

"So what is?"

"That it really is a formidable wall, and it's going to take a long time even to make a dent in it. Time which we don't have, because in two or three weeks Uthar's army will be here, and it'll attack us from behind. But then, let's let the people who understand all about besieged cities, assault weapons and military strategy deal with it."

"I'm sure you know all about all that."

Egil shrugged and smiled. "A little."

"I knew it!"

Egil smiled broadly. "Put on those clothes and armor. Now you're a Norghanian noble of the West."

Lasgol chuckled.

"And hurry up. We have to be at a very important meeting. My brothers are going to join Darthor and his people. They've invited us to form part of their retinue."

Lasgol felt his heart beating like a drum.

"Right away!"

Chapter 38

The party was made up of Austin, Arnold, Erikson, Svensen, and Malason, together with Egil and Lasgol. The meeting would take place on the eastern side, half-way between north and south, where both armies touched each other. From what Egil had told him, suspicion and tensions between the Western League and the Peoples of the Frozen Continent were still critical, even more so now that they were about to get what they both wanted so badly.

"My brothers say Darthor's having trouble making sure the leaders of the Peoples of the Frozen Continent honor the sworn treaty they agreed."

"But they swore on the white monolith. They can't back down now."

"It's not a problem of wanting to back down, quite the opposite," Egil said. He sounded worried.

"I don't understand."

"They see victory in their grasp, and they don't want to wait for anyone or follow any strategy. They want to hurl themselves straight at the city and destroy it."

"And they're not listening to reason?"

"It seems not. And my brothers are afraid of something else..."

Lasgol suspected that this would be something bad. "What?"

"That they won't be satisfied with victory, and they'll demand more."

"More?"

"All of Norghana for themselves."

"Oh, no..."

Egil nodded.

They arrived at the meeting and saw that the tent had been put up half-way between the two armies. The walled city watched them in silence more than a thousand paces away, although on its battlements and in its turrets King Uthar's soldiers were awaiting the inevitable attack.

The tent was bare except for its occupants, with neither table nor chairs. Lasgol recognized his mother as Darthor, in the middle. When she saw him come in her helmet turned in his direction, but she neither moved a muscle nor uttered a word. He had not expected a greeting in the presence of all the allies. On Darthor's right was Azur, Shaman of the Ice, leader of the Glaciers Arcanes. Beside him was Asrael, who nodded at him and smiled. On Darthor's left was Jurn, leader of the Wild of the Ice, and beside him Sarn, leader of the Tundra Dwellers. A little further back was the Arcane with violet eyes, Asuris, who might have been Darthor's shadow.

Austin went to stand in front of Darthor, Arnold in front of Azur and the other nobles in front of the leaders of the Peoples of the Frozen Continent. Lasgol and Egil kept to the back. Nobody spoke for a moment, and the tension was so great that it could be felt on the skin as though they were in the cutting winds of a winter storm. The contrast between the Norghanian nobles – being from the West, they were less ostentatious than their Eastern brothers – and the peoples of the Frozen Continent was profound. The Norghanians wore armor, cloaks and weapons of excellent quality, even wearing jewels here and there on their white-skinned bodies or their golden hair and beards. The Wild were far more primitive, wearing animal furs over their eerie blue-skinned bodies and frozen hair, and carrying basic weapons and animal bones as ornaments.

"Austin, Leaders of the West," Darthor greeted them, his voice deep and distorted by the helmet. He gave a slight bow. Austin returned the greeting.

Although both leaders seemed ready to negotiate, the faces of the others showed nothing of the sort. On either side. Lasgol shivered.

"We find ourselves at a critical moment," Darthor said. "We have Uthar surrounded and with no escape-route, hiding behind the walls of his great capital. We need to put an end to him now, once and for all."

"In this we completely agree," said Austin. "We've been informed that your plan worked in the East." He nodded towards Egil and Lasgol.

"Yes, I've just learned this. Uthar's forces will take two or three weeks to arrive. We need to make use of our advantage and destroy him once and for all."

"We've worked out a strategy," Austin said.

"Go ahead, I'm listening."

"We're going to build siege machines and catapults, then attack the walls with them. If we focus the attack on a single point, we'll be able to make a breach and enter the capital."

"That will take too long," Jurn growled.

Sarn shook his head. "If it works at all."

"It's a viable plan," Azur said, sounding unconvinced, "but even though it may work, it'll take too long to build the weapons and cause any damage to the wall."

"It's the safest way to take the capital," Arnold said, supporting his brother.

"Safe?" Jurn repeated. "We're not here to be safe. We'll storm the walls with a mass attack, then lay waste to the city."

"We'll kill them all," Sarn said. "Our spears will pierce them no matter where they may be hiding in the rubble. They won't be able to prevent the fury of the ice."

"That option would cost too many lives," said Austin. "Uthar has the Invincibles of the Ice and all the militia he may have managed to recruit. They won't let us take the walls in a frontal attack, that I can assure you. And nobody's going to lay waste to the city. There are thousands of innocent people sheltering there. They're not to suffer at our hands."

"Speak for yourself, Norghanian," Jurn said. "You do not speak for us."

"If you want to assault the walls, you can, but you'll pay dearly for it. They were built to withstand the attacks of powerful armies."

"They'll be powerless against the tide of ice," Sarn fired back. "We'll take the walls and the city."

"Don't count on us for an unprepared assault on the walls," Erikson said.

"Could it be that the Norghanians are afraid?" Jurn asked disdainfully. The semi-giant was so enormous and muscular that the Norghanian nobles beside him looked like children.

"We're not afraid," Svensen said. "But neither are we stupid."

"Who are you insulting, Norghanian?"

"You, you dirty brainless savage!"

Jurn beat his chest with both fists. "You've always been a cowardly race, and you still are!"

"There are no cowards here," Erikson said, pointing at Jurn and Sarn, "but there are certainly a bunch of idiots who're going to lead us all to our deaths!"

The discussion began to degenerate. Insults began to fly, along with threats and gestures from both sides. Distrust and hate were now so strong that it was impossible to have the slightest discussion without it turning into a heated argument. Jurn came to stand in front of Svensen, like a huge tower beside a boy. He glowered at him with his one eye.

"And what are you going to do, little Norghanian?"

Svensen reached for his sword. "I'm going to cut your balls off, since I can't reach any higher than that, but I think it'll be enough to teach you a lesson, you brainless mountain of muscle!"

"Try it and I'll crush your skull!"

Sarn meanwhile was arguing with Erikson, and although it did not look as if they would come to blows, it was a very close thing.

"Silence, all of you!" Darthor boomed in his cavernous voice. He spread his arms wide to separate both sides.

The arguments stopped, and they all turned to the Corrupt Mage of the Ice.

"We're listening," Austin said.

"There'll be no bloodshed between us. We all took a sacred oath, and you're bound by it." He pointed to each leader on both sides, one by one. "The Western League and the Peoples of the Frozen Continent will respect one another. That's not a request, it's an order. If there's anybody here today who doesn't agree, he can either leave with his people or fight me. I won't accept that we've come as far as this only to fail because of hatred, distrust and greed. We're one step away from victory, from a new beginning, a new world. I'm not prepared to allow anybody to ruin that. Many good people have died so that we could be here today, with Uthar only a step away from our hands. I'm going to see him dead at my feet, and nobody's going to deny me that. None of you! Not one!"

He spoke with such anger, strength and determination that a deathly silence fell on them.

Darthor came forward to the middle of the tent and spread his arms wide. He murmured something under his helmet, and from his body there began to emanate a heavy fog that fell to the ground. Everyone moved away from him. The fog fell from his head, his shoulders and his arms, as if something in his body were producing it, and surrounded him to form a circle two paces wide. He turned slowly, with his arms outspread.

"Does anybody want to confront me?"

Lasgol could not even breathe. He looked at Azur, thinking that if anybody could go against his mother or betray her, he was the one. Or perhaps Jurn. He did not like any of them, particularly Azur. He could see in his eyes that the old Shaman was dangerous.

Neither of them moved. They stared back at Darthor without a word, keeping their intention hidden.

"This is the time to step forward. If anybody wants to dispute my leadership, now is the moment."

Lasgol glanced aside at Austin. Would the King of the West allow Darthor to take command at that decisive moment? Would he fight Darthor for power? He glanced at Egil, whose expression was somber. His friend was equally worried, perhaps even more so. His two brothers were there with him, and they were risking everything. Would they allow Darthor to take command now?

There was a long silence.

"Do any of the leaders of the Peoples of the Ice wish to defy me?"

Lasgol bit his lip hard. He could not help fearing the worst.

Darthor waited a moment, but nobody said anything to challenge him.

"Do any of the leaders of the Western League wish to defy me?"

Silence reigned again.

Arnold made to move, but Austin stopped him.

"We won't oppose your leadership," Austin announced. "What we need now is a single leader who'll guarantee us the final victory. Not two divided sides, led by rivals. The Western League will follow Darthor to victory."

The nobles beside him exchanged glances. They were not truly convinced. Arnold wanted to protest, but his brother did not let him.

"It's the best thing for the North," he assured his people. And the nobles acquiesced, and accepted the fact.

Darthor turned to the other side.

"We'll follow your leadership to the final victory," Azur said.

Jurn and Sarn exchanged a glance, but after a moment they nodded in agreement.

"Very well," Darthor said. "Then it's decided. I'll be the leader in this war from now until victory."

"And afterwards?" Arnold asked.

"Afterwards we'll meet again, as we've done today, and we'll sign a peace treaty with our blood."

"How will lands and riches be shared out in this treaty?" Azur wanted to know.

Darthor stopped emitting the fog and stared hard at both sides.

"Austin will be King of Norghana, and his kingdom will reach as far as the Mountains of Eternity. The Peoples of the Frozen Continent will regain their northern lands and keep the Frozen Continent. The capital will neither be destroyed nor sacked. It will go to Austin, and with it its riches."

The decision did not please either side. Once again protests and arguments broke out. The League did not want to give up the north of Norghana, and nor did their rivals want to give up the capital and its riches.

Darthor remained unflinching for a long time, while the others argued.

Abruptly he spoke. "The Norghanians and the Peoples of the Ice will sign a treaty, and there will be no more bloodshed between them. The hatred and distrust will pass. Both peoples will respect one another and live in peace. And thus it will be because thus we will swear, all of us here."

"You ask for a great deal," Azur said.

"I ask what is fair for both peoples."

"You're asking us to give up part of Norghana," Arnold objected.

"Just as I'm asking them to give up the capital. In it Uthar has all the riches of the realm hidden away. I believe it's fair. Both of you give up part of the conquest, both of you end up winning."

"And what do you ask for yourself?" Jurn asked him.

"Justice," Darthor said. "Uthar's life and peace for the North, that's what I seek."

"I accept the terms as King of the West," Austin said. "It's fair, and I want peace as much as you do."

His people murmured, but nobody opposed him, even Arnold. Darthor nodded.

Azur looked at Jurn and then Sarn, who nodded reluctantly.

"The Peoples of the Frozen Continent accept," Azur said.

"In that case, everything is now decided."

"So what is the plan, War Leader?" Austin asked.

"We'll do as you've proposed and attack with siege weapons. We won't tackle the walls until we have those."

Jurn and Sarn protested, but Azur made them accept it.

"Go back to your camps and prepare the siege weapons," Darthor said.

Austin stared at Azur. "Prepare?" he repeated.

"We Peoples of the Frozen Continent have siege weapons too," Azur said.

"You do?" Austin said in puzzlement.

Instead of replying, Azur turned to Asrael. "When will they be here?"

"In a little over a week."

Austin was still surprised, but he asked no more questions. "Let's get down to it," he said, and with a respectful bow to Darthor and the other Leaders, he left the tent with his own people.

Lasgol wanted to stay with his mother, but he knew it was impossible; her secret might be found out, and in that situation her life would be at risk. Azur, Sarn, Jurn and the other leaders of the Frozen Continent would never understand. He threw her a glance and left with Austin's party.

Chapter 39

The forces of the Western League worked day and night in shifts, felling trees and getting everything ready for the construction of the great siege weapons. Arnold was in command, and Egil did not move from his side. Lasgol's impression was that Arnold had a little of Egil in him, even though he was a warrior rather than a thinker. He had a good mind, and it was because of this that Austin had put him in command of that crucial operation. If they did not have the weapons ready in less than a week, Uthar's armies would arrive and attack them from the rear. Unfortunately you cannot lay siege to a city and defend yourself against an attack from behind at the same time. Everybody knew this, and was afraid of it.

Lasgol had made friends with Ilvarson, the captain in charge of the horses. He came from the same county and served Count Malason, so it had not been hard to establish a bond, particularly when Lasgol had volunteered to help look after the horses. Not many soldiers or militia would have taken on the job gladly. The amount of food several thousands of Norghanian ponies and horses needed, and the manure they generated, was overwhelming, but Lasgol did not mind, and he took the night shift for a reason: to be with Camu. The little creature was resting inside Trotter's saddlebag. Lasgol did not dare take him to the war camp, with thousands of soldiers everywhere. The huge pen they were in was a little apart from the camp, to the south, to keep the smell from the soldiers. So Lasgol and Camu played at night until they both fell asleep beside Trotter. During the day he went back to Egil and the nobles to see how the siege was progressing.

On the sixth day, as expected, and to the great satisfaction of Arnold and Egil, who had labored hard in the construction of the machines, Austin announced that they were ready. Messengers were sent to Darthor's camp on the other side of the city, and they waited for the reply. Everybody was very nervous, even the Norghanian nobles. Lasgol could tell that after a week of tense waiting, the orders they gave their men were now snapped out more brusquely.

The messengers came back: Darthor had ordered the attack on

the walls to begin.

"Attention!" Austin cried, raising his sword to the sky.

The whole camp was silent as the thousands of Western Norghanians listened attentively.

The Leader of the Western League, the King of the West, as his people called him, approached his brothers Arnold and Egil. In front of them were twenty catapults. They were awesomely large.

"Set them up!" Austin ordered.

Arnold turned and gave the order. More than five hundred men began to pull on them with ropes, their enormous wheels reluctant to turn but unable to avoid doing so. They had chosen the biggest and strongest Norghanians of all the camp. The catapults advanced to a mark Egil had drawn on the ground, exactly five hundred paces from the great wall: safe from Uthar's archers, but close enough to allow the missiles to reach the wall and the lower part of the city.

"Order to attack!" Austin said to his brother.

Arnold unsheathed his sword.

"Load!" he cried.

The men pulling the machines loaded them with the projectiles of stone and wood which had been brought from a nearby quarry during the previous few days, a tremendous mountain of rocks.

Arnold brought his sword down sharply. "Release!"

The catapults shrieked, and the projectiles shot out through the air with a strange whistling sound. As he watched them fly, Lasgol wondered what would happen next. And the event left him stunned. The huge rocks struck the walls, battlements and towers, but the walls withstood the punishment; the stones that crashed against it did not even make a dent. Not so the battlements. They were shattered to fragments, and with them the soldiers who were protected behind them.

The besieging soldiers were shouting cries of victory and joy at the top of their voices at these first signs of damage.

"Adjust the aim of the catapults! Those battlements must be demolished!" Arnold called to his men.

Lasgol saw new projectiles being loaded with the help of small cranes with pulleys and horses. The men maneuvering the catapults moved levies and wheels which Lasgol guessed were to fine-tune the aim of the enormous weapons.

Arnold waited for all of them to be charged and calibrated. The process took some time, with the entire army watching, as absorbed in what was going on as Lasgol was himself.

Arnold brought down his sword. "Release!"

The projectiles flew out again, one after the other, all along the line of fire. Lasgol tried to imagine what it would be like to be in those battlements watching those monstrous rocks fall upon them, seeking to kill and destroy everything on impact. His skin turned to gooseflesh and he had to shake off a shiver.

Once again the missiles fell on battlements and wall. New loads of stone and rock tore down part of the battlements, while the wall stood up firmly to the impacts.

"It's incredible, seeing the destructive power of those machines," Lasgol said to Egil, who had come to his side.

"They're devastating. I'd read about them, but never seen them in action."

"Do you think Uthar will surrender when he sees their power?"

Egil shook his head. "I doubt it. He knows the wall will hold. We'd need months of steady punishment to breach it."

"Is it as strong as that?"

"According to my calculations, yes. We'd need far more powerful war machines to bring them down."

Lasgol found this hard to believe. "These aren't powerful enough?"

Egil smiled. "Norghanians aren't known in Tremia as great builders and thinkers. The machines we've put together are very basic and rudimentary."

"They look enormous and incredibly powerful to me."

Egil smiled again. "There are some which are much more so than these. The Nocean Empire or the Confederation of the Eastern Cities have them. They really are advanced. Even the Rogdonians of the Western Plains have better siege weapons than us. But I think they'll work, all the same. They'll weaken Uthar's defenses, and we'll be able to get in."

"You really think so?"

"Let's hope so."

"And don't they have siege weapons?"

"They do, but their range is shorter. It's the disadvantage of being inside the city. There isn't enough space to set them up on the walls."

Lasgol nodded.

"But when we get closer they'll attack us with them, you can count on that. That's why the more we damage their battlements and the interior of the city, the less damage we'll sustain when we try to go in. And I can assure you that even so it'll be a harsh punishment. Many people are going to die."

"While they're breaching the walls?"

Egil nodded.

Lasgol looked around at the men and women who were shouting in delight at the victory they expected to gain, and felt deep sorrow for them. Many would die at the hands of their own brothers, of other Norghanians. This was something his soul could not reconcile itself to. He shook his head. He only wished that it would be over soon, and with the least possible bloodshed.

Austin ordered his brother to continue the attack day and night, without a break. And they used another destructive ally, one which respected neither friends nor foes and destroyed anything in its reach, one that men feared more than death: fire. During the night they alternated rock missiles with others of fire. The huge balls spread the fire on impact to everything in their reach. Lasgol, with sinking spirits, watched the entire southern part of the city burning: wall, battlements, and the most southerly districts. Egil had told him they were using wood, hay and oil. The fire was consuming men, animals and buildings alike. It was horrible. It was war.

On the fourth day of constant attack, Darthor's order to take the walls was brought by three giant Wild of Ice to the League camp. Austin read it carefully, summoned his people and passed on the order. Uthar's army was less than three days away. They needed to take the walls now, or else it would be too late. The great moment had arrived.

Austin came out leading the lines of his men, armed and ready for the offensive. They were carrying ropes, hooks and long wooden ladders and spears. Arnold rode beside his brother Austin, after them Dukes Svensen and Erikson and Counts Malason, Bjorn, Axel and Harald, followed by several lesser lords.

"The moment has arrived!" Austin shouted. "Today we'll take Norghania for the North! Today we'll regain the crown for the true Norghanians!"

The Western army cheered their leader with cries of: "For the West! For the legitimate king of Norghana! For a strong united

Norghana!"

"Let the horns sound!" Austin shouted. "Let Uthar know that his ill-fated rule has come to its end!"

The horns sounded in the wind.

"Forward! For Norghana! For the true King!"

The western armies moved on under the blast of the horns, each noble followed by his men, and Arnold turned to Egil.

"You won't be joining in the fight. I forbid you."

"But I must be with you. It's my duty as an Olafstone."

"You've done more than enough, little brother. You'll stay in the camp. I'm not going to let anything happen to you in the battle."

"I'm no longer the weakling I used to be. I've been trained as a Ranger. I can take care of myself."

"I have no doubt about the fact, but even so, you're not going into battle. If Austin and I should fall, you must save yourself. You're the last of our bloodline."

"You won't fall. You're both great warriors, born leaders."

"Nothing is certain in battle, and this is going to be a hard and bloody one."

"Arnold, let me take part..."

"No, and not another word. I'll have you summoned as soon as we have Uthar."

"Those are his orders," Arnold said. "You can't disobey your King."

Egil sighed. "All right," he said, without much conviction.

"That's my boy." Arnold was mounting a black Rogdonian stallion as he spoke. "See you at the victory celebration," he said, and rode to join their brother.

Lasgol could see disappointment on his friend's face.

"They do it to protect you."

"I know, but I'm no longer the person I used to be. I've already been in battle."

"And you helped save your brothers from Uthar."

"True. I should've said so to Arnold."

"It wouldn't have changed a thing."

"I know, it's Austin's order."

"Look at it this way: they don't want anything to happen to you. They're protecting you."

"But it's my duty to fight for my people."

"Fire!" came the order from the captain in command of the catapults.

Lasgol started in surprise. "Why are they releasing now? Our people are on the move, they'll be hit!"

Egil watched the missiles flying over the troops in their advance and crashing against battlements and towers.

"They're to protect the advance. Uthar's forces will go up to the battlements to cause as many casualties as they can while our people get closer. The catapults will delay the enemy as much as possible. Which doesn't mean that some missiles won't hit our forces by accident as they're advancing. They're not exactly weapons of great precision."

Under the din of the war-horns, the Norghanian victory chants and the noise of the siege machines, the Western armies moved toward the southern wall. Suddenly there came terrifying roars, guttural cries, braying of beasts from the North, on the far side of the city. Darthor's forces were moving in to take the northern wall.

Good luck, Mother. Be careful, Lasgol prayed, and like his friend, he felt useless, there amid one of the greatest battles in the recent history of the North of the Continent.

Chapter 40

The black and blue tide of the Western Forces broke against the southern wall like the icy violence of the stormy sea on the cliffs of the north coast. From the damaged battlements the defenders were releasing everything they had. Thousands of arrows showered down on the western forces, seeking to kill anyone who might try to take the wall.

"Shields!" Austin shouted after his men.

A sea of round shields rose above the attackers' heads. The arrows struck shields, armor and flesh, and many fell wounded or dead.

"Stay together, keep yourselves covered with the shields!" shouted Arnold.

Once again the arrows rained from the wall and the defensive towers, which although in ruins were still standing. Uthar's soldiers hid behind them as best they could. The arrows were followed by javelins which fell on the men at the foot of the wall.

Suddenly two ballistae came into action against the attackers. There were tremendous explosions of wood and blood when the huge projectiles, almost the size of a pine-tree, hit the soldiers. Several dozen died at once, and as many others were wounded.

"We've got to take the wall!" Austin snapped at his brother.

"Erikson, ladders!" Arnold ordered.

The Duke gave the order, and his men ran to the wall carrying wooden ladders, in the area furthest to the west.

"Svensen, ropes and hooks!"

The Duke sent his men to take the most easterly section.

"We've got to divide them so that their defense is broken up," Austin said.

"Remaining forces, to the middle!" ordered Arnold.

Thousands of men ran to take the wall, yelling as they went. From the top of the wall they were riddled mercilessly with arrows, javelins, rocks and stones.

The western soldiers used their shields for protection while they tried to climb ropes and ladders. Suddenly, in the central section of the battlements, several cauldrons appeared. By now, the soldiers were almost at the top.

Austin realized what they were intended for.

"Look out!" he yelled. "Boiling oil!"

Those who were about to reach the top of the battlements saw the boiling oil being poured on them. Amid screams of horror, they fell.

"Hell!" Austin cried.

"We've lost Count Bjorn and many of his best men," Arnold said.

In the western section Erikson's men had managed to climb the ladders to the top of the battlements. But there something worse than arrows and oil awaited them: several hundred men, neither very tall nor very strong, with winged helmets and snow-white attire, holding swords in one hand and white shields in the other.

The Invincibles of the Ice!

The soldiers hurled themselves at them with axes and spears, but the Invincibles soon began to pick them off with the efficiency of trained assassins. Erikson's men were no rivals for such magnificent swordsmen. For every Invincible they managed to bring down through brute Norghanian force and courage, a dozen Western attackers were killed.

"Uthar's sent the Invincibles to defend the wall," Austin said to Arnold.

"It's going to be very difficult to take the wall with them defending them."

"They can't all be defending the south. Darthor's forces must be taking the northern wall this very moment."

"Let's wait, then."

And Austin was not mistaken. At that same moment a horde of Wild of the Ice was climbing the northern wall, using hooked ropes and rudimentary ladders, while from the base of the wall the Tundra Dwellers protected them by hurling javelins against the defenders on the battlements.

Jurn, at the head of the semi-giants and the Wild of the Ice, led the offensive amid the deafening shouts of his people in the strange language of the Frozen Continent. They were so huge and powerful that they were able to climb the wall easily. Above, the militia was waiting for them with Uthar's Invincibles of the Ice. The first fell, hacked to pieces and frightened to death in a matter of moments.

The second put up fierce resistance.

Sarn protected the Wild Ones with his Dwellers, who threw javelins at the Invincibles with amazing strength and precision. He yelled orders right and left, while he gesticulated with his whole being. The beasts of the frozen Continent, Trolls, Ogres of the Snow and unidentified creatures, waited amid roaring and braying that froze the defenders' blood. Behind them were the Arcanes who controlled them.

Two Ice Mages attacked the forces on the battlements with spells of Ice and Frost. They were unable to kill them thanks to the natural resistance of their blue bodies, but what they could do was slow them down, preventing them from fighting and thus giving the Invincibles an advantage.

Azur, the leader of the Arcanes, realized what was happening. He, Asrael and Asuris cast a spell on the wall, on the exact spot where the two Mages were standing. When the Mages saw this, they raised protective spheres around themselves. They attacked the three Shamans from the battlements, by hurling ice and frozen blasts against them. Their defensive spheres held and the two shamans strengthened them with more energy so they would not collapse. The Mages intensified their attack with ice tridents followed by shearing ice stakes that came up from the ground. The Shamans' defenses were gradually weakening under the power of the spells of the Norghanian Mages.

Azur called about twenty Glaciers Arcanes for support. A moment later these were casting a spell at the protective spheres of the Mages while the latter went on punishing the Shamans who could barely keep up their defenses.

The Arcanes cast a joint spell and created a colossal monster of the frozen caves over the battlements. The creature attacked the Mages snapping its gigantic crystal jaws. The Ice Mages fought back but saw with chagrin that their spells had no effect upon the monster, as if it were not there, although its bites shook their whole bodies and weakened their defenses. The Arcanes sent more energy to their creation and although the Mages of the ice defended themselves they could not bear the pressure of the attack. Their defensive spheres weakened further and finally collapsed. Both Mages were devoured by the ice monster. A moment later the creation vanished.

And that was the beginning of the end for the defenders of the wall.

Amid the savage yelling of the Wild, the northern wall fell into the hands of the Hosts of the Ice.

A moment later, the southern wall fell into the hands of the Western League.

Chapter 41

Egil and Lasgol watched the horrifying spectacle of the battle from the rearguard. Screams, pain, blood and terror reached them so strongly that their senses were numb. And yet despite that, the only thing they wanted was to join the action.

"I'm sorry," Egil said suddenly.

"What are you going to do?"

"I can't just stay here seeing my people die without doing a thing. I have to try and help."

"But you heard your brothers..."

The horns of both sides sounded over the yelling of the battle.

"They've opened up a breach. I can't stay here. I need to help Austin and Arnold."

"I had no idea you were so brave you'd jump into the fray at the worst possible moment," Lasgol said with a smile.

"I can assure you I'm not, but if I stay here and anything happens to my brothers, I'll never forgive myself."

"I can understand you. I feel the same way. If anything were to happen to my mother..."

"So are you coming?"

"Of course."

"Look who's the brave one now."

Lasgol laughed nervously. "I'm as brave as you are."

"Then we're screwed."

They both smiled determinedly. They were going to war.

"We'd better arm ourselves." Lasgol said, and they went to the tents to fetch their weapons.

Lasgol had a talk with Camu. He could not take him into battle – it was too dangerous – so he told him he would have to stay in the tent and rest. Camu did not agree at all and shook his head. Lasgol was not very sure whether he understood how serious the situation was; probably not, however much he tried to get the message across to him. He could not risk the naughty little creature deciding to follow him, as he had done before, so he used his Gift to order him to stay. It seemed to work, or at least that was what Lasgol hoped. He petted Camu one last time and prepared to leave.

"Wait," Egil said as they were going out. "Let's take our Ranger scarves."

"To hide our faces?"

"Exactly. That way my brother's men won't stop us."

"Won't we look suspicious?"

"I don't think so. Part of the city is burning, and there'll be plenty protecting themselves from the smoke with scarves. We'll be two soldiers of the west doing the same."

The two friends walked across to the wall, following the last reinforcements the West was sending to secure it. As they went on, with the wall looming larger in front of them and the noise of combat growing ever-closer, Lasgol felt his stomach clench. He glanced aside at his friend, whose face showed his own nervousness. They were heading into battle, death, and suddenly it all became very real.

They had to pass the bodies of those who had fallen in the attempt to reach the base of that gigantic stone structure. The wounded begged for help, screaming in agony, but the reinforcements did not stop. They had to reach the top of the wall and make it safe for the remaining forces of the West, which were already on their way to the Royal Castle. They had to jump over the dead and wounded or avoid them altogether, which was increasingly difficult as the plain was covered with them.

When Lasgol looked back, he saw that the stretcher-bearers and healers were hastening to attend to the wounded, and felt rather better. They climbed to the destroyed battlements via the ladders that now hung along much of the southern wall. At the top they saw another scene that took them aback. The battlements – or what was left of them – and the top of the wall were covered in blood, and there were bodies everywhere: thousands of dead along the wall and on both sides of it, in the plain and inside the city. A dreadful hopelessness came over them. War was something truly horrible, no matter how honorable the ends might be, no matter how much poets and bards might clothe it in acts of heroism in their odes and songs.

"Take your positions. We need to protect the access," said the officer in charge, a lesser noble whom Lasgol did not recognize.

The castle in the center of the city was a walled fortress which rose, regal and magnificent, on a hill. It was surrounded by thousands of steep-roofed stone houses. From their vantage-point on the wall they could distinguish the different parts of the city, its quarters, squares and streets. The southwest, the poorest part, where the common people lived, was burning. From it great columns of fire rose to the sky. The northern area, the noble quarter with its grand houses, was not burning, but it was covered with a strange frost, streaked with black, as if the ice had been corrupted. This was the work of Darthor and the Glaciers Arcanes in their advance toward the royal castle. It did not look as if contact with that substance was anything to be wished for.

"Let's climb down and go to the castle," Egil whispered to Lasgol.

They waited until the officer was distracted and slid down two ropes. Once inside the city they moved on among the dead into a wide street, where a group of western soldiers was on their way to the center.

The fighting in that part of the capital was over. The Eastern forces were retreating to the castle for a final defense, while both the Western forces and those of Darthor were closing in on the castle from the south and north respectively. In the streets people were trying to flee from those areas where there was still fighting and others where fires were out of control.

"The scarf," Egil said.

Lasgol put it on, so that only his eyes were visible. Egil did the same. They held their bows in their left hands and several arrows in their right. Neither of them wanted to fight. But if they found themselves in a situation where they had no choice, they would do so. Lasgol hoped they would not need to.

As they moved along the streets they saw more people trying to escape the fighting and the fire. They sheltered where they could, since the ways out of the city were shut. They were trapped inside the wall, which was now controlled by the Western Forces and those of Darthor.

Suddenly they heard cries on their left and turned, nocking arrows. Several of Uthar's soldiers, in retreat, were trying to make their way toward the castle. They were fighting Duke Erikson's men. Lasgol and Egil exchanged a glance. They were within shooting range, less than fifty paces, and they could both be killed. More of the Duke's men hurled themselves towards Uthar's men and blocked their line of fire. Lasgol and Egil lowered their bows and breathed out heavily in relief.

They followed the Avenue of the Snows, which was the main street of the city, and went on uphill toward the gates of the castle. Their route took them past a few skirmishes, but they left the soldiers of both sides fighting and went on. They met more and more forces of the West on their way, and went on unobtrusively.

They passed through Count Malason's men, and suddenly the great royal castle was in front of them. Being on a steep hill, it could only be reached by an equally steep ramp that gave access to the barred gate.

"Surround the castle!" Duke Erikson ordered his men.

"Keep out of shooting range!" Svensen said to his own as they took up their positions.

Lasgol saw Austin and Arnold studying the ramp and the castle gate. They did not seem to have decided to launch a frontal attack, which would cost many lives. Uthar's remaining forces were in the towers and on the battlements with bows and arrows and boiling oil, ready for the final defense. They would need a battering ram to bring down the gate, and that would take time. Lasgol had seen at least two battering rams among the weapons that had been built. But he did not know whether these had survived the attack on the wall.

Egil went to stand behind his brothers at a safe distance, trying to overhear what they were discussing. Lasgol joined him.

"Uthar won't surrender," Austin was saying.

"He's got no way of escape," said Arnold. "He's surrounded."

"He'll stay hidden in the castle, waiting for his armies."

"We've got to finish him off now. We won't get another opportunity."

"That gate's even going to stand up to one of our battering-rams, I'm afraid."

"I've ordered the one that's left to be brought here. It's rather damaged..."

"In that case, the situation gets complicated."

"We don't need the battering ram," came a deep, distorted voice.

Lasgol recognized it at once. It was that of Darthor. He was coming towards them, accompanied by Jurn the semi-giant of the Wild of the Ice, Sarn of the Tundra Dwellers and Azur of the Glacial Arcanes. Behind them were Asrael and Asuris, followed by the Hosts of the Ice.

The presence of the Leaders of the Ice was so impressive that the Western soldiers moved aside to let them pass. Dukes Erikson and Svensen and Count Malason came quickly to escort their lords. Austin and Arnold remained calm and let Darthor and the other leaders come to them.

"So how are we going to get in?" Austin asked. "Time's pressing, and our siege weapons are either at the camp or damaged."

"Forget them," said Darthor. "We'd take too long that way. I have a much more effective solution."

Austin yielded the leadership with a bow. "Very well, go ahead."

Darthor made a sign to Azur and Asrael. The Shamans of the Glaciers closed their eyes and concentrated, intoning a litany in some incomprehensible language while they moved their staves in front of them.

Suddenly the earth quaked: a tremor as if a giant were treading heavily on the ground they were standing on. Something was coming near. With each step the shaking increased. Some people lost their balance and even fell to the ground. Lasgol began to remember that he had already experienced something like this. The tremors intensified, and Austin's expression darkened.

"What's this? What's happening?"

"Don't worry, King of the West," Darthor said. "You'll see."

Suddenly Lasgol remembered where he had felt this trembling of the earth before: at the Pass of the Oriental Mountains.

Then, in front of where Darthor was standing, the ground began to fly through the air. An enormous hole began to form, and the tremors were followed by massive eruptions of earth and rock shooting up into the sky. The Western soldiers felt sudden terror, including the nobles.

"Relax, everyone," Darthor said.

And from the hole there appeared a surprising creature. Blind white eyes above an enormous mouth preceded an enormous reptilian body. It was covered with crystalline white scales, and as it came it gave a cry that sounded more like a high-pitched shriek.

"This is Gormir," Darthor explained. "He's our ally and will make a way through for us. Forward, my friend. Do your work."

Azur and Asrael intoned another litany and pointed to the castle gate. Gormir began to advance toward the ramp on his four short legs, with everybody watching in puzzlement.

From the castle came the order to bring the creature down. Hundreds of arrows fell on it, but to everybody's surprise, they failed in piercing it.

"His skin is as hard as diamond," Darthor said to Austin.

Uthar's soldiers launched arrows against the creature as it advanced slowly uphill. It appeared to feel neither the arrows nor the rocks they launched at it when it came closer to the gate.

Arnold was staring in astonishment. "Can anything harm him?"

"Every being has a weakness," Darthor replied. "There's not a single one which is invulnerable."

At that moment Gormir was attacked with arrows of fire, and these he did feel. He roared with his strange shrieking sound. A few paces from the gate, with the portcullis down, the soldiers poured boiling oil from the wall. When this reached him, Gormir shrieked again.

"Protect yourself!" Darthor called out to him.

The creature began to dig a hole with its enormous mouth, and the tremors broke out again. As it dug, Uthar's men set fire to the oil and the whole ramp began to burn. Gormir howled with pain.

"Come, my friend, protect yourself," Darthor urged him.

Gormir vanished inside the hole he had made, while the tremors went on with increasing force.

"What's he doing?" Austin asked.

"Protecting himself against the fire."

The tremors went on, and a hole began to form exactly under the gate to the castle. Suddenly it broke apart into a thousand pieces. Gormir's head appeared beneath it and gave a high-pitched shriek, a shriek of triumph.

"The gate has fallen," Darthor said. "It's time now to take the castle and put an end to Uthar once and for all."

Chapter 42

Darthor gave the order, and the hordes of the Frozen Continent hurled themselves at the castle entrance. From battlements and towers, the defenders tried to halt them with a shower of arrows and javelins.

"Arcanes, send the beasts," Darthor ordered.

Azur and his people called upon the enormous Ogres and Snow Trolls which hurled themselves up the ramp followed by other creatures as ugly as they were strong. Death rained upon them from the battlements but they were so tough and powerful that the defenders could not kill them. They ran up to take the fortress like beings from a nightmare, and they kept going with arrows and spears clinging to their bodies, seeking to kill those that hurt them. Their roars of pain and rage chilled the blood. None stopped, they all barged in to slaughter any defenders that tried to stop them.

The Wild of the Ice joined in the attack, climbing the ramp amid guttural roars. Many fell from the onslaught of arrows and rocks, many others were wounded, but despite this they kept going like unstoppable beasts of the ice.

Jurn and his semi-giants waited below. They were too big to go up the narrow ramp and would cause a lethal jam if they tried to. That was the defenders' hope, but Darthor made sure this would not happen.

"Jurn, you and your people will be the last to go up," he had told him.

Jurn growled in rage. "I must lead the Wild. It's my duty."

"I'm the War Chief, and you'll do as I say."

Jurn clenched his enormous fists and roared, but did as Darthor had ordered him.

"Semi-giants, with me," he told his people, and they fell back.

"Sarn, send your people to help the Wild take the battlements and towers, or else they'll go on picking us as we go up."

The leader of the Tundra Dwellers gave the order, and the Dwellers launched their attack amid war cries, javelins and knives at the ready.

From the towers and above the gate, Uthar's men started to throw down rocks and boiling oil. The ascent turned into a nightmare of death. But instead of stopping, the horde kept going despite the casualties, roaring as they went like wild beasts.

Darthor turned to Azur. "Protect them."

Azur nodded. He signaled to his people, and the Glaciers Arcanes moved toward the castle. They began to cast a spell, forming a long line as they did so. They were seen from the towers when they were less than two hundred paces away, and the soldiers released at them. Unprotected as they were, many fell dead or wounded.

But suddenly a blue fog appeared above the battlements to cover the towers of the Royal Castle. Uthar's men stopped shooting.

"It's done," Azur announced. "Now they see us as they would their own people."

"Very well done," said Darthor.

The first Wild Ones managed to enter the castle, where the last of the Invincibles were waiting for them in a defensive wall of white. The Wild Ones wielded their ice-blue axes and charged at them.

Leading the Tundra Dwellers who had avoided combat at the door, Sarn went up to the towers and walls to deal with the last forces who were defending the entrance and preventing the rest of their troops from entering.

"It's your turn now," Darthor said to Austin. "Go in and secure the courtyard and the barracks."

Austin pointed his sword at the gate. "You heard, men of the West! Forward!"

The Western Forces went up the ramp, which was half-filled with dead bodies, and entered the castle.

Lasgol was so nervous that he was behaving like Nilsa. He was trying to stay calm, but the situation was too intense. The battle was entering its final stage, and his stomach was as wild as the Northern Sea during a winter storm. Egil, watching the attack, was as pale as Gerd. Lasgol wondered how their friends were. *They'll be all right, they're strong and smart – if nothing bad's happened to them*, he told himself. Thinking about them usually had a calming effect on him, but in that moment, with all the shouts and death surrounding him, nothing could calm him.

The rest of the troops of the Western League and the Frozen Continent entered the castle, and the fighting spread throughout the fortress in the blink of an eye. The fighting was desperate; the defenders knew they were lost, but did not yield. The hosts of the Ice were brutal, and their beasts, axes and spears cut down whoever stood in their way. Still the Invincibles withstood, their skill with sword and shield wreaking havoc among the assaulting forces.

Darthor signaled to Austin. "It's time now to take the Throne Hall."

"Is Uthar holed up in there?"

Darthor nodded. "It's the safest place, in the heart of the fortress."

"In that case let's storm it and end this once and for all."

Lasgol gave Egil a questioning look, and Egil did not hesitate. He nodded, to indicate that he would follow Darthor and Austin. Careful not to raise suspicions, they went after the group where the two leaders were advancing. With them were the nobles of the West and the leaders of the Hosts of the Ice.

The fighting inside the enormous fortress of cold black rock was chaotic and desperate. The group led by Darthor and Austin did not stop to fight, but kept going to the Throne Hall. The door was locked from the inside.

"Now it's our turn," Darthor told Jurn, the semi-giant. "Bring down that door. Uthar and his minions are behind it."

Jurn smiled from ear to ear, and his single eye shone with the gleam of victory. "Bring it down," he ordered his people.

Several semi-giants hurled themselves at the door and started breaking it up with their huge double-edged axes. It was solid and reinforced, but it could not withstand the terrible violence of the semi-giants. With the sound of breaking wood, it split and fell off its hinges, and they roared with joy.

"Let's put an end to Uthar!" Darthor cried, and gave the order to go in.

The semi-giants entered, roaring, ready to destroy everyone inside. They were received with arrows that killed the first to go in. Inside the throne hall, Gatik the First Ranger of the Realm and his Royal Rangers were guarding the entrance. Uthar was beside the throne, with the Mage Olthar on his right and beside him another Mage of the Ice. The King was shielded behind the line of the Royal Guard. On one side were the nobles loyal to the King: his cousins Thoran and Orten, Count Volgren, and thirty or so dukes and counts of the East, all armed, wearing rich armor and red and white cloaks, with their personal retinues, ready to fight to the end.

"The hour has come!" Darthor cried. "To victory!"

His group went in after the semi-giants. A new wave of arrows reached the first to go in.

"Sarn, deal with the Royal Rangers!" Darthor ordered.

Sarn and the Tundra Dwellers charged against the Royal Guard, who released again. Many of the Dwellers fell.

"Swine!" Sarn yelled. "You're all going to die!"

Before the Royal Rangers could release again, the Dwellers threw their javelins as they ran. The Rangers, caught by surprise by the move, fell transfixed by those arrowheads of blue ice that were capable of piercing armor. The Dwellers charged with knives, and the Royal Rangers took out their own short axes and knives.

"Jurn, the Royal Guard!" Darthor shouted to the semi-giant.

"Follow me to victory, Wild Ones!" he yelled, and charged against the Royal Guard. The semi-giants were so large and terrifying that they would have intimidated the bravest of the Norghanians, but the men of the Royal Guard were the best of the best: strong, massive and very well trained in the use of weapons.

"Austin, Arnold, deal with the nobles!"

"With pleasure," Arnold said.

"And Uthar?" Austin asked.

"Uthar is mine. I'll deal with him," Darthor said in a voice so deep and distorted that Austin had no doubts about what awaited Uthar.

"Right. Follow me, nobles of the West. We'll teach our rivals from the East what a true Norghanian is."

The nobles of both sides fell to ruthless combat. Thoran and Orten fought together, side by side, both as big and brutal as they were ugly. Austin and Arnold confronted them, while Erikson and Svensen confronted Count Volgren and the other nobles. Count Malason supported them, with other, lesser lords of the West. They all fought with either sword and shield or sword and axe, in the Norghanian style. The fight turned to carnage in the blink of an eye. The nobles knew how to fight, and so they all did, fiercely, while the guards tried in vain to protect their lords.

"Uthar! Darthor yelled above the noise of fighting. "Turn yourself in while you still have time!"

"Turn myself in? Never! I'll have your head!"

"You're lost! Stop this and surrender!"

"You're wrong. My armies are about to arrive. And when they do, they'll put you all to the sword."

"They won't arrive in time."

"We'll see. You still don't have me, and they're almost in the city."

Darthor raised his sword and pointed it at Uthar, who was twenty paces away from him.

"Bend your knee and surrender!"

"Never! Sooner death!"

"If that's what you want, that's what you'll get!"

Uthar turned to Olthar and the other Mages of the Ice. "Kill them all!"

Darthor signaled Azur and Asrael. "Get ready!"

Immediately Olthar and the Mage of Ice raised two protective spheres, one against magic, the other covered with ice and frost as a defense against physical attacks. Darthor in turn raised a protective sphere, white streaked with black. It appeared to be covered in ice which was in the process of being corrupted by the blackness of his power of Domination. This was the origin of his names *Black Lord of the Ice* and *Corrupt Mage of the Ice*. Azur and Asrael raised two very pale blue-and-white protective spheres and prepared for combat.

Olthar and the Ice Mage, in their snow-white clothes, using white staves, began to cast spells, intoning words of power as they did so.

Darthor, the most powerful of all and the fastest, was the first to attack. A golden rune appeared in his hand, and he threw it at Olthar's chest. It was a rune of Domination whose edges were golden and whose inside black. As it moved toward the Mage it left a black wake as far back as Darthor's hand. But before it reached Olthar it struck the ice mage's protective sphere and was unable to penetrate it. Darthor concentrated and sent more power along the black wake to the rune, which began to engrave itself on Olthar's sphere of ice.

Olthar had now finished conjuring, and above Darthor, Azur and Asrael he formed a winter storm. Suddenly the temperature began to drop massively around them, and icy hurricane winds whipped at them. Several Wild of the Ice who were behind them were frozen to death on the spot in a single instant.

Azur and Asrael sent power to strengthen their protective spheres to avoid ending up like the Wild of the Ice. The whiplashes of the storm winds, traveling at tremendous speed, were lessened by the spheres, but even so, they felt the blows in their bodies and shook within that protection. They felt the lashing of the hurricane winds as if a giant of the ice were hammering on their spheres.

The Mage of the Ice beside Olthar left his staff on the ground after casting his spell and created two beams of ice with his hands. These he directed at Azur's and Asrael's spheres. He kept them on the defense, increasing his power over them. The beams were trying to pierce the spheres, and if they did, their occupants would be dead, pierced by a sword of ice.

Azur raised one hand, sending power to strengthen his sphere and trying to maintain his balance within the sphere. He twirled his staff with his other hand and cast a spell at the Mage of the Ice. With it he created a blue cloud around the mage's sphere, which began to corrupt both defensive spheres, as if with its touch they were infected with some age-old arcane power from the abysses of the glaciers.

Uthar took advantage of this moment of combat between the Mages. Sword raised high, yelling like a madman, he ran to kill Asrael. His intended victim turned on him with a spell that was ancient, quick and effective. Suddenly Uthar found himself unable to move. His feet were stuck to the ground in two huge blocks of ice.

"You bastard!" he yelled as he tried unsuccessfully to free himself.

"It's an illusion, your Majesty!" Olthar shouted.

"He's frozen my feet!"

"It's all in your mind, your Majesty! There's nothing wrong with your feet!"

Asrael conjured again against Uthar, who was trying to reach him but was unable to move his feet. Yet where Uthar could see blocks of ice, in reality there was nothing.

"It's climbing up my legs!" he cried, eyes staring from their sockets.

Darthor took advantage of this and sent more power to his Rune of Domination. As if it were a hot iron it began to penetrate the outer of Olthar's two spheres of ice. The Mage, becoming aware of this, sent more power to the storm above Darthor, Azur and Asrael. The three felt it; it was not only affecting them within their spheres but weakening the spheres themselves. Azur and Asrael concentrated on sending more power to their defenses. Darthor kept attacking with all his power, ignoring the danger in an 'all or nothing' move.

The Mage of the Ice intensified the ice beams on Azur and Asrael's defenses. They were about to yield under the combined attack of both beams and the storm. Asrael suffered a great jolt and almost fell. The victory seemed to belong to Uthar's Ice Mages.

And the balance of powers tilted.

Asrael's sphere failed to withstand the punishment and shattered. A gust of icy wind brought him down and left him lying in the middle of the hall. He did not get up.

"Victory is ours!" Uthar cried.

And at the same moment Olthar's spheres were pierced by Darthor's rune of power as he attacked with all his power. Darthor projected the Rune on to the mage's chest, marking his flesh as though with a hot iron. Olthar screamed in pain and tried to cast a spell, but the pain would not allow him to. Darthor cast a spell on the Rune and Olthar was left motionless, his eyes staring ahead of him in horror.

"End your life," Darthor ordered.

"No!" Uthar shouted.

Olthar cast a spell on himself.

"Stop, don't do it!"

An ice stake appeared in front of him, but instead of hurling it at Darthor, he turned it against himself. The stake went through him and he fell to the floor, dead.

Azur sent his last drops of power to his cloud above the Mage of Ice, and his defense collapsed. The cloud enveloped him.

"Sleep," Azur said to him, and the mage fell to the floor.

Darthor turned to Uthar.

"No! No!"

Azur went to Asrael and helped him up. The old Shaman managed to recover and looked at Uthar.

"Asrael, let him go," Darthor said.

"Are you sure, my lord?"

"Yes, it will be a clean fight. He'll have a chance."

Asrael nodded. "As you wish." He canceled the spell on Uthar.

Uthar felt himself free. He shook his arms and legs to make sure there was no ice holding him, then he attacked Darthor, lunging at him with the sword in one hand and his dagger in the other. Darthor avoided him and blocked his sword with his staff, but Uthar was so big and strong that he destabilized his opponent and almost made him fall. Uthar thrust his dagger at Darthor's neck, but he threw his head back and dodged the dagger that was intended to cut his throat. He took one step back. Then, before Uthar could attack afresh, he intoned words of power. A spell issued from his hand, like a thick thread of blackness, and hurtled toward Uthar's chest as he raised his sword to attack. The dark thread reached his chest, and a gold and black rune engraved itself on him. Uthar looked down, seeing the rune piercing his armor and embedded in his flesh, and howled with pain.

"Stop," Darthor commanded.

Uthar tried to finish his attack with the sword, but was unable to. He clenched his jaw, making a tremendous effort to free himself.

"You are dominated, you belong to me."

"No... aghh..."

"Drop your weapons."

Uthar shook his head, but his hands unclenched and his weapons fell to the floor.

"A curse on you," he cried.

"I could possess your whole mind, but I want you to be aware of your defeat, of your end."

"Let me be, you accursed creature of the abyss!"

"I want you to know who I am and why you're going to die."

"Let... me... go...argh!"

"On your knees, you scum!" Darthor ordered.

"Never!"

Darthor turned his gloved hand, and the rune flashed black. Uthar cried out in pain.

"On your knees!"

Uthar knelt, amid grunts of pain.

"Reveal yourself!

"No! Argh!"

Lasgol could not believe what he was seeing. His mother had Uthar at her feet: beaten, about to reveal his true identity. It was all about to end. Finally the senseless killing would stop. Everything would be all right. At last! Victory was theirs. A feeling of relief, of joy, came over him, and he snorted in relief. The nightmare was ending, and ending well for them. His mother had won, Egil's family would rule, and there would be peace with the Peoples of the Frozen

Continent. Norghana would once again be a kingdom united under strong, honest leadership. He could hardly believe it.

Darthor twisted his hand again. The black spot on Uthar's chest shone with a blackish flash.

The King howled.

"I am Uthar, the true King."

"No, you're not. Reveal yourself," Darthor said. He was about to twist his hand again to force him to do so.

Asuris came to stand behind Darthor, and his violet eyes shone with a strange gleam.

Lasgol noticed and felt a shiver. In Asuris' hands were two daggers of blue ice. *What's he going to do?* Something was badly wrong.

Without a word, with a lightning-swift move, Asuris buried a dagger in Darthor's back, up to the hilt.

Lasgol cried out in horror. Darthor arched. The dagger had pierced his armor. He turned.

"Asuris..."

The shaman of the glaciers buried the second dagger in his chest.

"Treason..."

"It's time for a new leader, one younger and stronger," he said.

Darthor fell to the floor.

Chapter 43

"Noooooo!" Lasgol cried, and ran to his mother.
Egil armed his bow, to cover his friend.
"Mother! Noooo!" Lasgol cried in despair. He knelt beside her and laid his head on her legs.
"Lasgol... my son..."
"Mother, you can't die!"
He heard his mother's labored breathing inside her helmet.
"I'm... suffocating..."
Lasgol searched with his fingers under the neck of the helmet for the catch. When he opened it and took it off so that she could breathe, he held her head, and her blonde hair fell through his fingers. He looked at her face and saw death in her eyes, closing in on her, unavoidable. He felt that a piece of his heart was being torn from him and squeezed, causing him immense suffering.
Mayra took several breaths, with difficulty.
"Thank you..."
Her face had turned ashen, and there was blood on her lips.
Lasgol stroked her head and kissed her forehead.
"Hold on, Mother." He looked up at Azur and Asrael, who were watching the scene as though in a trance.
"It was you," Lasgol said to Azur, but the shaman shook his head in denial.
Lasgol turned to Asrael. "If you're our friend, defend your lord."
"What have you done, you fool!" Asrael said to Asuris.
"Are your eyes deceiving you? Does old age prevent you from judging right, old shaman?" Asuris pointed at Myra on the floor with one of his daggers.
"I see our leader," Asrael replied.
Asuris shook his head vigorously. "I see a woman, a Norghanian no less. I don't see a powerful sorcerer from far-away lands who came to help us against the Norghanians, as she made us believe."
"It's the same person."
"For you, maybe, not for me. For me she's a fraud and a traitor."
"She led us to victory, just as she promised."

"By establishing an alliance with the Western Norghanians, which we didn't need and which most of us didn't want. Look at her well, she's a Norghanian woman, with a Norghanian son, one of the King's Rangers." He indicated Lasgol. "He lied to us, and he'll sell us to the Western Norghanians before the day's done. You don't see it, old man, but I do."

"She would never betray us."

"She already has. I saw her talking to her son in the Norghanian woods. I never trusted Darthor, I never trusted anybody."

"Even so, she didn't betray us."

"You're a trustful old man," Asuris said. "We young ones are sharper." He threw one of his daggers and hit Asrael in the shoulder before he could defend himself. He fell to the floor.

"Stop!" Azur called. "This is no way to gain victory for our people!"

Asuris turned to his leader. "Your time is past. Now it's time for a young leader, with brains and vision."

"Are you defying me? Are you going to lead the Shamans of the Glaciers?"

"That's right, old man."

"They won't let you. I'm the Leader of the Shamans, and after Darthor, of all the forces of the Frozen Continent. You'll pay for your presumption."

"Who's going to stop me? You?"

Azur shook his head. "No, I won't soil my hands with a traitor. Jurn, leader of the Wild Ones of the Ice! Sarn, leader of the Tundra Dwellers!"

The two leaders, who had stopped fighting to contemplate what had happened to Darthor, came to his side.

"Kill the traitor Asuris," Azur ordered. Jurn raised his powerful two-headed axe.

Asuris took a step back and started to recite a spell. Sarn raised his spear.

"Kill him," Azur repeated.

Jurn took a step towards Asuris, then half-turned. Instead of bringing his axe down on the violet-eyed shaman, he brought it down on Azur.

He split him in two.

Lasgol was petrified, unable either to cry out or react. He was in shock. He could not believe what was happening.

Sarn threw his ice-tipped javelin with all his might. Egil followed it with his gaze. He saw that it was flying at great speed toward the Norghanian nobles, who were still fighting and had not realized what was going on.

And he realized who it was aimed at, in an instant of terrifying clarity.

"Austin!" he yelled.

The spear caught his brother in the back, piercing his armor and burying itself deeply.

"Noooo!" he howled, and ran to his brother.

Austin took two hesitant steps back. He raised his hand to his shoulder, but could not reach the spear.

Thoran saw the chance and lunged to finish him.

Arnold had realized that something was wrong. "Austin!"

Orten stepped in front of Arnold, preventing him from going to his brother. "You'll have to kill me first," he said.

"So I will," Arnold replied, and delivered a sword-thrust, which Orten avoided.

Egil launched an arrow as he was running toward his brother. It hit Thoran in the shoulder, piercing the coat-of-mail and burying itself. Thoran glanced aside at his shoulder and cursed. He delivered a blow at Austin, who managed to block it, but his legs failed him. He fell to his knees, staring blankly.

"No! Austin!" Egil shouted. He released again and caught Thoran in the wrist who groaned with pain and lost his grip. His sword fell to the floor.

Egil was two steps away by now.

With his left hand Thoran buried his dagger in Austin's neck.

"Nooooo!" Egil shouted as he reached his brother's side.

Austin collapsed.

Thoran smiled and picked up his sword. He made to attack Egil, but the Wild of the Ice were now attacking the Norghanian nobles of both East and West equally.

"Kill the Norghanians!" Jurn ordered.

"All of them, whichever side they're on!" Sarn added.

"Treason!" Arnold yelled. "The Peoples of the Ice are betraying us!"

Chaos took over the Throne Hall. Everybody was now fighting

against everybody else.

Egil knelt by his older brother.

"Protect... Arnold..."

"Brother, you've got to live."

"I won't make it... but Arnold must survive... he's the heir to the crown now..."

"I'll protect him, I promise," Egil said, brushing away his tears.

"For Father... for the Olafstones... for Norghana..." Austin said with his last breath.

Egil stayed mourning his older brother for a moment with a terrible pain in his heart. The shouting around him brought him back to reality. When he looked for Arnold he found he was in trouble; the brute Orten had him against the wall. Thoran was fighting a Wild of the Ice, both delivering brutal blows. Egil nocked an *Air Arrow*, aimed at Orten's back and released. The arrow exploded against the scaled armor, and the electric discharge sent him staggering backwards, shaking uncontrollably.

"Arnold! To me!" Egil shouted to his brother. A Tundra Dweller stepped into Arnold's path, and Egil put an end to him with a *Fire Arrow* which flared into a burst of flame over his heart. Arnold nodded his thanks.

"We need to regroup," Egil said.

Arnold was staring at his brother's body on the floor, his face contracted by pain and sorrow.

"Come on, Arnold! We need to regroup, or else we're lost!" Egil gestured at Jurn and Sarn, who were dealing death among the Norghanians like ice gods.

Arnold came back to reality, shook off his grief and nodded. "Norghanians of the West, with me!"

Hearing his words, Count Malason warned Erikson and Svensen, who were now fighting against both Wild Ones and Dwellers. They all withdrew to regroup around Arnold. The Eastern Nobles too were having a lot of trouble holding back their attackers.

"Listen... Lasgol..." Mayra said.

Lasgol felt an unfathomable pain boring through his soul. Tears were running down his cheeks.

"Yes Mother."

"Take this, it's important, I want you to have it."

He saw her reach for a pendant with a strange ice blue jewel which she wore round her neck. Mayra pulled it off and handed it to him.

Lasgol took it. "What is it?"

"You'll find out. Don't lose it."

"I won't."

"Promise me you won't seek revenge..."

"They betrayed you, they killed you from behind. They deserve to die a thousand horrible deaths."

"Revenge is a path you must not tread... it leads to suffering... to death. Promise me."

"I don't know if I can, Mother."

"Do it... I want you to be happy..."

Lasgol did not want to deny his mother this. "All right. I promise."

"That's my boy... I'm so proud of you... so, so proud... your father would be too..."

"Mother, I love you," Lasgol whispered as the tears blinded him.

"I love you too... my brave son."

"Don't leave me... we haven't been able to enjoy any time together, getting to know each other..."

"My time has come... we shared some intense moments... remember them fondly, and remember too that I always loved you and I always will."

"Mother..." Lasgol could not say any more. There was a lump in his throat and his soul was bleeding.

Mayra smiled at him and stroked his cheek.

And died.

Lasgol burst out into sobs. His pain was limitless.

In the midst of the confusion, Gatik helped Uthar to his feet. Uthar, unable to walk, grunted in pain. Gatik dragged him to the throne.

"Where is it?" he asked urgently, and Uthar looked at him without understanding.

"The secret passage. I know there's one here, but I don't know where."

"Here," Uthar said. He pressed a stone in the wall behind the throne. There was a click, followed by the sound of rock sliding over rock. A secret passage appeared.

"Thoran! Orten!" Gatik called. He was gesturing urgently at the open passage.

The King's cousins saw it and understood. "Volgren," Thoran called to the Count. "We're withdrawing."

The surviving Eastern nobles retreated toward the passage, following their lords.

"Don't let them escape!" Asuris shouted.

Jurn, Sarn and their people hurled themselves at them. Asuris began to cast a spell. He pointed his dagger at Uthar. Gatik let the King fall and nocked an arrow in a lightning move. Before Asuris could finish, he released.

Asuris saw the arrow speeding toward his heart. He tried to hurl himself clear, but it caught him in the side. He fell with a curse.

Gatik was about to finish him off when a Wild One threw himself at him. He dispatched him with an arrow to the heart, then seized Uthar and dragged him inside the passage.

"We've got to retreat now," Egil said to Arnold.

"But Uthar's getting away."

"If we stand up to the Wild Ones, they'll tear us to pieces."

"You're right, brother."

"Retreat!" Arnold shouted.

Egil ran to Lasgol. "Come on, old pal. We've got to get out of here."

Lasgol looked up. He did not want to leave his mother.

"To stay is to die," Egil assured him.

Lasgol nodded. The Wild Ones and Semi-Giants were wreaking havoc. He looked at his mother for one last time.

"Come on!" Egil called urgently.

The Western Nobles went out of the door, and Lasgol and Egil followed them. At the door Lasgol glanced back and saw the passage closing. The Wild were not pursuing Uthar and his men.

"Sound the retreat," Arnold said. "We're withdrawing to the war camp!"

Several Ogres and Snow Trolls were coming at them enraged.

They all ran. The Horns of the West sounded as they fell back toward the southern wall.

Chapter 44

As they arrived at the war camp the horns were echoing across the plain, calling the retreat. The betrayal had spread through the whole capital, and the forces of the Frozen Continent were killing any Norghanian they came across.

"Fetch the wounded!" Arnold called.

Two riders arrived at a gallop and leapt off their horses to pass on their message.

"My lord, Uthar's armies are less than a day away. They'll reach the city by sundown."

Arnold was thoughtful at this news.

"Let's regroup and prepare our defense," Erikson said.

"You want to confront them?"

"We still have a chance."

"What do you think, Svensen?

"We've had plenty of losses…"

"And in the open field..." added Malason.

Arnold looked at his brother.

Egil did not want his brother to appear weak in front of his nobles, so he said nothing, merely shaking his head.

Arnold sighed. "So close... we almost had it. We'll retreat to Estocos, our Western capital."

"Sir," Erikson insisted, "we could go on fighting."

"We're in no condition to do that, and we'd have to face two enemies at once without a position of advantage. No, this isn't the moment for sacrificing more lives. We retreat."

Erikson nodded. "Very well. You're the King of the West now."

"Pack up camp, get the wounded ready and we leave," Arnold said.

"You heard the King!"

While the orders were being carried out, Egil, Lasgol and Arnold stayed staring at the great city. There was sorrow and pain in their hearts.

"You'd better get ready for the journey," Arnold said.

"I'm not coming with you, brother," Egil said.

"What do you mean, you're not coming?"

"I'm going to stay and wait for Uthar's army."

"What sort of nonsense is this? You'll be hanged."

"No, I'll put on my Ranger gear and join them. They'll come with the army, including our comrades."

"But you took part in the battle, you spied, you fought against them."

"But they don't know that. In there I was just one more Western soldier, and I had my face covered by the scarf."

"Even so, it's too dangerous. Someone might have recognized you."

"Don't worry, we've been careful."

"Why do you want to do this, to join them? I don't understand."

"Because Uthar's escaped. Because Gatik's with him, and he killed our father. Because I want to know what's happening and avenge him."

"I want to avenge him too, but this isn't the way to do it. You're risking too much."

"The only way of knowing what's going on is to be here now. It's a crucial moment. The Hosts of the Ice will be fighting against Uthar's armies. I want to be there."

"They should retreat, like us."

"But they won't. Their leaders are young, fiery, treacherous, but they don't know anything about strategy. They'll fight."

"Are you sure of that?"

"Absolutely."

"I can't say I'd be too unhappy if they were to fight and kill each other. Who's going to win?"

"Uthar's forces."

"Whoever wins will be left very weakened."

Egil indicated the huge number of wounded. "Just as we are now."

"That's true enough. Are you sure you want to stay, little brother?"

"I am."

"Very well. I won't stop you."

"Thank you, my King."

Arnold smiled, but the smile was a sad one. "I wish Austin were here. He was the true King." He turned to Lasgol. "And what about you, Lasgol? What are you going to do?"

Lasgol thought for a moment. "I'll stay with Egil."

"So I imagined," Arnold said with a smile. "Look after him."

"I will, my lord."

Arnold hugged his little brother. For a moment they held their embrace, without a word, aware of the love and respect they felt for each other.

"Good luck!" Arnold called to them, and left.

The forces of the West left the field at sunset, in a single long column. Egil and Lasgol, watching them, were already dressed as Rangers, and Camu was playing at their feet, giving little shrieks of joy at having them back with him.

"At least he's happy," Egil said with the trace of a smile.

Lasgol bent down to stroke him. "Yes, I often feel I'd like to be him."

"A surprising, magical, charming little creature," said Egil.

"He's that."

"Ready for what we have to face now?"

Lasgol nodded.

They waited patiently among the trees, but not for long. The first mounted scouts of Uthar's armies arrived at a gallop. Among them they could see a group of Rangers, with Isgord among them. The scouts examined the area and went back to report. The armies appeared from the East and advanced until they were some four hundred paces from the damaged city wall. Commander Sven took his place at the head.

Egil pointed to the rearguard. "More scouts combing the area."

Lasgol could not see them clearly at that distance, so he used his Gift and called upon his *Hawk Eye* skill. He recognized one face at once, and his stomach lurched. It was Astrid with her group.

"Owls," he said.

"And that group that's searching the south of the city?"

Lasgol smiled. "Snow Panthers."

"Are they all there?"

"I can see Ingrid, Nilsa, Gerd, Viggo, and Molak too. They're still with Nikessen, and he's in the lead."

"So they're all right. What good news!"

As the two friends rode toward their companions, Nikessen saw them and ordered the group to ready their weapons.

"Don't shoot, it's us!" Lasgol shouted. He had no desire to be shot at by Nikessen, or by Viggo, who was prone to shoot first and ask afterwards.

Nikessen raised his fist. "I hadn't expected to find you still in one piece."

"Lasgol! Egil!" Nilsa jumped off her pony and ran to give them an affectionate hug.

Gerd gave them a stronger bear-hug, laughing joyfully. Ingrid held them by the shoulders, smiling from ear to ear, which was not usual in her. Molak, smiling in his turn, gave them a hug. The only discordant greeting was Viggo's. He did not even get off his horse, but simply nodded and stared at them sullenly.

"What are you doing here? What happened to you?" Nikessen went on.

"We were captured by the forces of the West at the Bergen Crossing," Lasgol lied as best he could. His voice did not shake, and as a result he sounded quite convincing. Or so it seemed to him.

"That's what I figured. Are you all right?"

"They shook us up a little, for information," said Egil. "As we didn't have much to give them, they left us in peace. We've been held prisoners in the Western camp."

"We managed to escape when they retreated, and hid," Lasgol added.

Nikessen pricked up his ears. "They've retreated?"

Egil nodded. "They're going back to their lands in the West."

"But they had victory at their fingertips. I don't understand."

"We heard shouts of 'treason'," Egil said.

"Treason?"

"We think the Hosts of the Ice have betrayed the Western League."

"That's really interesting news. Are you sure?"

"It's what we heard," said Egil. "And the forces of the Western League aren't there on the plain any longer."

"I need to take this news to Commander Sven at once. Molak, with me. You others, wait for me to come back and keep watch to make sure the Western Forces don't return. If they do, pass on the information immediately."

Nikessen and Molak left at a gallop. When they were out of reach, Ingrid turned to Lasgol and Egil.

"Tell us everything that's been going on, this minute."

"Everything!" said Nilsa, who was a bunch of raw nerves.

Egil and Lasgol told them everything that had happened, with as much detail as possible. When they finished there was a silence.

Gerd was the first to speak. "I'm very sorry," he said, and gave a heartfelt hug to each of them.

"My condolences," Ingrid said, and hugged them tight as well.

Nilsa was weeping. "I'm so sorry..." she said, hugging them in her turn.

Viggo dismounted and joined them. "I wasn't going to forgive you about the poison. But after hearing what happened... everything's forgotten."

Lasgol and Egil both mumbled their gratitude, trying not to break down in tears.

Ingrid was looking at the corpse-covered plain and the city burning in the background. "The battle must have been impressive."

"And horrible," Gerd added.

"It was both," said Lasgol.

Egil shook his head. "An experience we'll never ever forget, I can assure you."

It was not long before Nikessen and Molak came back.

"Commander Sven himself thanked me for the information. They weren't sure what they were up against. Now they have a better opportunity."

"Will they attack the city?" Egil asked. "The Hosts of the Ice are still inside."

"They're trying to find the King and his followers. There are rumors that they managed to escape."

Lasgol and Egil said nothing, as did their friends, who now knew what had happened.

Suddenly they saw a large group of armed men riding out by the southern gate, the one that had been under the control of the Western League, though it was too dark by now to make out very much.

"Mount and get ready. They're coming close," Nikessen ordered.

Lasgol used his Gift, and at once recognized Gatik, Thoran and Orten. They were carrying one man tied to a horse so he would not fall, with Count Volgren leading the horse. The man tied to it was Uthar. He had managed to leave the city.

Lasgol thought about the rage Asuris would be feeling at the sight of Uthar slipping through his fingers, and rejoiced. It was only a small victory, but it made him feel better.

The group approached them, unsheathing their swords as they did so. "Royal Rangers!" Nikessen shouted at the top of his voice in warning.

The riders reined in their horses and approached slowly. Lasgol and Egil waited tensely.

"Where's the King's army?" Gatik asked.

Now Nikessen recognized them. "First Ranger Gatik, sir, my lord Thoran. Your Majesty, your army is waiting for you east of the city. Commander Sven is waiting for your news so that he can attack."

Lasgol thought about shooting at Uthar. He had him there, tied to his horse, physically incapacitated, barely conscious. He could do it. He would not miss at this distance, even with darkness falling. He glanced aside at Egil and saw his friend's eyes shining. He was thinking about shooting at Gatik. They had them there, on the spot. Their revenge, in front of their eyes. There was only one problem, but it was a major one. If they carried out their plan they would condemn their friends, and they would all hang. And there was no way they could kill them all –besides which, Nikessen and Molak were loyal to the King.

The wind caressed Lasgol's face. He could not do it. He could not endanger all of them like that, without warning, not simply for revenge, not without a plan that would allow them to get away with their lives. He had seen those nobles fight, and they themselves would be destroyed.

Egil's bow was slightly raised in Gatik's direction. He glanced at Lasgol, and his friend shook his head. Egil hesitated; he half-closed his eyes and clenched his jaw. Lasgol made another brief, unobtrusive gesture, and Egil gently lowered his bow. Lasgol let out his breath in relief.

"The forces of the Western League?" Thoran asked.

"They've withdrawn to their lands."

"Cowards," Thoran said. "That gives us an advantage, we can still win this battle."

"Are you sure, Ranger?" Orten asked.

Nikessen looked at Egil and Lasgol out of the corner of his eye. "I am."

"On we go, then!" Thoran cried.

The group left at a gallop to rejoin Commander Sven and the King's three armies. Helplessly, Lasgol and Egil watched them leave. They had been so close, and their enemy had escaped.

"The King and the Nobles," Nikessen said. He sounded stunned.

"What do we do now?" Molak asked.

"We follow our orders. We watch this area."

"Will they attack the city now the King's escaped?" Ingrid asked.

"In this darkness? I doubt it. It'll soon be completely dark. They'll wait till dawn."

Nor was Nikessen wrong.

With the first light of day the Norghanian horns echoed and the army prepared to take back the capital they had lost. The group watched from their position. They had not received any new orders, so they followed their previous ones.

The Hordes of the Ice had formed a line in front of the wall. Asuris, who was still alive, and his Arcanes, were in the center. In front of them were Trolls of the Snow, Ogres and other, unfamiliar, creatures, controlled by the Arcanes. Jurn and the semi-giants were leading the Wild of the Ice on the right of the Arcanes. On the left were Sarn and the Tundra Dwellers.

"Why have they left the city?" Ingrid asked. "That way they lose the advantage of the walls, surely."

"Very true," said Nikessen. "I don't understand why they have. The logical thing to do would be to wait for the attack inside."

"There are two reasons for it." Egil was watching the movements of the armies. "The first is that their leader doesn't have enough experience for a battle like this one. The second is that they're a horde, and they don't know how to fight other than on open ground. They're not good at fighting in closed spaces. They wouldn't know how to hold the wall or fight inside the city, with houses and narrow streets around them."

They all looked at him as if he were an experienced general.

"So we're going to win?" Molak asked.

"I didn't say that. The Horde is still very strong. Victory isn't assured, but now Uthar's forces have more of a chance. Their numbers are greater, and they have better military training."

"I'm sure victory will be ours," Nikessen said, more in hope than anything else.

"We'll soon find out," Egil said. He was looking at the battlefield, where both armies were launching into the attack.

Sven led the attack, while Uthar and the Eastern Nobles stayed in the rearguard. The Thunder Army led the way, following their motto. They were followed by the Snow Army, and the tip of the attack was the Blizzard Army. There were not many strategic alternatives to confronting the Hosts of the Ice, who were advancing at a run, in a single mass.

The clash was massive. The soldiers of the Thunder met the Trolls, Ogres and other beasts commanded by the Glaciers Arcanes. They fought like men possessed, trying to survive the monsters which were destroying them with unparalleled ferocity with blows, or bites, or simply by splitting their opponents in half. The Thunder Army was made up of huge Norghanians who were fighting with axe and shield, but beside the beasts and semi-giants they seemed no more than children.

The Wild of the Ice and the Tundra Dwellers hurled themselves at the Snow Army. The Norghanians suffered many casualties at the hands of the forces of the Ice. But they had one advantage: numbers. The Norghanians had the Blizzard Army, nimble and fast, which began to attack the Trolls and Ogres in groups of ten, moving swiftly and causing heavy casualties. It seemed that things were beginning to tilt in their favor. Numbers and mobility began to have their effect. The noise of battle filled the air like a lethal storm.

At this point Asuris acted. He ordered the Arcanes to cast spells against the Blizzard Army. Groups of these started acting strangely. Disoriented, confused, they began to attack anybody who was near them, whether friend or foe. Their advantage began to turn into a disadvantage

Seeing that neither of the two sides was managing to defeat the other, and that the number of casualties was growing disproportionately, both Asuris and Sven called back their forces. The Norghanian forces regrouped to the east, the Hordes of the Ice to the north of the battlefield.

Lasgol watched, gripped by suspense. The fighting had been brutal. Would they attack one another again? Would they retreat?

The Horde started to march toward the north.

"They're retreating!" Molak cried.

"Will they go after them?" Gerd asked.

Nikessen shook his head. "Our forces have taken too much punishment. They won't be able to follow them, and I honestly doubt whether they want to."

Lasgol breathed out heavily. There was neither winner nor loser. And just as Egil had predicted, both sides had worn out their strength, saving his brother in the process. They would not be able to attack Arnold, at least not for a while. His choice to retreat had been a wise one. Lasgol gave thanks to the five Gods of the Ice that he had a friend as intelligent as Egil.

The battle ended, and all that was left was the moaning of the wounded and the silence of those who would never get back up again.

"It's time to go and help," Nikessen said.

For six weeks they helped with the injured, with the rebuilding the city and a myriad other tasks Nikessen gave them. Time was of the essence. At night, after working all day, they were so exhausted that they dropped asleep without even a chance to talk among themselves. These were days of hard work, but at the same time, days that filled their hearts; instead of fighting and destroying, they were helping people and rebuilding the capital.

Finally they were granted permission to go back to the Rangers' Camp. Nikessen led them there, more as a journey of farewell than because they really needed him. When they passed through the Camp gates, he took his leave of them.

"It's been an honor and a pleasure to have shared this time with you. You're a magnificent group, and I haven't the slightest doubt that you'll all graduate as Rangers."

The Royal Ranger's recognition touched their hearts. Nilsa threw herself at his neck and kissed him on both cheeks. Nikessen went red.

"Thank you, Royal Ranger," Ingrid said. "The honor is ours. It's been a privilege to serve under your command."

Nikessen thanked them with a slight nod in the military style.

They said goodbye with hugs and laughter, and Nikessen went back to the capital. He had to go and serve the King, more so now that so many Royal Rangers had died.

Lasgol, watching him leave, felt sorry to see him go. He was a good man and a great Ranger.

Chapter 45

Master Instructor Oden welcomed them at the stables with his usual lack of friendliness and informed them that Dolbarar and the other Master Rangers were extremely busy with matters to do with the war and were not to be disturbed. He also informed them that several teams had not yet returned, and that he would let them know when Instruction would resume. Viggo asked, not without sarcasm, if all the experience they had gained in the war would not be enough to make up for the rest of the year. From the shouts and curses he received from Oden it was clear that it would not be, and that they would have to finish their year of Instruction. They were not surprised. Such was the *Path of the Ranger*: an arduous one.

The first evening back at the Camp was strange. On the one hand it was comforting, as they were back in what by now felt like their home, and on the other it was disconcerting because of all they had recently been through. By the fireside, in the warmth of their cabin, the six friends sat down together to eat and talk.

"It feels strange to be back here after all we've been through," Nilsa said.

"It feels good," said Gerd, stretching his strong arms and torso.

Camu gave several happy shrieks and ran around the cabin.

"Tell the beast to keep still," Viggo said to Lasgol.

"Don't call him a beast, he's a fascinating little creature," Egil reproached him.

"Yeah, sure, and I'm an enchanted prince."

"Who knows?" Nilsa said. "With all those secrets of yours, maybe you are."

"This one here?" Ingrid said incredulously. "In your dreams!"

Viggo folded his arms. "I have a lot of surprises. You'll see."

Nilsa giggled.

"What do you think's going to happen now? With the war, I mean?" Gerd asked.

They all turned to Egil. He was the best qualified of them to give a political and strategic evaluation of the situation the kingdom was in.

"Now there'll be an uneasy calm, and the three factions will regroup and try to build up their strength again."

Nilsa was biting her nails. "I'm not clear who's won the war."

"Nobody's won the war as such," Egil said, "because there hasn't been either a clear winner or a decisive battle to tilt the scale one way or another."

"Then we're still in the same tangle," Viggo said.

"A very similar mess, that's right."

"But after all the battles, one or other side must have come out in a stronger position," Nilsa objected.

"Analyzing recent events and the current situation," Egil said, "that side would be Uthar's."

Viggo made a face. "Wonderful news!"

"You mean Uthar is the strongest now?" Ingrid asked.

Egil nodded. "The Western League has been badly hit, and they were the smaller force. The Peoples of the Frozen Continent are at a disadvantage in Norghana, so I'd imagine they'll cross the Northern Sea and go back to the Frozen Continent. They might stay in the North of Norghana behind the mountains, but that would look risky to me. That leaves Uthar as the best-placed. He'll control the East and part of the West, as well as the North of Norghana." He paused. "I might be wrong, but I think that's what'll happen."

"You're not often wrong, particularly in this sort of thing," Ingrid said.

"And our situation?" Nilsa asked. "How does that leave us?"

"Not well at all," Viggo said before Egil could answer.

"Exactly, not well at all. We're in a very tricky situation, even more so than at the beginning of the year."

"Because someone knows our secret," Viggo said. "Someone in the camp."

"Correct. And this puts us all in danger of death, no matter what happens among the three factions, because our past acts will be interpreted as treason and we'll be hanged."

"Astrid..." murmured Ingrid.

They were all silent for a moment,

"We ought to kill her and make it look like an accident," Viggo said nonchalantly.

Nilsa was immediately indignant. "Viggo!"

Gerd had turned white. "We're not going to kill her, are we?"

"Of course we're not going to kill her!" said Ingrid.

"I don't see why not, there's one of her and six of us. Which is better, one death or six? Because in the end that's what it comes down to, and I can assure you I'd rather live than die, even more if the numbers are on my side."

"Nobody's going to die here!" Ingrid snapped.

"There's something in what Viggo says..." Egil put in.

They all gaped at him.

"How can you say that, Egil?" Nilsa said. "You, who're always the most rational one?"

"That's exactly why. The rational thing is to save six, not one. If Astrid gives us away, we'll all be hanged. She could do it at any moment. In fact I don't know why she hasn't already."

Viggo gestured at Lasgol. "Because of him."

All eyes turned to him. "Because of... me?"

"Well, of course, because she's in love with you and she doesn't want you to be hanged."

"Oh..."

"But in many cases, falling in love is a fleeting thing," said Egil, "or one with a tendency to arguments and break-ups, in which case we'd die."

"I'm sure Lasgol will behave like a perfect beau with Astrid," Nilsa said.

"This one here?" Viggo said. "He doesn't even know which way the wind's coming from. We might as well leave our fate to luck."

"All he needs to do is be the perfect beau and not make her angry," Nilsa said.

"Me? Perfect beau? She doesn't even speak to me!"

"Better that way," Egil said. "Less possibility of confrontation."

"That's right," said Ingrid. "Keep away from her, don't even look at her."

Nilsa shook her head agitatedly. "No, no, not that either. If he ignores her she'll be even more upset, and –"

"I think the best thing you can do is start giving her presents," Gerd said.

They all looked at him.

"Eh? In my village, when someone courts a pretty girl, he takes her presents. A pig, for instance, or a goat."

Viggo made a face and rolled his eyes. "Yeah, perfect, get her a farm animal."

"We have to remember an added problem," Egil said. "We need to unmask the King, and we're the only ones who know he's a shifter. If we die, then he'll win and the whole North will suffer. Astrid mustn't be the cause of a tragedy like that. We need to free Tremia from Uthar, and that's more important than her life."

Lasgol looked at Egil in amazement. He could not believe that his friend was serious.

"Nobody's going to sacrifice Astrid's life," he said, very seriously. "If anything happens to her, I'll kill whoever's responsible myself! I swear that."

"Nobody's going to kill Astrid," Ingrid said after a long silence. "But you've got to convince her not to give us away. Our lives are at stake."

He nodded. "I'll talk to her."

"Better if you sing her a love song," Viggo said.

They all laughed, and the tension decreased a little. They went on chatting about personal things again, and laughter filled the cabin. Companionship and friendship reigned.

But Lasgol was not laughing. He was deeply worried about Astrid, as well as about all of them.

The following days were uneventful. There was no trace of the Leaders of the Camp, and Oden left them in peace. Lasgol decided that he could not wait any longer and looked for some opportunity to talk to Astrid. He waited until she was alone by the horses and went up to her.

"Hello Astrid," he greeted her softly.

She turned to him like lightning and fixed him with her green eyes, which were intense with hatred.

"Don't you dare say a word to me."

"Astrid..."

"Not a word. If you ever talk to me again, you or any of the Panthers, I swear I'll go straight to Dolbarar and give you away as the traitors you are."

Lasgol did not know how to react. He had expected her to have thought about it, seen the light, but it was too much to ask. All the evidence pointed against him, and Astrid obviously still thought the same as she had in the tent where they had been prisoners of the Hosts of the Ice.

"We're not traitors... I swear to you."

"From my position I can assure you that you are, all of you."

"I can understand that you see it that way... but one day you'll change your mind."

"Never! I'm loyal to the Norghanian crown, to the King."

"You may not believe it, but so are we."

"The only reason why I haven't turned you in to Dolbarar to be hanged is that you must all be under some form of spell that's stopping you acting rationally. It must be that, and I'm hoping the spell will wear off. All spells have a time limit, like our potions, according to Eyra. That's what I believe that you're bewitched. I can't come up with any other explanation. That's what I want to believe. And that's why you haven't been judged and hanged yet."

"Thank you..."

"Don't thank me. I'm watching you, and if I come across any action of yours that I consider to be treason, I'll turn you in. Is that clear?"

Lasgol nodded. "Don't worry, there won't be any."

"There'd better not be. Now go back to your cronies. And remember, don't speak to me again."

Lasgol gave a slight nod and left. An intense pain was strangling his chest, and he was sure he was leaving behind a trail of blood from his broken heart.

A week after this conversation with Astrid, Oden came to their cabins at sunrise and made them all line up.

"It's time to stop lazing about!" he told them. "As of today, Instruction is resumed until further notice. We'll follow the established program: physical training in the morning and Schools instruction in the afternoons, each one in his or her particular School."

"What fun we're going to have," Viggo whispered.

"I'm glad we're back to normal." Gerd muttered.

Nilsa shrugged. "Me too."

"That's because you don't remember what a hard time we had. You soon will, though."

"In addition," Oden went on, "there'll be certain missions in which you'll be given the opportunity to show your worth and gain the Oak Leaves you need in order to graduate at the end of the year."

"This gets better and better," Viggo whispered.

"Shut up, blockhead," Ingrid muttered.

Oden's bark commanded them all to be quiet.

"As for the war, which I know is your chief topic of gossip, I can tell you that our King Uthar has recovered from the wounds suffered in battle and is once again ruling Norghana with a strong arm. You have nothing to worry about, except to serve him well."

Lasgol and Egil exchanged glances. They were not sure how much truth there was in this, but it was not good news.

"And now, let's start Instruction!" Oden ordered.

Training and instruction became very intense once again. The days flew by, because as they had expected, the training in this last part of the year turned out to be both enlightening and exhausting. Training, learning, sleeping and practicing had become the motto of the autumn. The season passed so rapidly that they could barely enjoy it.

They soon found out what Oden meant by "missions to show their worth". They were sent in teams to scour the north, to make sure the Hosts of the Ice had really left and were not coming back. The Panthers found that Egil had been right and that the Hosts had withdrawn to the Frozen Continent. They scoured the coast very carefully and found no trace at all. Even so, they would be sent many more times to make sure: particularly in winter, because it was less likely that the Hosts would cross over at that time of year, hence less expected, and they might take advantage of this and risk it.

Lasgol enjoyed the instruction. He was learning a great deal, and whenever he could, he visited the other Schools to learn as much as possible from watching their training. This kept him very busy, which was good for his soul as he had lost his mother forever and Astrid as well, so he felt an empty void where his heart ought to be. It was worse at night, but luckily he had Camu, who always wanted to play with him, making him forget all his sorrows with his eternal smile and tirelessly playful spirit.

Winter covered everything in white, and though it might be beautiful to the eye, it was not so for their tired bodies, which suffered greatly in the snow and the cutting, icy wind. They were twice sent on missions to the north and had a very tough time, but luckily there were no accidents or unwanted encounters with Wild Ones, Ogres or other beasts of the Ice. When they returned to the Camp they were each awarded an Oak Leaf.

"We're not doing badly after all," Nilsa said joyfully as she toyed with the Leaf, which fell through her fingers.

Gerd smiled at his friend's clumsiness. "I'm really happy, and we haven't had either some weird scare or more trouble."

"Don't say it too loudly," Viggo said. "With our luck, something's bound to happen."

"Don't put a jinx on it," said Ingrid.

"Let's not get ahead of ourselves," Egil said. "There's not much left of the year, so let's stay united and on our toes."

A week before the year's instruction ended, Lasgol was practicing archery in a landscape that was both white and ice-cold. He was shooting at a tree three hundred paces away.

"How's that marksmanship of yours?" asked a feminine voice.

Lasgol turned. The girl was wearing a green Third-Year cloak which was covered in snow.

"Hi, Val. Trying to improve."

She pushed back the hood, revealing her golden hair and beautiful blue eyes.

"And are you succeeding?"

Lasgol smiled. "Not much. Archery has always been hard for me."

"I'm quite good at it. Traps, not so much."

"I bet you're also good at fighting with axe and knife."

"That's right. How do you know?"

He smiled. "I can tell."

"And how am I with animals?"

"I'd say not too good."

"Right on target!" she said, and laughed melodiously.

Lasgol shrugged.

"Let's see. Finally: how am I doing in School of Expertise?"

Lasgol looked carefully at her for a moment. She was too radiant and beautiful to go unnoticed.

"I'd say not too well."

"Jackpot!" she said and threw herself into his arms.

They stayed in an embrace, looking into one another's eyes. Lasgol could not help but feel attracted to her, because she was beautiful and delightful. The most popular girl in the Camp, unattainable for all, except for him, and he knew it.

Val put her lips to his own and kissed him. Lasgol felt the warm, gentle kiss and felt something so pleasant, exciting and narcotic that he was on the point of letting himself go. But he held back and gently moved her away.

"I can't..."

"Is it because of the brunette?" she asked. She showed no spite at the rejection.

"Yes, it's because of her."

"Everybody knows you're not together any longer, she doesn't even talk to you. I don't know what's happened between you and I'm not interested either, but you're not together and I know it."

"No, we're not together," he admitted, bowing his head.

"In that case... there's nothing to stop you from being with someone else," Val went on with both sensuality and spirit. Her smile would have enchanted anyone. "A blonde, for instance."

But he could not. It was not that he did not like Val, not only physically but because of her personality and spirit. But his heart was broken, and there was simply no way he could.

"It's not the right moment..."

"Are you sure? These moments don't come very often, and once they pass they're gone forever."

Lasgol caught the hint at once. He nodded a couple of times, without looking at her. "I am. Now isn't the moment."

"That brunette certainly put a spell on you," she said with a smile.

"It looks like it."

Val came close to him. She put her fingertip on her own lips and then on his.

"I have a potion that will heal your wounds and free you from spells."

Lasgol smiled. "I'm sure you have."

"When the time comes, we'll both drink it. Deal?"

Lasgol nodded. He could not refuse her. "Deal."

Val winked at him, kissed his cheek and left. He watched her go away, with his heart broken and a feeling of confusion in his mind.

And during a snowstorm that had already lasted for days came the day they had all spent four years waiting for, the most important day in their young lives, the end of the Fourth-Year instruction. Dolbarar called them to assemble in front of the Command House.

They left their cabins shivering, not because of the cold and the snow but because of the possibility that they had not made it.

Gerd and Egil both looked very worried. They had not done badly in the second part of the year, but they both knew they stood little chance. Viggo was protesting as usual, but he had done very well. Ingrid had no doubt that she would graduate. Nilsa was so nervous that she did not know whether she would get through or not.

The Owls, with Astrid in the lead, went by on their way to the Command House. Lasgol looked at her, but as she had done since the summer, she ignored him completely. Lasgol sighed. Then came the Eagles with Isgord in the lead. He was as strung-up as a tense bow.

He looked at Lasgol as he went by and with an air of superiority commented to his team: "Here are those losers, the Panthers. I bet you whatever you like that not even a couple of them'll pass."

His partners laughed at the joke, but Ingrid did not find it in the least amusing. She showed him her gloved fist. "Keep walking, or you'll get to the Command House without a nose."

"We'll see you there, losers."

"I'm going to kill him," said Ingrid.

"You wouldn't want to be expelled on your last day just for breaking an idiot's nose," Viggo told her.

"You're right... I'd better calm down."

Viggo smiled at her. "Let's go, and may the Gods be merciful."

Dolbarar and the four Master Rangers were waiting for them. They were not wearing formal garb, which surprised Lasgol.

"Welcome, all of you," Dolbarar said, spreading his arms wide like a father welcoming his children. He was carrying the *Path of the Ranger* in one hand and his staff in the other.

Nerves and unease floated in the air. The general feeling was one of doubt. Would they graduate? Would they be expelled? Would they be made to repeat the last year? In some cases the leaders tended to opt for this solution when the person had potential but had not managed to convince them with their behavior over the last year.

"I'm aware that you're all nervous. The day you've all been waiting for has finally arrived. And I have good news, news I'm sure will fill you with joy.

"This is going to go wrong any moment, you just wait," Viggo muttered.

"Shut up, you jinx, you super-jinx!" Ingrid snapped.

Dolbarar smiled proudly. "This year the Ceremony of Acceptance for the Fourth-Years will not take place here today but in a week's time at the capital, before the King. His majesty Uthar wants to preside over the ceremony, and so it has been arranged. He wishes to thank you all in person for the magnificent work his Rangers have carried out during the conflict. It's a real honor and privilege."

Everybody began to shout with enthusiasm, to laugh, to cheer the King's name in excitement and delight. All except six. The Panthers were not laughing, but very much the opposite. They were as serious as the dead.

Chapter 46

"You're the biggest jinx in the whole snowy north!" Ingrid muttered to Viggo. She was looking daggers at him.

He poked the fire in the cabin. "It's not my fault if I have a sixth sense about these things."

Gerd was looking through the window. It was dark and snowing. "I can't believe this is happening to us," he said, lost in his own thoughts..

Nilsa was pacing from one side of the cabin to the other. Camu was following her, thinking it was a game.

"We're heading into the lion's mouth," she said, and began to pace even faster. Camu followed her happily, one step behind.

"And the lion could easily close it and gulp us down," Egil said.

"Do you think we're in any danger?" Lasgol asked him.

"I'm sure of it. I'd go even further and say this might be a trap."

They all turned to stare at him.

"A trap? Explain yourself," Ingrid said, and folded her arms.

"It seems curious to me that Uthar wants to celebrate our Acceptance Ceremony at his castle. More than that, why just ours?"

"Because we're the final year," Ingrid suggested.

"Or because he knows who's in this particular course."

Viggo pointed to Egil and Lasgol with his dagger. "You two."

"Did he recognize you in the Throne Hall?" Gerd asked. He sounded very frightened.

Egil sighed. "I don't know. Maybe."

"We were wearing our scarves and we didn't take them off," Lasgol reminded him.

"True. But I don't know if that was enough to stop him recognizing us. We were only a couple of steps from him."

"You should have killed him there and then." Viggo said.

"If we could, we would have," Egil assured him.

"The opportunity didn't arise," Lasgol said sadly, remembering what had happened.

"So what do we do now?" Ingrid asked.

"I don't think you're in danger," said Egil. "You weren't there, they won't suspect you. It's Lasgol and me who could end up being hanged."

"We also have to remember that you two have a certain past history with Uthar," said Viggo.

"I don't follow," Gerd asked. "What history?"

"Family history. Remember who their parents are and everything that happened."

"Ah, of course!"

"Don't go," said Nilsa. "We can poison you so that you fall ill. It worked on Nikessen."

"Good idea," Ingrid said, "or else we could break something, as if you'd fallen off a cliff or something."

"I like that better," Viggo said. "Very subtle."

"Shut up, blockhead."

Egil and Lasgol were thoughtful.

"We have to go," Egil said suddenly, sounding very serious.

Lasgol too felt that they had to go, although he had his doubts.

"But you're risking death."

"We've come so far," said Egil. "I want to see it through."

"It might end very badly," Viggo warned him.

"I'm going to go, and I'm going to graduate as well. I've been through the four years, I've suffered and struggled to make it, to get to this point. I'm not going to give up at the last step, not after following the whole long path."

"I'm with Egil," Lasgol said. "We're going to go."

Viggo waved his hand. "You're insane."

"Think about it," Gerd said. "It's very dangerous, and I'm afraid for you."

"I support you both," said Ingrid.

"I don't know – yes – I mean no – I don't know," said Nilsa. She was still pacing round like a maniac, to the delight of Camu, who was following her like a lapdog.

"And suppose it's a trap?" Viggo suggested. "Suppose Uthar's waiting for you, to hang you?"

"Then we'll think of a plan to counter it," Egil said with sudden determination.

"That's right," Lasgol agreed.

Viggo threw his hands in the air. "You're absolutely mad."

"Do I have your support for a counter-plan?" Egil asked.

"You can count on me," said Ingrid.

"I'm scared to death about what might happen," said Gerd, "but you can count me in."

Nilsa suddenly stopped. Camu bumped into her leg. "You can count on me," she said, and started pacing again.

"Viggo?" Egil asked.

"You'll get us all killed."

"Is that a yes?" Ingrid asked him.

Viggo looked at the blonde Captain. "It's a yes."

The journey to the capital was rather uncomfortable, since the weather was not good and the company was rather overwhelming. The Contenders were travelling together with Dolbarar, the four Master Rangers and an escort of a dozen Rangers. They journeyed by day under the snow, which never stopped falling. Luckily there was no heavy storm. In the evenings they made campfires and slept around them. They avoided villages and cities at all times. Viggo was furious, unable to understand why they could not rest properly in a good inn with hot food and a bed. But according to what Dolbarar had told them, the *Path of the Ranger* laid down that the traveler must always seek the forest, not the village, when traveling. Viggo was utterly delighted with the comment, and even more so when he was given cold soup for dinner.

They reached the capital at dawn, with the sun just rising. The ceremony would take place at noon in the Throne Hall, which made Egil and Lasgol very nervous. The risk was growing by the moment, and things did not bode well at all for them. They entered the city through the Eastern gate, with the marks of the battle still visible on the walls and the buildings closest to it. Reconstruction work was still going on, and the city looked far better than the last time they had seen it.

At the Royal Castle the soldiers let them in once Dolbarar had identified himself. They were led to the Royal Stables to leave their mounts, and here Lasgol said goodbye to Trotter. He had the feeling that this would be the last time he saw him. He tried to keep calm. *Everything's going to come out well. You've already been here, in an even more complicated situation, and you're still breathing,* he reminded himself. But he felt an oppression in his chest that would not leave him.

They were led into the Royal Castle, which was closely guarded by soldiers. It did not surprise Lasgol in the circumstances. They went along corridors and stairs to a great hall. Here Gondabar, the Leader of the Rangers, was waiting for them. Dolbarar and the Four Master Rangers greeted him respectfully. When Gondabar asked to be introduced to the Contenders, Dolbarar introduced them one by one. When Lasgol shook the Leader's hand and looked into his eyes he did not feel any sense of threat, rather the opposite; Gondabar impressed him as a good-hearted man. On the other hand, he had already been mistaken before when it came to judging people.

When the introductions were over, food was brought to them.

"The criminal's last meal," Viggo said.

"Just eat and shut up," Ingrid said. "You're impossible."

Gerd had lost his appetite. Nilsa devoured what was on her own plate as well as his. She was eating for two, presumably because of nerves.

They had a moment to rest. Dolbarar was chatting with Gondabar beside the window and the snow was still falling. Lasgol had the feeling of something ominous.

"Don't fret, we'll make it," Egil said, as if he could read what he was feeling.

"Do I look as bad as that?"

"Pretty much. Try to pretend."

"I'm already trying."

"Well, you're not succeeding."

Lasgol's mouth twisted. "Thanks."

"Better. Everything ready?"

Lasgol nodded and jabbed his thumb at his sword.

"It'll all work out well," Egil reassured him. "It's a good plan."

"I always trust your plans and ideas."

"In that case all we have to do is to execute the plan."

"Couldn't you use another word? Does it have to be 'execute'?"

"You're right. How about 'follow the plan'?"

"Much better."

Egil smiled. He was trying to convey calm and confidence, but without success.

"Listen to me, Contenders," Gondabar announced. "The moment has arrived for the celebration of the Ceremony of Acceptance. Follow me to the Throne Hall, where King Uthar and the nobles of the kingdom are waiting."

Lasgol swallowed. The knot in his stomach was the size of a

melon. Ingrid signaled to them to surround her.

"Stay calm, we'll get out of this one," she promised with a look of determination. "We're the Panthers, we'll survive and win through."

Lasgol was grateful for her words, and he knew that his teammates were too.

They went into the Throne Hall through the door the semi-giants had brought down and which was now rebuilt, two by two, following Gondabar, who led the procession at a stately pace. Behind him went Dolbarar, followed by the four Master Rangers, all wearing their formal Ranger uniform. The Eagles came after them, with Isgord and Marta in the lead, then the Owls, with Astrid and Leana in the lead, then the remaining teams in order. The Panthers had taken their place at the end of the procession, with Ingrid and Nilsa in the lead, followed by Gerd and Viggo, with Egil and Lasgol bringing up the rear.

Standing watch at the door, along the corridor and behind the throne were soldiers of the guard, which made Lasgol more nervous still. The whole Court was present: the Eastern Nobles, Dukes, Counts, lesser lords and their families, all elegantly dressed: the men wearing formal armor with heavy full-length cloaks and swords forged by the best craftsmen of the North, their pommels decorated with jewels. The women wore long dresses in lively shades of red and green, and dark fur cloaks with collar and cuffs of mink and sable, typical of the North. They wore jewels round their necks and on their wrists, although these were not very ostentatious, as Norghanians preferred ornaments of gold and silver, with a few colorful jewels like rubies or emeralds. As was the northern custom, some of the women also carried knives at their girdles, except that being noble, these were finely-crafted daggers. All this luxury left Lasgol open-mouthed. Still, according to what Egil had told him, the luxuries of the North were nothing compared to those of the east of Tremia, and most of all with those of the south, where the Nocean Empire ruled. Egil had told him that the Noceans considered the northern nobles to be brutes without taste, clothed in uncured animal-skins: coarse, ignorant and without taste. The luxuries of the Nocean Empire were a dream, and unthinkable for someone from the North.

Gondabar stopped before Uthar, who was sitting on the throne. The King appeared to be totally recovered. He was wearing radiant gold-scaled armor, and on his head was the Crown of Norghana. An imposing sword rested on the right of the throne and a Norghanian shield on the left. On his right stood Commander Sven and First Ranger Gatik. Beside them was a young man wearing a long white robe. Lasgol, who was watching unobtrusively with his Gift from the end of the row, guessed that he was a Mage of the Ice, even though judging by his youth he seemed to be fresh out of school. Lasgol remembered that Uthar had lost Olthar and his Ice Mages in the fight against the Glaciers Arcanes, and realized that he had summoned another Mage. Considering how scarce the Gift was, replacing fallen Mages was not going to be at all easy for him.

Gondabar bowed deeply. The rest of the procession fell to one knee between the rows of people as they had been told to do on presenting themselves before the King of Norghana. On the left of the throne Lasgol saw the King's cousins, Thoran and Orten. A little further away was Count Volgren. All the trusted nobles of the King, in other words. Behind the throne stood the survivors of the Royal Guard and Rangers. Lasgol felt bile rising from his stomach; things did not look good at all.

"Your Majesty, the Rangers are pleased to announce their presence at the Ceremony of Acceptance," Gondabar said, his head still bowed in respect.

"Welcome to all!" Uthar boomed in his powerful voice. "Your King is grateful that you heeded his request to celebrate the graduation ceremony here at Court."

Gondabar did not raise his eyes. "It is an honor and a privilege," he said.

"I would have liked to go to the Camp, as I usually do those years I can, but this time it was impossible. I have been very busy bringing their just deserts to Wild of the Ice and traitors of the West."

The nobles cheered the King's words. "They ought to be put to the sword!" said Thoran. "Better gut them all so they suffer!" said his brother Oden.

The throne hall was huge, but it was packed solid, and the din of the discordant voices echoed against the black stone walls. Lasgol felt a shiver run down his spine. The nobles wanted blood and revenge, and they were not prepared to listen to reason. The atmosphere was hostile. He had the sense that things were getting worse all the time, and that if they were to get out of there in one piece they were going to need a lot of cool audacity and courage.

Uthar let the nobles yell their opinions at the tops of their voices. He was smiling, relishing the bath of hatred, rage and praise he was receiving from his nobles. They had all lost relatives in the war, and their feelings were understandable. He would use them for his personal plans and gain.

"Your King hears you and understands you," he said. His expression showed his concern for them. Lasgol, who was watching every detail, knew it was a false sentiment, a piece of theater to convince his own people.

"You will have the justice you seek, that which is owed to you. Your King will make sure it is so. The enemies of Norghana will be destroyed, be they internal or external, both equally."

The court applauded the King's words and renewed their cheers. The Norghanians were not exactly the best-mannered and most temperate of people, rather the complete opposite. They could bring out their axes at any moment and swing them at anyone's head, nobles included. All Tremia knew it.

Uthar made signs with his hands for the court to moderate their feelings and gestures. Little by little, the hall returned to silence. Uthar smiled. He had them under his control, like puppets at his bidding.

"Today we honor the Rangers, who have served me so faithfully in the past, and especially during the present conflict. I wish to honor them, and hence I have invited them here, so that the whole realm may know the incredible work they do for their King. Without the Rangers, today we would very probably not be here, but in a ditch. Such is the importance of the work they do for the kingdom. Hence I would like to thank their leader Gondabar for his magnificent work, and Dolbarar for his dedication and sacrifice in training the new generations so that they may serve the Kingdom."

Gondabar and Dolbarar bowed in acknowledgment of the King's recognition.

Egil looked at Lasgol. There was no need for him to speak. Lasgol knew what his friend was thinking: that Uthar was a master-manipulator. He was winning over the Nobles and the Rangers by means of this farce.

"The Rangers fill me with pride," Uthar said.

"We serve the King with loyalty and discretion." Gondabar replied.

"And I acknowledge that faithful work. Continue with the Ceremony. I will merely preside."

"It will be an honor," Gondabar said, and made way for Dolbarar.

"Master Rangers," called The Leader of the Camp, and the Four took their places on the King's left. "Your Majesty, if you would be so kind."

"Rise," the King said, and the Contenders rose at once.

"This is the most important ceremony of the Rangers," Dolbarar said. "It is time for new blood to take the place of that which was shed for the Kingdom of Norghana. Today you become Rangers and will serve the realm with valor, honor, loyalty and in secret, since that is our way of understanding the defense of our lands, and thus it is written in the *Path of the Ranger*." He raised the tome he always carried in one hand. "Master Rangers, the Tomes of the Schools, please."

Eyra, Ivana, Esben and Haakon each took out a tome. On their covers the symbols of each School were represented.

"Open them and let the new Rangers begin to form part of our history. I will call each one by name. Those who graduate will be inscribed in the book of the School they belong to." He glanced at Uthar, who nodded to grant his permission.

"Contender Isgord Ostberg, step forward."

Isgord stood as erect as he could, raised his chin and went to stand in front of the King. He bowed deeply.

The Leader of the Camp now asked the fateful question they were all dreading: "Master Ranger Ivana, is Isgord Ostberg worthy of graduating here today as a Ranger in the School of Archery?"

Ivana nodded. "He is."

Isgord snorted in relief. It seemed that he had not been as sure of making it as he had wished to appear in front of everyone else.

"Let this be entered in the tome of School of Archery," Dolbarar said to Ivana, who wrote the name in the tome.

"Isgord, from this moment you are now a member of the School of Archers," Dolbarar announced emphatically. "The medallion, please."

When Ivana went up to Isgord and presented the Medallion of Archers to him, he puffed himself up like a peacock.

"From this moment on," Dolbarar said, "you are a Ranger of the School of Archery in your own right. Give me your right hand."

Isgord gave him his hand, which Dolbarar placed on top of the *Path of the Ranger*.

"You will honor the Rangers until the day you die. You will respect the laws that rule us. You will defend the kingdom from every enemy, internal or external. You will be guided by the *Path of the Ranger*. Swear with honor on your name and your soul."

"I swear," Isgord said.

Dolbarar nodded. "You are now one of us Rangers. Walk the Path with pride."

Isgord bowed to Ivana and Dolbarar, then to the King.

"Your King acknowledges you as a Ranger of the Kingdom of Norghana."

Isgord moved aside, ready to burst with self-satisfaction.

"Contender Marta Iskbarg, step forward," Dolbarar called.

One by one, they all went through the same ritual in the presence of the whole Court. Those who were graduating went to stand on the right, the others on the left. As more and more teams went through the ritual of the ceremony, so the Panthers moved closer and closer to Uthar.

Lasgol had a very bad moment which required all his strength and will-power. As the Boars were before the King, he found that he was standing on the spot where his mother had died. His eyes moistened, he felt an unfathomable pain in his heart, and he almost lost control of himself. Egil grasped his wrist, looked at him fixedly and gave him a gesture of encouragement, the one Ingrid had been making for four years. Lasgol, regaining control of himself, glanced aside at his friend. He knew Egil was going through the same torment as he stared at the spot where his brother had died. Egil was proving to be the strongest of them all, the one with the frailest body but the strongest spirit and character. Lasgol felt deeply proud of his friend.

The moment passed, and they recovered their poise. One more team and it would be their turn. Lasgol was happy for Astrid and the Owls, who all passed. He was not surprised; they were a great team, as were the Wolves under Luca's leadership.

And the moment came. The turn of the Panthers of the Snow. There was so much at stake that they all made a tremendous effort to control their nerves. Ingrid glanced at Nilsa, then at Gerd and Viggo, and finally at Egil and Lasgol. In her eyes determination shone. Nobody could beat the Panthers, not even King Uthar.

"Contender Ingrid Stenberg, step forward."

Ingrid took a firm step forward until she was standing in front of the King. She bowed, though not exaggeratedly. The King nodded and looked at her up and down.

"Master Ranger Ivana," Dolbarar said, "is Ingrid Stenberg worthy of graduating here today as a Ranger of the School of Archery?"

Ivana nodded. "She is."

Ingrid sighed.

"Let her be entered in the tome of the School of Archery. Ingrid, from now on, you are a member of the School of Archers. The medallion, please."

Ivana went up to Ingrid and presented the Medallion of Archers to her. It was identical to the one Ivana herself was wearing, with the image of a bow in its center, but smaller. Ingrid was moved, but she did not allow herself to show it. She raised her chin, and Ivana placed the medallion around her neck.

"Welcome to the School of Archers," she said.

"Thank you, it means so much to me..."

Ivana nodded and smiled. It was unusual in a woman who rarely showed any emotion.

"From this moment on," Dolbarar told her, "you are a Ranger of the School of Archery in your own right. Give me your right hand."

She gave him her hand, and he placed it on the tome.

"You will honor the Rangers until the day you die. You will respect the laws that rule us. You will defend the kingdom against any enemy, internal or external. You will always be guided by the *Path of the Ranger*. Swear with honor on your name and on your soul."

"I swear," said Ingrid.

Dolbarar smiled from ear to ear. "You are now a Ranger. Walk the Path with pride"

Ingrid was so happy that she could barely contain herself. She clenched her fists in triumph.

"You may withdraw."

Her teammates were looking at her with enormous pride and happiness. Lasgol had never had any doubt that she would make it. She was the best of them all, probably the best in all the Fourth Year. And for him she was the best captain and partner.

Ingrid saluted Ivana and Dolbarar respectfully, then turned and bowed to Uthar.

"Your King acknowledges you as a Ranger of the Kingdom of Norghana."

Ingrid looked at him briefly, with a searching gaze, as if she wanted to check whether this was really Uthar, or whether there was someone else inside him.

"Contender Nilsa Blom, step forward."

Rather than merely stepping forward, Nilsa jumped and nearly lost her balance. But she regained it and stood up straight. She bowed twice to everyone instead of just once. Her nerves were devouring her.

"Master Ranger Ivana, is Nilsa Blom worthy of graduating here today as a Ranger of the School of Archery?

Ivana nodded. "She is."

Nilsa's arms shot up, and she jumped. She was beside herself with joy. When Ivana and Dolbarar made the presentation to her, she dropped the medallion. The look in Ivana's eye almost seemed to say that she was thinking of changing her mind. Like lightning, Nilsa put the medallion around her own neck, smiling at Ivana as she did so. When the time came for her to swear the oath, she was shaking so much that she nearly knocked the *Path of the Ranger* from Dolbarar's hand, so that he was forced to clutch the tome with both hands.

Once Nilsa was beside Ingrid, she did a light tap-dance for sheer happiness.

"Contender Gerd Vang, step forward."

Gerd's knees knocked together as he stood in front of Uthar. But with a superhuman effort he managed to maintain his composure. His right hand was shaking, but somehow he managed to hide his fear.

"Master Ranger Esben, is Gerd Vang worthy of graduating here today as Ranger in the School of Wildlife?"

Esben nodded. "He is."

Gerd snorted so hard that his breath stirred Dolbarar's hair. When he swore the oath he smiled, as he had not smiled for a long time, with all his heart. When Dolbarar told him to go back to the line, he stood up to his full size and showed himself as he really was, a giant. He received the medallion with the image of a bear and stroked it as if it were an incredible treasure. At that moment he was the happiest Norghanian in the whole north.

The next to be called was Viggo.

He had taken on a pose which suggested someone who did not really care in the least about all that sort of thing. He came very close to a lack of respect toward the leaders, and realized it. Lasgol knew that Viggo was smart, very smart. He made a very elaborate bow to Uthar, and like Ingrid, he took the opportunity of taking a good look at the King now that he was so close to him.

"Master Ranger Haakon, is Viggo Kron worthy of graduating here today as Ranger of the School of Expertise?"

Haakon nodded. "He is."

Viggo was left in a state of shock. He had always thought he would not make it: not him, a mere reject from the sewers. When Haakon and Dolbarar approached him he turned to them and for the first time since he had been at the Camp, he smiled a genuine smile, from the bottom of his heart, without irony or sarcasm, without suffering, with only happiness: a smile of pure joy.

He took the oath and became a member of the School of Expertise, the hardest of all, in his own right. He turned to Ingrid and smiled at her. When she smiled back, her eyes shone brilliantly.

And the moment of truth arrived. Egil and Lasgol stepped forward until they were two paces from the King. Lasgol was watching Uthar intensely, and at the same time Egil was watching Gatik at the King's side. Uthar and Gatik returned their gazes, penetrating, somber.

If we come out of here alive it'll be a miracle, Lasgol thought. He commended himself to the Gods of the Ice.

Chapter 47

"Contestant Egil Olafstone, step forward," Dolbarar called out.

Egil took a deep breath before he took his first step. He knew his life was hanging from a thread. He was walking into a trap, to death, and he knew it. But he did not hold back. He took strength from the pain of the deaths of his father Vikar and his brother Austin and approached the throne, calm, serene in mind. He would need to be, in order to survive that moment. He took his place in front of Uthar and bowed.

"Are you the Olafstone youngster?" the King asked suddenly.

Egil straightened. The moment of truth had finally come.

"I am."

"I am, your Majesty," Uthar corrected him. "Or perhaps you're nothing but a filthy traitor like the rest of your family, and that's why you don't show me the respect you owe your King and Master?"

The nobles let out a collective gasp when they realized who this was.

"Seize the traitor!" shouted Thoran.

"Kill him!" cried Orten.

Quickly, the Royal Guard surrounded him.

Dolbarar hastened to defend him. "Your Majesty, he's a Contender... he's sworn fealty to you, he has my approval. He's loyal to the Crown."

"Let him hang, him and all his family!" shouted another noble.

Uthar raised a hand. "Silence, I beg you. I want to hear what he has to say."

Egil looked at Uthar, then at Gatik. "I've sworn fealty to the King of Norghana. I'm loyal to the throne."

"Interesting," said Uthar. "And will you still maintain that loyalty when we finally defeat your brother Arnold and execute him?"

Egil took a deep breath and inwardly considered his answer. Lasgol, whose eyes were on him, was frightened to death on his friend's behalf. He hoped that he would keep his head. If not, he would lose his life.

"I'm a Norghanian. When a Norghanian gives his word, he keeps it. I'll keep my oath, come what may."

Uthar laughed. "I'd like to believe you. I really would. But I don't trust you. Besides, I gave the order to kill you in the Frozen Continent, didn't I, Gatik?"

Gatik bowed his head. "Yes, my lord."

"And what happened?" the King asked Gatik.

"Duke Olafstone took the arrow for him."

"The arrow that took his life."

"Yes, your Majesty."

"You're going to forgive me that too, because of loyalty?" Uthar asked Egil.

Egil clenched his fists and his jaw. "It's not my prerogative to question my King's decisions."

Uthar let out a guffaw. "He's smart, this little one, very smart. Good answer. It's a pity I'm smarter than you, you little weasel. No, I don't believe you. Gatik, take him. He'll hang at dawn. And this time, don't fail me."

"Yes, my lord," Gatik replied and seized Egil by the shoulders.

Egil did not resist. Ingrid was about to act, but Egil put his hand through his hair. It was the sign to let events unfold. Ingrid held back.

"One question, my dear Dolbarar. The little weasel, has he managed to graduate?"

"Yes, your Majesty."

"Curious. Which School?"

"Nature."

"That makes sense. He must have been plotting ways of poisoning me."

Gatik began to lead Egil away.

"Let him witness the end of the ceremony," Uthar called to him.

Lasgol did not like this at all. Uthar was planning something. Something to do with him.

Dolbarar now called Lasgol, who summoned up his courage. He had come thus far and he had to finish: not for himself but for Egil, for his mother, for Egil's family, for the North; he could not fail now. He took a deep breath and used his Gift. He glanced at the Ice Mage, who was around his own age. Not advanced enough to catch others using the Gift, or so he hoped. He tried. The Mage did not seem to notice. During the two steps he took forward he called upon all the skills he had developed. He did not know what was in store for him, so he called upon all of them at once. The green flashes ran through his body.

He stopped in front of Uthar and bowed.

"You I know well," Uthar said.

Lasgol looked up.

"I owe you my life, Lasgol son of Dakon Eklund."

"Your Majesty," Lasgol said. He was trying to guess what Uthar was planning.

"I'm sure you've graduated. Am I wrong, Dolbarar?"

"No, your Majesty. Lasgol graduates in the School of Wildlife."

"Wildlife?" Uthar said in surprise. "I'd put you rather in Archery or School of Expertise. You surprise me."

"It's my favorite School," Lasgol said.

"He's outstanding in all of them," Dolbarar said. "He's a special case."

"Well, well," Uthar said. "Just like your father. They say the apple never falls far from the tree, and I see there's truth in the proverb."

Lasgol did not know what to say. What was Uthar getting at with all this?

"I knew your father Dakon very well. I loved him like a brother. His death was a tragedy. Gatik is very good, but let me tell you that your father was three times better, at everything."

The comment failed to please Gatik, who frowned.

"And just imagine: after everything that happened, after thinking he was a traitor, after clearing his name – which you did, by the way, and very well, I have to admit – there's something that doesn't hang together in this story..."

And Lasgol knew in that instant that Uthar had found him out. He knew the truth. He was dead.

"And you know what doesn't hang together?"

"No, your Majesty," he replied, bearing up as best he could.

"That right here in this same hall, a few days ago, I discovered something that puzzled me, something I would never have imagined, something that made no sense. But now, at last, it does. Do you want to know what it is?"

Lasgol did not want to know. He could have wished that a bolt of lightning would burn Uthar to ash on the spot, but he was not going to be so lucky.

"Of course, your Majesty."

"I'll tell you. I'll tell everyone. I discovered that Darthor, Corrupt Lord of the Ice, was really not a Mage or Sorcerer, as we all thought... in reality Darthor was a Sorceress, a witch, and a woman."

The nobles gasped in disbelief.

He turned to Thoran and Orten. "Isn't that so, cousins? You examined the corpse."

"She was a sorceress," Thoran said.

"Unbelievable, isn't it? A woman, a Sorceress, was on the point of conquering all Norghana. But there's more. I knew this woman."

There were more gasps and cries of disbelief and outrage.

"Yes, I knew her, and do you know who she was? This is going to surprise you all." Uthar smiled broadly. "No less than the wife of my dear friend Dakon, the First Ranger."

The hall exploded in outrage.

"And now I ask you, Lasgol: if Darthor was Dakon's wife, that makes her your..."

Lasgol knew there was no escape-route. Uthar knew everything.

"My mother."

"Correct. And doesn't it seem strange to you that Darthor being your mother, your father would not be a traitor?

"I don't know, your Majesty."

"I've meditated deeply on this, and I've come to the conclusion that Dakon was indeed a traitor, as we initially thought. He was involved in a conspiracy with Darthor, his wife, and they tried to kill me and take over the realm."

"Treason!" came the shouts from the crowd.

Uthar raised his hand to continue.

"And if Dakon and Darthor were traitors? If your parents were traitors, what do you think you are yourself?"

"I'm Lasgol, son of Dakon and Mayra."

"Exactly! And therefore a bloody traitor like them. Don't think I didn't recognize you when you were grieving for your dead mother, because I did."

Lasgol knew they were doomed. It was the end.

"Sven, take him. He'll hang with his friend at dawn."

The Commander made to take hold of Lasgol.

At the same moment Egil gave the signal by raising six fingers.

Ingrid took two steps and hurled herself with all her might at

Sven. She and the Commander rolled across the floor, moving away from Lasgol.

Egil elbowed Gatik below the belt, and the First Ranger bent double in pain.

Nilsa leapt forward and ran into the Mage, who fell backwards.

Gerd hurled himself with the full weight of his body against the Royal Guards, who were beginning to react to the attack, and swept them in front of him.

Viggo slipped in behind Lasgol, covering him with his own body, and took out his dagger to protect him.

"What's this?" Uthar shouted. He got to his feet in front of the throne. The whole Court was staring at him.

The Royal Guard and Rangers ran to protect their lord. The nobles were shouting.

And in the midst of it all came the most crucial part of the plan. Lasgol used his Gift and communicated with Camu.

Now create the anti-magic sphere.

The little creature became visible on Lasgol's back, although Viggo's body was blocking him from view. He stiffened and pointed his tail at Uthar, then began to flash with golden pulses. Suddenly a translucent sphere took shape, with Camu as its origin and center, five paces across. Only those with the Gift could see it; as far as everybody else was concerned, it was simply not there.

Very good, Lasgol said. *You're doing very well. Keep it up,*

Thoran and Orten reached for their swords and moved toward him. Nobody was attacking Uthar, so the Royal Guard and Rangers were puzzled. They turned on Ingrid, Nilsa and Gerd, and overcame them easily as they were unarmed.

"You'll pay for this outrage!" Uthar said, furious that they should have attempted anything.

Thoran and Orten went up to Lasgol to kill him, but Lasgol pointed to Uthar.

"First take a good look at your cousin the King," he said.

The two nobles turned. What they saw left them speechless.

"Kill that traitor!" Uthar ordered his cousins.

But the two nobles were staring at Uthar with eyes wide as saucers. Suddenly all the chaos and shouting stopped. Everybody was staring at Uthar. The whole Court. In Shock.

The silence stretched out forever.

"What are you waiting for!" Uthar yelled. "Kill that traitor!" Then he noticed that everybody in the hall was staring at him. "Why are you staring at me? Kill him!"

Thoran stepped forward, with Orten behind him. He pointed his sword at the man standing by the throne. "Who are you? Where's Uthar?"

Uthar could not understand what was happening.

"What have you done to Uthar?" Orten asked.

Uthar pointed to Lasgol. And in so doing, he saw something different. His arm and hand were not the pale white of the Norghanians. They were the tanned brown of the desert lands. He had lost Uthar's form and regained his own.

"What's happening to me?" he cried.

Thoran took another step toward him. "You're not my cousin Uthar. What have you done with him?"

"Yes, yes, I am," the false Uthar said, trying to change himself back into Uthar again. But he was within the area of effect of the anti-magic sphere Camu was generating. And he could not manage to shift. Desperate, he tried again, and his sun-bronzed face and green eyes showed all the fear and despair he felt. He had lost his form in front of the Court, and that was impossible. His pool of power was still half-full and there was enough to let him stay transformed for days, so what was going on here?

And then he realized. He jabbed his finger at Lasgol.

"It's you, isn't it? How are you doing it? You don't have that power. You need immense power to counter other people's magic. How are you doing it?"

Lasgol said nothing. All eyes were fixed on the false Uthar.

"I asked you what you've done with Uthar," Thoran said, and threatened him with his sword.

"Nothing, I swear to you! I'm Uthar, I've been bewitched, it's true, that's why you see me differently, but I'm Uthar, I swear it! Kill Lasgol!"

Thoran looked at Lasgol, then at Uthar.

"I'd rather kill you." And with a single stroke he pierced his heart.

The shifter fell to the floor and died almost instantly.

Thoran, Orten and the rest of the Guard were left staring at him, unable to believe what had happened.

A mental message reached Lasgol: *Tired. Sleep.*

Lasgol knew Camu could not hold out any longer; the effort of generating the anti-magic sphere had exhausted him. The problem was how to get him out of there without being seen. He would not be able to do it himself, nor would his teammates.

Then someone came up behind him. "Hand him over to me," the newcomer whispered in his ear.

Lasgol turned and saw Astrid.

"Don't let them see what you're doing and give me the little creature. I'll hide it. You won't be able to. Do it now, or it'll be too late."

Lasgol considered this for a moment. *Camu, go with Astrid. Be good.*

He turned his back to Astrid, who took Camu and hid him under her cloak. She went back to the Owls, who were only a step away from Lasgol.

Thoran turned and pointed to Lasgol and the Panthers. "I don't know what's been happening here, but you can take all this lot into custody."

Lasgol turned to Egil, who smiled. Lasgol smiled back. Somehow they had survived, and the shifter was dead.

They had won.

Chapter 48

Viggo shoved hard at the bars of the cell. "I'm really getting a taste for all these messes we get ourselves into, especially your plans for getting out of them,"

"You won't be able to move them," Gerd said. "I've already used all my strength on them."

"Well, at least we're not dead," Nilsa said. There was a nervous smile on her face as she stared at the cell where they were being held prisoner.

"The plan worked," said Ingrid. "Better than expected, even."

Viggo looked horrified. "We end up as prisoners in the royal dungeons, and you call it a successful plan?"

"It could have turned out a lot worse. None of us is either dead or wounded. I'd call that a victory, considering it's us."

Viggo rolled his eyes.

"And we unmasked the Shifter," Lasgol put in.

"We certainly did!" said Nilsa. "Bloody mage with his dark arts!"

"I'd say he was a Nocean Sorcerer, a very powerful one," said Egil. "And a rarity, because Shifters aren't very common. Very few can use the Gift to change their shape. And to replicate another human being so exactly, even fewer."

"And a very powerful mage couldn't do that?" Gerd asked.

"Not necessarily. There must be an affinity with the type of skill needed for shifting. The same way Lasgol wouldn't be able to, even though he possesses the Gift. He hasn't got that affinity to change shape, or create elemental spells like the Ice or Fire Mages."

"Quite honestly," Ingrid said, "it was an amazing sight to see the whole Throne Hall staring at him when he didn't realize he'd changed back to his natural form."

Egil nodded. "He'd been in Uthar's form for so long that his mind took it for granted that he was like that all the time. He didn't realize our plan."

Viggo smiled. "The best moment was when he tried to shift back to Uthar and his magic failed him. That was great."

"How did you know Camu's magic would work?" Gerd asked

Lasgol.

Lasgol looked at his friend. "I didn't, but I had what Egil called *a well-founded suspicion*."

"From my studies of Camu," Egil explained, "I deduced that he could create a field of anti-magic around him. He'd already done something similar once to defend Lasgol, so I thought he must be able to."

"The difficult thing was rehearsing him and persuading him," Lasgol said.

Egil nodded. "Very difficult."

Viggo stared at them open-mouthed. "You're not telling me that we went into Uthar's trap and you didn't know whether the most important part of the plan would work?"

Lasgol shrugged. "The thing is, Camu's complicated…"

"But you did rehearse it, didn't you?" Gerd asked.

Egil and Lasgol looked at each other. "Yeah, we rehearsed it, several times."

"Oh, well then, there you are," Nilsa said dismissively.

Viggo arched one eyebrow. "Wait a moment. How many times did it work?"

There was a moment of silence. Ingrid, Nilsa, Gerd and Viggo stared at the two of them.

"Well, sort of successfully… almost once," Lasgol finally admitted.

Viggo waved his arms agitatedly. "By all the storms of the northern winter! And we risked our skins with that plan!"

"I couldn't think of any other viable plan," Egil said.

Vigo uttered a string of curses.

"What matters is that the plan actually worked," Ingrid said, making light of the matter.

"That's right," Nilsa agreed.

"I wonder where Camu is at the moment," said Lasgol.

"He'll be all right if Astrid took him." Egil said.

"It seems your girlfriend knew more than she let on," Viggo said to Lasgol.

"She's not my girlfriend, and yes, I wasn't expecting her help."

"It came just at the right moment," Egil said.

"Yeah, I only hope she was able to hide Camu. If he fell into the hands of the nobles, he's lost…"

"He'll be fine, don't worry," Egil said to Lasgol, who was looking extremely worried.

"It's a pity Thoran killed the shifter when we revealed him in front of everyone," Gerd said. "He ought to have been questioned, to find out all the evil things he'd done."

"Well," said Ingrid, "Thoran and Orten aren't particularly famed for their patience and skill with words."

"Thoran didn't want to interrogate him," Egil said with half-closed eyes.

Lasgol was immediately interested. "Why not? That would have answered many questions that are still unsolved."

"Thoran saw his chance, and took it."

"To kill him? He could have executed him after he'd questioned him."

"As they're going to do with us..." Viggo added under his breath.

"Don't put a jinx on it and let Egil explain," Ingrid snapped.

"The chance to crown himself King of Norghana," said Egil.

"A brutal man, but a clever one," Viggo said, nodding. He had understood. "He killed two birds with one stone. The impostor and the King – so now he's the next in the line of succession. Well played, I'll give him that."

Egil nodded. "He wasn't interested in taking him alive. That might have complicated things for him. He took a shortcut."

"But Uthar could still be alive," said Ingrid.

Egil shook his head. "I doubt whether the shifter would have kept him alive. And if he did, then by now Thoran will have found him, and guess what'll happen?"

Lasgol understood his friend's reasoning. "Thoran'll kill him to keep the crown, then blame the Shifter,"

"Master-stroke!" Viggo exclaimed.

"And we served it to him on a platter," said Nilsa.

"We did what we had to in order to survive," Egil said to her. "Remember, Uthar was going to execute us."

Viggo smiled sarcastically. "Well, you two, to be exact, but not us."

Egil shook his head. "Do you really believe the Shifter would have let you live and run the risk of you knowing his secret?"

"I suppose not..."

"We did the right thing," Nilsa said. "The Shifter got what he deserved."

"And the real King Uthar?" Ingrid asked.

"That's the game of politics: if you enter it, you might not come out alive. Uthar knew that. His cousins know that. My brother knows that."

"Won't Arnold claim the Crown for himself?" Lasgol asked.

"He will, but I very much fear he doesn't have enough support to go against Thoran and Orten and all the Eastern nobles."

"You're taking it for granted that the Eastern nobles will support Thoran," said Ingrid.

"Oh, they will. They can't let the crown go to the Western line."

"All this politics gives me a headache," Gerd grumbled.

"It must be an immense one, seeing how big the head is," Viggo said with an innocent smile.

"As big as the royal castle above us," Gerd shot back.

They all laughed, and the tension relaxed a little. They had spent the whole night locked up in that cell and nobody had taken any interest in them, which was not a good sign. Lasgol feared they were going to be hanged for treason, and there was a knot in his stomach. He was trying to stay strong, like Ingrid, but fear was running freely through his heart. Fear for his friends, fear for Camu.

Suddenly there came a screech and the sound of footsteps.

"Someone's coming!" Viggo muttered. "Watch out!"

To their surprise, through the bars of the cell they saw Dolbarar with Commander Sven, Gatik and several guards. They all stood up and waited. This did not look good.

"Rangers," Dolbarar greeted them with a nod. His face was very serious.

The six of them fell to one knee, looking straight ahead respectfully. With the excitement of the situation Lasgol had forgotten that now they were Rangers, even though the ceremony had ended in tumult and death. He prepared himself mentally to hear the sentence that would doom them to hang.

"Rise, please. King Uthar, the true one I mean, has been found dead in an isolated dungeon where the Shifter had him locked up. It appears that he used the King's blood to prolong the shift so that he didn't need to consume all his own power. He was a very powerful sorcerer, with advanced knowledge of Transformation Magic and Blood Magic. We believe he was of Nocean origin, because of his race and the type of magic he practiced. Those kinds of magic are forbidden in the North and West of Tremia."

"King Uthar is dead, may the Gods of Ice protect King Thoran," Sven said, confirming the name of the next king.

Egil and Lasgol exchanged glances. They had expected as much. Now would come their sentence.

Sven stepped forward and looked at them all, one by one. Lasgol was surprised to see Gerd and Nilsa so composed, barely appearing nervous at all. Ingrid remained stoic, which did not surprise him. Viggo was staring at them as if he did not care in the least, which was not true. Egil's eyes were fixed on Gatik, a sinister glare that frightened Lasgol.

"King Thoran," Sven began, "will be crowned in a week's time. His Majesty does not wish to stir up the matter of the Shifter and his cousin Uthar's death any further. These are two events that fill him with sadness, and he wishes them buried. Norghana is in mourning, as well as in a complicated situation. Now it needs a strong monarch with a hand of iron. The King wishes to look forward and lead the kingdom to glory, leaving behind these last few years of misery. After deliberating with his counselors, he has reached the conclusion that you six were not involved with the Shifter, and that in some way, during the tumult you created, you managed to unmask the Nocean sorcerer. The King does not know whether this was deliberate or by accident, but nor does he wish to look deeper into the matter. Whatever the case, his Majesty would like to thank you for your part in the unmasking of the Shifter, and therefore he grants you your freedom."

Lasgol was stunned. The expressions on his friends' faces were equally shocked. They had all assumed the worst. He looked back at Dolbarar to make sure he had heard properly. The Leader of the Camp smiled and nodded.

"Remember that as Rangers, you owe loyalty to the crown, to King Thoran," Gatik said, and it sounded like a warning.

"Guards, unlock the cell," Sven ordered.

The guards did so. The six were about to come out when Sven turned to them. He pointed a threatening finger at Lasgol and Egil,

"As for you two, the King knows very well who you are and whose sons you are, and he's not going to forget. Dolbarar has interceded for you before the King, assuring him that now that you're Rangers, your past life has been left behind and you're only guided by the privilege of serving the crown and the realm. King Thoran warns you to remember that. If he should find out otherwise, you'll hang, and Dolbarar with you, for having backed you up with his own honor. Is that clear?"

It seemed that Sven was not too happy with what had been decided.

Lasgol felt an enormous respect and admiration for Dolbarar at that moment. There had been no need for him to have done that. He was gambling his life on them. Lasgol felt his eyes moisten. As soon as he could, he was going to thank him from the bottom of his heart.

"We understand the King's message, it's crystal clear," Egil replied.

"His Majesty has nothing to worry about," Lasgol added.

"Very well then," Sven said, "you're free to go."

Chapter 49

A few hours later, Lasgol was looking out at the view from the northern wall of the capital. Snow lay over fields, forests and mountains, creating a beautiful and peaceful landscape. He exhaled, unable to believe that he was still alive. He huddled deeper into his hooded, green-brown Ranger cloak and looked down at the color for a moment: how he had wished he could wear it, and now at last he had got hold of it. It filled his soul with joy.

Dolbarar had given them the cloaks as a Fourth-Year graduation gift. He had also given them the Ranger medallions. Lasgol put his hand over his own, the School of Wildlife, which bore the image of a roaring bear. Once again he felt very happy to have obtained it, for having become a Ranger despite all they had been through. And happy also for his friends, and for Dolbarar, who had saved their lives. Lasgol and Egil had been able to thank him once they were alone at last.

"It wasn't very important," the leader of the Camp had replied.

"Yes, it was, very important," Egil had said. "Sven would have hanged us, and Thoran would have let him do it."

"They don't trust you two... because of your families," Dolbarar had explained.

"That's normal, up to a point," Lasgol said. "We're the sons of the enemy, both of us."

Dolbarar nodded. "But now you're Rangers, and all that's behind you. Your family is now mine, and your duty is to serve the realm."

"We understand that," Lasgol said.

"And accept it," Egil added.

"I trust you," Dolbarar said with a friendly smile.

"We won't disappoint you, sir," Lasgol said. He bowed respectfully, and Egil did the same.

"I know that. I know your hearts, and they're noble, pure."

"Thank you for saving our lives," Lasgol said.

"And for risking your own." Said Egil.

"We'll never be able to repay you," Lasgol insisted.

"Become Legendary Rangers and you'll do that." Dolbarar said smiling.

"We'll try," Lasgol promised.

Dolbarar said goodbye to them with a firm embrace.

"Is it true, what they're saying?" came a voice behind him.

Lasgol came back to reality. He recognized the voice, turned round slowly and saw the wild and beautiful face of Astrid.

"What are they saying?"

"Isgord is going everywhere shouting that you're Darthor's son."

Lasgol bowed his head. "Yes, it's true. Darthor, Mayra, was my mother."

"But how on earth is that possible?"

"It's a long story and this isn't the moment for it, but maybe someday you might want me to tell it to you."

"Now I understand what happened when we were captured. You weren't worried, you weren't afraid, but of course you knew Asrael and Darthor himself."

"That's right."

"And you knew that Uthar was a Shifter, and that was why you took action at the ceremony."

"I'll tell you the whole story, someday, if you want me to... but right now I need to know about Camu. Is he all right? Nothing's happened to him, I hope?"

Astrid took off the knapsack she was carrying on her back and handed it to him. When Lasgol opened it, Camu's head appeared, with his large eyes and his everlasting smile.

"Camu! Are you all right, little one?"

Camu gave several joyful shrieks and licked his cheek with his blue tongue.

Happy, he transmitted to Lasgol.

Lasgol stroked his head. "I'm happy to see you too."

Camu gave more little shrieks and wanted to get out of the knapsack.

"No, don't come out now, there are soldiers on watch duty, it's not safe."

Later? Play?

"Of course, we'll play later,"

"Can you communicate with him?" Astrid asked.

"You can manage to, with time and patience."

"I found it impossible. He's a charming little creature, he loves to play and he's very cheerful with those little shrieks of his."

"And very mischievous," Lasgol said as he put the knapsack on his own back. Camu licked his neck.

"How did you know about Camu?" Lasgol asked her.

"I've seen you with him."

"You spied on me?"

"Yes," she admitted. "As you wouldn't give me any answers, I went in search of them myself."

"And what did you find out?"

"That moron Isgord was going around saying you had some sort of weird creature, magical or something like that, so thinking it would be another of your secrets, I spied on you. I spotted you one night playing with him behind the cabin. At first I didn't know what you were doing because I couldn't see Camu, until he appeared as if by magic and I saw him."

"I couldn't tell you... I'd have put you in danger..."

"How many of your secrets would have put me in danger?"

"Almost all of them..."

"I finally understood at the ceremony. I saw Uthar change, I saw the little creature and I realized it was magical and that you'd need to get it away from there."

"You've always been very clever."

"Don't think I'm as clever as all that."

"Thanks for looking after Camu. He means a lot to me."

"Forget it, it was a pleasure. He's a charmer. Unlike you."

He tried to apologize. "Astrid... I... I'd have told you everything..."

"Yeah, but the danger of death, treachery, magic, shifters, wars and all that."

"Yes, exactly... will you ever forgive me?

"Why should I? You didn't trust me. It hurt. A lot." The brunette's eyes shone.

"I've learned my lesson. I'll trust you."

"Even if that puts me in danger of death?" she said, staring at him in disbelief.

"If that's what you want, I will. You have my word on it."

Astrid was thoughtful, looking out at the snow-covered fields from that high viewpoint.

"Show me."

"What d'you mean?"

"Until you show me, I won't believe you. Words and good wishes are just here today, gone tomorrow." She turned to leave.

Lasgol seized her hand. "Wait."

"I'm not going to forgive you just because you beg me to. You hurt me a lot."

"If you want proof, I'll give it to you."

"Go ahead," she said, daring him with her fierce eyes.

Lasgol sighed. "There's one thing you don't know about me."

"A secret?"

"Yes."

"Dangerous?"

"Could be."

"Then tell me. I want to know."

"I'm not sure you'll understand... whether you'll accept me..."

"I doubt whether it's worse than what you've already done to me."

Lasgol snorted in resignation. "Fine, I'll tell you..." He paused and then decided: he did not want to lose her, not for anything in the world. "I have the Gift, the Talent," he admitted.

Astrid's eyes opened wide. "You have magic?"

"Yes, though not much, really just a little. I'm not a mage or a sorcerer, but I can do certain things..."

"I always knew you were special. What I didn't know was how much."

"Special in a good way? Or special in a bad way?"

"That remains to be seen."

"Oh..."

Astrid came closer. Suddenly, as if carried away by a sudden impulse, she kissed him passionately. Lasgol, taken by surprise, was left breathless and on the brink of suffocating. But at that moment he would not have minded if he had died a little.

"Does this mean you forgive me?" he asked her hopefully.

"Of course not. This is for telling me about your Gift."

"Oh... and after that?"

"After that you still have a long way to go before I forgive you."

"But what do I have to do?"

"I'll let you know," she said with a smile, and turned to go.

"Where are you going?"

"To get ready for the journey back to the Camp. We have to be there in three weeks for the specialization tests, and first I want to see my family, know that they're fine, even if it's only for a few days."

"Are you going to try?"

"Absolutely. Aren't you?"

"I... well... I hadn't decided yet."

"Well, if you want to see me..."

"You're telling me what I have to do, aren't you?"

"Maybe?" she said with a mischievous smile, and left.

He watched her leave, feeling completely confused. He had not decided whether or not to take part in the tests for the elite school of specialization or start his new life as a Ranger at once. Now he could see clearly that if he wanted to be with Astrid he would have to apply.

On her way Astrid met the other Panthers, who were coming up to find Lasgol and to enjoy the view and the quiet. They exchanged greetings, then came up to where Lasgol was waiting.

"Has the brunette forgiven you?" Viggo asked.

"Almost..."

"And what's the situation with the blonde?" he asked ironically.

"Which blonde?" Gerd asked.

"The beautiful Val."

"Lasgol only wants to be with Astrid," said Nilsa. "Don't you?"

Lasgol nodded and went red.

"Let him be," Ingrid said.

"Sure, since you already have your Captain Fantastic," Viggo said.

"I've told you a thousand times not to call Molak that," she said angrily, and raised her fist.

"Freedom feels so good!" Nilsa shouted, spreading her arms wide to enjoy the caress of the cold wintry wind and put an end to the quarrel.

"You've only been a prisoner for a day!" Viggo said.

"Even so, it feels so good."

"I'm enjoying being free too," Gerd said, and followed Nilsa's example.

"You're just like children."

"So said the adult," Ingrid said.

"Look, for once I'll admit you're right, I'm not really an adult."

"Miracle!" Ingrid cried, flinging her arms into the air. "The first time in four years that you've admitted I'm right about something."

"Well, it looks like it."

They all laughed joyfully, happy to be alive and free.

Lasgol shook his head, unable to take it all in. "Can you believe it? We managed to graduate as Rangers."

"We're wearing Rangers' cloaks," Gerd said, looking at the cloaks Dolbarar had given them as graduating gifts. "So that's what we must be."

"When I stop to think about it, I can't believe it," Nilsa said.

"The first day I saw you, when they put us together, I knew we'd make it," Viggo said, trying to sound serious.

They all looked at him incredulously. "But we were the hopeless team!" Gerd said.

"We started out last, but in the end we finished," Egil said. "What matters is the journey, not the starting point or the end."

"I have to admit, there were lots of times when I thought we'd never make it," Ingrid said.

"You?" said Nilsa. "But you were always the one who was sure we'd succeed at everything."

"It was to cheer you up. Someone had to stay strong."

"Well, you did a fantastic job," Gerd said.

Viggo smiled. "It's been four fabulous years. I wouldn't change them for anything."

"Yes, the best ones of my life," Gerd agreed.

"For me it's been four fantastic years at the Camp, but not outside it..." said Egil.

"To some extent, for me too," said Lasgol.

"In spite of all they've made us go through?" Ingrid asked.

Lasgol and Egil looked at each other and nodded.

"In spite of everything."

"This deserves a group hug," Gerd said, spreading his arms wide.

"Here we go with the mushiness," Viggo protested.

"Shut up and give me a hug, you blockhead," Ingrid said to him.

Viggo smiled and hugged her. Then Gerd and Nilsa joined them, and finally Lasgol and Egil added themselves to the bear-hug.

"For the Snow Panthers" Ingrid cried.

"For the Snow Panthers!" they all shouted.

"For the elite specializations!" she shouted again.

"We're not going to apply, are we?" said Gerd.

"Of course we are!" said Nilsa.

Gerd looked at Egil for help, but his friend merely smiled and shrugged.

"For the specializations and the fools we're going to make of ourselves!" Viggo said.

"We'll make it!" Ingrid said.

Nilsa looked at them all. "You're the best partners anyone could wish for."

"The best friends," said Gerd.

"Panthers and friends forever!" said Lasgol.

"Forever!" they all cried.

And for a long while the six friends remained in their group hug, sealing what would be a friendship that would last their whole lives.

"Can we drop the embrace?" said Viggo. "I'm going to throw up. Must be all this touchy-feely stuff."

"Shut up, you blockhead!" they all shouted in unison.

---THE END BOOK 4---

The adventure continues in:

Pedro Urvi

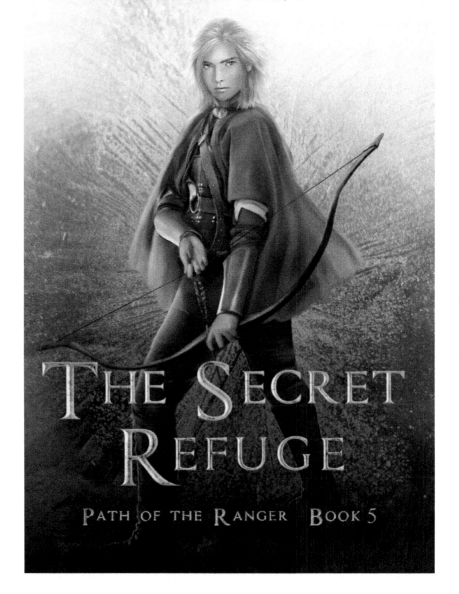

Note from the author:

I really hope you enjoyed my book. If you did, I would appreciate it if you could write a quick review. It helps me tremendously as it is one of the main factors readers consider when buying a book. As an Indie author I really need of your support.
Just go to Amazon to enter it.
Thank you so very much.
Pedro.

Note about the Series:

This series has 20 books and tells the beginning of the legendary story of the Snow Panthers of the Norghanian Rangers. It does not cover their whole life. Their adventures continue in other epic sagas that follow.

Other Series by Pedro Urvi

THE SECRET OF THE GOLDEN GODS

A world ruled by merciless Gods. An enslaved people. A young slave-hunter at the service of the Gods. Will he be able to save his sister when they take her?

This series takes place three thousand years before the events of Path of the Ranger Series.

Different protagonists, same world, one destiny.

PATH OF THE RANGER

A kingdom in danger, a great betrayal, a boy seeking to redeem his father's honor. Will he succeed in exonerating him and saving the realm from an enemy in the shadows before it is too late for the whole North?
The beginning of the legendary story of the Snow Panthers of the Norghanian Rangers.

THE ILENIAN ENIGMA

A powerful evil. A deadly destiny. Will a young warrior fulfill his calling or doom millions of lives?
This series takes place after the events of Path of the Ranger Series. It has different protagonists, but one of the Snow Panthers joins the adventure in the second book. He is a secondary character in this series, but he plays an important role, and he is alone…

THE PATH OF DRAGONS

A human with dragon blood who tries to hide it. A martial school where those who have dragon blood and manifest the Power are sent to learn to fight for their dragon lords.

This series takes place after the events of Ilenian Enigma Series. It has different protagonists, but all the heroes from the previous series will appear and will be critical in the outcome of the story.

READING ORDER

This is the reading order, top to bottom, following the main story of this fantasy universe. All series are related and tell part of the overall story.

Acknowledgements

I'm lucky enough to have very good friends and a wonderful family, and it's thanks to them that this book is now a reality. I can't express the incredible help they have given me during this epic journey.

I wish to thank my great friend Guiller C. for all his support, tireless encouragement and invaluable advice. This saga, not just this book, would never have come to exist without him.

Mon, master-strategist and exceptional plot-twister. Apart from acting as editor and always having a whip ready for deadlines to be met. A million thanks.

To Luis R. for helping me with the re-writes and for all the hours we spent talking about the books and how to make them more enjoyable for the readers.

Roser M., for all the readings, comments, criticisms, for what she has taught me and all her help in a thousand and one ways. And in addition, for being delightful.

The Bro, who as he always does, has supported me and helped me in his very own way.

Guiller B, for all your great advice, ideas, help and, above all, support.

My parents, who are the best in the world and have helped and supported me unbelievably in this, as in all my projects.

Olaya Martínez, for being an exceptional editor, a tireless worker, a great professional and above all for her encouragement and hope. And for everything she has taught me along the way.

Sarima, for being an artist with exquisite taste, and for drawing like an angel.

Special thanks to my wonderful collaborators: Christy Cox and Peter Gauld for caring so much about my books and for always going above and beyond. Thank you so very much.

And finally: thank you very much, reader, for supporting this author. I hope you've enjoyed it; if so I'd appreciate it if you could write a comment and recommend it to your family and friends.

Thank you very much, and with warmest regards.
Pedro

Author

Pedro Urvi

I would love to hear from you.
You can find me at:
Mail: pedrourvi@hotmail.com
Twitter: https://twitter.com/PedroUrvi
Facebook: https://www.facebook.com/PedroUrviAuthor/
My Website: https://pedrourvi.com

Thank you for reading my books!

Printed in Great Britain
by Amazon